The Nine Lives
of
Tito d'Amelia

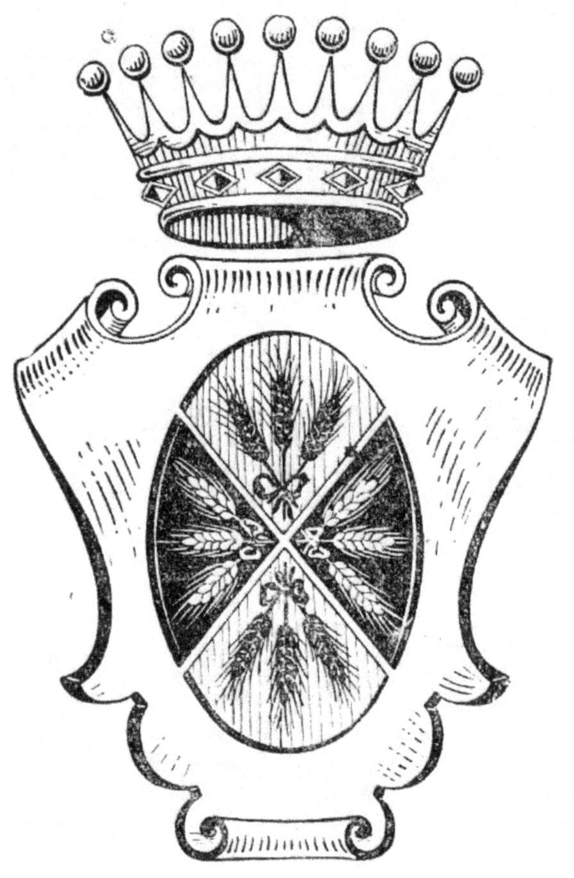

The Nine Lives
of
Tito d'Amelia

Ettore Farrattini Pojani

Books may be purchased by contacting the publisher directly at Bayou City Press, LLC, 10303 Scofield Ln, Houston, TX 7096 or by emailing Publishing@BayouCityPress.com.

Editing by Julie Gianelloni Connor | Cover design by Rob Williams
Peninsular Maps by Daniele De Vecchi |
Town Maps by Carter Norman Phillips

978-1-951331-10-8 (paperback) | 978-1-951331-11-5 (ebook)
Library of Congress Control Number: 2024943703

Publisher's Cataloging-In-Publication

(Prepared by Cassidy Cataloguing Services, Inc.)

Names:	Farrattini Pojani, Ettore, author.
Title:	The nine lives of Tito d'Amelia / Ettore Farrattini Pojani.
Other titles:	Nove vite di Tito d'Amelia. English
Description:	[First English edition].	Houston, TX : Bayou City Press, LLC, [2024]	Enhanced translation of: Nove vite di Tito d'Amelia. Rome: Gruppo Armando Curcio Editore S.p.A., 2022.	Includes bibliographical references.
Identifiers:	ISBN: 978-1-951331-10-8 (paperback)	978-1-951331-11-5 (ebook)	LCCN: 2024943703
Subjects:	LCSH: Cats--Italy--Amelia--History--Fiction.	Families--Italy--Amelia—History--Fiction.	Nobility--Italy--Amelia--History--Fiction.	Amelia (Italy)--History--Fiction.	LCGFT: Historical fiction.
Classification:	LCC: PQ4906.A77 N6813 2024	DDC: 853.92--dc23

First English EditionPrinted in the United States

Contents

Prologue

Meow. Meeow. Meeoow. Mee... mee-mee... MEEOOOW!

WHEN CATS WANT to communicate with humans, their sounds start with the letter "M," or at least we associate the beginning of their "words" with that letter of our alphabet. We pronounce it by making our lips touch each other—a movement that does not belong to cats but that generates the sound closest to theirs.

Cats have never needed to develop an explicit audible language that is understandable to us. Since the beginning of time, they have had superior intelligence. They very easily make themselves understood with a tilt of their head, a movement of a paw, or a twitch of their tail. More than anything, cats express their approval or disapproval with their gaze. A gaze that can freeze us, show their total superiority, or indicate their unconditional love: a gaze that is worth a thousand words. Their pupils can adapt to any kind of light, allowing them to see what is happening around them, even on the darkest nights. The magical flexibility of their eyes—from a perfect circle to a thin vertical line— gives their expression an intelligibility that is deeper than words.

This visual acuity is associated with a refined sense of smell and prodigious hearing. Even if soundly asleep, a cat can perceive any movement around it, any sign of danger, long before any other living being.

However, the biggest mystery lies in their whiskers, an incredible combination of radar, sonar, and extraordinary sensory perception that goes beyond any possible human understanding. No science will ever be able to understand, equal, or duplicate the perceptual abilities of a cat's whiskers.

It was undoubtedly the combination of these outstanding senses that induced the Egyptians to believe cats had divine characteristics. They idolized Bastet, the goddess with a human body and a cat's head, protector of the home and women, and goddess of fertility. A cult ruled with strictness: killing a cat could result in a death penalty. In all Egyptian tombs, even in recent discoveries, the presence of mummified cats is a constant, along with objects, amulets, and statues of cats of every form and size.

Every museum in the world with an Egyptian section has examples of this kind of object. Perhaps only the falcon was idolized as much as the cat, but the cat now remains undoubtedly the most admired animal in their culture.

Egyptian priests were the first to claim that cats had nine lives; they were convinced that a cat would reincarnate into a human being in its ninth life and then ascend to divinity. Over the centuries, the Egyptian belief has turned into a less-elevated concept that cats can survive nine fatal accidents during their lives. In some cultures, based on different traditions, the number has dropped to seven lives.

After the Egyptians, the ancient Greeks perpetuated the adoration for cats: for them, the goddess Artemis could transform into a feline hunter. The ancient Romans also followed the cult of Artemis, but they renamed the goddess Diana.

Cats were less fortunate in the Middle Ages, when their seemingly magical abilities were linked to witchcraft. The superstition about black cats bringing bad luck probably originated then. The tradition of cats having nine lives was also present.

In the late Middle Ages, Muhammad—the father of Islam— supposedly gave his cat Muezza magical powers by giving her a sleeve of his precious robe. By touching her three times on her back, he gave her the ability to always land on her four legs when falling from dangerous heights. "Three times three" would provide cats their nine lives, according to the mythological Islamic tradition.

Another cat admirer was the poet Petrarch, who synthesized his love for cats in the epilogue of his last letter sent to his beloved pupil Giovanni Boccaccio: "Humanity is divided into two categories: those who love cats and those who were punished by life."

Numerous cats gladdened the French royal court. At the end of the sixteenth century, Cardinal Richelieu had many cats in his rooms. He left them an inheritance upon his death. During the eighteenth century, King Louis XV granted more rights to his cats than to his princes.

Famous scientist and mathematician Isaac Newton invented the classic cat flap to allow his cats in and out of his house.

"Literary cats" have accompanied and inspired many writers and playwrights, such as Alexandre Dumas, Émile Zola, Lewis Carroll, Mark Twain, Ernest Hemingway, Italo Calvino, and many more. They all drew inspiration from their beloved felines.

And we cannot forget about the many cats involved in politics: Abraham Lincoln was the first American president to bring a cat into the White House, followed by Theodore Roosevelt, John Fitzgerald Kennedy, and, more recently, Bill Clinton.

England also had important "political cats": Nelson and Jock were Winston Churchill's cats, living with him at Downing Street, and today London's most famous cat is Larry, who can go in and out of the British Prime Minister's home more easily than the minister himself.

Divine, magical, supernatural, long-sighted cats. Friendly, hostile, mischievous, and loving cats. The many millions of cats that populate the earth are all different from each other, each with its own personality and magic.

In these pages, I will tell you the story of one cat, a very special cat—a cat that traveled through history and collected information from all of the humans with whom he lived in each of his nine lives.

This is the story of Tito, or rather, these are the nine stories of Tito d'Amelia.

Chapter 1
The Bronze Age in Amer
Year 1134 BC
Tito and Hephaestus and a Town Called Amer

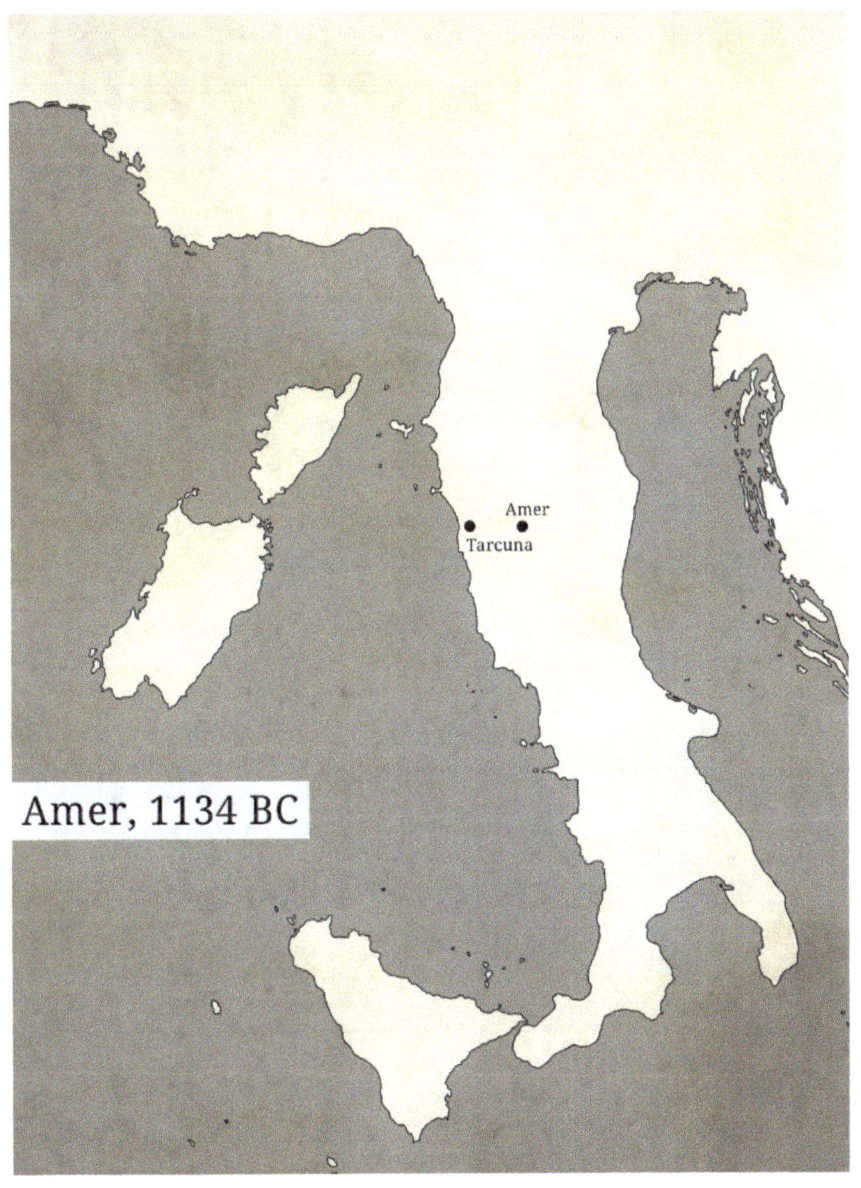

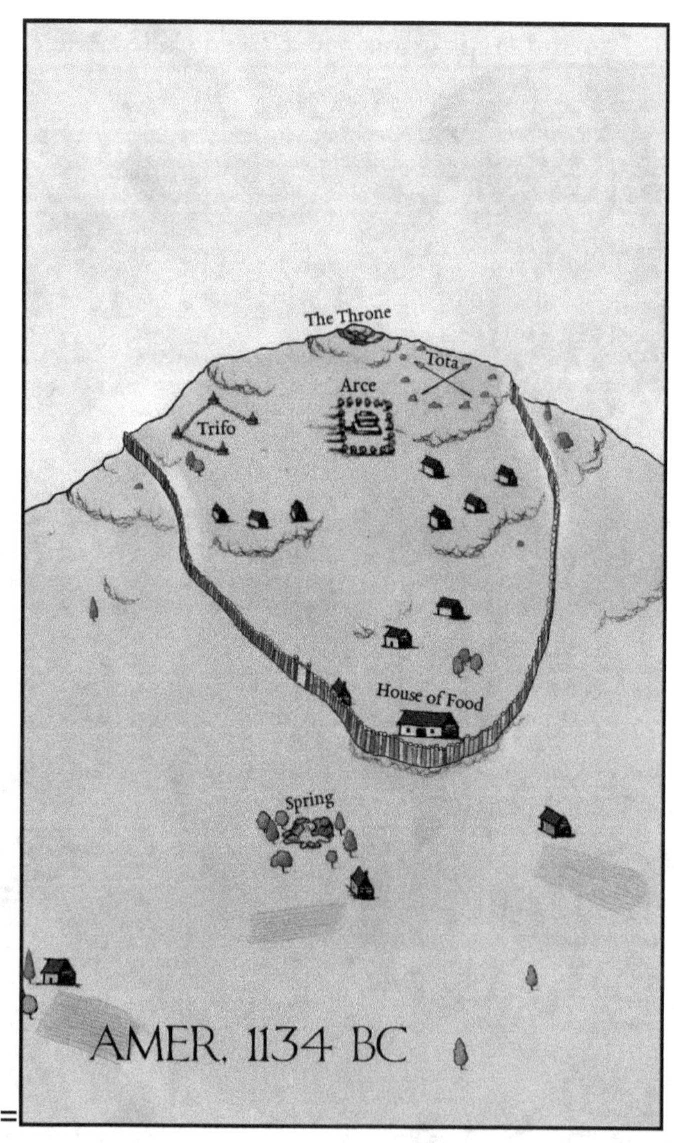

The Throne
Tota
Arce
Trifo
House of Food
Spring
AMER, 1134 BC

Cast of Characters

Family at the Start of the Chapter

Khepri: a hunter

Hator: the father of Khepri, former hunter, tribal priest

Hephaestus: the son of Khepri

Titolo/Tito: a cat

Other Principals

Plesia: the widow of a deceased hunter, a worker at the House of Food

Tidra: the daughter of Plesia

Amerians

Ameroe: the chief of the tribe

Mezente: a builder

Avile: the son of Mezente and a friend of Hephaestus

Olèo: a Servant of the Earth

Populations

Etruscans

KHEPRI HAD BEEN chasing a large wild boar for quite some time, but the beast showed no sign of slowing down—its survival depended on that. Armed with his sharp, bronze-tipped spear and his equally sharp-bladed dagger, the expert hunter ran among the thick bushes, waiting for the right time to deliver the killing blow to his prey. His tribe had been starving for meat for days now: that boar would feed them.

The summer had been a scorching one. Trees were still laden with plenty of fruit, but animals were hard to hunt. Many had moved down to the valley along the river, the only abundant source of water during the drought. Natural pools and streams near their village had almost dried up.

The elderly members of the tribe had discussed several times the possibility of leaving their hill and moving down to the valley like the animals did, but not everyone agreed. Hator, Khepri's father, a former hunter himself and now the tribal priest, believed that just as animals became more vulnerable in the valley, so too would they. The top of their hill was a much safer place. The chief of the tribe, Ameroe, listening to Hator's advice, knew they could not survive much longer if the drought persisted since there was no more water to drink and no animals to hunt.

Khepri was so focused on chasing the boar, waiting for the right moment to strike, that he did not realize how far he was advancing into an area he had never visited before. The severe drought had lengthened his hunting trips; he had to go further and further away from his usual hunting zones to follow the animals closer to the river. While his eyes were checking out rocks and trees, he did not realize his strong legs were not slowing down. He was the most expert and strongest hunter of his tribe and rarely missed a throw. This boar was particularly wily, and Khepri could not find the right moment to throw his spear.

Out of the corner of his eye, he saw a hill on the left. With a little luck, if he could push the boar toward that hill, it would slow down its run. He tried to push himself, running to his right. When his father, Hator, many years before was teaching him how to hunt, Hator successfully passed on to him his experience on how to prevent his prey's next move and advised him to attack only when sure of the perfect throw. While Khepri was still a young man, he had hurled his spear at prey counting on his considerable physical strength only, which he deemed sufficient to overpower the animals—but they had often escaped him.

With long and patient training, Hator taught Khepri how to think like a boar or a deer and how to predict their moves. Now a grown man at his physical peak with a well-trained mind, Khepri rarely returned empty-handed to his tribe. His instinct proved right: passed on the right side, the boar turned to the left, finding himself in front of a steep white rock wall. The boar's run was slowed by a moment of uncertainty. Khepri took advantage by throwing his spear, knocking down the boar, and giving him no chance to escape.

The hunter approached the wheezing animal and quickly finished it off with his dagger. Blood that had begun to flow copiously out of the boar's neck stopped after a few last spasms, and the boar inexorably breathed its last. After that long chase under the burning sun, Khepri was short of breath, so he sat in the shade of the tall trees at the bottom of the hill and rested for a while.

The sun was still high in the sky, so there was time left before darkness came. He hung the animal from a large branch to drain its blood and walked around that high hill to see what was behind it. It was a place he had never seen before—peaceful, quiet, and nothing like the hill he was living on with his tribe. Trees and bushes here were flourishing, while those on his hill were withered and dried out. He kept walking, finally turning around beyond a pointed spur of rock. He looked beyond and discovered an even flatter, greener area. He was amazed by the sight of so many green, leafy trees. He continued walking toward a huge fig tree. He picked a couple of figs and, tasting them, was surprised by their sweetness, while those in the trees near his village were smaller and almost dried out. After his long run, the two figs gave him an energy boost.

With the rocky part of the hill at his back, he realized how that high wall was a natural barrier from the cold winds of the north. The side that stretched in front of him, benefiting from the hill's protection against the winds, was incredibly green and flourishing. Trees were full of fruit. While he was admiring the apple and pear trees, suddenly, a pair of rabbits ran between his feet. He did not pay much attention to them.

On that day, the hunt was over for him, but it was not over for a fast cat that was chasing those rabbits and caught one not far from Khepri. The little hunter failed to deliver a killing blow to its prey, and although the cat held it tightly, the poor rabbit wriggled and almost freed itself. The cat knew that if it let the rabbit go to inflict a lethal bite, the rabbit would run away.

Khepri's eyes met the cat's. They were both at the end of an exhausting hunting day, but while Khepri had secured his prey, the cat was on the verge of losing the rabbit. Their gazes showed that they understood each other instantly. The cat remained still, while Khepri, with a swift gesture, knelt, grabbed the rabbit's head, and broke its neck, leaving it dead in the cat's jaws. On a different occasion, Khepri probably would have tied that rabbit to his belt and carried it back to his camp to roast for his son—but not that day.

That intense gaze between the two hunters established mutual respect, and Khepri had not even thought for a moment of appropriating the prey of that impromptu hunting partner. Instead, he felt beyond happy that he had helped the cat get its food. The cat loosened its grip, grabbed the dead rabbit with a more secure bite, and ran away, dragging it. Khepri followed it with his eyes until the cat disappeared into the bushes.

Khepri walked past those same bushes to discover an enchanting scene. A stream of clear water was flowing down the center of this side of the hill. He walked up the hill and reached a spring gushing from a rock. He bowed to sip the clear water, scooping it up with cupped hands. He had never tasted such good water with this particular mineral flavor. It was nothing like the water from the ponds or the river near his village, which now seemed flat and bland in comparison. Standing up again, he turned toward the valley, and from that higher position, he had a better and wider view of the place. It was unique, unlike any place he had ever seen before. Looking down the hill, he saw a family of deer grazing further away and heard the lively chirping of various species of birds on the tree branches.

Suddenly, he realized the sun was about to set, and he still had to walk back to his village. He quickly ran back to the tree where he had hung the boar. With a few branches, he began building a litter to drag the heavy boar back to his village. As he was working on it, the cat's image came back to him. It certainly had been easier for the cat to carry that rabbit back to its lair than for him since he now had a long way to go with the heavy litter.

He could not forget those eyes staring at him. The cat made no sound nor spoke a word, of course, but Khepri had clearly heard a request for help from that small hunter. Even if neither of them would have shared or yielded their prey to the other, at that moment, although they were a human and a feline, that difference just disappeared; they were two hunters, both busy with getting food for themselves and their loved ones. There were no barriers between them.

Walking back, he could not get out of his mind the images of that valley and the hill he had discovered by chance, and he could not wait to tell his son and his father about it. He arrived home late. The sun had already set, and many villagers asked him why it had taken him so long.

His son Hephaestus ran up to greet him. He was a beautiful young man who took the best from both his parents: the bright, deep eyes of his father and the facial characteristics of his mother, who had died when he was still a child. He liked to practice fighting and hunting, and sometimes, he went along on hunting trips with his father, but by the rules of his tribe, he was not allowed to follow beyond a specific area around the camp. Only after turning fifteen and passing a group hunting test could the new young hunters follow a more experienced hunter and then, later, venture out alone. Hephaestus was already very well-trained and strong for his fourteen years, but he was still not old enough to follow his father on hunting trips.

Villagers had already lit a big fire in the center of the field, and it was blazing in the pale twilight. Normally, everyone would already be in their huts for the night, but the excitement caused by that tasty boar meat roasting on the fire kept the entire tribe awake and ready to eat.

Khepri spread the word to everyone to gather around the fire, not only to eat but also to listen to him talk about what he had seen that day. The night fell quickly, but it was still hot, so everyone gathered a good distance away from the fire. The chief of the tribe, Ameroe, after giving thanks to the Sun God and to Khepri for finding food for all of them, invited him to talk. Khepri quickly told them about his hunting day and why it had taken him so long to return, describing the wonderful place he had discovered.

"I saw a place I did not know, and we have to go back there to explore. There is this high hill with a high rock side facing the north winds. On the other side of the rock, there is a slope facing the sun. A spring of fresh water comes out from the heart of the rock. It has a taste I have never experienced before. The water flows down toward the sun, and all that side of the hill is full of trees and green bushes full of fruit."

As he was speaking, he took out of his bag a few figs he had picked from the fig tree and held them out to Ameroe and the tribal elders.

"Look, have you ever seen bigger figs in this season? Taste them and tell me if they are not the best you have ever had! This juiciness means that water always flows. If not, those trees would not be so green and strong!" He then turned to Ameroe. "It is a place we could move to and have a chance to live a better life. And besides fruit and water, there are lots of animals. In the short time I was there, I saw deer, many different birds, and fat rabbits." He stopped for a moment. Speaking about the rabbits reminded him of that cat's gaze.

Hator spoke, interrupting Khepri's words. "How can we know it is not a territory belonging to another tribe? We cannot risk starting a battle now that we have so little food and no strength."

"Father, I did not meet anyone the whole time I was there, not going there and not coming back here. I did not see signs of people passing or signs of the presence of others, not a single trap. We must go back to that hill and explore."

Hator was not very supportive, but Ameroe, knowing the hardships they were experiencing, decided to organize an expedition the next day at sunrise.

After entering his hut with his son, Khepri could not sleep. He was constantly thinking about how beautiful it would be to live in that valley. Always worried about not being able to give the best of everything to his only son Hephaestus, Khepri knew that life on that hill would be easier for everyone. His son asked Khepri to tell him more about what he had seen. After describing the beauty of that place again, Khepri also told Hephaestus about the cat, how he had helped it, and how the cat almost spoke to him with its deep eyes.

Hephaestus admired cats. His grandfather often called them the perfect hunters and said that Hephaestus should observe them to become a good hunter. His grandfather taught him to imitate how cats lurk at the sight of prey and wait for just the right moment to launch a fatal attack. How they use all their senses and exercise patience. His grandfather often repeated the same favorite observation: "The haste the prey has to save itself will always be greater than the speed you must use to attack it." It was one of the reasons Hephaestus had always wanted to have a cat for himself, but he never had the opportunity nor the courage to obtain one. He saw people from his tribe in these times of shortage killing and roasting cats, and he was afraid that if he could domesticate one, it would suffer the same fate.

Hephaestus kept asking about the wild boar and how Khepri had chased it. Khepri began to feel exhausted from all those questions and his long day. He started to fall asleep, lightly snoring. Hephaestus then retired to his bed, imagining that valley and its feline inhabitant he wanted so much to caress.

The next day, at sunrise, Khepri joined Ameroe and three other tribe members. They set out on their horses toward the hill with the source, as everyone started to call it. With his experience and knowledge of the region, Khepri had no problems going in the right direction.

Once they arrived at the white rock wall which was already so familiar to him, everybody discovered how accurate Khepri's description had been. He led them around it, reaching the valley on the other side. They remained ecstatic before the view of the stream and the intense green of the vegetation. They walked up to the source and drank the water while looking around at the vastness of the valley, which was surrounded by other small hills but was predominantly flat and rich. Many birds chirped serenely, and a small herd of deer peeked out in the distance and calmly drank at the edge of the stream. The tribesmen saw the burrows of wild rabbits and the many trees full of fruit.

They crossed the stream to have a glimpse of the other side of the hill. From that point of view, the rocky hill was strong and tall, perfect as a natural barrier from the strong north winds, with a front-facing slope leading gently from the source toward the valley.

Ameroe touched Khepri's shoulder and said, "You are right. Here, we could be safer and have enough food and water for everyone. We have to convince them to move here."

The group lingered to drink more of that tasty water, and before heading back, they began filling their bags with figs and other fruit. Khepri tugged on a branch to pick some apples that still hung tightly to the branch. A few fell down and rolled away, and a couple stopped by a large boulder between bushes. Khepri reached out for the apples, only to be scratched by a quick feline paw. A cat hissed fearlessly. Khepri also heard the tender meowing of a few kittens. Looking behind the boulder, he immediately recognized that gaze. It was the cat he had helped the previous day. The feline was frightened, mostly about defending its kittens. Khepri soon realized that the hunter was a mother hunting to nourish her young ones that were not yet big enough to be independent.

Khepri and the cat stared at each other for a few moments. She recognized him and left her defensive position to lie down and welcome the kittens to her small teats. Very slowly, so as not to scare her, Khepri reached out to stroke her head. She sniffed his fingertips, recognizing that smell she had been so close to the day before. It was not usual for a feral cat to trust and allow a human to approach her. She, however, was doing it and began to purr to thank him for the help she had received.

Ameroe's strong voice echoed in the valley. He was calling everyone to head back home. Khepri stood up, said goodbye to the small family, and ran to join the others. On the way back, the group decided to take a longer route home in the direction of the big river to see if there might be other tribes around. Before deciding to move to a new place, they had to be sure no one else was claiming that valley.

Ameroe was well aware that, on the other side of the big river, there was a wealthy and well-organized population called the Etruscans. He had heard of them and knew their camps were much more than a simple cluster of huts. They had buildings that were solid and vast. He was concerned they might have already crossed the river on the side where the sun rises. If so, his tribe could never successfully compete against them.

Back home, Ameroe invited the entire tribe to listen to his decision. He knew he was putting himself in a very complicated position and that many would oppose it, but seeing that valley made him increasingly certain it would be a very comfortable place to live.

After a lengthy discussion, a plan was worked out. Hator advised the chief and finally agreed to the plan. Four small groups of selected tribe members would set off in opposite directions. The first group was to head toward the mountains of the cold winds. The second one toward the valleys where the sun rises. The third one toward the valleys where the sun sets. Their task was to talk to the leaders of the other tribes and summon them to an enlarged council to convince them all to move together to the valley with the source. Only with more people and more hands could they build a new settlement before the winter. The fourth group was to cross the river, a task made easier by the drought, to visit a city called Tarcuna, founded by the population on that side of the river, by the great sea.

Ameroe wanted to build something more permanent and lasting than a simple village. Not having enough experience, he sent his best men to investigate what the Etruscans had already built.

Very proud to have contributed to this breakthrough for his people, that evening in his hut, Khepri told his son about the cat family and how the mother cat had recognized him, remaining calm in his presence.

Hephaestus was very excited about this news and could not wait to move into the valley and take care of those kittens. If there was plenty of food, the cats were less likely to end up roasted.

After several days, all four groups returned, but not all success-fully. Those who had crossed the river were full of information and stories about the city they had visited. The others reported some acceptances and some refusals from the other tribes.

Another two weeks of an even stronger drought and unbearable torrid heat were enough to help change many people's minds. The vision of that fresh water source crept increasingly into everyone's mind.

In those weeks, Khepri had returned several times to the valley with the source, always coming back with game and fruit. Hephaestus tried every time to convince his father to let him go along, but he never succeeded. Eventually, Khepri had to surrender, and after his son promised he would only collect fruit, they walked together to the valley.

Arriving there, Hephaestus was enchanted. As much as his father had described the valley in detail, it was even more beautiful than he had imagined.

Hephaestus asked immediately where he could find the family of cats. While approaching the spot, Khepri realized the mother was absent, probably looking for food. The kittens had grown considerably since the last time he had seen them. They were very playful, trying to catch each other's tail. As soon as the father and son approached, they hid in their den. Hephaestus reached in to catch one, but his father immediately stopped him.

"Do not touch them! If their mother perceives any human touch, she might abandon them! Let's go grab some fruit and then come back later before going home."

Hephaestus looked at the kittens with an unbridled desire to caress them, but he obeyed his father. The three kittens were all alike, more or less, brindle and piebald white, with curious and beautiful little eyes. One in particular looked at him with his deep yellow-green eyes. He half-closed his eyes, almost in a sign of submission.

After Khepri and Hephaestus filled their two bags with apples and figs, having eaten a few, they passed again by the den. The mother cat had returned with a kill that the three little ones were voraciously devouring. She recognized Khepri and walked toward him, keeping a certain distance. He sat down, stretched out his legs, and leaned his arm on the ground. The cat sniffed his fingers for a long time, finally rubbing against that same hand that had helped her get the rabbit. Khepri took his son's hand and rubbed it for a few moments in between his. He did this to leave his own smell on Hephaestus's hands. He then brought Hephaestus's hand closer to the mother cat, who allowed Hephaestus to caress her.

They remained like this for a while until the three kittens, now full of food, also approached the two humans. They were suspicious but reassured by the presence of their mother. Khepri told his son to move slowly and stay silent so as not to scare them. Hephaestus also sat down and stretched out his legs. A little later, the three kittens were on his lap, playing with the strings of his robe and tunic while the mother cat was resting on Khepri's thighs, happy that someone else was taking care of her rowdy kittens for a while.

Sunset was approaching. They had to leave. Hephaestus did not want to go and made his father promise they would move there soon. He did not want to give up those kittens.

After several meetings filled with discussion, Ameroe managed to convince many more people than he had initially and finally fixed a date for the transfer. Three whole tribes followed him in this exodus, together with a few smaller groups. Time was running out. If they wanted to have time to build new homes before the winter, they had to move quickly.

Once they arrived in front of the white wall, many were perplexed and disappointed, but as soon as they passed the rocky spur, the luxuriant nature present freed their minds from uncertainties, leaving them amazed and happy to have embarked on the journey.

Hephaestus immediately ran to the cats' den, finding it empty. Saddened, he told his father, who tried to console him. "One day, you, too, will leave our home. You will see, the kittens will be around here. We will find them again."

After several days, while exploring around, Hephaestus found one of those little cats behind some bushes. The cat had grown up and was independent from its mother. Hephaestus sat down as his father had taught him and slowly stretched his hand on the ground. The cat carefully sniffed each finger. Hephaestus stayed still, giving the cat all the time it needed to familiarize itself with and remember his scent.

After a while, calmed by his silence and stillness, the cat rested its paw on the thigh of the young man, and shortly afterward, it jumped on his lap. Only then did Hephaestus start to caress the cat, whispering a few words so as not to scare it. Hephaestus lowered his head to get closer. The cat sniffed his chin and slowly started to rub its head against it. Mutual trust was established. Hephaestus started to stand up, holding the cat in his arms. The cat tried to escape, but with a few reassuring whispers, Hephaestus managed to calm him, and with a quick gesture, he put the cat on his shoulders. In that position, the cat was free to jump, which it did not do. From that moment, the cat usually rode on Hephaestus's shoulders for their entire life together.

They marched back to the camp. Hephaestus could not wait to show his father that he had found one of the kittens, now grown up. Frightened by the villagers, the cat jumped down and ran away. Hephaestus tried to follow the cat but lost it again. It was late and time to go to sleep; he would look for the cat the next morning. During the night, he stretched out his legs and with one foot he felt something warm and soft. He sat up and saw the cat peacefully sleeping at his feet. Happy to see the cat there, he caressed it gently so as not to frighten it. The cat also stretched out with a long sigh and lay beside his human.

After a few weeks of intense work, the new camp was taking shape. More and more wooden huts with roofs made of branches were now standing on the flat part of the valley near the source. Slowly, the community was becoming a small town with a considerable number of innovations compared to what they had been used to until then. The great availability of wood, stones, and rocks allowed the building to go faster. The ideas stolen from the city beyond the river proved to be very useful.

When almost everyone was more or less settled with a roof over their heads, it was time to give direction to the small new community. Ameroe was recognized as their leader and made king of the new town, which was named "Amer" in his honor. He proved to be a great leader, giving his people a well-structured organization. He decided to give every single person who excelled in a specific field a title so they could guide the others. That gave him the idea of calling them "Titolos."

Khepri was given the "Titolo" of Chief Hunter. Not only was he in charge of organizing the hunting trips, but he also had responsibility for the equal distribution of meat and fowl among the citizens. For this purpose, a House of Food was created, a construction where the kills were brought to be processed, cut, and treated. Plesia, a widow of a hunter killed by the tusks of a huge boar, was in charge, along with other women, of the conservation and distribution of the collected food.

Others were assigned different tasks, all aimed at the good functioning of the community. Another group of citizens collected fruit and various grains. They had the Titolo of Servants of the Earth. Those in charge of creating arms had the Titolo of Defenders. Another group had the Titolo of Builders: they were assigned the task of designing the new buildings and the fortifications of the city to make it safer. The high white rock was a natural defense barrier on the back side of the valley. They needed to create one on the front, toward the flat part, starting from the left side of the rock, all along to the right side, up until the spur. That wall would take a much longer time to construct, so Ameroe decided to build a long barrier made of strong, tall tree trunks to keep everyone safe inside.

One of the Builders, Mezente, began making bricks using a technique he had picked up during his visit to the Etruscan city of Tarcuna. He set up a furnace in an area not far from the House of Food. His workers built a grid of planks in the forecourt where the bricks were placed to dry in the sun before putting them in the firing kiln. Mezente's son, Avile, was a close friend of Hephaestus. They had grown up together, but Avile was not interested in hunting like his friend Hephaestus was.

With his new furry friend on his shoulder, Hephaestus came to greet Avile at the furnace. While they were chatting, the cat jumped off and landed on the edge of one of the still-soft bricks, leaving his pawprints on it. The brick ended up in the furnace, but when Avile saw it, he threw it on the scrap heap. Back home, Hator asked his grandson if he had given his cat a name.

"I will call him Titolo!" Hephaestus said.

"And where does this name come from?" Hator asked.

"King Ameroe called the chiefs 'Titolos.' He is 'Titolo,' the chief of all the 'Titolos'"!

Hator smiled at his grandson and placed his hand on the head of the purring cat. "Titolo, you will be the soul of this city, and you will be part of it for centuries." He then placed his hand on Hephaestus's head, saying, "And you, my grandson, you will watch over this land, and your descendants will for generations make this city beautiful, strong, and alive."

With his new name, Titolo became the lucky charm of the new city. Everyone loved him. They all greeted him and wanted to pet him anytime he was passing by on Hephaestus's shoulder. He got used to this, overcoming his initial fear of other humans. He no longer ran away. Now and then, he would disappear for a few hours, sometimes for an entire day or two, but he always returned home to Hephaestus, who was now used to the cat's getaways. When Titolo was gone for the whole night, Hephaestus worried something might happen to him and could not sleep. Khepri tried to calm his son, telling him Titolo was having a good time with some beautiful female cat, adding that Hephaestus, too, should start to look around and choose a girl for himself.

Hephaestus smiled at his father and replied, "You should do it, too! I noticed how Plesia looks at you down at the House of Food. I do not have time for girls now. I have to train for the final hunting test. I want to be as strong and as good as you at hunting!"

Indeed, every day, Hephaestus got up early. He trained in running, throwing a spear, and combat. He also helped in the House of Food to skin and prepare the slain animals for distribution. Titolo was always with him, quickly getting used to living with humans. He was perhaps the first cat in history to live comfortably and peacefully in this way. He became a bit lazy since Khepri often brought him some meat scraps, as did many others, to win his favor.

As the name "Amer" came from an abbreviation of Ameroe's name, so, too, did Titolo begin to be called more affectionately with a nickname. Even Hephaestus ended up calling him as the other villagers did. Soon, he was known as "Tito" by everybody.

Even though spoiled and now living with humans, Tito did not lose his wildness and often returned home with a bird, a mouse, or a rabbit. If he was hungry, he ate them outside the front door.

Otherwise, he would bring them inside for his humans to eat. It was his way of being part of the family.

A year went by, and the city had already taken shape. The chief builders were constantly busy, and more and more huts turned into houses with more resistant stone and brick walls. The top of the hill was slowly cut down to make it flatter. The stones were reused in new buildings. Now, from the top of the hill, they had a clear view of the north valley and could check all around their new city from all sides.

A Hunter's Training

The long-awaited hunting test finally arrived for Hephaestus and the other young future hunters. If they passed, they could hunt with other senior hunters for the following five years. Then, from the age of twenty, they could go on hunts by themselves. On that testing day, the five most experienced hunters organized a deer hunt for the aspiring young hunters. Khepri was, of course, one of them. He believed in his son's abilities. Khepri had trained Hephaestus physically, while Hator had shaped his psyche, molding his impetuosity, as Hator had done with Khepri, teaching Hephaestus how to get into the prey's mind. It was not an easy task with a young, energetic boy eager to be noticed and to contribute to the survival of the community.

The path the young hunters had to take was not an easy one. To prepare for the final test, they had to practice developing individual senses in a specific way to be able to dominate their prey. To improve sight, hearing, and smell, each young hunter spent long days in a specific setting without moving. One of the adult hunters, unexpectedly, from a random and distant location, would wave a small rabbit skin just behind a rock or a log. They might not appear at all on one day but then maybe two or three times on another day. The boys had to report each movement. They needed to hold their concentration for those long hours to catch even the most hidden prey.

On other days, they had to sit blindfolded in the same position. The master hunters, at their discretion, would or would not make noises near or far from them. A broken twig, a rolled stone, or the creaking of a branch had to be recognized just by listening and perceiving its direction or distance. This exercise would help them to understand how near or far the prey was.

In another training exercise, with the young hunters always blindfolded, the master hunters would pass by them with different animals' skins: once a wild boar, another time a deer, then a fox or a wild sheep known as a "mouflon." At first, the master hunters would wave the skins close by, then further away to get the young hunters used to smell the different scents in a gust of wind in order to identify the prey before seeing it.

The most challenging part of the training was running blind-folded in the woods to acquire sensitivity in arms and feet, allowing runners to avoid crashing into obstacles. It was a skill that needed considerable practice. It was, however, essential to master these blindfolded runs using the sensitivity of the feet to recognize the morphology of the roots on the ground; deciphering from just the touch, a runner could work out the distance of the trunk from that point and be able to avoid it. The arms served as antennas: the left hand, kept free, was used to recognize the surrounding elements such as hedges, logs, rocks, and bushes, while the long spear held in the right hand allowed the runner to identify obstacles by the touch of the blade before the obstacles got too close to the body.

After the long initial training, the young hunters continued to increase each of these sensitivities to higher levels. Being able to combine them all together would make them infallible hunters.

It had not been easy for Hephaestus to undergo these long training sessions since he was a very impetuous youth. If he succeeded, he had his faithful companion to thank. Tito had stayed close to him every single day, helping him practice with his senses. With his wide eyes and lively ears, he scanned the horizon next to his human. Whether sitting on rocks, looking toward open spaces, or hidden in the middle of the woods, Tito never moved from Hephaestus's side, inducing in him a patience that was certainly not his strong suit.

It was during those long days that the deep connection between them was established. During the countless hours spent side-by-side, Tito's whiskers developed a sensitive connection with Hephaestus's skin and a genetic map of his cells. The high tension they both experienced during the training sessions created a profound, invisible bridge so that Tito's whiskers would vibrate whenever he got close to his human's skin. Hephaestus very much preferred days of physical training to sitting-down days, even when he would come home with his head bandaged or his arms and legs bruised.

Tito ran alongside Hephaestus, and after months of training, they established an impromptu code: while running in the woods, the feline made a more guttural sound if the obstacle was on the right, a short "meow" if it was on the left. His fellow aspiring hunters were jealous and reported the matter to the masters. Khepri made his son promise that Tito would not follow him on the day of the final test.

Becoming the best hunter of the tribe had not been easy for him. He had managed to bring the combination of his senses to its highest level. He could sense the presence of an animal even in the slightest breath of wind. He knew which direction to take to intercept the animal even before seeing it. His strong and sinewy legs responded immediately to every little signal received from his running feet so he could run with eyes fixed on the prey, not worrying about possible obstacles, unlike everybody else. He was an example that was followed and admired by everyone.

Khepri was worried Hephaestus would fail after training with Tito for too long. When the day of the final test arrived, Hephaestus stopped for a moment and talked to Tito. He asked for his protection before taking him to his grandfather's, telling Tito he had to wait there.

Tito was not happy to be locked inside, knowing his human was going hunting. He was meowing behind the closed door when Hator took him in his arms and spoke to him. "Tito, you have done your duty; you have been by his side, teaching him patience and sagacity. Now he has to put your lessons to good use. Be patient, and he will come back victorious."

Listening to Hator's words, Tito stopped meowing and jumped on the bed, crouching over his paws. Eyes fixed on the door, Tito waited for his human to return home.

At sunset, the five master hunters and the young hunters returned, exhausted but satisfied. They dragged two litters carrying three deer and two wild boars which they had chased and killed. With the entire tribe gathered around, Khepri climbed on a rock, shouting that each aspiring hunter had completed the test excellently. Shouts of joy and enthusiasm followed his words. The young hunters, including Hephaestus, were battered, full of bruises, but happy.

After the dinner, the celebration was over, and everyone retired to his own hut. Khepri congratulated his son before falling asleep. "I am proud of you. You did an excellent job, even if you could not avoid falling between those two rocks while chasing the second deer. In the future, if that happens again, remember to wait before launching your spear. Coming out of the bushes into an open space, a deer will always seek a place to hide. You threw your spear too early, thinking the deer would continue in a straight line, so you missed it just when it turned back toward the bushes. If you had waited longer, you would have caught it then instead of having to chase it farther. However, you succeeded, and you should be proud. Now get some well-deserved rest!"

Hephaestus was still so excited and full of adrenaline that he could not sleep. He was lying on his bed with Tito on his chest. Tito's eyes were made even larger by a profound darkness only interrupted by the few rays of a pale moon. He listened to his human with a mixture of a slight reproach for having been left home and contentment for feeling Hephaestus's beating heart.

"You should have seen how I ran after that deer! I left it breathless. You would have had such fun! Today, I could not take you with me, but I will from now on. We will be a very good pair of hunters, you and I!"

Tito tapped Hephaestus's chin with his paw. It was a sign of approval, his way of saying, "Agreed, human. That is a promise!"

The Meeting of the "Titolos"

Ameroe wanted always to be aware of what was going on in his community. To do so, he gathered the "Titolos" every ten sunsets to learn about work progress and to listen to suggestions or new initiatives his men proposed to improve life for the citizens. In the months following the move, other tribes knocked on the new city walls, asking to be let in. The king welcomed them without hesitation. More towns-people made the city safer and more prosperous, even if there were more mouths to feed.

The place chosen for the meetings was the top of the hill, the one that had been made flatter by breaking the rock. There was a spur of stone left. Sitting on it, Ameroe could see everyone and be seen at the same time. Behind his back, there was a small wall with a small ledge. Beyond this highest part of the hill, there was the emptiness of the valley facing toward the north winds.

After the hunting skill test, the new hunters were also allowed to participate. Hephaestus arrived with Tito on his shoulders. When he sat down, the cat jumped down and walked toward Ameroe, walked in front of him, and then jumped onto the stone ledge towering above him. Ameroe turned his head, looked at Tito affectionately, and then said to his citizens, "I see we have a new king today!"

Tito ignored Ameroe and continued in an arrogant way to watch the people gathered there, thinking how nice it was that they were all there to serve him. This hill was his home. He was born there before any of these humans arrived. He was happy they were working to make "his" hill more beautiful. He was very proud of it.

Tito sat on that ledge for the entire meeting, maintaining a solemn and dignified bearing, never diverting his attention from what was happening in front of and below him. He sat with his front legs perfectly aligned, and never once did he curl up or fall asleep like he did when at home. His composure was regal and showed his superiority. When Ameroe ended the meeting and stepped down from his stone throne, Tito jumped down and then up onto his human's shoulders. He did not understand what they were saying. He did not care. He knew they were there for him, there to make his territory a better place.

At that specific meeting, the group decided to devote a portion of the upper part of the hill as a place to worship the gods. It was called "Arce." An altar was built for sacrificial ceremonies. Hator was confirmed as the community's spiritual leader and named Supreme Priest with the delicate task of evoking the gods' protection of the city and its inhabitants.

Amer's hunters would make regular trips to the woods to get

enough game, but with the increasing population, there was a greater need for food. There was a flat area at the lower part of the hill, between the creek and another small hill. The Servants of the Earth decided to deforest it. The Builders needed wood to build more houses and huts, and that area could then be used to grow a greater quantity of the puffed wheat called "farro" or spelt. The Servants of the Earth had devoted a lot of effort to cultivating the precious cereal that was so valuable to everyone's livelihood.

On the other side of the creek, they planted grape vines. With a slight slope and exposure to the south, it was the ideal place to transplant long lines of vines to produce juicy and sugary grapes.

It became necessary to enlarge the House of Food, which was doubled and divided into three sections. One was called the "*Sala del Farro*" (Farro Room) and was filled with large terracotta jars to store the puffed wheat for winter. In the middle section, three large basins were hammered out of the stone to provide a place to press the grapes. The resulting delicious wine was kept in smaller terracotta jars. The third basin was left for the hunters to dissect prey and distribute the meat, fur, and skin. In a building nearby, skilled craftsmen treated the coat and skin to make clothes, blankets, and accessories.

One of the Servants of the Earth named Olèo noticed some evergreen trees with small, elongated leaves. At the end of the summer, those trees were filled with small green and black fruit. The fruit was bitter and inedible. He picked up a small quantity, thinking he could press the fruit like they did with grapes, though certainly not in the same way. Grapes were pressed by using feet, and the liquid juice was then poured into the jars. These small berries were much harder. To press them, the berries' pits had to be removed, and the pulp crushed between two flat stones.

Olèo tried to savor the resulting juice with some farro and *focaccia*, but it was so bitter it almost burned his throat. He put the berry juice in a small jar and forgot about it. After several months, he came across it again and noticed some slush at the bottom of the jar. The juice had a better flavor, a more transparent color, and a nicer taste. He asked the others to try it, and everyone was enthusiastic about it. At the end of the following summer, they harvested all the berries, pressed them, and placed the liquid into several jars. After a few months of settling, the liquid became a delicacy served on important occasions on *focaccia* or on roasted meats. It was also used to heal wounds.

The larger House of Food was also entrusted to Plesia and a few other women, wives of hunters or Servants of the Earth. One of Plesia's daughters, Tidra, was tasked with preserving and storing different foods. She had to make sure the older stocks were used before new ones, both the stocks from hunting and harvesting.

Tidra had a soft spot for Hephaestus. She watched him discreetly whenever he returned from hunting, but she never dared talk to him. She was also intimidated by the crush her mother had on Khepri. The thought of her mother flirting with Khepri, chief hunter and father of Hephaestus, made her reluctant to follow her own feelings for the son of her mother's possible mate.

However, her attraction to him grew steadily, and Tidra decided to talk to her mother, who was already well aware of her daughter's feelings. One morning, Tidra discovered that a few wooden plugs used to close the terracotta jars filled with farro had been gnawed by mice. The pesky rodents had discovered the treasure stored in the House of Food.

When Hephaestus returned from a hunting day, Tidra asked him if he and Tito could spend the evening with her in that room. To preserve their stocks for the winter, they had to kill those mice, and there was no one better than Tito to do the job. It was the perfect opportunity to spend time with Hephaestus and simultaneously solve the mouse problem.

Hephaestus showed up at sunset with Tito on his shoulders. Tidra showed them where the tiny four-pawed thieves had started to gnaw the wooden plugs. Hephaestus took the cat off his shoulders, placed him on the top of the jar, and said to him, "Look closely, smell them! These mice are stealing our food. Find them and kill them! Scare them! Kick them out!"

Tito did not seem very involved. He gave Hephaestus a smug look, then yawned and stood there cleaning himself by licking his paws and wiping his head.

Tidra said to Hephaestus, "Are you sure he is a good hunter? He does not seem very interested!"

Hephaestus stood up for him. "It is just that he is used to hunting in the woods for rabbits and other animals. Maybe he is not interested in mice."

A couple of hours went by. Tidra had a *focaccia* and a small jar of the green juice, which had been named "oil" after the name of its discoverer, Olèo. She also brought some wine. While they started to get to know each other more intimately, after initial shyness, they exchanged stories. She told him how she had lost her father, and he told her about losing his mother. They both shared their contentment at having moved to this valley and recounted many more stories. They did not realize Tito had jumped down from the tall jar and wandered into the large hall.

Darkness fell, the right time for mice to arrive. The two youngsters talked about their remaining parents and about how nice it would be if they could finally get together as a couple. Tidra reached out to touch his hand, and their faces were getting closer in what would be their first kiss when they heard a great commotion among the jars. In the dim light, Tito's white paws appeared.

When he got closer, they noticed the big mouse he had in his jaws. He left it near them and turned back. Before Hephaestus could say anything, Tito returned with a second mouse, dropping it next to the other one. He sat next to his prey with a look full of pride and defiance as if he was saying to the girl, "And you doubted me? You do not hunt on command! You have to wait for the right moment." All those months of training had proved to be useful for him, as well, in knowing when it was the right moment to capture the prey. He had gotten two in a very short time.

Tidra and Hephaestus had an impromptu laugh, looking at Tito seated there like he was saying to them, "So, what? After my effort, do you not even want to eat the dinner I caught for you?"

Not to disappoint him, Hephaestus caressed Tito, thanked him, saying he had done a great job, and took the two mice to show he had accepted the gift. Tito understood it was time to go; he turned around and left the hall, showing the young people his butt, with his tail straight up. Tidra and Hephaestus then exchanged their first kiss.

Hephaestus and Tidra

Soon enough, everyone knew about their love. A ceremony was celebrated in the upper part of town in the presence of King Ameroe and all the Titolos. Hephaestus intended to follow in his father's footsteps. While Hator spoke words of blessing and consecrated their love to the gods to bring many progeny to the city, Tito remained seated on the rock ledge behind the king, always erect and dignified. Hator then raised his arms to the sky and invited the couple to kiss. Everyone screamed with joy and celebrated the newlyweds. Tito jumped down from the ledge and leaped on Hephaestus's shoulders, rubbing his head on his human's nape.

The festivities continued with a huge banquet in the House of Food, with different roasted meats seasoned with the green juice called "oil." Tito preferred to stay away; he knew that when many humans gathered together and drank too much, they became loud and out of control. Since, on another similar occasion, a drunken man had stepped on his tail, he had been keeping a safe distance at such events. He went home and waited on his bed.

Much later, when Hephaestus and Tidra arrived, he was asleep. He barely opened his eyes, looking at them crossly like he was saying, "You woke me up!" He dozed off again while the two started to discover the secrets of their bodies on their first night as husband and wife.

They tried to be quiet so as not to wake Khepri, who they thought was sleeping in the next room.

Only the next morning did they realize Khepri had never returned home. Hephaestus thought his father got drunk and fell asleep in the House of Food. Opening the front door, they saw him walking toward the house.

"So, Father, how much wine did you drink last night? You could not find the way home?"

Khepri smiled at him. "I found it, but not yours. Now, this is your and Tidra's home. And Tito's. I will miss you, little one," he said to Tito.

"Why, Father? Where will you go?"

"I will be staying with Plesia. We have decided to leave this house to you."

Father and son embraced while Tidra watched from behind, holding Tito in her arms.

Hator's Prophecy

Ameroe's wisdom was very appreciated by his people, who listened to him and supported him. It was not easy for him to reign over several tribes with different backgrounds and ways of communicating and make them all live together peacefully. At every meeting of the Titolos, conflicts were raised with heated discussions. His incredible patience and foresight always brought about solutions, and he had each meeting end with at least one new project to improve the city and the lives of its inhabitants.

The new rules were not always welcomed unanimously, but in the long run, they always proved to be constructive for the community's growth. In addition to individual homes for each family, Ameroe wanted to unite his people, trying to ensure that everyone had enough to live well. His benevolence and the esteem he received from everyone made his task more manageable, even though someone was always there to dispute his authority. He tried not to impose too rigid rules, but it was necessary to take something away from those who had more and give it to those who had less.

The House of Food was created for this exact task. All agricultural production converged in it. Harvest foods; products from vegetable gardens, vineyards, and farms; and meats from hunting were collected and divided to make food available for everyone. No one could withdraw more than was necessary to feed himself and his family.

Ameroe struggled to explain the rule with serenity and clarity. The survival of all citizens and the community's future, especially during the winters, depended largely on avoiding food wastage. Sharing all resources allowed everyone to carry out his or her work and contribute to the well-being of the whole community.

To improve the city and make it safer, in one of the meetings, the townspeople decided to excavate the rock on the top of the hill even further in order to expand the flat part to accommodate more people and activities. The Defenders, the Titolos in charge of providing hunting weapons, suggested that they had to train young people to defend their land. If news about the wealth and beauty of their hill spread, they could be attacked. They also needed young people to be trained to defend, not just hunt. The upper part of the Arce was dedicated to this purpose and was called "Tota." There, the youngsters were trained in hand-to-hand combat, fighting with daggers, and other defensive disciplines.

The other side of the Arce was dedicated to public life and the government of the city. It was called "Trifo." Each citizen could go there to submit problems or suggestions and attend each meeting of the Titolos, which were now open to everyone. The large stone boulders that had been removed from the top of the hill were moved further down the hill, to start replacing the wooden city fence. This more resistant and impenetrable wall, built by superimposing these huge chunks of rock, was a huge project strongly desired by Ameroe, even though he realized he would not live to see it finished.

As Supreme Priest, Hator, every three sunsets, prepared a sacrifice to the gods to gain their goodwill for the city. As appropriate, he prayed for a copious harvest or for needed rain in the warmest months. Hator's offerings seemed to be well received by the gods.

The city infrastructure was enriched with new buildings and new activities. Many artisan shops opened: ironsmiths and carpenters, seamstresses, goldsmiths, shoemakers, and ceramists. Their products made Amer's homes more beautiful and elegant. This wealth made the city a much more advanced place than other nearby communities.

Years had passed since Khepri had first discovered the valley, and while he continued hunting, he was not as agile as before. The time came to pass the Titolo of Hunting Chief to his son, his worthy successor. In those years, however, two significant events had forever changed Hephaestus's life: he became a father himself, and his faithful hunting companion Tito was also reaching the end of his life. When Tidra gave birth to their third child, her pregnancy and Tito's decline went side by side.

Tito no longer followed his human on his hunting trips. The passing years proved to be even harder for him than Khepri. When Hephaestus called him, he stayed on his bed or by the fire. Hephaestus could not accept that Tito was growing old and missed him terribly when hunting. His father tried to comfort him, saying that one day soon, both he and Tito would pass to the afterlife underground.

The year after the birth of Hephaestus and Tidra's last child, Tito, now confident his human's lineage would continue, gently died in Hephaestus's arms. Their last look was full of mutual understanding and deep love. The entire city mourned Tito's death.

Hephaestus's friend Avile then remembered that brick with Tito's footprints from so many years before. He ran to the furnace and began to search for it in the pile of cast-offs where sometimes somebody went to recover some imperfect bricks for minor repairs. Avile was on the point of giving up when he found the brick and brought it to Hephaestus. Seeing Tito's two small pawprints made Hephaestus very emotional. He brought it to his heart as tears flowed down his face.

A solemn ceremony was organized to give Tito a last farewell. Hator placed Tito's remains in a special small shrine carved into the rock on the top of the hill. He closed it with the brick with Tito's pawprints while pronouncing a majestic prophecy: "Tito, you were in this land before us; you welcomed us here to share the richness of your valley. Now that you have left your mortal life, your soul will remain among us forever in this valley to protect it and lead it toward a glorious future. We ask for your protection and your intercession with the gods, while awaiting your return to us. Protect our King Ameroe, your Hephaestus, and all his progeny for the centuries to come. Protect our city, Amer."

The legend of Tito of Amer was remembered for many of the following generations. Hephaestus recounted it to his children, and they continued to pass it on. Tito was remembered by everyone as the first inhabitant of the valley, or at least the first that, by his actions, had won him the name "Titolo," his legendary name.

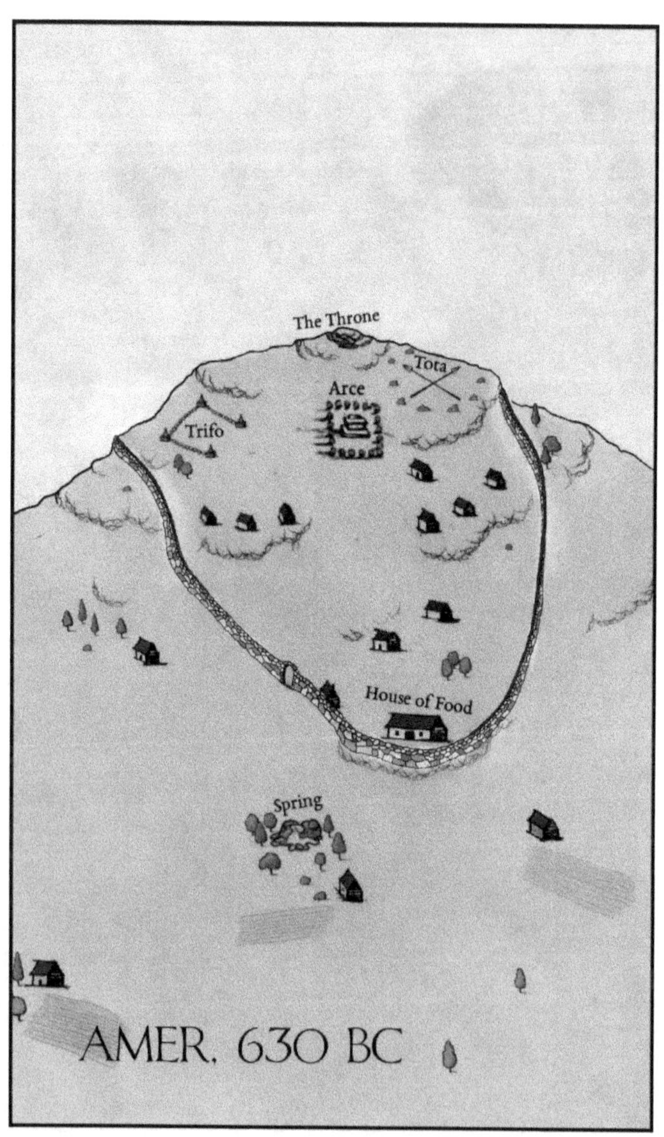

The Throne
Tota
Arce
Trifo
House of Food
Spring
AMER, 630 BC

Chapter 2
The Pre-Roman Era in Amer
Year 330 BC
Aker and Tarzio: The Engineers of the Walls

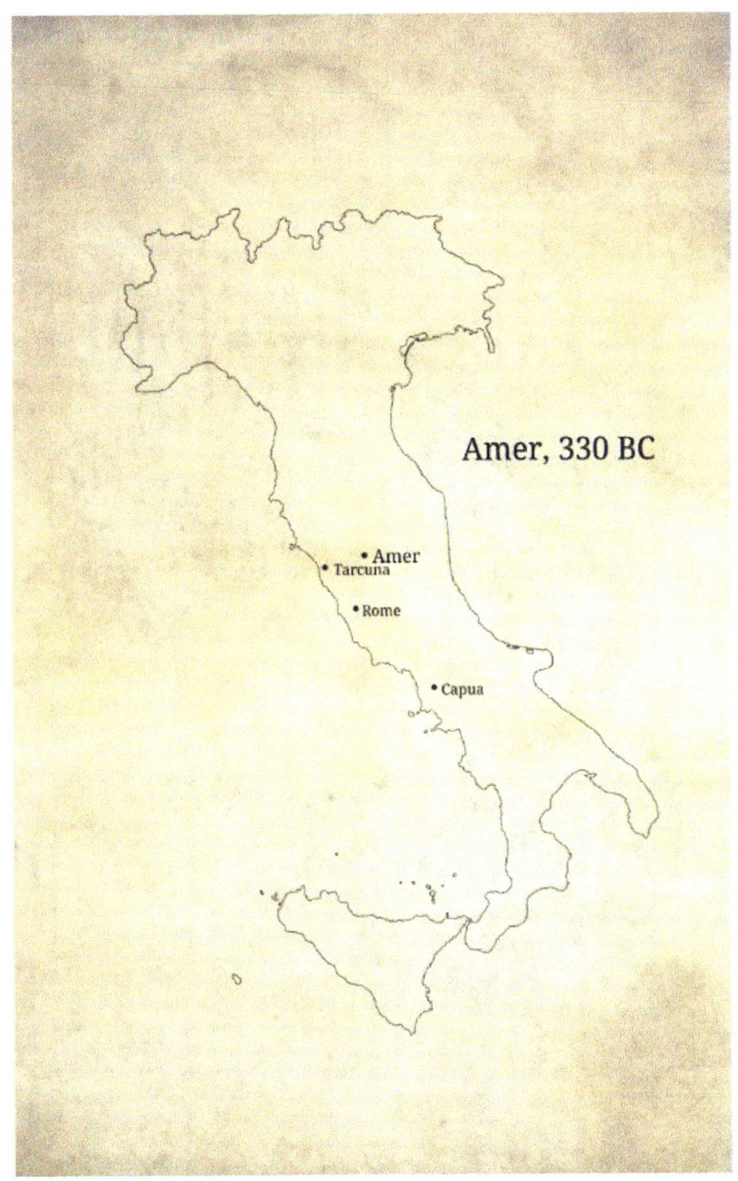

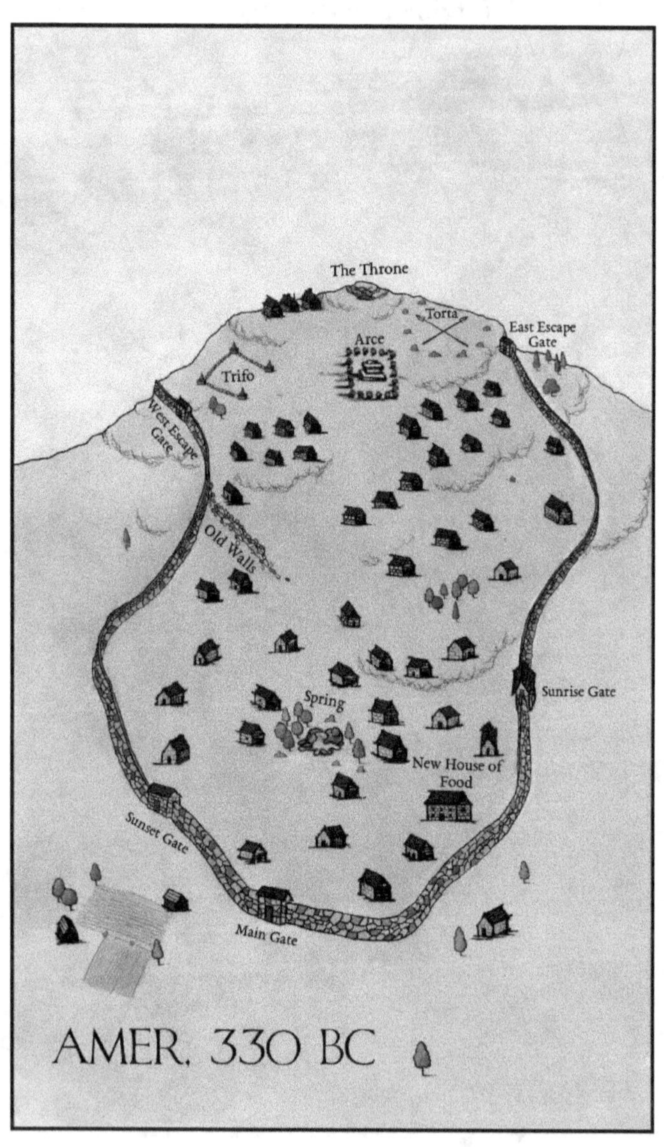

The Throne
Torta
Arce
East Escape Gate
Trifo
West Escape Gate
Old Walls
Sunrise Gate
Spring
New House of Food
Sunset Gate
Main Gate
AMER, 330 BC

Cast of Characters

Family at the Start of the Chapter

Xeste: a descendant of Khepri, a farmer

Setonia: Xeste's wife

Tarzio: the son of Xeste and Setonia

Tito/Aker: a cat

Other Principals

Laertes: the twin of Laertia, a friend of Tarzio

Laertia: the twin of Laertes, a friend of Tarzio

Other Amerians

Arcite: the king

Pompeus: the chief worker at the construction site

Aulus: a rope merchant for the construction site

Velio: a construction site worker

Tolumne: a second construction site worker

Historical Figures

Marcus Valerius Corvus: the consul of an expanding and aggressive
   Rome

Populations

Samnites: a population living in the Apennine Mountains south of
    Rome

Family at the End of the Chapter

Elaxantre

Introduction

Nowadays, when we look at the walls of Amer (today called Amelia) and wonder about their history, we are told that there is no documentation of any kind about the origins of the walls. We can only refer to the legend about King Ameroe, who hired a Cyclops. Only a Cyclops could move boulders of such enormous dimensions. But if Ameroe founded the city of Amer in 1,134 BC, he would have had to be immortal or lived for several centuries to be able to witness the construction of both walls of the city: the *"Ciclopiche"* dating back to the 6th century BC, and the *"Poligonali"* dating to around the 4th century BC. No one will ever be able to know the truth about the construction of the walls. Perhaps Tito is the only witness left to the true story.

~

Loud, overlapping noises echoed over the entire valley—people's cries, logs screeching, horses neighing, and oxen bellowing. The construction site of the new city walls, which were being made of massive, squared blocks of grey rock, was in full operation. It had started months before and was supposed to continue for a long time.

Ameroe had died almost five centuries before, but no one had forgotten that great man who had founded one of the first organized cities of central Italy. His legend was handed down for generations and made him immortal.

In Amer, there were no direct descendants of that legendary king, but there were still families who could boast of having ancestors who lived in his time and contributed to the birth and beauty of their city. One of those families was Xeste's. His wife was Setonia, and their son was named Tarzio. They could not trace themselves back to every ancestor they might have had, but for generations, they had been considered descendants of Khepri, the great hunter who discovered the valley with the spring. Ameroe's dream of surrounding the city with an impenetrable wall had never been abandoned and was finally coming true.

Amer had become a very populated city, and its first stone walls, built some three hundred years before, were not sufficiently expansive to secure the growing number of inhabitants. On the top of the hill, the area devoted to worshipping the gods was still there. On the side of the hill, Trifo was the area where the king and the city elders ran the city's public affairs. Close to Trifo was Tota, where the city guards resided.

The old House of Food no longer existed. Now, there were mostly private homes in that spot. Another bigger building down the valley replaced the old House of Food and was specially built to store essential goods—crops, wine, and preserves. It was closer to the fields and the grazing areas.

The current king, Arcite, decided to protect these areas with new, more extensive, stronger walls, which would include the precious spring, left outside of the original walls.

Amer was now the principal city for a very large region. Merchants and travelers never failed to stop in this ever-growing city. All the houses were now built of stone or bricks, with the last remaining wooden huts only used for farm animals or wood storage. The citizens had consistently advanced socially, both in manners and lifestyle. Houses were elegantly decorated.

Women wore fashionable dresses made with precious linens that were either woven locally or bought from the numerous merchants who sold goods in the big square at the base of the hill. The elegant dresses were enriched by elaborate jewels, proof of the community's wealth. Finely crafted earrings with precious stones, refined gold necklaces, and arm and forearm bracelets were common among Amer matrons who flaunted them on all public occasions and at the numerous private banquets.

During those opulent banquets with tables full of delicacies and delicious wine from nearby vineyards, important decisions for the town were often made. On those banquet days, the expansion of the walls was frequently the main topic. That complicated and expensive proposed venture would involve the entire city's financial and labor resources for a very long time.

King Arcite had to not only convince everyone to contribute financially but also assure everyone that he would find and entrust the project to someone who was sufficiently experienced to design the project and direct the construction of the new city walls. Not a single "Amerian" had those skills. It had been easier for him to decide to have the walls built than to find someone who could manage the project, until a young Amerian called Tarzio proved he could handle it.

The problematic design of the walls and the complicated building machinery composed of tree trunks, beams, and tie rods—all necessary for the construction—came from the brilliant mind of this young, until-then-misunderstood genius.

Competence to build city walls was not a goal Tarzio had achieved easily. From an early age, he had been a very silent and shy child. Teased by his peers for not participating in group games, he was not interested in sword fights or in playing with children of his own age. He preferred to stay at home building toys made of wood and rope for purposes no one could understand. He spent whole days making small wooden carts that could move tiny stones and pebbles. Along with the carts, he created small homes, bridges, and turrets.

Tarzio's parents worried about him being so isolated and not playing with other children. His father, Xeste, was a farmer who culti-vated the community fields where the townspeople grew farro. Xeste took Tarzio along to the fields, trying to interest him in agriculture and teaching him about the proper times and methods for sowing and harvesting, as well as techniques for storing grains.

None of that seemed to interest Tarzio. One morning, watching the peasants struggle to lift heavy sacks of farro onto carts, he had a brilliant idea: he looked around him and found two long, wooden boards, which he placed on two boulders. In a very short time, Tarzio had created a slide to make their job quicker and less difficult.

Tarzio's father was delighted to see him interested in something outside the house and was thrilled with his design for that simple device. Using the slide Tarzio had created, Xeste managed to get many more sacks to the House of Food in a much shorter amount of time.

Returning home for several days in a row, Xeste noticed a white cat with a striped coat sitting near his front door. The cat was always there, and Xeste started to give him some leftovers from the family's meals. Sometimes, the cat slept on their windowsill. Setonia started to find him there every morning when she opened the shutters. Xeste then remembered the legend of Tito, his ancestor's cat, a legend his grandmother used to tell him when he was a child. He also remembered Hator's prophecy, which gave Tito the task of protecting the city of Amer for centuries to come.

Xeste's first thought was that the cat could be good company for his son and help Tarzio out of his isolation. Certainly, Xeste did not know that the cat was indeed Tito, who had returned for his second life to accompany Tarzio for one of the most legendary and important projects in the city's history. Tito's reincarnation was not regulated by strict rules or predefined deadlines, especially given the delicate task the gods had assigned him, that of protecting the city, Hephaestus, and Hephaestus's progeny. Tito's spirit had wandered around in his valley until his presence had become essential again.

When the reincarnated Tito opened his yellow-green eyes after being weaned from a new mother, he recognized the sky, the scent of the air, and the place where he had been born for the first time several centuries earlier. He explored the surroundings, observing the changes and evolution of the place he had known. There was less green than when Tito had closed his eyes at the end of his first life. Lots of buildings had been built in areas where he used to run freely together with Hephaestus. While drifting in the spirit world, he had strongly felt the call of his land and experienced an unconscious but determined feeling of having to return for an important reason, a decisive mission.

Xeste soon managed to win Tito's trust. He took him in his arms and walked him into his home. Tito's whiskers started to vibrate at the touch of those hands. The cat immediately recognized the sensation established in the past with Hephaestus's skin. He had the confirmation he needed; he had found the descendant of his old pal.

Xeste entered Tarzio's room.

"Look, my dear son, this kitty needs affection. I found him out there alone and sad. Do you want to keep him company?"

When Tarzio and Tito's eyes met, something magical happened between them. Tito immediately understood that he had to make friends with Tarzio rather than Xeste. The boy squeezed him in his arms, and at that touch, Tito's whiskers vibrated even more intensely. He knew he was in the right place.

Xeste asked Tarzio if he wanted to name the cat.

"I will call him Aker!"

"Why that name?" Xeste asked.

"It comes from the name of our city, Amer." Tarzio looked deeply into Tito's loving eyes and said, "You are Aker of Amer!"

Tito looked at Tarzio, a bit disappointed, as if he were saying, "My real name is Tito, but never mind! Aker will do just fine!"

The two became inseparable. Aker stayed patiently by Tarzio's side during the long hours he spent in his room playing and planning his little games. Tarzio immediately started to talk to Aker like he was human, something Tarzio wasn't used to doing with real humans. He described each step of his games to Aker. The cat patiently listened and sometimes played with a bit of stone or those strange gadgets; he pretended to follow Tarzio's comments, but often, he dozed off. He knew the moment had not yet arrived when his presence would be essential.

~

A few years later, during harvest season, Xeste, now approaching old age, was complaining about how long it took to bring the numerous heavy sacks of farro to the House of Food. Seeing his father tired and often angry about that difficulty, Tarzio began to think of how he could help. He spent several days making drawings on pieces of parchment, and one night at dinner, he spoke to his father about a mobile platform. It was intended to elevate loads of sacks right in front of the House of Food instead of having to transport them on carts pulled by donkeys up that steep cobbled street.

Even with Tarzio's detailed explanations, Xeste could not follow what his son was saying and told him it was unfeasible madness. Setonia was very disappointed with her husband's behavior. She herself also could not understand how the machine would work, but her mother's instinct told her she had to support her son. She had to act quickly and let him show his capability before he could isolate himself even more.

She wondered what she could do. Going to sleep that night, she passed the slightly opened door of Tarzio's room. She saw him at his table in the candlelight with the parchment pages laid out in front of him. He was talking to Aker, who was seated in front of him, listening attentively.

"Nobody understands me! You are the only one who listens to me!" he said, caressing Tito's fur. "I know it can work if only they gave me a chance to prove it. Then I know they would be grateful." Aker pushed his head toward Tarzio's chin, rubbing it several times.

That image brought tears to her eyes. She said to herself, *If that cat listens to Tarzio's words, I have to find a way to show my husband our son's genius.* She walked slowly to her bedroom, lay down next to her already-asleep husband, and remained awake, thinking about how to convince him.

Rain started to pour down and continued for several days, delaying the already-planned harvest. It was not possible to gather the grain with such wet fields. Xeste was worried and came back home every night deeply demoralized; with the delay, he could not ensure enough supplies were being stored for the community for the following winter. He had to find a quicker way to harvest and store the farro soon after the fields dried. Storing wet farro would not be safe; it would get moldy during the winter.

That was the right moment for Setonia to intervene with her husband. She was not only worried about her son's isolation but also preoccupied about her husband's health since he pushed himself too hard on his job. She repeated insistently to him, "Let Tarzio try! Give him a chance!"

When the rain stopped, Xeste called his men back to the still-wet fields. They would have to wait at least ten days before the sun dried the fields. The harvesting technique was well established by that time: a line of workers with sharp scythes moved in parallel formation, cutting the stalks and leaving them behind. A second row of workers followed. They collected the stalks, tying them in bundles. The bundles were then brought to a flat area and piled up in haystacks, with the stalk heads facing outwards so they could dry more quickly.

When the grain started to fall from the stalks, the workers placed large sheets of canvas jute on the ground. The stalks were scattered on the sheets and covered with another layer of canvas. Workers leading mules would walk back and forth on the canvas. Thanks to the weight of the men and mules, the farro grains detached from the stalks, which remained on the bottom of the canvas. The stalks, with no grain remaining, were then removed with rakes. The grain left on the canvas was then poured into numerous sacks after being separated from any remaining straw, leaves, or stems. After that, the sacks of grain had to be carried to the House of Food, poured into terracotta jars, and kept for the winter.

To speed up at least this last phase, Xeste finally allowed his son to build his elevating platform, leaving a few of his workers with him to help. Tarzio created a large cage made of solid tree trunks. Four of them were placed vertically and tied together by four others situated horizontally, creating two high rectangles. This way, he could overcome the difference in height between the lower level and the House of Food.

He placed the rectangles next to the hill, anchoring them on the floor and the side with solid pins stuck into the rock. In the center of this cage, he placed a platform made of strong wooden planks, to which heavy ropes were attached and fixed at the four corners. The ropes were then elevated to the top of the cage, from which they fell down on each side. Two large oxen, slowly driven in opposite directions, pulled the ropes.

Sliding over the beams, the ropes raised the platform, which was loaded with sacks, from the valley to the top of the hill. Tarzio stood at a distance from where he could have a clear view and was able to shout to the peasants guiding the oxen, letting them know if they had to slow down one of the oxen or speed one up to keep the platform balanced and prevent any sacks from spilling.

As soon as the platform reached the top, two workers secured it with four large pins. They could then unload all the sacks and carry them inside. After unloading the grain from the platform, the team lowered it again, and with only three or four raisings of the platform, they managed to do in one day the work that would have taken a much longer time.

King Arcite came to witness Tarzio's invention, and he was as mesmerized by it as everybody else. Tarzio himself was not very happy with the result; he knew he could do better. The ropes were quickly worn out by friction and needed to be replaced often. Even if the tree trunks forming the platform were smooth and coated with animal fat, the heavy weight of the sacks created friction, which caused the ropes to break. An entire load of sacks could potentially be lost if a rope broke and the platform tilted, spilling the sacks to the ground.

One evening, Tarzio was sitting at his table in front of a parchment sheet on which he had drawn his invention. No matter how much he looked at it, he could not find the right solution. On his table, in addition to a mug of wine, a few old toys, and other items, Aker was dozing off.

Tarzio lost his patience and swore nervously, slamming his fist on the table. He knew the solution was there, but he could not see it. Disturbed by his swearing, Aker got up, walked over, and sat next to one of the small carts Tarzio had built several years before. The cart was upside down, its wheels in the air, and Aker started playing with it. With his paw, Aker began to make one wheel turn noisily, again and again.

Tarzio was not happy and screamed, "Stop it! You distract me! I cannot concentrate!"

Aker began to spin the wheel even more insistently, looking at Tarzio with demanding eyes as if he were saying, "You idiot! Can you not see I am suggesting the solution to you?"

Tarzio was about to explode and moved to push Aker off the table when his eyes fell on Aker's paw, turning the wheel. He instantly got the enlightenment he was searching for. He realized that if he could fit four wheels at the corners of his structure, the ropes would not suffer from the friction caused by the ropes rubbing over the edges of the platform but instead would glide on those four flywheels. Pulling the platform up would also be easier.

The next morning, he placed four sections of a huge tree trunk, each with a hole drilled in the center, at the platform's four corners. He thought of having the trunks carved with an edge to prevent the ropes from sliding out over the sides, but there was no time. To make the process quicker, he nailed small boards around the wheels on both sides to contain the ropes during their rotation. The lifting became faster and easier.

He also attached boards around the platform's edge, creating a railing, so more layers of sacks could be loaded on each trip. On each side of the cage, he built two fenced paths to give the oxen a mandatory route to follow, allowing better management of their strength.

Xeste was delighted to see his son so enthusiastic and busy. He would never have thought that Tarzio's childhood toys could evolve into such large and useful structures admired by everyone.

It did not take long for many citizens of Amer to ask for smaller versions of his elevating platform to help them build their own houses or repair roofs, allowing them to save money and time.

The Project for the Walls

Tarzio had just turned thirty when the Council of the Elders and King Arcite, having admired his inventions, summoned Tarzio and asked him to study a project to realize Ameroe's dream: create the strongest and most resistant walls anyone had ever seen. New settlements and new cities had begun to be built in surrounding areas, and more and more travelers and merchants reported news about some of the towns beginning to get bigger and to be possible threats to Amer. One of those new cities was constantly talked about. Called Rome and founded almost four centuries after Amer, it was a fast-growing city on the left bank of a big river. Stories of battles and guerrilla fights between Rome and other cities near it circulated more and more frequently and were worrying.

King Arcite was convinced they needed to quickly build a strong, impenetrable defensive wall. The one built nearly three centuries before on the upper part of the hill proved not to be very durable, suffering damage several times from the frequent earthquakes in the area. What they needed were solid walls capable of resisting any attack, walls everyone would admire for their beauty and for the strength they would offer for the centuries to come.

Tarzio was very proud of this assignment and shut himself in his room for days and days, drawing on parchment. It was a challenging task, and many details needed deep study. His mother understood she could not disturb him while he was working; only at mealtimes did she knock on his door to bring him a plate with food.

Aker would immediately jump on the table when Setonia arrived. He knew that there was always something for him on the plate, too. The two friends ate quickly, and then Tarzio returned to work while Aker dozed off on his lap or on the table next to him. Aker never left Tazio's side except to go outside to tend to his needs or for a short walk.

Aker felt his presence was essential to Tarzio, helping Tarzio to maintain his concentration. Preparing the rock blocks became Tarzio's obsession. Before long, he understood that every block had to be cut precisely to match the surrounding ones perfectly. The old walls had been built with irregular rocks, and the gaps between them had been filled with smaller stones and lime. Over the succeeding centuries, the walls had had to be restored several times.

After studying the walls closely, Tarzio knew their weaknesses. Natural events such as earthquakes or heavy rains caused parts of them to collapse or wash away. The solution came to him almost by accident. It was not the same for his cat, who was only waiting for the right moment to act and show Tarzio what to do.

To avoid disturbing Tarzio and have his own little spot to nap, Aker started squatting on the fireplace mantel. He enjoyed the warmth coming from the chimney's bricks, and from that high position, he could observe every movement made by his human.

For his research, Tarzio filled two baskets with different kinds of stones he had collected from the fields. He built a miniature wall on one side of his long table, similar to the one on the top of the hill. He had drawn the wall stone by stone, rock by rock, and replicated it in this miniature model to discover why the walls did not last over time.

Aker was very happy to have this new game displayed on the

table, where he occasionally climbed up to be next to his human. He loved those little stones. He often batted them with his paw, making them fall from the top of the small wall.

Tarzio encouraged him. "Go for it, Aker! Let me understand where the weaknesses are!" An insight came to him when he saw Aker enjoying himself by knocking some stones off the top: those old walls had been built with the heaviest rocks at the base and with gradually smaller rocks going upwards. The smallest ones at the top were the ones Aker's pink paw pads could easily bat to the floor. Tarzio had the inspiration to mix the position of the stones, placing some smaller ones at the bottom and some heavier ones on the top. Aker could also dislodge the larger rocks, but he needed more strength. Tarzio concluded that it was their irregular size and shape that made them fall.

He began to build another miniature wall on the other side of the table. He started to mix small and large stones. The weight at the top of the wall made the wall more resistant. The more he went on, the more he realized the adherence of the stones to each other was the secret to strengthening the wall. He started to rub them together, molding them with a hammer and chisel, smoothing their surfaces, and giving them precise shapes to fit perfectly one beside the other. He then sat on his bed where he could peer at the two walls, moving his eyes from one side of the table to the other. He was evaluating the differences and all possible solutions. With almost closed eyes, he imagined himself on the top of a hill, looking at those two walls like they were real.

Aker was dozing on the fireplace mantel on the other side of the table. He was, in a way, happy about this new second life, which was much quieter than the previous one. Aker had loved being a hunter and accompanying his human, Hephaestus, on those exciting hunting trips. He often accompanied his human when Tarzio was visiting his father's fields, but those were simple walks, and Tarzio would carry him in his leather shoulder bag.

During those walks, Aker sat comfortably, watching the surroundings with his paws resting on the edge of Tarzio's bag. He did not miss the long and exhausting runs in the woods. He had had a lot of fun hunting with Hephaestus, but with Tarzio, life was definitely more peaceful. Both Tarzio and Tarzio's parents fed him enough. He no longer had to hunt to survive and liked being spoiled.

With these thoughts in his mind, Aker suddenly felt hungry. To get some attention from his human, who was so concentrated on those two small walls, Aker jumped from the mantel right onto the middle of the table. His weight jostled the long wooden boards.

Tarzio yelled, "Nooooo!" and shot Aker a menacing look, ready to reproach his cat, who leaped off the table and ran toward the kitchen. Instead of following him, Tarzio stopped at the door and looked back at the table.

Aker also stopped, turned around, and, as was usual when he was certain he had done something right, he sat down and started licking his paw to clean his muzzle, a sign of self-satisfaction.

That thud on the table had an earthquake-like effect. The wall built with irregular stones was almost completely destroyed; only a few stones remained in their original positions. The other wall, built with smooth and skillfully alternating stones, was virtually intact and still standing. That was proof that his studies on the positioning and shaping of the stones were the secret to giving the walls the strength that King Arcite and the council had requested.

Was it a coincidence that Aker had jumped on the table at that very moment? He could have jumped on the floor or on the stool right below the fireplace mantel. His instinct guided him to make that revealing leap right there, right at that moment.

Tarzio was ready to repeat the test before the king and the council, although in this instance, he would have to recreate that vibration on the table with a solemn punch to the center of the table. He was sure Aker would have jumped at his command, but he could not risk a failure if Aker refused.

Tarzio brought his own table to the council room. Before the King and the Elders arrived, he carefully rebuilt the two walls, paying even more attention to the position of every stone. Before the assembled council, he provided a detailed explanation about how those two walls were built roughly in the same way and how the shape and location of the stones would affect their resistance. Many could not follow his explanation, but when Tarzio delivered that strong punch in the middle of the table, everyone was surprised to see how the one built with the irregular stones completely fell apart. In contrast, the one with the well-joined and smooth stones remained standing.

After the test, King Arcite put Tarzio in charge of designing the walls, determining their layout, and directing the project.

Tarzio ran back home and hugged Aker, holding the cat against his chest. "My friend! Without you, I would not have been able to end my research!" Tarzio squeezed Aker even more, kissing him on his head while Aker purred loudly. "Now, let's get back to work! The bulk of the work is yet to come, and you must help me!"

Aker's "meow" response meant, "Sure, that is why I am here!"

Xeste and Setonia were delighted to see the passion their son was putting into this massive project. Worried that he would not be up to it, his mother offered to help even though she could not understand any of his drawings or calculations. Despite her lack of understanding, she still asked if she could help him.

Tarzio did not want to exclude his mother, and he knew he needed to form a smart, capable team to share the important tasks he could not carry out all by himself. Tarzio knew he needed at least two collaborators to survey the area, measuring land and distances to establish the direction of the walls, their extension, length, and precise positioning. He mentioned to his mother that he needed at least two assistants.

Setonia became very concerned. Knowing her son very well and, above all, knowing he could not deal with strong personalities, she knew she needed to find individuals similar to him or at least an assistant who would put him at ease. She started to investigate among their neighbors and her husband's workers to see if they could help her find someone that she and her son could trust.

After a few days, she introduced her son to the two perfect people with whom he could collaborate. Laertes and Laertia were twins, brother and sister, children of one of Xeste's workers. Their father, returning home, often told his children about Tarzio's inventions. He also took them to see the platform Tarzio had created, and they were charmed by it.

Although of different genders, the twins looked very much

alike. They shared a very intense relationship with each other to the point of being held up by many, not as a miracle but as a joke of nature. Some people avoided them, saying they were possessed since their minds seemed to be connected to each other, and they reacted in the same ways. The harmony of their actions, words, and faces was frightening to some people instead of beautiful.

Setonia saw their marginalization as the necessary element to attract her son's trust. The three understood each other very quickly, and while the twins felt honored to work with him, Tarzio perceived the feeling of exclusion in which they, too, lived. It made him feel comfortable and pushed him to open up to strangers for the first time.

Laertia soon fell in love with Aker and often carried him in her shoulder bag. The twins immediately began long and detailed inspections to determine the route of this impressive project. They climbed the hills around Amer and all the other viewpoints they could reach, like the big rock on the sunset side of the town and the hill to the sunrise side. The white rock wall behind the valley provided the well-known natural barrier that had attracted Khepri many centuries before. That barrier needed to be accompanied at its front with a large "hug."

The positioning of the walls was essential; they had to be visible from afar, from every path leading to Amer. From the very first look, everyone had to understand their strength, and that belief was needed to deter any attack on the city.

Aker quietly accompanied the twins for several days during those expeditions. Occasionally, he recognized places he had passed by in his previous life when he used to run side-by-side with Hephaestus. Memories of those years came back to him. He had had a different view from Hephaestus's shoulders from the one he was seeing now, comfortably seated in Laertia's leather bag.

Aker got emotional, remembering how Hephaestus and he understood each other and created that unbreakable bond when they were together. In absolute silence, their hearing, sight, and smell had sharpened to make them into infallible hunters. Still, being carried around in a soft bag was definitely better.

Once the three collaborators had an accurate idea of the area they needed to enclose in the new walls, they asked permission to dig a deep trench indicating the course of the walls to show to King Arcite and the council. In their imaginations, the white rock wall was like a giant stretching his two strong arms to encircle Amer at the front and to defend the city within those arms.

The next step was to put together an impressive team of workers. It took a very long time to discuss the project with the stone-masons, who were the group of citizens who provided the stones to build houses and other buildings. The number of stonemasons had to be increased, and their skills improved. It was not just a matter of the stonemasons providing regular- and small-sized correctly shaped stones. They now needed many more workers who could move and shape huge blocks of rock. They also needed to smooth the stones accurately to make each rock face perfectly fit with the next one on every side.

Other related needs had to be considered and improved, such as the wagons used until then to transport rocks. The wagons had to be reinforced with two more wheels in the center to support the massive weight of the heavy boulders and prevent the wagons from breaking in the middle.

The perimeter they laid down would include the spring previ-ously left outside the old walls. It was essential to have water if they were attacked. For the same reason, Tarzio decided to enlarge the area within the walls to include spaces they could dedicate to agriculture. In case of a siege or natural disaster, the farmers could provide food to the community locked inside the walls, cultivating vegetables and legumes.

It took Tarzio a whole month before he was ready to present the final project to the King and his fellow citizens, a month in which he hardly ever slept. After the long days spent measuring, drawing, and discussing issues with Laertes and Laertia, Tarzio continued to work at night in his room, reviewing his drawings and perfecting every detail, with Aker always at his side. Sometimes, annoyed by the light of the lanterns, Aker curled up on the bed, turning his back to Tarzio, but he was always there, listening to Tarzio when he talked to himself.

Sometimes, Tarzio questioned Aker, knowing he would not get

an answer. He did not realize Aker was answering him silently. Every time Tarzio reasoned aloud and turned toward Aker, the cat's calmness and intense gaze opened up Tarzio's mind and helped him find the right solution. The influence Aker had on him was almost hypnotic. Aker's feline brain could not understand anything about buildings, machines, or project requirements, but Aker certainly understood one thing: he was there to help his human achieve the best he could. Aker derived no advantage from his assistance to Tarzio, but the cat felt the pleasant weight of Hator's prophecy deeply within his soul.

The day to present the project to the King and the council finally came. After his presentation, many took him for a fool. They did not believe he could carry out such an extensive project. Some of the elders accused him and the twins of witchcraft and feared the citizens would all die in a large, open-air grave without any exits. King Arcite listened attentively and asked a few specific questions about the project. Despite protests from some of the council members, the King entrusted Tarzio with this colossal task.

The first days of the project were spent at the quarry, where the boulders were prepared and shaped. They had to be measured one by one with wooden planks on each face. They also had to be branded with a specific sign to indicate their exact positioning, like they were part of a mosaic. Tarzio was utterly convinced that careful positioning was the secret to achieving greater stability. The boulders could not be cut, transported, and placed randomly. Each had to have a pre-established position, and they had to be carefully positioned at the site to perfectly match on each side the ones that had already been placed there.

In addition to extending the walls for a huge linear distance, the walls also had to be built to a considerable thickness, almost four human steps, especially in the lower part, the foundation. The foundation stones were then later covered with wagonloads of dirt. Initially, that same dirt also served to build artificial hillocks to transport the rocks up the inclines that had been created so as to heighten the walls. The city farmers would later reuse that same dirt to create terraces for cultivating gardens and areas for the breeding of small animals inside the city walls.

Many workers started to complain about working so hard to shape so precisely those first stones that would then be hidden away. For them, that exacting work seemed a waste of time. Tarzio had to insist, to convince them of the importance those very first stones had for the stability of the whole texture of the walls. Despite all the criticism, he made sure each block fit perfectly.

The stonemasons and other workers derided Tarzio and his orders. His theory of alternating smaller and larger boulders in all directions and positioning them on non-parallel lines with no perpendicular angles gave the whole structure the ability to absorb the thrusts coming from possible earthquakes. That was perhaps too subtle a concept for the minds of workers used to supplying blocks more or less similar to one another without having to spend days shaping them one by one, with no stone the same as the previous one.

Tarzio lost his temper on several occasions, and Laertia had to intervene more than once to calm those heated discussions. In the beginning, it was not easy for her to put herself forward in addressing the workers, who were not inclined to take orders from a woman. When she started to send back boulders that were not shaped as requested, they began to listen to her and realize they could not make fun of her.

The twins gradually gained Tarzio's trust. They soon became essential to him. Setonia had had considerable intuition in getting together those three decidedly smart but marginalized individuals. Their joint minds complemented each other perfectly. More importantly, together, they formed a strong front in giving orders to the workers. Even if the twins did not share or understand Tarzio's directions, they did not try to object, at least not in front of the workers. Often, when the twins left the quarry, the workers enjoyed making jokes at their expense, behind their backs.

Once the first layer of boulders was set in place, the workers, using the dirt dug out on site, started building the hillocks needed to raise the first section of the walls. One side of the wall was left steeply inclined, while the other was given a gentle incline. The slope was then covered with well-oiled tree trunks to enable the workers to drag the blocks upwards with less effort as they began putting in place the upper layers.

Tarzio then developed a new version of his lifting platform, with a simpler structure but based on the same concept. Placed on the vertical side of the walls, with only two flywheels at the top, the ropes pulled by the oxen carried the blocks to a higher level much faster than was possible by manpower alone. In this way, construction of the wall was speeded up considerably. Nevertheless, criticism of the project spread from the workers to the common people.

Many people told him it would be easier and quicker to decrease the size of the boulders as they were getting to the top. He had to explain over and over again that a heavier weight on the top would give more stability to the entire wall. An earthquake would dislodge smaller stones, while heavier ones were more likely to stay in position. Only a few people could understand the concept.

One evening in his room, with Aker curled up on his chest, Tarzio vented his frustration to his friend, who listened attentively. To show his support, Aker reached out with his paw and caressed Tarzio repeatedly on his chin. Aker knew that the walls would stand for a very long time. Maybe he would not be able to see the walls completed in his lifetime, but he was sure he would admire them in his next life and remember his human, Tarzio, the creator of this immense project.

The Accident

Several months later, the wall's perimeter was almost entirely laid out. From the top of the city's hill, the walls could be easily admired, joining the two opposite spurs at the back of the hill. The foundation stones had been laid down for the entire perimeter, and on the sunrise side, several upper layers were already in place. Entrances to the city had to be considered so that people entering the city could reach and connect with the internal streets.

Laertes' contribution became essential in this phase. In his younger years, he trained as a soldier and studied defense in the Tota, where the soldiers lived and trained. He had ultimately abandoned the military, tired of the continuous mockery he received from his companions. His physical and intellectual resemblance to his twin sister was a subject of recurrent jokes. Their genetic affinity was such that in both of them, there were attributes of the opposite gender. While in the case of Laertia, some of her more masculine behavior could be tolerated, the more feminine aspects of Laertes' character were unacceptable, especially to his fellow soldiers. Only the profound strength of their distinct but deeply- connected personalities allowed them to deal with the ignorance of those who feared their intimate connection.

Laertes' military experience had been limited but proved useful when they started to position the access gates to the city. In the beginning, they set out three gates, with the main one placed in the center of the perimeter of the walls facing south. The other two entrances were almost equidistant from the main gate but in two opposite directions, one facing the sunrise, the other the sunset. From these two gates, the walls continued their path to reach the top of the rock wall in the back.

Laertes had the idea that two more escape gates were important in case the city came under siege from the valley. Having two more emergency exits would enable a possible exodus of the citizenry. These additional exits would reassure those elders who were afraid of getting stuck inside what they ironically started to call "the great common grave."

The three project bosses spotted two different paths on the back of the hill, one on each side, where two walkways could be constructed to let the population escape to the valley behind the hill and thus be safe in the event of a siege.

Yet even at this advanced stage of the construction, a large part of the population of Amer complained to the king and the council. They nicknamed Tarzio, Laertes, and Laertia "the three little boys," alluding to their similarity to each other but differentness from other people, which was incomprehensible to many. Seeing them always together every day and often at night preparing for the next day's activities, the townspeople gossiped about them, risking the positive outcome of their project.

Construction and delivery delays started to pile up due to the envy and ignorance of some workers who still did not take the three seriously. Declarations like, "I will not be bossed around by those three little boys," and "The only real male of the group is that cat they always carry around with them" distracted Tarzio and the twins, causing them to lose the concentration they needed to maintain—until the day a terrible accident dramatically halted the works.

One of the ramparts had to be elevated two more feet to place the shaped stones at higher levels. At each higher elevation, the structure of the wooden platform also had to be adjusted in height, and the ropes had to be exchanged for longer ones.

That day, Tarzio, Laertes, and Laertia were studying the placement of the fifth gate on the west side of the hill. The chief workman, Pompeus, had been instructed to wait for the new ropes to be delivered. Tired of waiting, his lack of understanding pushed him to tie together two of the ropes he had used until then. He then gave orders for the oxen to pull up the two large boulders already waiting at the bottom of the wall. The two large stones had not yet reached the top of the wall when the knot between the two ropes got stuck in the flywheel. The workers guiding the oxen made them go back a few steps to try to free the knot, but the knot was caught between the flywheel and the wood below it. That short retreat by the oxen created slack in the rope on one side. The two large stones on the platform, no longer level, slid downwards at high speed, sweeping away two workers standing behind the stones. Their bodies were nothing but a long trail of blood, with the remains of flesh and bones completely mangled under the weight of the boulders.

Tarzio and the twins were immediately accused of causing the accident and charged with the death of the two workers. In front of this macabre scene, they were insulted and attacked by the population. They shut themselves in Tarzio's room, waiting for the evening to be able to go out and investigate the accident scene.

King Arcite ordered his soldiers to guard the workplace while waiting for the remains to be removed the next morning. Tarzio could not rest. He was upset and could not believe his machine had failed. That night, he decided to go by himself to the construction site to see what had happened. In the dark, he left the house and walked there with Aker at his side. The twins had wanted to go, too, but he preferred to go alone. He could not risk attracting attention and letting every possibility of self-defense vanish.

Everything was mostly as it had been when the accident occurred. The slope of tree trunks had since been washed with buckets of water, but a penetrating smell of death had remained in the air, and the blood of the two victims had soaked the trunks and poured onto the ground underneath. The water had not been enough to wash the two large stones, which probably still hid more body parts beneath them.

As soon as he reached the base of his machine, Tarzio found that it was perfectly upright, well fixed to the embankment, and had suffered no damage. He could not find an explanation as to what might have happened. He turned to Aker with a questioning, almost desperate look. Aker immediately understood what he had to do and began to climb one of the trunks. In a few seconds, he had reached the top and sat next to the flywheel.

Tarzio followed Aker with his eyes, but he could not clearly see. He could not climb up himself for fear of attracting the soldiers' attention. While Tarzio remained hidden behind the embankment, Aker began sharpening his claws on the wood next to the flywheel, creating an echoing noise in the silence of the night. One of the soldiers took a torch and approached the embankment, raising it as much as he could.

When the soldier realized it was a cat, he took a stone and threw it at him. Aker anticipated him and jumped across to the other side, meowing strongly, pretending to be hit. That light beam was enough for Tarzio to see the big knot stuck in the flywheel. The dynamics of the accident became immediately apparent to him.

As soon as the soldier returned to his position, Tarzio turned away and went back home with Aker running beside him. Once in his room, he woke up the twins, who, exhausted, were asleep on his bed. Tarzio explained in detail what he had just discovered.

Laertia was furious! With tears in her eyes, she felt responsible for the accident, repeating over and over again that she should have stayed on the construction site and waited for the new ropes to arrive. Laertes tried to calm her, saying she had told Pompeus several times to wait for the ropes. It was not her fault that he had not waited.

Laertia was still crying bitter tears when Aker jumped on her lap and began rubbing his head on her chin.

"See? He agrees. It is not your fault!" her brother told her.

"But those two men died because I was not there to check, and I will never forgive myself for it!" she repeated, sobbing. Tarzio sat next to her on the bed and, for the first time, wrapped his arm around her shoulder to calm her. She reciprocated the embrace. Laertes sat on her other side and did the same. He was also crying, sharing his sister's pain.

Aker began pacing back and forth on their six legs, paired as they were next to each other on the bed, tickling their chins with the tip of his tail. Every now and then, he stood up on his back legs, nudging his head repeatedly against their chins. They smiled at the cat's impulsive attempt to console them and to lessen their sadness. Exhausted, the four lay down on the bed, and all four fell deeply asleep, their limbs entwined.

The next morning, the council and the king gathered at the site. Almost everyone in the town came to the hearing. When Tarzio, Laertes, and Laertia arrived, everyone started to yell at them, "Murderers! Incompetents! Buffoons!" Some even threw mud at them.

King Arcite stood up and tried to silence the crowd. When told about how the accident had occurred, he called the crew chief, Pompeus. Pompeus babbled, trying to justify himself, saying he only followed orders and that the three project directors were not there when it happened. He declared it was not his responsibility.

When Tarzio was called to the podium, the crowd began to riot, requiring the king to restore calm once again. Tarzio had his leather bag on his shoulder, with Aker hidden inside. Tarzio had his hand inside the bag, touching Aker's paw to draw strength.

He approached the king and started to talk. "King Arcite, members of the council, citizens of Amer: I, Laertes, and Laertia—the three of us—were not present when the accident occurred. We were on the top of the hill to check the positioning of one of the gates in the back. Before leaving this worksite, we carefully instructed crew chief Pompeus that he had to wait for master Aulus to bring the new longer ropes to raise the stones. Since we had had to raise the embankment, the old ropes were not long enough. Master Aulus delayed the delivery.

"Our mistake consisted of not waiting for his arrival. Crew chief Pompeus did not wait for the delivery and decided to tie together two of the old ropes with a knot. He did not consider the fact that the knot could not pass through the flywheel. When the knot got blocked on one side of the platform, the platform tilted, and the large stones slid down the incline.

"Laertes and Laertia had instructed him in the presence of all the other workers, who are witnesses, to wait for the new ropes, but he decided to avoid waiting. King Arcite, he is guilty of having taken this initiative without considering the consequences.

"We, for our part, are guilty of failing to consider his ignorance of how the flywheels work. But none of us purposely sabotaged the lifting mechanism or willfully caused this terrible accident. We ask for forgiveness from the families of the deceased workers and permission to continue the project, taking greater care.

"We ask for more respect, more collaboration, and more trust toward us. We are continuously attacked and mocked, and this does not allow us to work with serenity.

"We have already completed all the dawn side of the project, and we are now raising the twilight side. We cannot stop now."

With his hand inside the bag, Tarzio kept his fingers on Aker's paw. The cat, for his part, was licking Tarzio's fingers to show his support. At the end of Tarzio's speech, the square fell into an eerie silence.

The king asked one of his soldiers to climb to the top of the embankment to check if Tarzio had told the truth. Once at the top, the soldier tried to get the knot out of the flywheel without succeeding. He then took his sword out and cut the rope. He raised the knot to clearly show it to all present.

King Arcite stood up and proclaimed, "No action will be taken against Tarzio, Laertes, and Laertia. Their dedication to accomplishing one of the most important tasks in the history of our city of Amer is not questioned. If Pompeus acknowledges his mistake, he will not be punished but will be returned to being a simple worker.

"I, King Arcite, order that every worker engaged in the construction has to fulfill his duty. Any hostility toward our ingenious builders must be ended.

"The families of the two deceased workers will be supported by the community, and their sacrifice will always be remembered. I order that their names, Velio and Tolumne, be carved onto those same two stones which now contain their souls.

"Thus, I have decided. The work will start again in five dawns from today."

Tarzio, Laertes, and Laertia bowed before the king, thanked him, and embraced each other. They returned home and found Setonia waiting at the door. She had not had the courage to go to the square to witness the meeting. Seeing them arriving with smiles on their faces gave her great relief. She pampered them with a good meal, also putting on the table a plate for Aker, who was happy to have been pivotal in discovering the truth.

The three friends decided to take advantage of those five days to relieve their stress. Laertia took her brother aside and asked him if he had anything against leaving her alone with Tarzio that evening. She told him she had felt something in his embrace and wanted to be alone with him.

Her brother had a peeved, jealous reaction, feeling excluded from her and Tarzio's companionship. "As you wish!" he answered abruptly. He turned around and walked home.

Left alone, Tarzio and Laertia both acted shy. Getting closer to Tarzio, Laertia took his hands in hers and spoke to him with tenderness. "I want to thank you. Today, you did not just defend our work with profound braveness; you defended each of us. You showed them that my brother and I are not different or dangerous. And you, Tarzio, we all know very well that you have problems relating to others, but your genius is undeniable. You have great courage, more than you even imagine."

Tarzio remained silent and lowered his eyes, shy before such closeness to another person, something he had never experienced before. To relieve his embarrassment, he asked, "Where is your brother? Why did he leave? We could have worked a little."

"No, Tarzio, we cannot work now," she replied. "We have to think about ourselves for once." She got closer and kissed him on his lips. It was the first kiss for both of them, and they experienced a new, unprecedented sensation.

Aker looked at them from the top of the fireplace mantel. He lay down and slept peacefully now that everything was going in the right direction. His human was working hard for the city, and he was opening himself up to life. In his feline heart, Aker knew his second life was coming to an end. He was happy to see that Tarzio and Laertia would possibly continue Khepri and Hephaestus's lineage.

But neither of them was ready for that yet. Tarzio's primary purpose was to complete the walls, while Laertia had to deal with her brother's jealousy. After that night, a latent tension arose among them. This time, the tension was not created by outside forces but came from within them. As much as his sister tried to reassure him that nothing had happened between them except for that innocent kiss, Laertes was always alert and kept an eye on each of their interactions. Tarzio had to scold Laertes every now and then, telling him that he needed to be more focused on his duties. But Tarzio was so caught up in his own duties that he did not understand what exactly was going on between the twins.

Despite the tension, construction on the walls continued, and the sunset side was almost finished. The names of the two dead workers had been carved on the two "murderous" stones. As the king had requested, they were now part of the monumental work in memory of their sacrifice.

On the sunrise side, the terraces had also already been built. Looking out from the top of the walls, townspeople had a different view of their beautiful valley, which could be seen and admired. Word started to spread about the beauty of the new walls, and many people from nearby communities began to come to Amer to look at them. Merchants and travelers altered their journeys to pass by Amer to see them.

The growing tension between Tarzio and the twins pushed Tarzio to avoid them as much as possible. He tried to assign them tasks they had to share, like checking mechanisms, rope, the shape of the boulders, and other details, so that he could dedicate more time to critical aspects of the project. He preferred to be alone with his cat to concentrate on the new difficulties they met while constructing the last part of the walls on the sunset side.

The foundational trench previously laid down had been excavated in soft, flat ground while now they were on steep, rocky ground. Digging on the rocky hill to create a solid foundation required more attention. He could reuse many of the rocks excavated on the site, but the increasing slope of that side of the hill made every action more complicated than those he had faced on the flat part of the project.

At the end of each working day, the three met to discuss what had been done and to plan the next day's activities. Personal feelings disturbed the atmosphere of these meetings at times. Laertia, secretly in love with Tarzio, was always hoping to be alone with him. Laertes did everything to avoid leaving them alone, always finding a new topic to discuss or a detail to study, giving Tarzio a chance to talk about work or anything else.

But Laertia understood her brother's game and played it, too. After a few nights, after she and her brother had left Tarzio's house, she would later return, unseen by Laertes. These encounters worried Tarzio, who was preoccupied about how Laertes would react if he found out. Tarzio insisted on secrecy. One night, after a few kisses, they both lost their virginity on Tarzio's bed, under Aker's sly and attentive gaze.

The already unstable equilibrium between the three completely changed after that night. Laertes sensed the change immediately. One night, he pretended he was going to see some friends at the tavern to drink wine. Instead, he hid not far away and saw his sister knocking on Tarzio's window and entering his room through the window. He felt betrayed and wanted to scream or make a scene, but instead, he started to cry and kept everything inside his bleeding heart.

Over the following days, Laertes tried to ignore what had happened, forcing himself to work even harder and not to think about it. He realized, above everything else, that it was more important to make Tarzio happy and proud of him. He tried to avoid his sister as much as possible and started to undertake different tasks from hers. By working separately, each of them had to concentrate more, and they got better results. Ultimately, this dynamic favored the project, which progressed quickly and was nearing completion.

The End of the Project, the End of the Story

King Arcite often visited the site and was extremely pleased with the results. Messengers and travelers reported that the Romans had started a war against the Samnites, a population living in the Apennine Mountains south of Rome. In 342 BC, a bloody battle took place on Mount Gauro. The Romans sided with the city of Capua, which was threatened by the Samnites. That battle drastically changed the politics of the Roman government, which until then had only focused on the normal protection of their city limits.

Elected consul four times in a row, Marcus Valerius Corvus began an extensive, expansive military campaign, strengthening his army and fighting neighboring populations. The quickly increasing number of Roman citizens required greater supplies of food, which the area south of Rome and the fertile region toward the sea could provide. Those areas were easy and desirable conquests.

King Arcite worried about the Romans' possible expansion toward the "nuerte" (the north) after they conquered the south. The rich Amer valley and the lands belonging to the Etruscans on the other side of the big river might be of interest to the Romans. Amer did not have a large army; only a few legions were trained for defense. The unfinished walls were a protective shield that needed to be completed quickly.

After another late-night meeting, the trio said goodnight and planned to meet the next morning at the quarry. When Laertes was sure Laertia would not return to Tarzio's, he knocked on Tarzio's bedroom window.

"Here I am, Laertia. I wasn't sure you were coming back," Tarzio said while opening his shutters. He stood still when he saw Laertes.

"Disappointed?" Laertes asked.

"No, no, I am sorry. Come in. What is going on?"

Laertes climbed over the windowsill and found himself very close to Tarzio's face. "I know you and my sister are secretly meeting, and you do not know how much it hurts me."

"I am sorry, Laertes. We were afraid you would not agree with our relationship, and I did not want to have problems complicating our duties."

"Yes, I know, and that is why I stayed silent, but I cannot bear this anymore. Tarzio, you know how much I admire you and how much I want you to be proud of me and proud of our achievements. But in these last weeks, I have realized a very important thing. I am *not* jealous of your relationship with my sister, but I *am* envious because I am in love with you, too." Laertes stood still waiting for some brutal reaction from Tarzio.

Tarzio took Laertes' hands instead and kissed him on his lips. "I was hoping you would say that. I have been hoping you would say it for a long time. You are so much like her and at the same time so different… Sometimes, I confuse you two in my mind and in my heart to the point I cannot distinguish my feelings for her and for you."

They embraced and kissed again. Utterly happy about Tarzio's reaction, Laertes got lost in Tarzio's arms. A few moments later, Tarzio freed himself and turned around, searching for Aker's eyes, into which he looked deeply to seek focus.

"Nobody, absolutely nobody, must know. Laertes, we must be even more careful. If we let ourselves go, we will compromise all the work we have not done so far. Promise me that until the walls are finished, there will not be a single chance of us getting caught. We cannot risk being called 'the three perverts' instead of 'the three little boys.' You know how cruel people can be. We cannot give them the chance to destroy our work."

Tarzio turned back to face Laertes and added. "Promise me, please!"

"Yes, I promise," said Laertes. "You can count on my loyalty and fairness."

They kissed again as Aker watched from his usual position on the mantelpiece. Crouched with his head resting on his outstretched paws and eyes huge in the pale light of the fireplace flames, he was wondering what was going to happen now. He was happy to see his human so radiant in both Laertia and Laertes' arms. That was fine with him, but what about the continuation of the lineage? This new situation could put at risk his task now that he was feeling close to his second departure.

Tarzio told Laertes he could not stop making love with Laertia; she would be suspicious.

"I understand," Laertes answered. "Do not worry; I will bear it. But only once, only tonight, please let me stay with you. Then I will not bother you until the end of the project."

They undressed, and as with Laertia, Tarzio also took Laertes' virginity in a long and passionate night that left him happy but deeply disturbed. The physical resemblance and the similarity in the twins' gestures and movements were such that, when reopening his eyes after loving Laertia, he was unsure to which of the two he had made love.

Laertes kept his word and never sneaked back to Tarzio's room again. He spoke to Tarzio when he was sure they were alone, saying he could not wait for the construction to be over, but he showed great self-control.

Aker calmed down, too, seeing only Laertia come to Tarzio's bedroom at night.

Finally, the day came when Laertia announced to Tarzio that she was pregnant. He was extremely happy but scared at the same time. When she started to show, they had to tell Laertes, who was indeed very happy for them. He knew his relationship with Tarzio had to be kept secret. He saw in that pregnancy his chance to maybe spend a few more nights with Tarzio.

The joy of the pregnancy was sadly interrupted by the sudden death of Aker. One morning, he started to be wobbly on his paws and failed to walk. Coming back home that night, they found him lifeless on the bed. They mourned him together all night long, hugging each other, holding Aker, and caressing his fur, which was gradually losing its softness.

The next day, Tarzio went to the quarry and ordered the workmen to prepare one large stone with a hole on one side. When the stone was put in place, he laid Aker's body in it so Aker could forever rest in the walls he had helped build.

That stone was positioned almost exactly where Khepri had first found Tito centuries before. The closeness between the place where he was born in his first life and the place where he was buried in his second life would ensure enough energy for Tito/Aker's soul to hover in his valley so that someday he could return for his third life.

Three months after Aker's death, Laertia gave birth to a boy they named Elaxantre.

Soon after, the last stones were put in place, and the walls were considered finished, even though they still lacked some final, finishing details.

King Arcite congratulated the three on this huge achievement. Whether looking down from the top of the hill or up from the valley, the walls were imposing, solid, and majestic. They filled him with pride. His city was now protected and safer.

Though happy to have accomplished this immense task, Tarzio now felt utterly drained of all energy. He could not find a new purpose as nothing could match, let alone surpass, the grandeur of what he had created with the walls of Amer.

Without his cat, he felt alone, abandoned by his first real friend, who had helped him in his work and in opening up to others. He was again closing himself off from the world. He could not even get excited about his little boy. Ever since the baby had been born, he was spending less and less time with the twins. He was attracted to both and could not tolerate the idea of having to choose between them. Most of all, he did not want to make either of them suffer because of him.

At this point, Laertia knew about Tarzio and Laertes. Her mind was so similar to her brother's that she intuited what was going on. She understood that the distance Tarzio was keeping from her was because of his feelings for Laertes. The deep connection between brother and sister prevailed, and she did not resent Tarzio. She did not even ask him to marry her. She knew he could not have done so. She was happy enough to be the mother of a wonderful child and continued to live with him in her parents' home. She was also happy to see her brother spending a lot of time with her son, as if the baby were his own.

Tarzio decided to leave Amer. He never returned to his city, and no one ever heard of him again. He left a letter for the twins.

"Laertia and Laertes, life has been extremely generous to me. It has given me two people I have loved with all my heart, even more than myself. Maybe I have not shown that love as I should have, but I will be forever grateful because, without you two, I would never have accomplished this miracle that will remain for centuries to come as a testimony of our work and our love.

"That grandeur has left me completely empty, and I do not have anything more to give to either of you or to my son Elaxantre. Please give him the love you both feel for me. Laertes, please raise him like your own son. Tell him his father was so afraid to hurt the two people he loved most in his life that he decided to go away.

"Tell him about Aker, his cleverness, his love, and how important he has been for me and for us. I have only loved three beings in my entire life, and I know for the rest of my days I will never love again as I have loved you two and my Aker."

Over the following centuries, nobody remembered Tarzio and his work designing and building the city walls. His story was lost within a few generations. The only one who remembered this misunderstood and forgotten genius was Tito, who would always carry in his heart the memory of his second human—life after life.

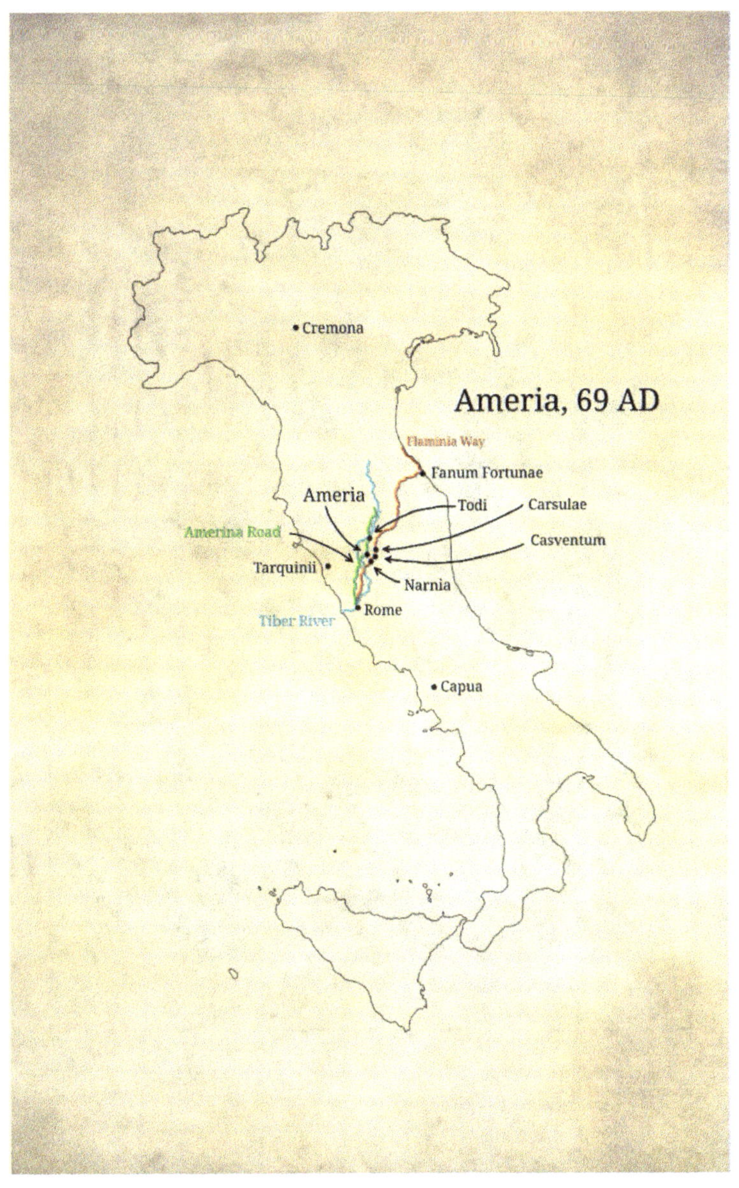

Cremona
Ameria, 69 AD
Flaminia Way
Fanum Fortunae
Ameria
Todi
Carsulae
Amerina Road
Casventum
Tarquinii
Narnia
Tiber River
Rome
Capua

AMERIA, 69 AD
Temple of Saturn
Porta Pusterola
Porta Vallis
Old Walls
Porta Iliona
Public Baths
Porta Pantanelli
Porta Romana
Amphitheater
Germanicus Square

Cast of Characters

Family at the Start of the Chapter

Marcus: Ameria's chief military tribune, a descendant of Khepri, Tarzio, and Elaxantre

Aleste: Marcus's father

Tito/Bebio: a cat

Other Principals

Fulvia: a masseuse at the public baths

Other Amerians

Matron Lydia: a manager of the public baths

Darius: the head gardener of the public baths

Donna Vistilia and Donna Sertoria: public bath clients

Cuspius: a wealthy merchant and public bath client

Bianchina: a little white cat who lives at the public baths

Romans

Emperor Nero: died by committing suicide

Servius Sulpicius Galba: Nero's successor as emperor

Marcus Salvius Otone: Galba's successor

Vitellius Germanicus Augustus: followed Otone as emperor

Vespasian: overthrew Vitellius

Germanicus (Nero Claudius Drusus): the adopted son of the Emperor Tiberius; he died at only 39 years of age in 19 AD

Agrippina: the wife of Germanicus

Gnaeus Calpurnius Piso: a trusted friend of Tiberius; appointed governor of Syria by Tiberius

Antonius Primus: the commander of Vespasian's legions

Ambassador Sabinus: a Roman official

Domitian: the son of Vespasian

Populations

Umbrians

Family at the End of the Chapter

Claudius, Lavinia, Valerianus, and Emilia

Introduction

ROMAN INFLUENCE STARTED to spread, and with Latin becoming the common language, the name of the city of Amer changed to Ameria. The exact reason and time for this change are utterly unknown, but it is traccable to the Romans' conquest of the lands of Central Italy belonging until then to the Etruscans, Samnites, and Umbrians. The Roman Empire had, by 69 AD, extended to almost the entire European continent and was spreading toward the East.

Ameria retained its governmental autonomy after accepting Rome's supremacy, to which it had submitted without being conquered militarily. Given its location and beauty, Ameria was an important center for Roman culture in the first century, reaching splendor. It was at its very best in this period of ancient history.

~

Tito's soul hovered in the valley until he felt a strong call to reincarnate around 69 AD. His presence became necessary to assure the continuation of Khepri's lineage, which was in danger because there was only one living descendant at that time, a military tribune named Marcus. Tito had to come back.

A female cat, almost entirely white except for two or three small gray-brown spots, wandered between the hedges and the colonnade of the great and quiet public baths in the center of the city of Ameria. She felt the time she would give birth approaching and was looking for a den in which to welcome her kittens. She knew the area well but needed a safe spot to nurse and raise the newborns in peace.

She slipped into a small cave at the base of the sidewalk along the long line of white columns that surrounded the large garden of the baths. That space seemed perfect: barely visible from the outside and quite deep to prevent her little ones from climbing out when she had to leave to get food for herself.

Matron Lydia was the manager of the baths. She would leave a bowl with leftovers for the cat outside the back door. Before going there, the mother-cat-to-be had to be sure her babies would be safe when left alone. A few hours after she had holed up, the cat lay down and prepared to give birth. One by one, four kittens started meowing and fussing around her to nurse. While they were sucking her life-giving milk, she kept on cleaning the placenta from them. After a long job, the four kittens were perfectly clean. Two of them dozed off; another one was still sucking, while the fourth one started to take some faltering steps.

The baths of Ameria consisted of a vast building with large pools both in the garden and inside the building. They were supplied by the water source Khepri had discovered centuries before. The colonnade of the baths surrounded a beautiful garden full of well-kept trees and hedges. Exposed to the south, the building was graced by the sun all day long, warming up the waters of the pools where many Amerians plunged to seek cleanliness and relaxation. During hot summers, they would also dive in at night to cool off after a day of hard work in the heat.

Matron Lydia had managed the baths for several years now. She was a cheerful woman, very open but rigorous in her duties and very demanding of her workers. She asked for the same degree of commitment from every worker, covering all aspects of the baths: maintenance of the gardens; cleaning of the pools; and respect for schedules and appointments by masseurs, stokers, and cleaners.

Matron Lydia had a plump, smiling face, a sign of her serene soul and love of her job. That same face could turn into a non-forgiving grimace if rules were not followed. She loved cats. She had more than twenty in her own home, the cats filling it with love and joy. At work she fell for a cat she named Bianchina (“Little White One”). She tried to take Bianchina to her home, but the cat always returned to the baths. Lydia decided to feed her there, always keeping Bianchina out of the rooms where her customers enjoyed relaxing massages. Matron Lydia was afraid her clients would be annoyed by an animal wandering in the rooms she kept as clean and tidy as shining mirrors.

A few days after being born, the kittens, with their eyes now wide open, started to be able to climb up and exit the den. They took their first steps outside in the daylight between the tall columns of white travertine. Still uncertain on their paws, the four siblings played in the sun.

One of the kittens was Tito, who realized he was back home. He recognized the scent of the place, the fragrances from the trees and bushes he had smelled in his previous lives. Looking beyond the colonnade, he identified the hills and fields where he had spent time with Hephaestus and the location where he had studied the walls of Amer with Tarzio. Those memories were imprinted on his mind. This large space he was exploring around him was situated where he had lived his two previous lives. Khepri's home, where he had lived with Hephaestus and Tidra, was a bit higher up the hill, while Tarzio's house was built exactly where the central part of the building for the baths was.

Those moments of sweet remembrance were suddenly interrupted by the playful attack of two of his brothers. They all started to roll around on the gravel of the path, biting each other. Right now, his focus was to play with his siblings, suck as much milk from his mother as possible in order to become a strong cat, and get ready to face his new life.

Fulvia and Marcus

A young woman named Fulvia walked quickly along the path leading to the back door of the baths. She heard meowing and saw a mother cat and her kittens. She approached the cat and stroked her head tenderly. "There you are! Now I know why you disappeared! You needed to hide to have your babies! They are beautiful!" She continued to caress the purring mother, who was proud to show off her kittens. "Now, I must go to work. I will return later and bring some food for you and them."

The mama cat rubbed herself on Fulvia's white tunic without taking her eyes away from her babies. Fulvia planned to spend more time with those kittens, but she knew she was late and ran inside the building.

Matron Lydia was there, waiting impatiently for her. "Where

were you? Hurry up! Tribune Marcus has been waiting for you for a while now!"

Fulvia washed her hands and quickly prepared her basket with small bottles of scented oils and soft linen cloths. She told Matron Lydia why she was late. "I must apologize. Do you remember Bianchina, that white cat you said was missing? I just saw her on the path along the colonnade, near a small cave. She has given birth to four wonderful kittens. I could not help but stop and look at them."

"My little Bianchina!" Matron Lydia said. "I thought she might have come to a bad end. But now, hurry up! Do not keep Tribune Marcus waiting. You know how impatient he is to see you!" Matron Lydia said this with a blunt but not malicious tone. Nothing could make her happier than to see Fulvia get involved with the city's most admired tribune. Lydia could not tell who was shyer or more reserved, Fulvia or Marcus. Both lacked the courage to take the first step.

Fulvia entered a small room that was sealed off by heavy white curtains. Lying on the cot face down, Marcus was ready for his massage. "Where were you?" he asked abruptly. Realizing he had been too aggressive, he raised his head and apologized. "It is just because I was afraid I would not see you today. You know you are the only one I want for my massage."

Fulvia remained silent and placed her basket on a stool. She then put her hands on Marcus's head, pressing it slowly back down onto the cot. She picked up one of the small bottles and poured some drops of an expensive perfumed oil on his shoulders. He shivered a little and began to relax, emitting quiet moans under the pressure of those expert hands.

Fulvia was, in fact, in high demand for her experience and particular expertise. She had a natural gift and could figure out where her customers had a problem, felt pain, or had annoying tension. She placed her hands on their shoulders or chest and moved her hands slowly toward their arms, back, or other parts of their bodies without asking a single question. Her hands were guided by an innate sensitivity to the exact point that needed treatment.

At the end of each massage, everyone was mesmerized by how she had found the aching part of their body without even asking them about it. The other masseuses often asked her how she did it, jealous of her popularity among the clients. She herself did not know the answer. Whenever her hands rested on a body, she felt herself detach from her hands, letting them move as if they were not hers. They followed their own path as if she were not responsible for their moves.

The energy released through her hands soothed aching spasms and brought such a high level of muscle relaxation that, stepping down from the cot, clients felt like they were flying instead of walking. Marcus had had that feeling since the first time she had massaged him. He also understood he had to be completely silent for the entire duration of the massage. Some talked to her, giving information about their problems; others, even worse, tried to touch her thighs when she approached the cot.

In those situations, her hands continued to do their job, but less efficiently. The first time Marcus tried to talk to her, she responded with a long "Shhhh," followed by a very unique pressure on a specific part of his shoulder. He immediately understood that he had to remain silent if he wanted the best from her and to connect with her. Those sessions with her became an almost transcendental experience he could not live without anymore.

At the end of each massage, after their goodbyes, Marcus always spoke with Matron Lydia to arrange his next appointment. Every time Marcus left the baths, he felt like he was reborn.

She, on the other hand, felt empty, like she had been drained of all her energy.

Neither of them had ever had the courage to go beyond their professional relationship and deepen their obvious bond. Marcus was falling in love with her. As a chief military tribune, he was a strong, confident, and inspiring soldier for his companions, with an imposing and well-muscled physique. As a man, he was shy and reserved. Marcus was a descendant of Khepri, the hunter who had discovered the hill with the spring; of Tarzio, the engineer who had built the city walls; and of Tarzio's son Elaxantre. Even with these prestigious ancestors, he was a kind person, not at all pretentious.

Completely absorbed in his position as a military leader, he was not thinking of getting married. The continuation of Hator's lineage was thus in danger of ending. Completely engaged by the responsibilities of his position as a tribune, he did not have the time or an interest in forming a family. What he was feeling for Fulvia took him by surprise. He never would have expected to be entranced by the hands of a woman.

After meeting her, he had stopped going with his fellow soldiers to the city brothel. He had been a longtime and well-received guest there. Now, he had lost interest in those kinds of meetings. The last times he went, when he undressed to lie with the brothel prostitutes, Marcus was always thinking of when he undressed to be massaged by Fulvia. Nothing sexual had ever happened between them, but the satisfaction he was getting from her hands was more intense than the orgasms he had at the brothel. For that reason, he stopped his visits to the brothel and increased those at the baths.

Marcus lived with his father Aleste in a large house not far from the baths, so anytime he could, he grabbed the opportunity to stop and have a refreshing swim, especially during that hot summer of 69 AD.

Fulvia, on the other hand, was of humble origins, the only daughter of a peasant working in the vineyards. Fulvia and her father lived in a small house in the lower part of the city. This difference in social class intimidated her. As much as she was attracted by Marcus's beautiful and sensual body, she would not dare to think of herself accompanying the most admired Amerian tribune. Very recently, he had also been appointed the chief military tribune, with the specific task of maintaining contact between the legionnaires and the local government. His increasing power was another reason for her to keep her distance from him.

After massaging Marcus that day, Fulvia had some free time before her next client. She ran out to take some food to the cat family near the colonnade. Bianchina voraciously ate those leftovers while two of her kittens were still attached to her teats. The other two kittens were peacefully sleeping. Fulvia caressed them gently so as not to annoy their protective mother.

One of the four kittens caught her attention. His four paws were perfectly white, as was his belly. His head, back, and tail instead were covered by beautiful, streaked brown and black fur. It was the particular look of this dark part of his fur that struck her. It seemed like he was wearing a cloak. It reminded her of those ancient drawings of feasts where hunters wore the furs of wolves or other animals on their heads and backs.

The other three kittens were also white with brown and black spots, but their markings were not as defined as the first one's were. Fulvia had no knowledge of the legend of Tito and did not know that the little kitten who attracted her so much was indeed Tito. He had come back to make sure Hator's lineage would continue.

Fulvia said her goodbyes to the cats with one last stroke on their heads. Walking back inside, she met Darius, the head gardener of the baths. She told him about the family of cats hidden between the columns to make sure he would not shoo them away. He replied that he must do it, or Matron Lydia would complain to him.

She reassured him. "No, Darius, that is Matron Lydia's cat, a cat she loves very much and thought had gotten lost. I have come to tell you because Matron Lydia would be upset if you threw them out of the garden!"

He thanked her for sparing him a sure scolding. He was well aware of how much Matron Lydia cared about the thermal baths. Every detail had to be attended to meticulously. The garden and its flower tubs had to be impeccable. The beautiful black-and-white mosaic floors had to be perfectly clean and well-polished so as not to bother customers' naked feet as they walked from room to room. The big curtains, which served to shelter guests from the hot sun and at the same time let in refreshing breezes, were changed every day and had to be absolutely clean and perfumed.

The wonderful reputation of Ameria's thermal baths was so well known that many customers traveled from nearby cities to enjoy its attractions. And Fulvia's precious hands were one of those attractions. Fulvia was not a young girl; she had turned thirty recently and had dedicated her whole life to her work. Many men had asked her to marry them, probably under the spell of her massages. Those proposals became a reason for her to ask specifically to have only female customers. Often, Matron Lydia could accommodate her as there were many wealthy matrons in Ameria who asked for massages. Only to Marcus could she not say no to an appointment with Fulvia. He always booked in advance to ensure that Fulvia would be the only one taking care of his body.

Fulvia did not mind Marcus. She was at ease with him as he was always respectful and silent during their sessions. He greeted her when he arrived and thanked her when leaving, never interrupting her while her hands kneaded his muscles. Fulvia understood that he had feelings for her, but she never encouraged him. Their dialogue was essentially tactile—she spoke to him with her fingertips while he answered with the passive movements of his skin and muscles that she so expertly stroked.

Not a word passed between them, just the non-verbal connection made through those perfume-scented oils she poured on him, the well-calibrated pressure of her hands, and his total abandonment to her touch. At every meeting, both of them hoped that the tension between them would lead to something more, but even if the communication between them was at a very high level, it remained silent. Marcus reached heights of subliminal relaxation but said nothing. For Fulvia, professionalism was more important than anything else. All the intimacy they shared remained unexpressed, although they each were extremely happy after every encounter.

Week after week, the kitten Tito became more independent and took long walks away from his den and siblings. He began to discover the changes made to his land since his last life. Humans had made it different but beautiful. He was not very excited about that long line of perfectly aligned white marble trunks, mainly because he could not climb them as he used to scale the dark wooden ones.

He wondered what the purpose was in erecting leafless trunks that nails could not penetrate. The columns seemed useless to him. However, arriving at the end of the colonnade and looking out toward the valley, he felt deep happiness. He recognized the places he had run through with Hephaestus, his first human. He remembered those long days of training, all those long hours seated next to his human for what for him was both a game and a survival matter.

One day, he wandered much farther away than usual and,

returning to his den, found it empty. He knew the time had come to think about his own new life. He would probably run into his mother and siblings again, but they had most likely moved away. They were not as attached to that place as he was. Maybe his mother, Bianchina, would stick around, but for sure, she would no longer treat him like her kitten.

He did not ask himself if any of his brothers were in their first, second, or other lives. It was not customary for cats to reveal such personal mysteries. The reincarnation of a cat remained a very well-kept secret between three essential elements: the animal, the place, and the chosen human being. Only by following those rules could a cat's life be perpetuated over time. Certainly, Tito did not know or understand this dogma nor who had established it. It was a rule guided by innate feline instinct. And it was his instinct to tell him what to do without further questions. He also did not care much. He was a young cat now interested in exploring his valley and making it his own once again. Time would tell him why he had returned at that precise time.

The Fight for Power in Rome

AD 69 was a very difficult year in the history of Rome. News arriving from there was not reassuring. Not a year had passed since Emperor Nero, loathed by most, had committed suicide. The Roman Senate appointed Servius Sulpicius Galba as the new head of the empire. However, his government was very unstable. After Julius Caesar's dynasty ended, the competition between Roman leaders turned into a full-blown civil war.

Ameria was an independent municipality with its own government, and it was not directly involved in those battles. A possible request from Rome to send Ameria's legions into the battles concerned Marcus, who took his duties as a tribune very seriously. Despite his ever-growing feelings for Fulvia, with news of the possible involvement of his legions in the conflict, he did not have time to start a family.

With his position and his imposing physique, every unmarried woman would fall into his arms without him having to ask. But Fulvia was different from all the other women in town. The feelings he was experiencing for her commanded him to show her respect. She could not just be an object of sexual pleasure. At the same time, he did not want to commit to her, given the looming possibility of having to go to war.

This thought became even more insistent when news broke that Emperor Galba had been killed a few months earlier by the legions of Marcus Salvius Otone, who proclaimed himself emperor but did not last long. Otone kept the throne for just three months before being defeated and killed by Vitellius Germanicus Augustus in March.

Vitellius was proclaimed emperor in April but had to make his way to Rome from Germany, where he had been a commander for a long time. Ameria's consuls were worried and were very attentive to the news arriving about Vitellius's progress toward Rome. The ever-growing city of Rome was only fifty-six miles away, and the road called the "Amerina," which led from the town of Todi toward Rome, was increasingly traveled by troops and legions coming from the north. Ameria's strong walls were a notable protection, but a well-organized and trained military legion was essential to protect the city and its citizens.

Every defensive aspect of the city was on alert. Every day, Marcus spent countless hours exercising with his legionnaires. He was not just a soldier but also a good leader and a profound connoisseur of his city and its surroundings. He used to take his young recruits around the walls and into the surrounding valleys to show them strategies to surprise and defeat whoever might attack the city.

In June, while on his way to Rome, Vitellius rode along the consular road Via Flaminia after defeating Otone's legions in a cruel battle near the city of Cremona. He stopped in Narnia, only a few miles from Ameria, and the inhabitants of that town were obliged to organize a two-day-long sumptuous banquet for him and his legionnaires.

A messenger reported the news to the worried Amerian consuls, who were afraid he might also stop in Ameria. They were somewhat reassured by the fact that he was in a hurry to get to Rome and probably would not stop again in another nearby city. And so it happened. After halting in Narnia, Vitellius continued on his way to Rome, making a triumphal entrance, but not without leaving behind a tragic trail of blood. Roman citizens who tried to stop his arrival suffered another bloody massacre. Seven months of civil war with three different Emperors—Galva, Otone, and now Vitellius—had passed, and the fighting was not yet over.

The citizens of Rome did not welcome Vitellius's arrival. His legions, mostly made up of mercenaries and rough barbarians, took Rome by storm, robbing it of its riches. Vitellius's lack of authority and control had transformed Rome into a huge brothel where continuous celebrations and gladiatorial games often turned into riots and carnage.

The new emperor was not much appreciated. He did not consider it a fundamental task to furnish the city of Rome with enough food supplies. Most of the legionnaires arriving from the east were close to exhaustion and controlled by another general, Vespasian. The Roman people were starving and ready to rebel. Throughout that summer, messengers who stopped in Ameria to refresh or change their horses reported that Vespasian was returning from the east, where his legions had stopped fighting wars. After leaving the command of those areas to his son, Vespasian began moving his legions back toward Rome.

Informed by the Amerian consuls about all this news, Marcus kept any thoughts of marriage out of his mind.

Matron Lydia had witnessed the strength of the feeling between Marcus and Fulvia, and although they met three or four times a week, Matron Lydia could read the sadness on their faces every time they parted.

Marcus's father, Aleste, urged him to marry. "You are my only son," he kept repeating to Marcus. "If you do not give me a grandchild, our lineage will die out. We have been part of this land for centuries. You must continue our lineage! If your mother had not died giving birth to you, I probably would not have been so demanding!"

"Father, I know. But how can I have a child if I have to go to war? What if I do not come back? A father can raise a child; you have been exemplary in that. You have given me everything. However, a single mother cannot do the same alone. Who would protect the child?

Who would give him strength? He would become a pawn of others, and I do not want your grandchild to be a pawn."

"Son, you are right. I was able to protect you and direct you in your military career. You have grown to be a strong and respected man. But I am getting older, and nothing would please me more than seeing you have a family of your own. I know brothel prostitutes are a pleasant diversion, but you deserve more."

"Oh, Father! The brothel? I have not been there for a long time now!"

"So then, where do you go almost every day? I see you coming home perfumed and with a relaxed face."

"Not to the brothel, Father. I go to the baths. There is this woman there who is gifted with amazing hands. When she massages me, I feel like I am born again. She is in such high demand that I almost have to bribe Matron Lydia to ensure I can have her and only her as my masseuse after my daily training at the military camp."

"And is this special feeling about her perhaps called love? Your eyes lit up when you mentioned her."

"No, Father, I assure you. Ask the Matron. People come from Narnia, Carsulae, and Casventum to get a massage from her."

"And what is the name of this massage sorceress?"

"Her name is Fulvia."

"Is she very young?"

"Not very young. She is maybe thirty years old, but very beautiful. I do not think she likes me anyway. She does not talk to me. Those few times I have asked her something, she has always silenced me. But I have to confess that when her hands glide over my skin, it is as if I am hearing her talking to me. I think that I know everything about her, as she does about me, without saying a single word."

"Marcus, you are a proud and brave soldier, but you are a man who is still closed off to love. And I do not mean sexually. I mean to the spiritual meaning of love. Next time, try to talk to her, and if she talks to you, just listen. She might be intimidated by your reputation as the most important tribune in town. She may not consider herself worthy of being with you, as I suppose she comes from a humble family. I am sure she might be afraid that after copulating with you, you will not look at her in the same way. I understand from your words that she must be a very proud woman."

"Father, even if you are right, I do not want to start a relationship with her, maybe have a child, and then abandon her to go to war. Rome has had three emperors over the last six months, and the civil wars have caused more deaths in this period than throughout the entire history of the empire. And it is not getting better. I do not feel like I can start a family now."

"She respects you, and you respect her. If this is not love, then I have just turned into a groggy old man!"

Marcus understood that he was not going to win this argument against his father. They were very close to each other, so he preferred to end the conversation. "Good night, Father. Sleep well. I will see you in the morning." Marcus retired to his bedroom and lay awake for a while, watching the pale rays of moonlight penetrate the thin curtains. He enjoyed the night breeze. Thinking of Fulvia, he fell asleep imagining holding her in his arms and kissing her passionately.

If neither Matron Lydia nor Aleste could push those two into taking the first step, they needed a more subtle, more mischievous, more effective intervention—a sneaky one.

At the back door of the baths, where Matron Lydia used to feed Bianchina, now the only cat that showed up was the one with the white paws and belly and the streaked coat. Having refamiliarized himself with his valley, Tito was now ready for his mission. Guided by his instinct, he did everything he could to conquer the heart of Matron Lydia. He knew he needed her in order to meet his new human and fulfill his destiny.

It turned out not to be that hard. Matron Lydia, however demanding with her workers, was a woman with a kind heart and was easily duped by the affectionate purring of a nice, loving, and insistent cat. Tito succeeded in achieving something his mother Bianchina had not: in a short time, he was allowed inside the first room of the baths. He did not need to be aggressive. With a constant calm presence, he was awarded a nice, padded basket where he spent hours sleeping comfortably.

When the baths closed at night, Matron Lydia let him out

when she went to her house. Every morning, he was back at the door waiting for her. The cat became well-known to all the workers, and they pampered and caressed him all the time. While accepting all that attention, he ran toward Fulvia anytime she came in.

One night, when she was returning home, she realized the cat had followed her. "What are you doing here!" she exclaimed. "Come in, and tomorrow morning, I will take you back to the baths!" And so she did, leaving him in the gardens.

"Have you seen that cute, big cat?" Lydia asked when she saw Fulvia enter the room. "I put down a bowl of food for him, but I did not see him. He is usually always there waiting for me."

"Yes, Lydia, I just left him out in the garden. I am sure he will be here asking to come in soon."

"What do you mean 'left'? Why?"

"He followed me home last night and slept in my bed. I kept him in the house so he would not get lost."

"I do not think he could get lost! I think he knows very well what he is doing. I guess he has chosen you as his owner."

"I do not think so, Matron Lydia. He likes it here. He would be bored at my house… What clients are on my list today?"

"If you say so. But I do not think you will get rid of that cat so easily. Let me see, you have Donna Vistilia, then Donna Sertoria, and after lunch, you have Marcus, the tribune." As she pronounced that last name, she looked at Fulvia to catch her reaction. Fulvia lowered her eyes, and Matron Lydia said, "When will you finally show him your feelings?" Just then, Tito appeared beside them.

Fulvia decided not to answer. She turned to Tito, took him in her arms, and told him, "Perhaps now I should give you a name, my big, beautiful cat!"

"Right, yes, change the subject!" Matron Lydia winked and smiled.

"Let me see now… What can I call you?" Fulvia looked into his deep yellow-green eyes, and Tito returned that look, trying to send her a very clear message: "My name is Tito! My name is Tito!"

"I will call you… I will call you… Bebio!"

"Bebio?" he thought. "What kind of a name is Bebio? All right, human, for you, I will be Bebio!"

Bebio and Marcus

Bebio was dozing in the comfortable basket Matron Lydia had given him. Sometimes, he tried to follow Fulvia on her shifts in the different rooms in the baths. She scolded him: "No! You must stay here; you cannot follow me. I must work!" He sat behind the closed door and waited for her to return between one client and the next. Clever as he was, he noticed her different attitude when she had an appointment to see Marcus—she was tense and nervous.

To regain her concentration Fulvia used to lean her back against the wall with her eyes closed. She inhaled deeply, letting every breath start at her toes and rise up along her legs and body, reaching her forehead. At that moment, she let her breath flow behind her head like she was throwing it away. That breathing exercise gave her a liberated feeling, leaving all negativity behind. Despite the breathing exercise, which gave Fulvia some control over herself, when she had to see Marcus, Bebio felt her anxiety and started to think about how to intervene.

One hot afternoon, Marcus arrived early for his appointment at the baths. Matron Lydia accompanied him to a cubicle, leaving some linen cloths there for him. She suggested that he go bathe in the outdoor pool, which was still in full sun at that time of day. Bebio watched from afar. Marcus got undressed, tied a towel around his waist, and headed outside. He saluted some fellow citizens already pleasantly enjoying the coolness of the water. He recognized Cuspius, a wealthy merchant. Cuspius approached Marcus, asking for the latest news from Rome.

"Not good," he replied. "Vitellius is not a good emperor. He has no control over his soldiers. He had every single one of his opponents killed. He is not very different from Nero. He is more interested in organizing huge banquets with all the senators."

"I see," Cuspius answered. "In Narnia, they are still complaining about how much preparatory work and how many expensive items were required to please him. Maybe he thinks that is the only way to keep the Senate quiet."

"Probably, but he is not dealing with the problems of the people, and they are rebelling. It is still not confirmed, but it seems that Vespasian will return to Italy. His legions made him emperor a few months ago. He made his son commander of the eastern lands, and he is traveling back to Rome to be recognized as emperor by the Senate. The civil war, dear Cuspius, is still not settled."

"He would be the fourth emperor in less than a year! What a messy situation… But our legions! You will not be involved in these struggles, will you?"

"Nobody knows. Up until now, our consuls have not been asked to take part because various factions cannot decide whether to request reinforcements. If they do, we will have to enter the fight. Now, please excuse me, Cuspius, but the time for my massage is approaching. I must go inside."

"Enjoy it! Who will do the massage? Fulvia?"

"Who else?" he said, smiling.

Alone in the small cubicle, Marcus wiped the water off his tanned skin. He lay down on the cot, covered his waist with a cloth, and closed his eyes, waiting for Fulvia. He was almost asleep, dreaming of the moment he would feel her hands on his body when he felt a sudden weight on his abdomen. He opened his eyes and saw a big, beautiful cat sitting on him, staring into his eyes.

"*Ave*, big cat, you startled me!" said Marcus, starting to caress the cat. "You have very soft fur! Where do you come from?"

As soon as his paws touched Marcus's skin, Bebio's whiskers began to vibrate, his senses recognizing in that contact those cells that were so familiar to him. His new mission became immediately clear to him. He crouched on Marcus's abdomen and started to knead Marcus's stomach with alternate paws. Bebio purred loudly, making Marcus happy with this sensual "appetizer" to his massage.

Bebio, eyes half closed, was very careful not to hurt Marcus with his nails, not to annoy his "target." Marcus continued to caress him and talk softly. Their connection was established.

Fulvia entered the cubicle and jumped in embarrassment,

putting her hands on her cheeks. "I am so sorry, Tribune Marcus! Bebio, down! Right away! Now! Out! I have told you many times you must not come in here when I am working!"

"I see you know this cat very well," said Marcus.

"Indeed, I do. I cannot separate myself from him anymore. He was born here, and now he follows me everywhere. But I assure you it will not happen again! Please do not tell Matron Lydia. Even though she loves the cat, she does not want him to bother our clients."

"No need to worry, Fulvia. He did not bother me at all. In fact, I must say I should have guessed he was your cat from the way he was massaging me. You taught him well! He does not have your skills, but he is very good!"

A beaming smile lit up her face as Bebio, now seated on Marcus's legs, gave no sign of wanting to get down. Fulvia had kept her eyes looking down until that moment when she raised them and glanced into Marcus's eyes. They both realized they had exchanged more words in those few moments than in all the time they had spent together since they had met more than a year before.

"Bebio! Enough now! Come on, get off the Tribune, out!" She used her hands to push him off Marcus and out of the cubicle.

"Goodbye, little fellow, come see me again, and many thanks for the massage!" he said, watching Bebio disappear behind the drapes while lying down again for his massage. He took advantage of their conversation and added, "Please, Fulvia, I would like you to stop calling me 'Tribune,' now more than ever since your Bebio and I have become friends."

She smiled gently, placing her hand on his eyes to make him close them. Only in this way could she regain concentration and start the massage.

Bebio was very happy: a first step had been taken. Marcus and Fulvia had talked. When evening arrived, on their way home, Fulvia scolded Bebio, telling him how ashamed she had been that afternoon. He listened and occasionally answered with little meows of approval or disapproval, knowing she would not understand the difference between the two.

He had to concentrate on the next step to achieve his purpose.

With Hephaestus, he had exploited his own enormous patience to get him used to enduring the long days of training. With Tarzio, tired of seeing him looking at those two small walls on the two sides of his table, he had made that crucial jump. Now, with Marcus and Fulvia, he had to find a way to make them confess their mutual feelings, which neither of them had the courage to express.

If he failed, Marcus's bloodline, the bloodline of Tarzio, Hephaestus, and Khepri, would not continue. Bebio could not allow Hator's prophecy to be unfulfilled. Bebio's plan was to be precise, meticulous, and decisively successful.

Bebio's Plan

Over the rest of the summer, messengers on their way to and from Rome delivered troubling news about what was happening. Vitellius's legions had brutalized many areas of the empire's capital. His soldiers became rapists and thieves terrorizing the population. Aware and worried about this recurrent news, the consuls of Ameria often gathered the popular assembly to keep everyone informed about what was happening outside their walls.

At that time, Ameria had reached one of the most glorious periods in its history. The imposing polygonal walls had been completely restored and raised for more security. During that restoration, the engineers did not follow the technique used by Tarzio of alternating big and small stone blocks. Thanks to the Romans, they had developed considerable knowledge in the use of cement mortars. The parts of the walls that needed to be consolidated or raised were integrated with smaller stones kept together by very resistant mortar, which provided the necessary stability and resistance to bad weather or possible attacks.

Bebio occasionally descended from the garden of the baths and took long walks along the top of the walls. Once in a while, heading east, another time going west, he remembered sitting comfortably in Tarzio's bag while the walls, stone by stone, grew under Tarzio's feet. Bebio loved to admire the length and strength of the walls, feeling very proud of his human who had completed this incredible, monumental project even though he, Tito, had left him before the project was finished. At the end of his second life, the houses of Ameria were almost exclusively inside the walls; only the necropolis and a few rural buildings were outside the walls.

From the top of the walls, Bebio now looked at all the roofs well outside the city gates. Looking south, almost opposite the main gate, he could see the large square complex where the young inhabitants of Ameria trained in fighting, wrestling, and sports. The square was dominated by the large bronze statue of Nero Claudius Drusus, known as Germanicus, who died in 19 AD at only thirty-nine years of age. He was the adopted son of Emperor Tiberius.

The death of Germanicus was a big blow to the empire since he was Tiberius's rightful successor. In addition to being an outstanding commander, loved and respected by his legions, Germanicus was a kind human being—the perfect combination for him to be an excellent emperor. Elected consul when he was only twenty-eight years old before he turned thirty, he was given the command of the Rhine territories. He was so successful that he was sure to win another important assignment in the eastern regions of the empire.

Germanicus's increasing popularity became a threat to Tiberius himself. The emperor had no faith in Germanicus's wife, Agrippina, an ambitious woman who was impatient to return to Rome and sit on the throne. Tiberius decided to send to Germanicus's side the newly appointed governor of Syria, Gnaeus Calpurnius Piso, a man he trusted. Germanicus and Gnaeus did not get along, nor did their wives, who were also competing with each other, as wives do. Piso decided to return to Rome.

A few days after his departure, Germanicus fell ill and died, leaving Agrippina with the certainty that he had been poisoned. His deeds of valor and popularity were then exploited by Tiberius, who needed to eliminate every suspicion of his being involved in the death of his adopted son. He ordered that bronze or marble statues of the dead leader be created in the main Roman municipalities. Thus, in 22 AD, the military square of Ameria was enriched with a ten-foot-tall bronze statue of Germanicus to which all young legionnaires had to pay respect every morning before starting their training.

Continuing his walk to the east, Bebio saw the big amphitheater. On some days, the frightening screams of excited masses of chanting humans rose up from it. Bebio never ventured beyond the walls of the amphitheater, and he certainly did not care for what was going on inside that building. He was scared when there were large groups of humans about. He had seen them attacking and killing each other.

Bebio was not a coward; he often fought with other cats that violated his territory. More than once, Darius, while trimming the hedges, had to intervene to separate him from the attacks of other cats. But Bebio always kept away from humans fighting since nothing good could come of that.

Returning home from one of his walks, he slipped into the cubicle where Marcus, already naked, was stretched out on the cot, waiting for Fulvia. "*Ave*, little fellow, come here!" Marcus said, tapping softly on his belly to ask Bebio to jump up. Bebio did not wait for a second request and immediately leaped up on him. Marcus had covered himself with a linen towel and started to caress Bebio while Bebio started to massage Macus's abdomen, purring loudly.

When Fulvia entered the cubicle, she saw them and, putting down her basket, exclaimed, "Oh no! Tribune Marcus! Again! I am so sorry. Bebio! Get down immediately!" Bebio did not pay any attention to her at all, continuing to purr and massage his target.

"Do not worry, Fulvia, he does not bother me. In fact, I have to say that it is very pleasant! And please forget the titles. Please just call me Marcus."

Not listening to him, she approached the cot and picked up Bebio with both her hands in order to put him down. With a very quick gesture, Bebio stuck out his claws and dragged the linen towel with him, leaving Marcus stark naked in front of Fulvia. She was so embarrassed. In all the times she had massaged him, she had never seen him totally naked. Shy as she was, she could not help but look at that one part of his body she had never yet touched. He covered himself with his hands while she remained motionless, still holding Bebio in her hands, and Bebio was still gripping the towel with his claws.

Their first embarrassment turned into laughter, first half-volume, then louder. Turning toward the door, Fulvia placed Bebio on the ground and handed Marcus a clean towel. He was still laughing but clearly embarrassed.

Marcus covered himself. "Quite mischievous, your Bebio! I hope you did not teach him that kind of trick!"

"Of course not, Marcus! I hope you do not think that!"

"I am not so sure!" he said, laughing without looking her in the eyes. Then, to reassure her, he added, "I was just joking. Do not worry. Now let's try to pull ourselves together and start the massage."

She turned to get the oil with a smile still on her lips and the image of his naked body still in her eyes. She had often tried to imagine him without that towel covering him. Now that she had seen his nude body, it would not be easy for her to do her job.

Quietly, Marcus said, "Quite a smart rascal, your kitty!"

They started giggling again and could not stop. When Fulvia began to spread oil on his skin, her lips puckered as she shushed him to restore silence and her concentration. When the sand of her clepsydra had completely run down, indicating the end of the massage, she exited the cubicle silently to let him get dressed. She could not wait for him to come out so she could bid him goodbye. She ran to Matron Lydia to tell her what had just happened. Matron Lydia laughed out loud and told Fulvia she certainly was not the first girl to see him naked.

Fulvia lowered her eyes and blushed, while Matron Lydia turned to Bebio and said, "Well done, my dear! You surely know what to do! Thanks for organizing this beautiful show for Fulvia!" Matron Lydia petted Bebio and gave him a well-deserved bowl of milk.

A few evenings later, going back home after finishing work, Fulvia was alone. Bebio did not follow her. She was worried that he might have followed some female cat in heat, and so after waiting for him at the door for a while, she went to bed. When she woke up at dawn, she looked around, but he was not there. She decided to go to the baths earlier than usual to look around for him. She looked everywhere in the gardens and the rooms but could not find him anywhere.

It was almost time for her first client when she suddenly saw Marcus arriving with Bebio in his arms. She ran toward him and took

Bebio from his arms. "Where did you find him, Tribune Marcus? Bebio! I was worried about you!" In public, in front of others, she could not avoid being formal with Marcus. She did not want to encourage gossip about their relationship.

"He actually found me," Marcus said. "During the night, I stretched out my leg and felt this soft ball of fur on my bed. He was watching me sleep. I immediately recognized him. I called him, and he came next to me, lying beside me all night long. I brought him back because I was certain you were worried."

"Thank you, Tribune Marcus, thank you very much. So kind of you."

He smiled, without words understanding her desire to keep their relationship hidden. Respecting her wish for privacy, he saluted her, saying they would meet the following day.

Fulvia immediately told Matron Lydia, who teased her. "Too bad Bebio cannot talk! It would be nice if he could tell us what it is like to share a bed with the handsome tribune!"

So now Bebio knew how to get to Marcus's home. At least two or three nights a week, he would show up at Marcus's window and sleep with him. Amused, Marcus commented, "You are lucky that it is summer now! I will have to teach you how to get in when the windows are closed in winter."

When Bebio did not go back home with her, Fulvia was not worried anymore; she knew he was with Marcus. She was a little jealous knowing that Bebio was there next to Marcus's naked body, that body she knew so well but still wanted to get to know better. In the morning, when Bebio returned to the baths after sleeping at Marcus's house, she would pick him up and put him close to her face to smell whatever scent remained on his fur.

Aleste asked his son about this cat that showed up frequently at their house. In the beginning, Marcus did not want to tell him the cat belonged to Fulvia, knowing very well that his father would start up again with his lectures. When autumn arrived and the windows had to be closed, Marcus had to let Bebio in through the front door and had to confess to his father that the cat was Fulvia's. His father laughed out loud and told him, "My son, I have nothing to add! That cat is doing my job! Let's see how long it will take you to understand that it is a sign sent by the gods!"

"Father, the situation has not changed; in fact, it is getting worse. Vitellius's legions were massacred in Cremona, and he is now taking shelter in Narnia. I do not know how he managed to get help from the Narnians again. Vespasian's legions are marching toward Rome. If Vitellius does not surrender, we will have war at our doorstep. It is not the time for me to be thinking about love."

"Marcus, there is always time for love. And that cat is telling you so! Why do you think he sleeps one night with you and another one with her?"

"Father, you are being ridiculous! A cat cannot be that clever!"

"Of course, he can! Do you not remember the legend of Tito, the cat belonging to our ancestor Hephaestus? Your grandmother used to tell you that tale when you were a little boy, along with the story of Aker, the cat of the city walls. Cats are animals sent by the gods for specific tasks."

"Oh, Father! Those are legends, made-up fairy tales!"

"Do as you wish, Marcus, but if I were you, I would investigate this affair more deeply. I will bet you fifty gold coins that if you and Fulvia sleep in the same bed, that cat will no longer commute between your two houses."

Vitellius Surrenders in Narnia

That November was very cold. Snow had already fallen abundantly on the Apennine Mountains. Emperor Vitellius had returned to Rome, leaving his legions in Narnia with two of his commanders. Vespasian's legions, led by Antonius Primus, were marching toward the south and were already near Fanum Fortunae. Consuls from Narnia sent two messengers to the leaders of Ameria to keep them alert in case they were to suffer an attack. The defeat of a nearby city could have severe repercussions on the political and economic stability of the entire region. Rome and many other towns had suffered vast devastation. It would be a very hard blow for Ameria if it were attacked.

Vitellius proved once again he was neither a good strategist nor a good emperor. His total lack of sagacity, together with his choice of incompetent military commanders, led him to make the wrong decisions, which weakened any chance of resisting an attack from Vespasian's legions.

Upon his arrival in Narnia, Vespasian's commander, Antonius Primus, did not have to start a battle. Vitellius's commanders laid down their arms and surrendered. Their soldiers joined Vespasian's legions, and half of them were redistributed to the legions left to guard Narnia and the region, while others joined the troops marching toward Rome. Their undisputed strength and support from many of the empire's provinces were so great that Vitellius's resistance completely disintegrated.

In Ameria, the usual December Saturnalia celebrations were in full swing. The traditional banquets to honor the Titan god Saturn and his golden era had been arranged throughout the city, including several sacrifices to the gods. Marcus had to attend the one organized at the military camp, the *Saturnalicium Castrense*.

Before joining his fellow soldiers, dressed in his formal uniform, Marcus went to Fulvia's home for the first time. He knew where it was but had never been there. On the windowsill, he saw Bebio crouched in a corner, his paws tightly curled under his breastbone in an attempt to stay warm. "*Ave*, Bebio! What are you doing out in the cold? You would be better off inside, close to the fireplace!"

Bebio stood up, stretching himself and letting his back form the typical high curve while maintaining a straight tail. Bebio then extended his paws forward in a stately welcoming bow to his Marcus.

Marcus, smiling, bowed in front of Bebio at the exact moment Fulvia opened her front door to depart to meet her friends at the banquet at the Temple of Saturn.

"Marcus! What are you doing here?" she said with surprise and embarrassment, looking around to be sure nobody could see them together.

He remained for a few moments in that bowing position, feeling somewhat ridiculous. He stood up and approached Fulvia, handing her a little red cloth bag tied with a leather string. "This is for you, Fulvia, a little gift to celebrate the Saturnalia."

She untied the string and unrolled the cloth, finding a painted terracotta statuette of a seated cat. "Marcus! This is so beautiful! Thank you! Now, I am embarrassed. I do not have anything for you. I did not think, I did not know…"

"Shh… Shh… Shh… I am sorry the sculptor could not exactly replicate the colors of Bebio's fur, but I think the statuette looks a lot like our Bebio."

Marcus pronounced the word "our" with emphasis, and Fulvia felt a shiver that did not derive from the cold. "I have to go now, but I hope to see you again very soon," she said.

Marcus took her hand in his to pull her closer for their first long kiss. She had no choice but to kiss him back.

Bebio was there watching the scene with his eyes wide open. As soon as Marcus and Fulvia ended their kiss, Bebio yawned, jumped down from the windowsill, ran into the house, and curled up in his basket next to the fireplace. He had suffered quite a bit from the cold while waiting for Marcus to arrive, and now that his plan had advanced another step, he could warm up and let the humans go celebrate.

Fulvia waved goodbye to Marcus while holding the statuette next to her heart and walked away to join Matron Lydia and the other bath masseuses at the Temple.

On the third day of Saturnalia, which usually lasted a whole week, news arrived from Rome that the Temple of Saturn on the Capitol had been destroyed by a huge fire lit during the ferocious battles between the opposing legions of Vespasian and Vitellius. The latter and other officials like Ambassador Sabinus tried to repress the fighting, but their attempts dissolved like the smoke from the fires.

On the 19th of December, Rome experienced a defeat that echoed throughout the entire empire. Vitellius was killed, beheaded, and his body thrown into the Tiber. Antonius Primus's soldiers paraded through the city with Vitellius's head impaled on a long spear to show the Romans that Vitellius had been defeated. Terrible days followed as Primus's legions devastated the city even more than Vitellius's legions had.

Finally, on December 21st, the situation seemed to take a turn for the better when the Senate appointed young Domitian, the son of Vespasian, as praetor, with Vespasian being confirmed as emperor. With the fourth emperor proclaimed in just over a hugely bloody, violent, and destructive year, the end of the Saturnalia season seemed to coincide with the hope of finally seeing a lasting peace restored.

Ameria had been spared from these conflicts and wars, with its soldiers staying out of any battles. The citizens placed new hope in Vespasian, who was still in the east. He informed the Senate he would return in a few months, a delay that worried the consuls of Ameria, and not only them since other political or military leaders might take advantage of his absence to seize power. The situation calmed down, however, and tempers did, too, and Vespasian arrived in Rome in the spring of 70 AD. His rule lasted for ten long and peaceful years, during which Rome and the entire empire had unprecedented cultural and legal growth.

With this more tranquil situation, Aleste became more insistent with his son, assisted by Bebio, who continued to switch between Marcus and Fulvia's beds. "Son, you have no more excuses. The civil war is over. Vespasian is proving to be a wise emperor, capable of giving stability to the empire. Give me a grandchild! Please propose to Fulvia! I am asking, as is Brebio!"

"Bebio, Father, not Brebio"!"

"Yes, Bebio, whatever. Please, do propose to her!"

Marcus's feelings for Fulvia completely overwhelmed him, but he was still uncertain of her reactions. They belonged to two different social castes, and even if Fulvia had never been a slave, she belonged to a much lower social class. Marcus knew how cruel certain Ameria matrons could be, especially those who wanted their own daughters married to the city's most renowned tribune. They would never forgive Fulvia or treat her with respect.

Marcus wondered how to find a way to prevent any possible rejection from Fulvia because of their different upbringing. He thought of moving to another city where nobody knew them, but he could not leave his father alone, especially now that he was approaching old age. One night, when Bebio was sleeping with him, Marcus asked Bebio for advice. "If what my father affirms—that you were sent by the gods—is true, then you must help me find a solution!"

Bebio stretched out on his back, paws in the air, showing his soft, white belly. Marcus imagined caressing Fulvia's hair and fell asleep embracing Bebio, who was already planning his next move.

Bebio's New Family

On a crisp March morning, Marcus was preparing to go to the military camp for a long day of training. Approaching the door to let Bebio out, he turned around to say goodbye to his father, and he did not see that Bebio quickly hid under a chest. When Marcus exited and closed the door, he looked around and did not see Bebio. They usually walked together for a while, and he then would turn toward the military camp while Bebio continued on the street to the baths.

Aleste was also getting ready to go out and was wearing his *subligaculum*, his long winter tunic, and his sandals. As he was about to wrap himself in his woolen toga, completing the complex turn of the fabric around his shoulder and body, he felt some resistance right when he was raising his left arm to wind the toga under his right arm.

Bebio had climbed on the part of the toga still on the floor, and his claws were caught in it. He ended up rolled in the toga, and to free himself, he slipped between Aleste's feet. The poor man lost his balance and was about to fall to the ground. To avoid hitting the floor, Aleste stretched out his arms toward the bed, rotating his chest sharply. His muscles felt a sharp snap. He remained motionless, with his face in a pained expression. He finally managed to slide onto the bed, where he stayed immobilized.

Bebio got on the bed and lay down next to him, feeling guilty but satisfied. He began licking Aleste's fingers like he was asking for forgiveness.

Upon his return home, while opening the door, Marcus saw Bebio running out between his legs. "That's why I didn't see you this morning; you were still inside!" He had not finished his sentence when he heard his father groaning. He rushed into his father's bedroom, visibly worried.

Aleste reassured him that it was nothing serious but that he could not move. He explained that he had fallen and that Bebio kept him company. He did not say anything about how he had fallen so as not to put the blame on Bebio.

Marcus tried to move his father, but he only increased his father's pain. Marcus told Aleste he would go immediately to bring Fulvia. Only her hands could release the magic that would dissolve the pain. Before leaving, he chided Aleste. "Father, let me be clear with you. Please do not say anything to Fulvia about us. You will only embarrass her."

Aleste nodded, gesturing with his hand as if to tell Marcus, "Yes, yes, go. I am not listening to you anyway!"

Arriving at the baths, Marcus immediately entered Matron Lydia's room. He saw Bebio lounging in his basket, licking his paw with the utmost indifference. "Matron Lydia, may I ask you the great favor of having Fulvia come to my house?"

Surprised, she replied, "Tribune, it was about time you took this step!"

"No, no, what are you thinking? It is about my father. He fell and has bad back pain. He cannot move. I am sure Fulvia can ease his pain. I will pay for the whole working day."

"Do not worry, Tribune, I do understand. As soon as Fulvia finishes with Matron Livia, she will accompany you. I will cancel her other appointments." With his air of superiority, Bebio watched Marcus falling like a trout caught in a net and was pleased as only a cat can be. He was in his third life and was learning more and more about how to manipulate a human.

Soon afterward, Fulvia was in Marcus's home next to Aleste's bed, her hands working their magic on his aching back. He was moaning under the healing pressure, emitting sounds that Bebio had never heard before. Bebio looked at Aleste, tilting his head with an intrigued expression.

After almost an hour, Aleste felt more relaxed and could move a little without feeling excruciating pain. "Thank you, Fulvia. Now I understand why Marcus cannot do without your hands. They are truly magical. And let me tell you, I am convinced he cannot do without you at all. Nothing would make him happier than welcoming you under our roof as his wife, and I am sure Bebio would also be very happy to see you two together."

Fulvia blushed and smiled at Aleste without being able to utter a word. Bebio yawned like he was saying to Aleste, "I hope that my work and your pain will bring some results!"

As she was leaving the room, Fulvia told him, "I will be back in the morning for another massage, Domus Aleste. Please rest and try to move every now and then. The muscles have to stay active."

Fulvia joined Marcus in the atrium before returning to the baths. Thanking her, he embraced her, and the two shared a long kiss. "I hope my father behaved and didn't embarrass you."

"It is fine, but I think he joined the list of people who want us together. Marcus, I am in love with you, and this is not a secret anymore, but you are a patrician while I am a plebeian. Marriage would damage you and be an embarrassment for me. There are too many families who want their daughters married to you. How many times have I had to endure those matrons' wicked insinuations that make me feel bad? One of them had the nerve to ask me if I were your concubine."

"Fulvia, I do not want to lose you. I could not be with anyone but you. And I would never make you my concubine. I want to marry you. We will show them that love has no social class and silence their rumors about our love." They embraced with another passionate kiss under Bebio's attentive gaze. Seated on the top of a column in the garden, he did not miss a single aspect of their conversation.

"Say you will marry me, Fulvia, and we will make the announcement right away. Together, we will be stronger than them."

"Yes, Marcus, yes! I will!"

At that point, Bebio jumped down from the column, stretched his legs, and walked to the garden to do his business. He knew that from that moment on, he would do it there most of the time.

The wedding was celebrated in May. In the following years, they were gladdened by four beautiful children: Claudius, Lavinia, Valerianus, and Emilia. Bebio welcomed them all with joy, delighting in full days of naps in an always-full cradle. He was always in the company of the children, sleeping, playing, and eating with them.

They all adored Bebio, and he was very happy he had accomplished his mission of extending Khepri's lineage. After the birth of their fourth child, Bebio, now eighteen years old, fell ill. He permanently closed his eyes for the third time. Marcus and Fulvia were devastated by the loss of their matchmaker, who had worked so hard to make them fall in love. They organized a funeral that was worthy of a consul and kept his ashes in a marble urn in the *peristilio* of their house.

With the help of one of his gardeners, Marcus began to shape four laurel bushes at the four corners of the garden. He had planted one of them for the birth of each of his children. He was now slowly shaping them one by one into big cats to invoke Bebio's protection over his four children. After a few years, each of them had a large laurel cat in the garden, where they often gathered to read, play, and remember their Bebio.

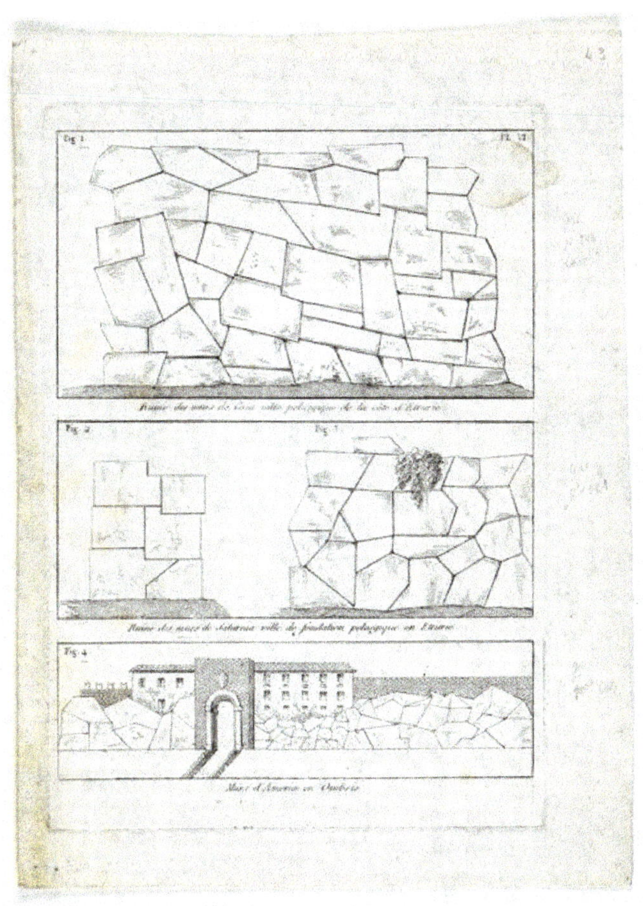

Drawing of Ameria's walls

Statue of Germanicus in the Archeological Museum of Amelia. The statue was rediscovered in 1963, buried near the Amelia city wall. It was in pieces and had to be reconstructed.

Chapter 4
The Early Middle Ages in Ameria
Year 548 AD
Pirro the Diplomat/Strategist and Lucius the Lover

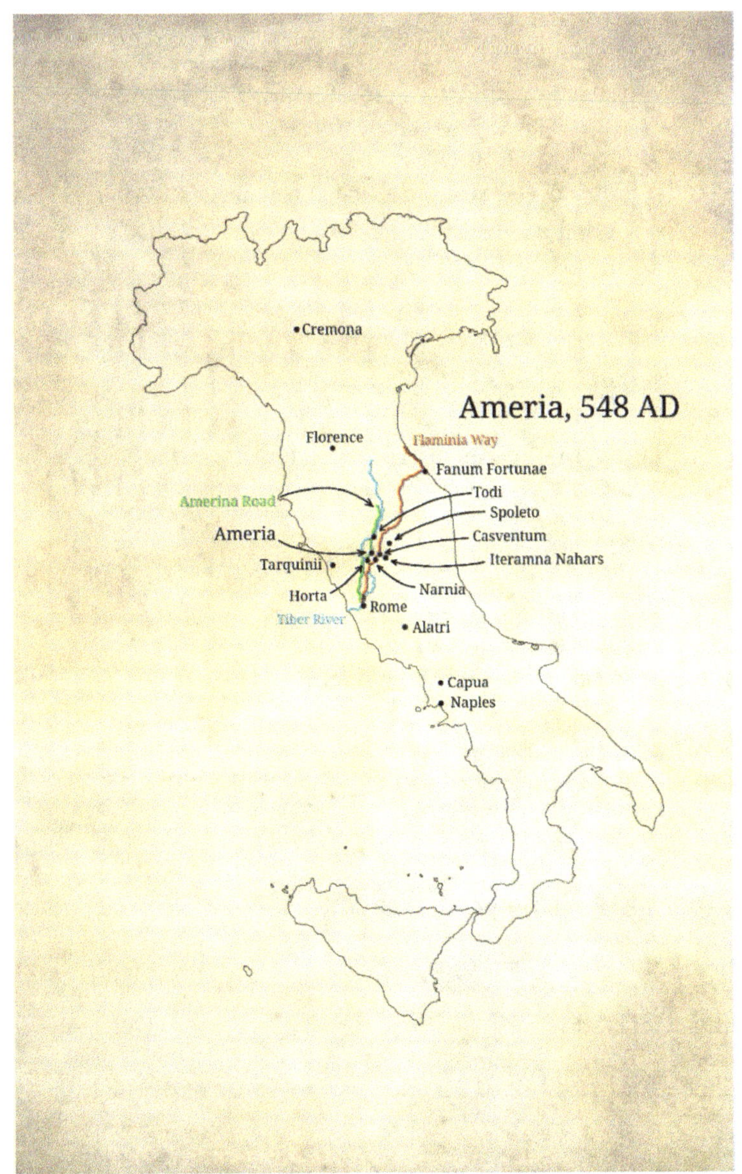

Cast of Characters

Family at the Start of the Chapter

Petrus: runs the family flax business; the older brother of Lucius

Lucius: the younger brother of Petrus; handles deliveries and sales for the family's flax company

Gnaeus: the father of Petrus and Lucius; formerly a soldier; an elder in the Council of Ameria

Tito/Pirro: a cat

Other Principals

Scilla: the widow of the Narnia commander of guards

Other Amerians

Appianus: the consul of Ameria

Caius: the head teamster of the flax company

Artusia: the family cook and maid

Others

Mamertio: a wealthy Roman trader

Pelagius: a deputy to the Pope

Maximus: Scilla's brother

Benedict: a monk; abbot of Monte Cassino; founder of the Benedictine Order; a saint

Ostrogoths

Theodoric: the king of the Ostrogoths

Baduila (better known as Totila): the general and later king of the

Ostrogoths

Vult, Ruderic, and Blidin: Ostrogoth generals

Family at the End of the Chapter

Totila, Eusebia, and Pirro

Totila

110

Introduction

T HE SPLENDOR AMERIA reached in the first century AD, which was maintained over the following three centuries, was slowly fading. The end of the fifth century marked the inexorable decline of the Roman Empire. The Italian peninsula had been subjected to continuous invasion from populations coming from the north: the Huns, the Visigoths, and the Vandals roamed the peninsula, often descending along the Via Amerina, the alternate road of the Roman consular road system.

In the early years of the sixth century, Ameria was under the command of Theodoric, King of the Ostrogoths. The last devastating wars had made the provision of wheat and other essential goods, usually imported from the eastern territories of Theodoric's kingdom, very difficult. For this reason, many cities, including Ameria, could not rely on imported goods and had to go back to the cultivation and production of their own staples in order to survive.

Theodoric died in AD 526, leaving no male heir. Uncertain years followed, in which General Baduila, better known as Totila, gained more and more power. "Totila," in the Gothic language, meant "immortal." Crowned King of the Ostrogoths in AD 541, Totila besieged Ameria in AD 548. It was precisely then that the spirit of Tito felt the call to return to life to protect his city from possible irreparable devastation.

Petrus and Lucius

Petrus and Lucius were two brothers, sons of Gnaeus, an elder member of the Council of Ameria. Their father had been a valiant soldier, a worthy descendant of the tribune Marcus. Gnaeus's sons did not follow in their father's or their ancestors' footsteps. When Gnaeus ended his military career, he was awarded a few lots of land. The two brothers had acquired some more fields and dedicated their lives to the cultivation and processing of flax.

Flax production had been steadily growing over the years. Workers prepared flax in two large rooms of a building which was said to have been the House of Food in the ancient city of Amer. In those rooms, the two brothers supervised several workers who were skilled in different uses of the precious plant. Their main activity was the creation of linen threads that were turned into fabric for dresses, or towels, or sheets.

Another team of workers was in charge of processing flax seeds for alimentary use. A team of three alchemists worked on separate quantities of seeds for medical and cosmetic use. The production and sale of flax-related products, however, had taken a severe downturn because of the invasions of recent years.

Petrus, the elder brother, was more involved in directing the overall business. Lately, he has been in a constant state of stress since the whole family survived, thanks to his work. Married with two children, he was an attentive family man.

Lucius, the younger brother, was not involved in overall business responsibilities. He loved his job but was less committed to it than his brother was. His main task was dealing with deliveries and the sale of finished products in the markets of nearby cities. He also kept in contact with wealthy merchants to sell them the family's goods. At least twice a week, riding horseback, he led two wagons loaded with linen and other products to the markets of Narnia and Carsulae, where the brothers had many customers.

Lucius was not married yet and knew how to use his charm and overflowing youthful vitality to better sell their products to the matrons of the cities he visited. Those ladies often asked him to deliver the goods in person, ending those visits in the matrons' bedrooms. Once a month he headed south to Horta, where he would meet Mamertio, a wealthy merchant who bought large quantities of fabrics to resell to rich Roman patricians.

After their meetings, Mamertio would transfer the items he had purchased from his wagons to his *caudicaria*, flat-bottomed riverboats. His purchases included bales of fabrics and crates containing small terracotta bottles filled with precious oils and cosmetics. Descending the river, Mamertio would then dock at the Portus Tiberinus in the heart of Rome to reach the Roman markets and his own customers in the big city.

The meetings between Lucius and Mamertio in Horta happened at the local tavern, Seripola, located in the port area. Lucius was so persuasive that he always succeeded in selling Mamertio at least a couple of lots more than he actually needed. Mamertio often told Lucius that he had to go to Rome with him. That day, Mamertio insisted, "With your charm and ability to sell, in Rome you will be rich in no time!"

Lucius was fascinated by the tales he had heard of the Roman lifestyle. The thought of leaving Ameria for Rome was tempting; more than once, he had thought about venturing toward a new life, but it was just not the right time.

After King Theodoric's death, many cities had closed themselves up within their walls and isolated themselves for fear of the continuous raids by barbarians and military deserters. Without a central authority, these thieves and destroyers sowed terror wherever they went. Uncertainty about who was in control of the empire resulted in battles and devastation.

In those troubled times, merchants were the best source of communication between local governments. However, they were also the main target of attacks and theft. Mamertio told Lucius about two years before when Totila's soldiers had attacked him while they were besieging Rome. The soldiers seized all his merchandise. Mamertio miraculously managed to preserve his *caudicaria* from their destructive fury by offering no resistance and letting them rob him of all his goods, a loss from which he had struggled to recover.

At the end of their meeting, Mamertio paid Lucius with a bag full of coins. Lucius said his goodbyes to Mamertio, jumped on his horse, and, without waiting for his workers who were taking the wagons back to Ameria, started off on his way home. He told Caius, the head teamster, that they would meet up in Ameria before he raced away on the road along the river.

Tito Meets His New Human

Lucius rode fast across the fields to shorten the distance home and then returned to the road closer to Ameria. Not too far from the city, a group of mercenaries ambushed him. They had stretched a strong rope between two trees on opposite sides of the road. Lucius's galloping horse suddenly swerved to avoid the rope, and Lucius crashed to the ground.

Five or six robbers jumped on Lucius, beating him up with repeated kicks and robbing him of his money and his horse. Lucius passed out and remained unconscious. Thinking he was dead, the robbers left him on the side of the road behind a big tree. They ran away, very happy to have acquired a bag full of shiny coins, much more money than they could have expected from a lone rider.

When Lucius gradually regained consciousness and opened his eyes, the first thing he saw was the two yellow-green eyes of a cat staring at him and smelling the tip of his nose. "I hope you will be kinder to me than your friends!" Lucius said. In response, the cat meowed gently. Lucius tried to get up, but with the cat not moving from atop his chest and the excruciating pain all over his body, he could not move. "Well, are you comfortable? I am sure you were waiting for me to die to have a nice dinner!" he joked in a faint voice between spasms of pain.

Lucius finally managed to lean up against the tree trunk and began trying to determine if he had any broken bones. He decided he must still be all in one piece since he could move his legs, hands, and arms. The atrocious pain in his ankle, however, did not allow him to stand. He must have landed with his entire body weight on that foot when falling off his horse.

The cat, now sitting on his thighs and still staring at him, was thin but with lovely, soft, pure white fur on his paws and belly. The cat's back and face were streaked with colored fur. He had a very intense expression, more that of an adult cat than of the youngster he obviously was.

Yes, it was him; it was Tito, who had returned to his valley for his new mission. As soon as he had approached that human lying on the ground, he had felt that revealing vibration in his whiskers. He was then certain he had found the right human.

Sore and weakened, Lucius was about to lose consciousness again. Tito knew how dangerous it could be for an unconscious person to remain on the side of a road for the night. Given the many wolves and wild boars roaming around the woods at night, the man might not survive. Tito stood up, placed his paws on Lucius's neck, and started licking his face while loudly purring. Tito also gave Lucius little butts with his head to keep him awake.

Lucius caressed the cat and spoke to him softly with the little bit of breath he had left, almost fainting again. In the silence of the woods, they started to hear the noise of wagons approaching. Lucius tried to attract attention by calling for help, but the sound of the hooves and wheels covered his weak voice. Lucius rolled on his side and tried to crawl toward the road. Having recognized his workers heading back to Ameria, Lucius shouted Caius's name, but his effort was choked off by a resulting deep spasm caused by his broken ribs, and he could not make himself heard.

Tito had to intervene. He started running and stopped right in front of the lead cart horse, straightening his tail and raising his fur. An incredibly loud meow erupted from his mouth. The howl was even louder than the combined one that two male cats utter to get the attention of a female cat in heat.

The poor horse, taken by surprise, reared and swerved to the right, taking a few running steps toward the woods. Caius pulled on the reins and stopped the horse in time before the wagon crashed into a tree. Thanks to repeated "Whoahhhs!" and "Shhhhs!" he managed to calm down the horse. As soon as the horse stopped, Caius jumped down from the wagon and went to soothe and check on his horse.

"Damned cat!" he yelled at Tito, who was now running toward Lucius. Caius followed the cat to scare him away. "If I catch you, I will strangle you!" He had hardly finished his sentence when he saw Lucius on the ground, trying to raise an arm to be noticed. "Master Lucius! By the love of the gods! What happened to you?"

In a few words Lucius told Caius about the attack and begged him to take him home. Caius and the others carried Lucius to the wagon, laying him in the back, and left for Ameria.

Turning his head and looking between the wooden slats of the wagon, Lucius saw the cat still sitting next to the tree where they had met. "Come on, little one! Jump on! I owe you my life. You deserve a nice dinner, even if you wanted to eat me, do you not?"

Tito did not wait to be asked a second time, and with a few bounding leaps, he landed next to Lucius in the wagon that was carrying them toward their adventure together. Once they arrived back home, Lucius, with a swollen foot, collapsed on his bed. He could not walk for several days. The chief alchemist of the brothers' flax company applied compresses with linseed oil to the foot in the morning and evening to soothe the pain and the swelling.

What better way for Tito to begin his new life than staying comfortably in bed with his new human? After being reborn in the woods around the city, now he was settling down in this house and beginning to appreciate its comforts.

Petrus was not very happy with the huge loss they had suffered from the robbery and scolded his brother. "Was it too much of an effort to return with the others? No, of course, you had to venture all alone, did you not? You know very well that we are surrounded by barbarians everywhere! The situation is already complicated, and you, you have thrown away an entire month's profit!"

"Petrus, calm down. They almost killed me. If it were not for this cat, I might never have returned, and maybe you would have thought I ran away with your money."

"*Our* money, not mine, *ours*! Yes, the workers told me how this cat led them to you. It is incredible. Where did he come from?" Petrus asked while caressing the cat. Tito, paws in the air, was enjoying those soft linens that reminded him of those he had slept in with Marcus and Fulvia. Petrus smiled, calming down. He loved his little brother very much and always ended up forgiving him, especially now that he saw Lucius so battered. "I do not think we will be able to move this cat out of your bed. You will have to give him a name."

Hearing that, Tito immediately got on all four paws and looked Lucius straight in the eyes, thinking intensely, *My name is Tito! My name is Tito!* He tried his hardest to convey that thought telepathically to Lucius.

"I do not know. I must think about it… But I have an idea!"
Tito waited anxiously.
"I think I will call him Pirro!"
"And how did you come up with that name?"

"Because Pirro was a great strategist and also a great diplomat. This kitty has proven to possess both those qualities in how he acted to save my life." Lucius picked up Tito and moved him closer to his swollen face. "What do you say?" he asked, looking into those deep yellow-green eyes without sensing the cat's reluctance to have to get used to yet another new name. "Would you like to be named after a smart strategist?"

Tito had little choice and limited himself to a soft meow, followed by prodigious purring.

The Fall of Narnia

After several days, still with black-rimmed eyes and various bruises all over his body, Lucius began to walk again, even if heavily limping. He slowly started to work again. Pirro followed him everywhere: to the warehouses, to the loom room, and above all, around their house. Pirro mostly traveled between Lucius's bedroom and the kitchen, where their maid Artusia stuffed Pirro with food. His strong meows echoed all over the house when she held his bowl before placing it on the ground for him to eat the succulent dishes she had prepared for him. Lucius teased her, saying she was now cooking more for Pirro than for the family. Pirro was, of course, very happy with this treatment. Artusia reminded him of Lydia, the matron of the baths. She had the same chubby, sympathetic face, and she loved cats as well. Pirro felt at home with her, now that he had found the object of his new mission in his fourth life.

Over the next few days, the consuls of Ameria assembled the council to report the alarming news delivered by messengers arriving from Rome. After a two-year-long siege, Totila, the king of the Ostrogoths, had managed to enter Rome with a stratagem: he bribed the guards of the city gates, who let him pass through without any resistance. To avoid devastation and mass killings, Pelagius, the pope's deputy, began impressive diplomatic moves and saved the city from a massacre of the citizens and senators who did not submit.

Totila had shown the same mercy and spared the citizens of Naples from a possible massacre in AD 543. Nevertheless, he seized all the treasure and riches he could find. On the other hand, another city, Alatri, was razed by his troops and not given any chance to surrender. Totila had a reputation for inconsistency and took decisions based on the spirit of the moment. He could be sympathetic or ruthless. The cities he conquered could, in equal measure, either be saved or razed to the ground. The possibility that Totila would send his soldiers and mercenaries to conquer the main cities of central Italy one by one became a reality, and every consul was on high alert.

The council in Ameria deliberated about beginning to store provisions, wood, and anything that might be useful in case they were besieged within their walls. Everyone was involved and ordered to contribute. Every warehouse, every cellar, every available space had to be set up to store food and all the other necessary items. Everything from the fields and orchards, even if not completely ripe, was collected and safely stored. Many trees ended up being cut down to have enough wood to burn. Whoever possessed any kind of oil—olive oil or linseed oil—had to give it up for use by the city, such as boiling it and then pouring it down on attackers from the top of the city walls.

This news enraged Petrus, who lashed out at his father. Their family was the largest producer of linseed oil in the city, and Petrus was furious that his father had not defended their family's interests in the council.

Lucius answered very calmly. "Petrus, you do understand that if Totila attacks the city we will not have much of a chance to resist, and we will lose that linseed oil anyway?"

"Sure! What do you know about how much work I have put in to produce that linseed oil, which gives you the means to lead your good life!"

"Petrus, listen. The situation is dire. None of us will remain alive if we do not use every resource we have!"

"You have been hearing too many stories and reading too many manuscripts while I was working!" Petrus replied.

"And you should have studied more history instead of only thinking about accumulating wealth."

"Well, someone had to think about supporting the family!"

Gnaeus tried to restore the peace between the two brothers. "My sons, this is no time to quarrel. Each of you has undertaken a different path. Each of you excels in his own field. Try, you two, to understand how much more effective you are together. You complement each other. Do not fall out with each other. Your minds together can be much more effective than either of you can be by yourself.

"I know I gave each of you a different education. You, Petrus, are a hard worker, an organizer, and a good manager. And you, Lucius, are a good merchant, storyteller, and salesman of goods and ideas. Together, you are a winning team. Do you remember when I used to read to you about the achievements of Pirro? He was an unprecedented strategist and diplomat—he had both qualities—but the two of you together can replicate what Pirro did by himself!"

When Gnaeus mentioned Pirro, the two brothers instantly turned and looked at their new four-legged friend and he, too, focused his hearing by turning his head to one side when he heard his new name. Gnaeus smiled. "No, not this Pirro! I am talking about the Pirro who resolved insurmountable situations ages ago with work and diplomacy." Exiting the room, he added, "Think about what you two can achieve together. Do not disappoint me!"

Lucius picked up Pirro and placed him on his shoulders. He also exited the room; it was not the right moment to argue with his brother. The cat felt immediately at ease in that position, regaining in an instant the balance he had gotten used to with his first human, Hephaestus.

In a very short time, Pirro took possession of the whole house and moved around it with ease. Petrus's young sons were glad to have him at home. They often played with him. Pirro showed great patience with those two little devils, even if he had to give them a couple of scratches when they went too far. In the evening, his bed was with Lucius.

If that cat had not saved his life, perhaps it would have been an embarrassment for Lucius to have a cat with him day and night—the handsome Lucius, argued over by many women, sleeping with a cat in his bed. But he did not care. Many times in his dreams, Lucius relived the nightmare of the attack in the woods. Waking up all sweaty, he found comfort in those yellow-green eyes looking at him.

After several iterations of the nightmare, Pirro began to realize when the nightmare was returning to Lucius's dreams. When Pirro felt the dream starting, he would lick Lucius's face to wake him up before the dream became too unbearable. Then Lucius would regain his calm, thanks to Pirro's steady gaze and strong purring. When his human was relaxed again, Pirro would lay down again and fall into a deep sleep.

After a few months, the inevitable happened. Totila's army headed out toward the Umbrian lands to join up with other troops arriving from the north. Going up the Via Flaminia, they stopped in the valley opposite the town of Narnia, briefly besieging it. Even though it was perched on the top of a high hill, with high slopes as a natural defense, Narnia did not have walls as strong as Ameria's. It was not difficult for Totila's soldiers to infiltrate and open the gates of the city, which then underwent ruthless devastation. Its walls were destroyed, an act to demonstrate that nothing could resist his savagery. The same destiny befell Iteramna Nahars, the Roman-era walls of which, built out of blocks of tuff, were swept away without much effort.

A few hundred Narnia citizens gathered outside Ameria's gates, now hermetically sealed to shelter the city. The Narnia refugees who were massed under the walls begged for help. Even if more people would be helpful in defending Ameria, the consuls did not trust letting them into the city. Knowing how Totila had entered Rome and Narnia, deceiving gullible dupes and bribing gate guards, they were afraid a few of his soldiers might infiltrate the town among the Narnia refugees. If Totila's spies could get inside Ameria, they would be able to give access to the city to his troops.

From the top of the walls, Lucius, with Pirro on his shoulders, was looking down at those desperate people. Suddenly, he heard a woman's voice calling him. Lucius recognized Scilla, one of his clients to whom he had sold linens and beauty products that he had personally delivered to her—right to her bedroom. Lucius told his brother he wanted to find a way to save Scilla and her people.

Petrus was skeptical but decided to help Lucius. At sunset, they made their way to the top of the hill, and while Petrus distracted the guards, Lucius attached a rope to the top of the wall and began his descent to the valley. On his shoulders, Lucius carried a sack containing a dozen daggers. Pirro, standing on top of the wall, had no intention of being left behind. Suddenly, he leaped, twisted in the air, and landed on the sack, using his claws to anchor himself. Surprised by the sudden additional weight on his back, Lucius looked over his shoulder. "Pirro! You crazy cat! I should have known you would not have missed it. Hold on tight. We have a ways to go before we are down." Once near the ground, Pirro jumped down the rest of the way and then waited for Lucius. Reaching the bottom, Lucius scooped up Pirro, hugged him, and placed him in a small gap in the walls. Lucius told Pirro to stay there and wait for him. He repeated it four times and added hand signals.

Pirro gave him a look that could easily be interpreted as, "I got it! Once was enough!" By then, Pirro understood humans very well. It was Lucius who still had to learn how to communicate with him!

With his bag on his shoulders, Lucius started running along close to the walls. He approached the group of refugees, hiding his face under a hood. Mingling among them, he reached Scilla, who started to react in a way that would reveal his presence. He covered her mouth with his hand, and with his other hand, he put his finger to his mouth to ask for silence. He took her by the hand and slowly left the group.

"Lucius! Thank all the gods you are here. Please let us in! They have killed so many of my fellow citizens. If they come here, and they will, they will kill us all as you watch from the walls. Please help us!"

"That is why I am here, but it is you who must help me if you want to save your people. The consuls will not let you in for fear there might be spies among you."

"What do you want me to do?"

"You must choose a dozen of your most trusted friends. Each of them will have to go around and make sure all of the people who are here are citizens of Narnia; you must be sure there are no strangers. Only if we are sure of that can I arrange to get you into the city. Behind that tree over there, I left a bag with a dozen daggers. Give one to each of your chosen friends and kill anyone you are sure is not a Narnian. Now I must go. I will be back tomorrow at the same time. Good hunting for the Ostrogoths!"

He ran back up the valley and reached the gap where Pirro was waiting. He whispered, "Pirro, go inside and let Petrus see you so he will understand he has to pull me up."

Pirro immediately slipped through the long gap, then raced to find Petrus and rub on his legs. It was the signal that Lucius was climbing up. Petrus saluted the guards and went to the other side of the turret. When he was sure he had not been followed, Petrus reached over the wall and pulled his brother up, asking how it went.

"We will find out tomorrow: Scilla is a very smart woman and loves life in all of its various aspects. No one can trick her. Come on, Pirro, let's go home." The three strategists walked back home, visibly worried about the success of their mission but determined to risk it for the safety of all those lives.

The Narnians, crowded next to the walls, were preparing to spend another night under the stars. Scilla walked among them and occasionally stopped to talk to someone already stretched out on the ground. Then she walked toward the big tree to collect the daggers. With her walked her brother Maximus and a few of his closest friends. She explained the plan and gave each one of them a dagger. Almost all of them had escaped Narnia without being able to take along any of their belongings, much less their weapons.

As the sun rose, the group began to wander among the people of Narnia, searching for people they did not recognize. Asking questions, they were able to identify a group of six or seven people who had remained a bit separated and had never been seen by anybody else before. One of them, fearful of being discovered, tried to escape. He was caught and killed while Scilla's recruits, most of whom had stayed close to the other suspects, took them by surprise and killed them mercilessly.

Other citizens, not knowing about the plan, started to yell, fearing for their own lives. Scilla climbed on a spur of rock and shouted to everyone: "Narnians! Do not be afraid! We killed some traitors! They infiltrated among us to try to enter Ameria and turn over the city to the invaders. Now that we have killed them, we hope the Amerian consuls will open the gates and let us in. If you have any doubts about anyone, do not hesitate to say so. Our safety depends on this!"

Meanwhile, Lucius and Petrus, along with the faithful Pirro, were arguing with the consuls. They had to reveal their plan and work hard to convince them to let the Narnians inside the city. Consul Appianus was not very inclined to do so and declared before the council that he would strangle the two brothers with his own hands if even a single enemy managed to enter the city.

In the late afternoon, Lucius went through the gate on the hill to reach Scilla. When he arrived, she and her men had created a bottleneck using some large branches, and they were making everyone go through this passage one by one to make sure they could recognize every single person. Those who had already passed through the bottleneck were quickly marched toward the upper gate in order to enter the city. Lucius told her to hurry since there was little time before sunset. There were still a few dozen people waiting to pass through. "We must hurry. Soon it will be dark!"

"I cannot hurry! I have to be sure I eliminated all of the imposters."

"How many were there?" Lucius asked.

"Seven, so far," she replied angrily. "Those bastards destroyed my city. I could not bear for them to do the same to yours."

A sudden shout arose at the back of the line. Two men had tried to steal some clothes to better disguise themselves. They had been discovered and detained. Once they were taken in front of Scilla, without a moment of hesitation, she killed them, cutting their throats right in front of Lucius, who discovered a new aspect of his passionate lover. Looking at the two corpses at his feet, he whispered, "I have got to remember to come armed the next time I enter your bedroom!"

"Just bring your cat," she replied, smiling. "From what you have told me, he is the smartest one around. He could defend you from my attacks!" She gave him a look full of meaning, wiping away the blood left on her dagger with the robe of one of the victims.

They walked toward the others, who by now had all passed through the last control. The Narnians quickly hid the nine imposters' bodies, throwing them off a cliff to the lowest part of the valley. Totila's generals had to think the imposters had managed to enter the city. Waiting for their spies to open the gates would allow the Amerians extra time to better organize their defense.

When the Narnians were all inside, they were confined in one of the squares in the lower part of the city to make them easier to control. It took a couple of days to house them and to arm them in anticipation of the arrival of the enemy soldiers, who inevitably showed up at the entrance to the valley a few days later.

From the top of the town, the guards blew their trumpets to warn everyone of the arrival of the Ostrogoths. The entire council, along with Petrus and Lucius, hurried up to the edge of the walls. They were amazed by the massive deployment of men approaching.

The Siege

The encounter between Totila's forces and the Amerians came as a mutual surprise, even if from two completely opposite points of view. The Amerians were terrified to see the vast quantity of men starting to camp in the valley before their walls. The Ostrogoth soldiers were pitching their tents and setting up a command post, while all around the walls, large groups of soldiers were gathered in sections spread out to control every single city gate.

The generals, for their part, were struck by the beauty of the walls of Ameria, but mainly, they were concerned by their visible strength. The Amerian walls looked much more challenging to conquer than those of Narnia, Interamna Nahars, or other cities they had conquered. The Ostrogoth generals had the exact feeling Tarzio had wanted them to have centuries before. It would be a long and tiring siege unless their imposters had succeeded in infiltrating the city. For now, the generals decided to stall, hoping for some action from within. In the following days, there was no interaction between the two opposing factions.

A very rigid schedule of lookouts was established in Ameria, with continuous shifts. Not a single yard of the city's perimeter could be left unguarded. Stations to boil oil were organized on the edge of the walls in various strategic locations. Piles of logs were placed near the winches built to move the huge copper cauldrons filled with the many gallons of linseed and olive oil, ready to be boiled and thrown down on the invaders. All of the city's archers were in position with large stocks of arrows.

The Ostrogoths were resting outside the walls, recuperating from the many battles in which they had been involved. The generals took several walks around the city to find points of weakness. It was not an easy task; those walls looked impossible to breach. The generals ordered their engineers to build new attack machines. One team was in charge of building a new ram, while another was busy extending the arms of their existing catapults to give them more strength and range.

Lucius was watching the enemy camp with Pirro on his shoulders. With his attentive eyes, Pirro was also looking at all those soldiers and their machines. They reminded him of the toys built by Tarzio. Something told him the contraptions were not for peaceful purposes.

Petrus and Scilla joined Lucius and Pirro. Without having to say anything, they all realized that Ameria could not hold out very long against such a massive deployment of forces.

Pirro jumped down from his human's shoulders, climbed to the highest point of the turret, and looked out to the west. His eyes were fixed on a particular spot. There was movement in the bushes near the sloping cliff toward the valley, under the big rock. A group of soldiers was climbing up, carrying the bodies of the spies killed by Scilla and her friends.

"I knew we had to bury them or take the bodies inside the city!" Lucius exclaimed. "Now they know their spies are dead and will not help them from the inside. They will attack."

Scilla answered, "There was no time! Who would think they would go down that cliff!"

"We must act somehow. We will not survive a siege. We need to talk to the consuls."

"They will never listen to us—two merchants, a beautiful woman, and a cat! Who would listen to us?" Petrus muttered more to himself than to the others.

Scilla took up the initiative. "We must try! Pirro, come with me! You have more courage than these two!" She set off quickly, followed by Pirro, toward the location where the consuls were discussing strategy with the chief military commander. After exchanging dumbfounded looks, the two brothers quickly followed her.

Pirro knew precisely how strong the walls of Ameria were. He had been there for most of their construction in his second life and studied the restoration made by the Romans in his third life. The walls were, in fact, very solid, so the only chance for Totila's army to penetrate into the city was through its gates. The townspeople needed to strengthen the wooden doors. But how to pass these thoughts to the humans?

As soon as Scilla neared the consuls, the guards stopped her from trying to appear in front of them unannounced. "I wish to talk to the consul," she yelled at one guard who was pushing her away.

Lucius and Petrus stepped forward. "Consul Appianus! Let her talk! She is a refugee from Narnia, and she has something to say. We beg you, listen to her!"

The consul motioned for the guards to let her pass. Scilla came closer with the two brothers at her sides, while Pirro stood next to the consul in a position where his three allies could clearly see him. He thought he could then pass them his message.

"Who are you?" Appianus asked.

"My name is Scilla. I was the wife of the commander of the guards in Narnia. My husband was killed on the third night of the siege of my city, which, as you perfectly well know, has been destroyed. What I saw was dreadful. Men, women, and children slaughtered, beaten, and raped by those barbarians. They destroy everything they can put their hands on, and the longer the siege lasts, the greater their violence grows. Your walls are much stronger than the ones we had in Narnia. Believe me, the longer it takes them to climb them, the more ferocious they will be once inside."

Pirro stared at her and tried his best to pass her his thoughts. *Tell him about the gates… Tell him about the gates!*

"Then what do you suggest, Matron Scilla?"

"Your weak points are the gates. You know very well they can break them down. The wooden doors are not strong enough and will not resist their rams. They will get in and destroy Ameria as they did Narnia!"

Pirro was delighted, approaching Scilla and rubbing himself on her legs. He attracted everyone's attention even if he felt a bit irritated. Pirro wondered why he could sometimes convey his thoughts, but so far, he had never succeeded in communicating his real name. He was, in any case, by now used to being called by names other than his own.

Lucius started to talk to the consul in support of what Scilla had said, while Pirro, still a little annoyed, walked toward a pile of logs to scratch his claws. It was his way of letting go of his disappointment.

"Consul Appianus, we must try to make a deal with the generals if we want to save our city and our fellow citizens. The generals' goal now is to establish their supremacy in Rome, and they need as many soldiers as possible. If we can talk to them and negotiate a deal, they will save money, men, and time, and in the end, they will be grateful to us."

"And what would your suggestion be, Lucius?"

"Consul, send a delegation to talk to the generals. Find out their intentions. Seek an agreement with them!"

"Do you think they will listen to us? Especially now that they have discovered that you have killed nine of their men? We can be sure they will kill anyone who tries to exit our gates!"

Appianus was right. Lucius had not considered possible retaliation for the loss of those nine men. On the spot, Lucius could not think of a good answer.

"Come back to me with an effective plan, or we have no choice but to fight and resist," Consul Appianus said.

The four headed home, disappointed and worried, their heads full of different thoughts. Over bowls of farro soup and a jug of wine, the three humans were mumbling about a possible plan. Next to the table, Pirro was enjoying a plate filled with well-roasted chicken livers and hearts that Artusia had just prepared for him.

"How come he eats meat, and you just get soup? No wonder he is the smartest one!" Scilla teased them with a smile.

"Artusia adores him, and he deserves her regard," Lucius added, slightly moving away his empty soup bowl.

At the same time, Pirro, with a full belly, grabbed the last remaining chicken heart in his jaws and jumped on the table. He set it down in his human's bowl and sat down beside it.

The three of them looked at Pirro, surprised, trying to understand the meaning of his gesture.

Scilla's smile faded gradually, her face acquiring a much more thoughtful expression. She had a clear insight. She took the bowl with both hands, stood up, and with conviction exclaimed, "That is it! We must appeal to their hearts and at the same time impress them with our cooking specialties!"

"What do you mean?" Petrus and Lucius asked in unison.

"We will invite the generals to a banquet especially set up for them. We will let them taste our best specialties, and we will have children as waiters to soften them up. With all that savory, delicious food, they will be reminded of peaceful times, and being surrounded by children will remind them of their own. Maybe then they will be more willing to negotiate and spare the city!"

That ball of fur Pirro had once again sent a relevant message. He gave a big yawn, got off the table, and, satisfied about his contribution to the discussion, began his usual after-meal toilet before laying down for his nap.

The following day, the fourth one of that still peaceful siege seemed to be on the edge of becoming the beginning of the attack. With one catapult launch, the generals sent a message tied to a stone. The stone hit one of the guards, and his companions reacted instinctively, shooting arrows. The commander stopped them just in time before this skirmish turned into the beginning of the end.

The message tied to the stone was loud and clear: "People of Ameria, lay down your arms and give up the battle, or nothing will be left of your city."

There was no guarantee that the Ostrogoths would respect the implied promise to spare the city after surrender. Consul Appianus feared they would destroy the city even if the Amerians did surrender. He had to find a solution before the generals turned the siege into a real attack. He sent for Lucius and Scilla and showed them the message.

She immediately spoke up. "This is the opportunity we have been waiting for!" With great fervor, she described in detail her idea to appease the generals with the best quality food and wine and to make them open to generosity by using the children of Ameria as servants at the feast.

"It seems to me to be a very risky and difficult plan to implement. It will not be easy to convince mothers to let their children serve those barbarians." After a few minutes of deep reflection, Appianus then said, "But we do not have many alternatives. Who made up this plan?"

"It was Pirro's idea!" Those words rushed out of Scilla's mouth before she realized exactly what she had just said. She caught Lucius's stunned expression while he rolled his eyes in consternation.

"And who is this Pirro? Do I know him?" the consul asked.

"He is… my… cat, Consul Appianus," Lucius reluctantly replied, throwing an angry look toward his mistress. "It is a long story, Consul. One day, I will tell you all about it. But now we must act; there is no time to waste."

Appianus once again remained silent for a few minutes before announcing his decision. The first problem was where to set up the banquet. The generals would never willingly enter the city walls, given the obvious danger of being arrested and killed. The banquet would have to be held outside the city walls, after agreeing beforehand that the reason for the banquet was to sign a peace treaty. After talking to himself for a while, Appianus gave his orders: "The three of you will go and convey the invitation to the generals and lay down the bases for the negotiation."

"We… three?" Lucius stammered.

Appianus pointed first at Lucius, then at Scilla, and then down at Pirro. "Yes, you two and the cat. Actually, do you have children?"

"No, Consul, we are not married. Scilla is a refugee from Narnia, do you not remember?"

"Well, it does not matter. Find yourselves two children and present yourselves to the Ostrogoths as the perfect family. That way, the enemy will not hurt you. And do not forget the cat. His presence will make the peaceful nature of the invitation more convincing."

That afternoon, the Porta Romana opened slightly to let out Scilla and Lucius with his brother's two children, followed by Pirro.

They were immediately surrounded by enemy soldiers, and for a moment, they feared for their safety.

"We come in peace! We have a message for your generals from the consul Appianus. Let us talk to them."

The guards escorted them to the largest tent, which had in its center a wide table with a rudimentary rendering of the walls of Ameria drawn on parchment. It was an image that was familiar to Pirro. It reminded him of the numerous drawings made by his second human, Tarzio.

Three generals were sitting around the table, and at the head was a tall, imposing man. The guard that escorted them introduced them: Counts Vult, Ruderic, Blidin, and finally King Totila. Not expecting the presence of the king himself, Lucius shivered instinctively, hugging his nephews close to him as if to protect them. Scilla bowed, keeping her head down, while Totila started to speak. "I was expecting soldiers as messengers, not a little family! Speak! What is your consul's response?"

Lucius took a deep breath, and with a newfound tranquility, he managed to keep any tremor out of his voice. "King Totila, I bring you the greetings of Consul Appianus and the entire city of Ameria. My name is Lucius, and these are my wife, Scilla, and our children, Cirene and Damocles. We have come here to invite your Majesty and his generals to a banquet where we will serve you our most delicious dishes as a sign of peace. Ameria does not want a war. Ameria does not want death. Not anymore. We ask for the safety of our city and our people in exchange for a surrender without fighting."

"Who is this?" Totila almost screamed when Pirro jumped on the table and sat on the parchment maps at a specific point, near the spot designated for the Porta Pantanelli.

"His name is Pirro. He is part of our family, and he follows us everywhere," Cirene said.

The eyes of Pirro and Totila met, remaining fixed on each other for long seconds. No one was able to understand what happened during that time. Pirro then approached the head of the table and sat next to the king, who started to caress him, never taking his eyes off of Pirro's. He then turned to Lucius. "Why should I accept a peace proposal? You have no hope of holding on for long after we attack."

"Your Majesty, Ameria is not a rich city. It is a peaceful city, a city that has always maintained its independence, a city that occupies a strategic position at the crossroads of the consular roads. It will serve you better as a functioning town than as a ruin. Perhaps we have no chance of resisting your siege, but how much of your resources and how many of your men will be lost in this battle? Men who will be more valuable to you in your war against Rome. Do not lose men and time against us. Our walls are very strong; it will not be an easy task to breach them. We have the men and resources to resist for a long time, but we do not want to jeopardize our children's future. Consul Appianus follows the doctrine of Monk Benedict and believes in his teaching to pursue peace and do good."

At the sound of Benedict's name, King Totila suddenly reacted. Monk Benedict had died only a year before, and the two had met a few years earlier. Totila had been very impressed by the personality of that monk, who had predicted Totila's glory but also his death. Benedict had also scolded Totila for his excessive violence and desire for destruction, saying to Totila during the meeting: "You have done many bad things, and you will do more. Put an end to your wickedness."

Totila looked at the two children, then looked at Pirro, who, noisily purring, was rubbing his little head on the king's hand, which was still suspended in mid-air. "You can go and tell your consul that I will be honored to attend your banquet. We will discuss the terms of your surrender there."

His generals looked at Totila suspiciously, disappointed to see the possibility of severe devastation and the substantial spoils of war vanish. But the three of them had also been present when Totila met Benedict, and they, too, had been strongly influenced by him. They could understand their king's reaction to that monk's name, a man who had impressed them all with his outstanding personality.

Lucius bowed to the king and took a step back toward the tent's exit, taking the children with him. Scilla softly called to Pirro, who, after licking Totila's hand, quickly ran across the table and joined her, leaving the tent. They returned to the Porta Romana, and once back in Ameria, they conveyed the results of their mission to the consul. Shortly afterward, Consul Appianus issued the order to set up the banquet.

Looking west, a whole area next to the walls was covered with large swaths of cloth anchored to the stones. Townspeople set up and elegantly decorated a big, rectangular, low table. In the center of the table, a complex floral arrangement augmented with fruits and acanthus leaves was placed. On each side of the table, there were *triclinia*. On the two short sides were the *triclinia* for Consul Appianus and King Totila, and on the two longer sides were those for the three generals and the three chosen council elders.

On the table were elaborate, sumptuous dishes prepared by the best cooks in Ameria. Finely decorated, they offered a taste of the excellent Amerian cuisine. On two sides of the table, two roasted piglets were surrounded by honey-crusted roasted onions and apples. At the corners, in perfect symmetry, were four dishes showcasing a triumph of roasted pheasant dishes, each decorated with flashy plumage arranged in a radiating pattern. On top of each platter towered a stuffed pheasant with spread wings. All around the table, many other dishes featured various specialties—quails with a fig crust, wild boar stewed in sweet prune sauce, farro soup with herbs, and chickpea soup with Cameline sauce.

Upon the arrival of the illustrious guests, the musicians began to enliven the meal with their music. Totila was impressed by the group of children, instructed by Artusia very quickly but with much care. They moved with attention, carefully keeping every glass filled with the best wine. They cleared the dirty plates and served whoever asked for more of this or that dish.

Above everything else, Artusia made sure, based on Gnaeus's strong recommendation, that the king and the generals could see they were served in exactly the same way and from the same dishes as everyone else. Every time they served drinks to the Ostrogoths, they immediately afterward served their consul and elders from the same jug. This procedure was to remove even the slightest suspicion of a possible poisoning of the food or drinks.

The children proved to be very attentive to the guests, and the king and his generals felt reassured by seeing the Amerians drinking and eating from the same dishes as they did. Throughout the banquet, Pirro moved from one *triclinium* to the other, accepting juicy morsels from all the guests. He remained munching for a long time on the quail bones the king gave him. This also reassured the king that they were not poisoning him. He understood how much they loved that cat; they would not have risked poisoning their pet, too.

King Totila and his generals very much appreciated the meal. Artusia had organized every single detail. When they had finished eating and everyone was happy and relaxed thanks to the excellent food and wine, the conversation turned to the possibility of Ameria surrendering.

Appianus asked King Titola to spare the city and its citizens. Lucius had told him how Totila had reacted to hearing the name of the monk of Monte Cassino, and the consul took the opportunity to recall Benedict's saying, "Violence is not force, but weakness, nor can it ever create anything good, but only destroy it." Repeating those words, Appianus said that Ameria could serve time and time again as an outpost for the king's troops as they traveled from north to south and could repeatedly function as a resupply depot. In contrast, a destroyed city could only serve as a spoil of war once and then could offer the Ostrogoths nothing more.

Under the influence of that good wine and remembering Benedict's words, Totila accepted the surrender terms. After his mystical encounter with the monk of Monte Cassino, Totila had not converted to Christianity. Still, the monk had deeply affected Totila's soul, and he could no longer carry out his conquests, massacres, and devastation with the same lightness of heart as before.

In his more recent conquests, he had behaved under the influence of decidedly opposite moods: Alatri, destroyed; Naples, spared. Florence was also devastated, while Spoleto was conquered but preserved. And now Narnia had been destroyed, but Ameria was to be spared. Those different outcomes were also caused in part by his presence at battle sites. When his generals were alone, though following orders, they did not care about saving cities, letting their soldiers ravage and kill as they wished. When Totila was present, his better side, the one Benedict had discovered and influenced, took over, and his desire for destruction was consistently diminished. In this case, Pirro and his allies' mediation had kept Ameria from certain devastation.

The surrender came with a high price in men and goods. Totila demanded eight wagons filled with sacks of farro and legumes to feed his soldiers and as many wagons loaded with barrels of wine and olive oil. He also claimed a substantial supply of arrows, spears, helmets, and shields, which left the Amerians practically unarmed. Finally, he asked for fifty men to join his forces to replace his losses in the battles with Narnia and Interamna Nahars. If the consul consented to these requests, the city would be spared.

Appianus was very hesitant. Giving away men and weapons would leave them much weakened, especially if Totila did not keep his promise. Appianus wondered if it was all just a ploy to disarm them and have an easy conquest.

Before accepting these conditions, Appianus consulted the council, and they agreed that there were few choices. Signing the agreement, Appianus referred once more to the words of Benedict and declared, "The people of Ameria surrender to King Totila. In return, we ask for protection and grace for our city and its citizens, trusting that the words of Monk Benedict will be respected. As Benedict said, 'Ask God with constant and intense prayer to carry out the good things you are about to do, so that one day, when he receives us among his children, he will not be angry at our unworthy conduct.'" With this statement made, Appianus approached Totila, and the two gripped forearms in a sign of mutual acceptance.

The surrender document bearing the agreement's text was signed by the consul, the king, and his generals. When it came time to seal it, Pirro, who had been watching the entire scene and discussion but was quite bored, jumped on the table, hitting the inkwell from which a few drops ended up on the table's surface. The scribe quickly caught the inkwell before the whole contents could spill out. His gesture scared Pirro, who ran along the table, wetting one paw in the spilled ink. Racing over the parchment, Pirro left a perfect paw-print next to the signatures of the consul and the king. Gnaeus immediately said, "In the name of the Council of Ameria, I apologize for this inconvenience!"

Totila laughed loudly, exclaiming, "In all my life and all my reign, it has never occurred to me to have the signature of a cat next to mine. People of Ameria, I, Totila, bow before your expert strategist!"

Pirro ran toward Lucius, who picked him up and wiped off his paw before Pirro could lick the ink. Over the many steps Pirro had taken, the ink had dried out, but his usually pinkish paw pads were now more brown than pink.

The agreement was honored. Ameria fulfilled its part, and so did Totila. In the following years, moving along the Via Amerina and Via Flaminia, Totila's troops came and went without incident. Totila himself never returned to Ameria.

Four years after the siege, news arrived that he had died. Meanwhile, Lucius and Scilla got married and named their first child after that king with whom they had come face-to-face in one of the most legendary diplomatic successes in the city's history. They had two more children, Eusebia and another boy who was born right after Pirro's death. To remember this incredible strategist and diplomat cat, they named their third child after him.

Pirro spent the last year of his fourth life at Lucius's side and in Lucius's bed, even after Lucius's marriage to Scilla. His death was a great sorrow for the whole family. He was buried next to Gnaeus, who died shortly before him, in the necropolis outside the walls of Ameria. When Pirro exhaled his last breath, he knew he would be back; he just did not know when. His spirit would hover among the alleys and in the valleys around his city, waiting for the moment when his reincarnation would be necessary again.

In the following centuries, Ameria lost even more of its former glory. Several earthquakes occurred, and continuous invasions from different barbarian tribes brought dangerous epidemics. The first historically documented bubonic plague arrived in Italy in AD 540, recurring at intervals of ten to twelve years and decimating the population. In the year AD 570, smallpox, another very deadly illness, made its first appearance in Europe. It was not an easy time for small cities whose survival was based mainly on agriculture, craftsmanship, and commerce. A weakened economy would not allow cultural and architectural growth as occurred in bigger cities. But Ameria, differently from many other towns that were abandoned or fell into disrepair, managed to maintain its identity even though struggling through a dark and difficult era.

A clear sign of recovery was the construction of the Civic Tower, which rose on top of the hill. It was built in the early years of the XII century, signaling an important new beginning and the acquisition of a leading position among the municipalities of central Italy. In the late Middle Ages, however, Ameria once again was the site of another massive siege.

Tito would not miss this important new adventure.

Recipes for Cameline Sauce

Cameline sauce is a condiment that was used for boiled meats in the Middle Ages. The old recipe is still used sometimes: Soak seven slices of bread without a crust in two glasses of strong red vinegar. Add salt, a spoonful of cinnamon, a teaspoon of ginger, a half teaspoon of cloves, a pinch of black pepper, and crushed cardamom. Then, mix the ingredients to get a creamy sauce with a nice caramel color that tastes strongly of spices.

Another version of the same recipe accentuates a sweet and sour taste by adding a puree of grapes and crushed almonds.

Chapter 5
The High/Late Middle Ages in Ameria
Year 1240 AD
Otto Saves Colao and Ameria

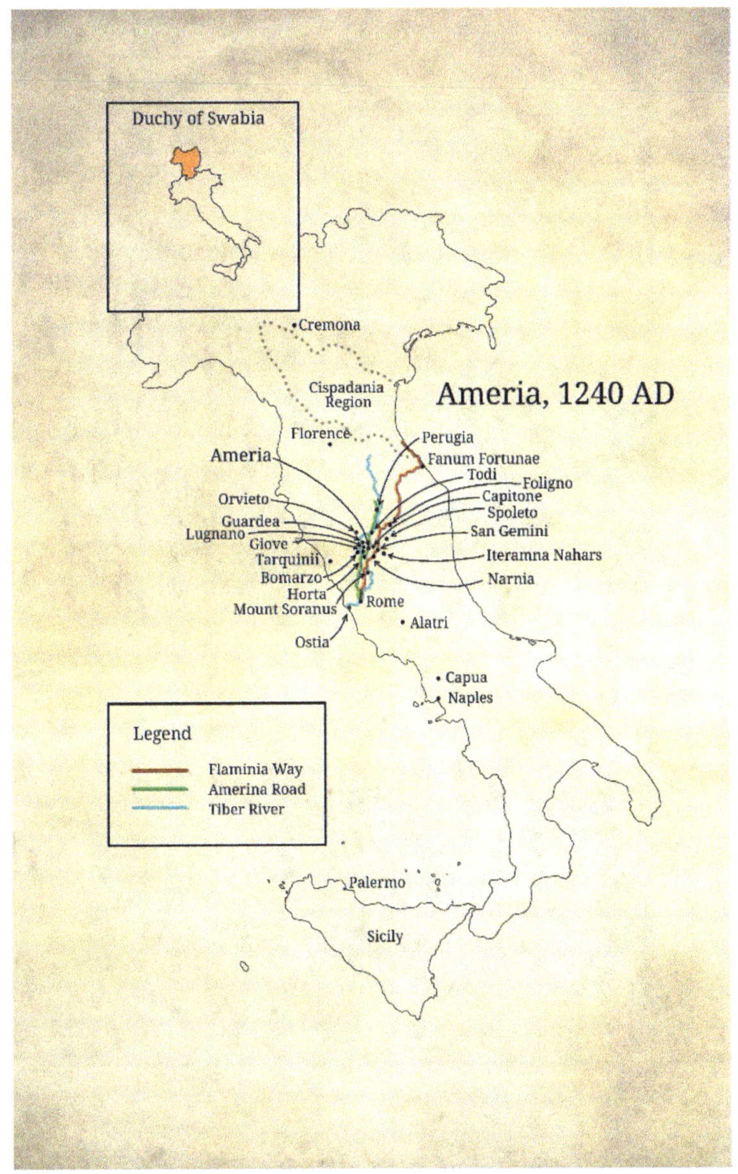

AMERIA, 1240 AD
Porta Pusterola
Civic Tower
Cathedral
Porta Vallis
Old Walls
Porta Leone
Porta Pantanelli
Porta Romana

Cast of Characters

Family at the Start of the Chapter

Giulianus: Consul of Ameria

Nofria: wife of Giulianus

Roscio: the elder son of Giulianus and Nofria; a member of the city
guards

Colao: the younger son of Giulianus and Nofria

Tito/Otto: a cat

Others

Alaric: a soldier

Montemarte family: of Ovieto

The Wonder of the World and Staff

Frederick II of Swabia: a nephew of Frederick Barbarossa; King of
Sicily; King of the Romans; Emperor of the Holy Roman
Empire; enemy of popes

Pier ("Piero") Delle Vigne: Frederick II's secretary

General Simone: the general left in charge of Ameria after Frederick's
departure

Historical Figures

Charlemagne

Pope Leo IV

Pope Innocent III

Pope Gregory IX

Pope Innocent IV

Alliances

Ghibelline cities: Perugia, Gubbio, Orvieto, and Iteramna Nahars

Guelph cities: Todi, Foligno, and Ameria

Cities changing sides: Giove, Lugnano, Guardea, Capitone, and Narnia

Populations

Lombards

Franks

Family at the End of the Chapter

Leandra: the wife of Colao

Tommaso, Uliviero, Bartolomeo, Polissena, and Mirabile

Introduction

THE CENTURIES THAT followed Totila's siege were not peaceful for the tormented Italian peninsula. After the Ostrogoths, the next conquerors were the Greeks. Then, in the second half of the eighth century, the Lombards invaded the Italian peninsula, followed by the Franks under King Charlemagne, who was crowned Emperor of the Romans on Christmas Day of AD 800. After he acceded to the throne, Charlemagne made a deed of donation to the church of Rome known as a *Promissio Carisiaca* with which he reassigned various territories to the pope. Among others, the donation included lands in the Cispadania region and in Umbria. Ameria was among those Umbrian lands given to the pope.

Returning to the control of the Papacy gave the city a new stimulus for growth. In AD 882, Pope Leo IV heavily restored the city walls. The gate to the east, until then called the Iliona Gate, was renamed Porta del Leone (Leo's Door) in his honor. Despite being part of the "Patrimony of St. Peter," the Amerians managed to establish themselves as a free municipality with their own jurisdiction.

More centuries passed. The beginning of the XIII century saw a new wind bringing wide-ranging changes. The rise to power of Frederick II of Swabia, a nephew of Frederick Barbarossa, certainly brought new wars and destruction but also significant cultural development. Nicknamed *Stupor Mundi* (Wonder of the World) for his innate curiosity and great interest in culture, he was given the title "King of Sicily" at birth. He then became King of the Romans and later Emperor of the Holy Roman Empire.

Born in Jesi, he was first raised in Foligno and then in Palermo. He was tutored by Pope Innocent III when he was residing in Perugia at the beginning of the XIII century. Throughout his entire life, he remained very attached to his childhood homes, always keeping the Umbrian region in his heart. A man of great intelligence, he was loved and hated with the same intensity. He was excommunicated twice, and his contemporaries often misunderstood his willingness to enlarge his views about all of the political and administrative aspects of his reign.

He tried to spread religious tolerance by opening up his

territories to Islamic immigrants. His contribution to the enrichment of arts and architecture was essential, creating the bases of the modern Italian language. Frederick II was also a lover of good, healthy food. Everywhere he went, he identified recipes based on fresh ingredients and ended up collecting them into two volumes.

His other big passion was birds. He was most passionate about falcons, about which he became an expert. He always traveled with his birds of prey, for which he invented the *chaperon*, the leather cap used to cover their eyes during training. Until then, it had been customary to sew closed the eyelids of the falcons, a practice that he considered brutal.

In 1240, Emperor Frederick arrived in Ameria. Tito did not miss the opportunity to meet this incredible man who pushed the Italian peninsula out of the Middle Ages and toward the Renaissance.

The Wars between the Guelphs and Ghibellines

In the first decades following AD 1200, several wars broke out among the cities of Umbria, which broke into two opposing factions. Perugia, Gubbio, and Orvieto were Ghibellines cities. On the Guelph side were Todi, Foligno, and Ameria.

The alliance with Todi slowly turned Ameria into a subservient town. Weakened by human and material war losses, Ameria could not rely only on its strong walls. Todi's army became essential for its defense. To complicate this precarious equilibrium, changes in alliances frequently happened. The various lords of smaller territories supported one side or the other, depending on who won this or that battle. Giove, Lugnano, Guardea, Capitone, Narnia, and many other places became pawns in a game ruled by the two greatest players, the pope and the emperor. These struggles resulted in the two excommunications inflicted by Pope Gregory IX on Frederick II, the first in 1228 and then again in March 1239.

After the second papal excommunication decree, Frederick began a series of offensive maneuvers against the Umbrian cities that were loyal to Rome. The emperor's troops marched south along the

Via Flaminia. Numerous messengers and travelers talked about the massive numbers of soldiers.

The Consul of Ameria, Giulianus, convened the council to discuss the city's unfortunate resource situation and the emperor's strategic moves. Returning home after that meeting, the consul was extremely worried. His wife, Nofria, noticed it right away.

"Did something go wrong during the council? You look upset."

"We had to make many concessions. Among them, we had to accept being ruled by a *podestà* (commander) sent by the pope from Rome to control us. I do not like us Amerians being subjected to the whims of a stranger who knows nothing about us and our customs. But we could not refuse. We are in a weak position, financially and militarily speaking. On top of that, the pope wants to assign the manor of Lugnano to the Montemarte of Orvieto. For us, it is a big loss. But I do not want to bore you with this. Where are the children?"

"They are already asleep. You will see them tomorrow morning. But please, Giulianus, tell me sincerely, are we in danger?"

"I wish I could reassure you, dear wife, but the situation is serious. According to the messengers, the pope and the emperor are fighting like cats and dogs. I am afraid Frederick does not want to come to terms with the pope, and with his massive army, Frederick could easily defeat the pope."

"Perhaps you should propose to the council the possibility of submitting to the emperor? Remember the tales of Totila's siege of Ameria? Could not we do as they did then?"

"That is only a legend from centuries ago. Nobody knows what really happened. Ameria belongs to the pope; we do not have the political strength nor the resources to rebel."

Giulianus did not know that there was a being out there in his garden who knew very well what had happened with Totila, a being who was now ready to fulfill a new and very dangerous mission: saving the life of Giulianus's youngest son, the only person who could continue the lineage Tito had been instructed to protect.

Giulianus's family was one of the wealthiest in Ameria. His ancestors owned the land used for flax cultivation. In recent decades, the same land had been used to grow farro, which was more helpful in feeding the people of Ameria. His lineage and wealth assured him an important social position. He was an honest and loyal man, and he had been elected consul for the second time in a row.

Growing farro earned him his nickname "Farratino," a name that became attached to his family name and to that of all his descendants. Giulianus and his wife Nofria had two children who were years apart in age: the elder, Roscio, was already twenty years old and part of the city's armed guards, while the younger, named Colao, had just turned eight and spent almost all of his time with his mother.

Roscio was constantly on alert with his fellow city guards, while his father was frequently engaged in legal matters. Colao admired them both very much. Roscio was, for him, a model of strength and bravery. Meanwhile, on the few occasions his father spent time with Colao, he spoke to him about his responsibilities in managing the city's resources for the good of the community. Colao listened to his father with curiosity, sometimes asking very on-point questions that left his father speechless.

In the evenings in bed with his wife, talking about his son, Giulianus sometimes told her that even some of the council elders could not ask questions as intelligent as his son's. "I am sure one day he will be a good consul," he said, giving her a goodnight kiss.

Before he fell asleep, Nofira had the time to say, "I just hope he will not get in trouble due to his overabundant curiosity!"

It ended up not being a good night for the consul. At 4:00 in the morning, he was suddenly summoned to the council headquarters. A messenger had arrived, seriously wounded, from Interamna Nahars, a nearby city that was under siege by Frederick II. The messenger reported that Spoleto had already been conquered and set on fire. If Interamna Nahars also fell, then in the emperor's path toward Rome, Ameria would be the next victim of the emperor's violent repression against all the cities loyal to the Papacy.

The morning after, following a long night of discussion, Giulianus ordered a group of chosen guards to observe from a distance the events in the valley of Interamna Nahars. They were to report every development daily in order to prepare for the possible arrival of the emperor's troops. Meanwhile, the council warned the city's population about the danger and instructed them to store all goods like wood, poultry, farro, and fruit in every possible space in order to be able to withstand a potential siege.

Ameria had large green areas inside the city, the areas Tarzio had created more than fifteen centuries before. Even if no one remembered their names, many now blessed those individuals who, in the past, had thought of leaving such open spaces to serve the community.

Tito did remember that planning very well. Now that he was back in his valley at a very perilous moment, he was ready to defend the work of his second human and, most of all, to fulfill the prophecy guiding his reincarnations.

He wandered around the alleys and streets of the city he had left so many centuries before. After four lives, his instinct was well-honed, and he had a remarkable ability to recognize dangerous situations. Tito noticed great ferment around him and perceived the nervousness of the people. He often had to hide, feeling threatened by people who were running or dragging carts loaded with wood and vegetables and cages full of chickens and rabbits. Tito was always scared when humans were agitated. He remembered that he had always wanted to avoid large groups of people, especially in the evenings when they got drunk and were out of control.

But it was daylight now, and they did not look drunk—just very worried. Tito hid between two large pots placed next to the entrance of a house. Looking at the sky and following the sun's position, he knew exactly where he was. A woman opened the door of the house, and Tito saw the woman telling a child to wait there for the arrival of two of his father's workers, who were carrying sacks of farro and legumes for storage in their home.

While she returned inside to make room for the huge sacks, the child sat on the step, waiting for the workers. From that position, he noticed two big eyes staring at him from behind two large pots. Tito meowed and laid down on his side. Colao approached and stretched his arm between the pots to caress the cat. Tito's soft and fluffy fur always made an impression on people at their first contact with it. Colao then immediately reached out and sat the cat on his knees. "You are scared, too, with all this activity and people running around, are you not?" he said to the cat.

When the two workers arrived with the enormous sacks, Colao walked them inside while still holding the cat and said to his mother, "Mother! Look what I found out there! He is scared. May I keep him?"

"Colao, this is not the right moment! Put him back outside. I do not have time to care about a cat right now!"

"But, Mother, you will not have to. I will take care of him. And if Roscio has to go to war, at least I will not be alone."

"All right, all right, we will talk about it later. Now let me go. I have so much to do!" Nofria replied while walking away, followed by the two men and their loads.

With his new friend in his arms, Colao walked into his room and lay down with the cat on his bed.

Feeling the tension and the fear of the young boy, Tito understood he had to act quickly: he had to gain this boy's trust to be able to help him. Tito's purring was already at the highest level, and with quiet and mellow meows, he tried to bring calmness into Colao's heart and gain a place in it. The vibration of Tito's whiskers told him he was in the right place with the right person. It was the same genetic code handed down from generation to generation, and his whiskers recognized it every time he was close to it.

That young boy was the only chance to continue Hator's lineage. His brother Roscio was probably destined to fall in the coming battle, leaving Colao the only heir.

The two lay on the bed, with the boy speaking gently to his new friend. "There is going to be a war soon. My elder brother is a soldier, you know? He is strong and brave; he will defend us." Tito listened, purring softly.

That evening at dinner, Giulianus decided it was time to be frank with his family and prepare them for the worst. "Nofria, dear wife, Colao: I can no longer hide the truth from you. I am very worried about what is going on." Giulianus continued talking to them, recounting what the messengers had reported from Iteramna Nahars. That city, part of the Ghibelline coalition, was governed by families of Germanic descent and had submitted to the emperor without opposition. Frederick II rewarded their loyalty with a golden eagle symbol to affix to the city flag and banner.

The cities in the Guelph alliance were suffering a different fate. "We are now isolated," Giulianus explained. "Spoleto was burned down. Todi, too, was conquered. We cannot surrender, nor can we defeat such a strong army."

"But Father, our walls are very strong! They will never destroy them!" Colao said, holding his furry friend in his arms.

"You are correct, my son. Our walls are very strong, but the emperor has a massive army. They can beat us. No walls can resist." He stopped momentarily, then added, "Who is your little friend?"

"I found him just outside our door. May I keep him, Father? He is a good cat."

"Yes, you can, my son. He will keep you company. But now listen to me very carefully. There are some important things you need to know. If the emperor's soldiers enter the city and you find yourself alone, you should not wait for me or Roscio. You will have to find a way to keep safe on your own. I will leave Alaric to guard the house; he is a trusted and faithful soldier. He will guide you to the underground tunnels that lead beyond the walls to the valley behind the hill. You can escape from there."

Giulianus made both his wife and son promise over and over to escape, knowing that if that moment arrived, then he and his elder son would have probably already been killed. To change that sad subject, he stretched his arm toward his son to caress that handsome, big cat that Colao, feeling the tension in his father's speech, was holding close to his chest. "Did you give a name to your friend?"

"Not yet, Father."

It was getting late, so Nofria told her son to go to sleep. He asked if he could take the cat with him. At a different time, she would have said "no," but given the situation, she did not object. Probably soon, they would not sleep in those beds anyway. While still in the corridor, before entering his room and closing its door, Colao heard his mother say, "Giulianus, have you not gone too far in talking to him like that? He is only eight years old! *Otto* (eight)!"

Colao could not hear another word, and so his father's answer remained behind the door that Nofria had closed. The word his mother had emphatically repeated—*otto*—remained stuck in his head. He looked at his cat and said, "I will call you Otto, so we will have something in common: my age and your name." He kissed the cat's head and then lay down on his bed beside Tito for their first night together. They would share many more, and Tito once again had to get used to a new name.

In the following days, the tension around Ameria grew dramatically. Colao spent a long time at their doorstep talking to Alaric. He asked Alaric why he, being a soldier, was not ready to fight with the others. Alaric told him that he had gotten badly wounded in a battle against the people of Orvieto and could not lift his right arm. For that reason, he could not fight and so had become involved in training the young soldiers.

Colao asked Alaric many questions, mostly insisting on one specific matter: he wanted to know about the entrances to the underground tunnels leading outside the city walls. In the beginning, Alaric told him not to worry and that in case of danger, he would lead Colao and his mother to the closest entrance. But Colao was so insistent he had to answer him. Alaric first told him about one tunnel that started not far from the city spring, then joined up with another one that started from the opposite side of the city and was hidden in the cellars of another building.

Colao could not figure out where that tunnel entrance was; he did not know all the streets. Alaric continued by describing a second tunnel located in the upper part of the city, one whose entrance was in the cellar of the palace of the guards and that led from there to outside in the valley behind the hill.

Alaric realized that Colao was a little lost with his descriptions, so he thought it might be easier to focus on the most recognizable one. "To reach its entrance you first must go to the Civic Tower. The tunnel entrance is in the building next to it. You know where the tower is, don't you?"

Colao nodded, saying he knew it very well. He had gone there when his brother Roscio took his oath to become a soldier. Everyone knew the Civic Tower; it was visible from everywhere. It had been built only a hundred years before, but it was already considered the symbol of Ameria. Colao made Alaric promise he would show Colao all three entrances, although some were secret and known only to the city's military leaders. Alaric, in turn, made Colao promise he would keep the entrances secret; they could not risk too many citizens slipping into the very narrow tunnels and blocking them.

One day before the one the messengers had predicted, Frederick's troops arrived within sight of the walls of Ameria. From the top of the Civic Tower, the guards started to ring the city bells and blow trumpets to warn the population. Everyone still outside the walls immediately returned, and the city gates were promptly bolted. In a few hours, the entire city was surrounded by the emperor's soldiers.

Nofria locked herself inside the house with Colao and Otto. She knelt in front of a large painting of the Madonna in their private chapel. She began to pray to the Virgin for protection. Colao was impatient; he wanted to go out with Alaric and see the tunnel entrances, but she prevented him from leaving. The attack was imminent. It would not be safe to leave the house.

Ameria Versus Frederick II

All the men, military or not, were on alert and on watch on the walls. The next morning, the first fighting started. The consul and the members of the council could see, with considerable concern, three large catapults and two tall siege towers approaching the walls. In front of the Porta Romana and Porta Leone, Frederick's generals placed two long rams, each with an impressive iron head with large, twisted horns. All around stood thousands of men in their shining armor holding large swords. Behind them were arrayed crossbowmen and archers with quivers full of arrows. Without any help from allies, most of whom were already beaten or annihilated, Ameria had no chance of winning.

With no pause for mediation, those first small engagements morphed into a ferocious attack on the second day. The catapults began to launch large stones at the city, causing several places at the top of the walls to collapse. One of the two siege towers was brought as close as possible to the walls, but the width of the moat was greater than the length of the tower's access bridge. The emperor's soldiers could not jump across the empty space without risking falling into the moat. They started to bring logs, stones, and dirt to fill in the moat so the tower bridge could reach the walls. It was not a difficult task, but it took the entire day.

During the third day of the siege, hand-to-hand fighting began between the soldiers of the opposite factions. At first, the fighting was limited to small groups at the top of the walls, but the battles quickly grew in number. The rams pounded continuously on the two doors, causing a dangerous loosening of the door hinges. Even if reinforced with tree trunks placed to block the opening, with the destruction of the hinges, the doors would collapse anyway.

The battle continued for nine long days, with heavy losses on both sides. Giulianus had not returned home for three days. He lost track of his son Roscio and did not have the courage to tell his wife he had seen Roscio fall, wounded, at the bottom of the moat. There was not much hope that he had survived. Some Amerians were already leaving the city through the tunnels. Finding themselves out in the valley, they dispersed into the woods, trying to reach the towns of Giove, Bomarzo, or other smaller cities north of Ameria.

Nofria did not dare leave the house, and Alaric was still guarding the front door. Even if she had told him that she wanted to go look for her husband, Alaric would have replied that he had specific orders to keep her inside.

Starting to suspect that Giulianus would not return, to reassure Colao, Alaric made a drawing of the tunnels that Colao could reach if he found himself alone. Alaric repeated several times, "If you are in doubt, set your eyes on the Civic Tower and run until you reach it." Otto was also carefully listening.

The twelfth day of the siege was the fatal one for the city. Many blows from the catapults had badly damaged the city's walls and buildings. The Amerian defenders were weakened by the long siege, decimated in numbers, with few weapons left and even less hope.

Almost simultaneously, the two gates collapsed, and the two siege towers, now next to the walls, started pouring dozens and dozens of soldiers into the streets. Worn out by the siege and thirsting for violence and the spoils of war, the emperor's soldiers began to destroy everything they came across.

Alaric rushed into the house, grabbed Nofria and Colao by their hands, and began to run toward the tunnel next to the spring. Colao had Otto inside his tunic. His mother yelled at him to leave the cat behind so as not to cause any delay in their escape, but Colao could not abandon Otto. When they turned the corner between the main street and the alley leading to the spring, a screaming group of soldiers was running up the street from the other side, killing and destroying.

Alaric shouted, "Go back! Go to the tunnels on the top of the hill!" He drew his sword to shield them but was overwhelmed and killed. Colao did not witness Alaric's death as he had already gone back up the alley and turned into the main street. After a few more steps, he turned around and, not seeing his mother behind him, started to go back. He stopped when he saw the soldiers coming around the corner. At that moment, Otto began to squirm to free himself from inside the tunic. He jumped to the ground, meowing loudly, and ran up the street. Scared of losing him, Colao followed the cat, calling him repeatedly. The more he tried to grab him, the more Otto ran ahead, making sure Colao was following him.

Thus, they arrived at the top of the hill, at the Civic Tower. That area had almost been abandoned for days now. The Amerians were all busy in the lower part of the city and on the walls. The priests and the few inhabitants of the upper part of the hill had already fled through the tunnels, and the imperial troops had not yet arrived. Otto stopped at the bottom of the tower. Colao managed to grab him and ran toward the guards' headquarters to look for the tunnel entrance so they could leave the city. He struggled to find it; its entrance was blocked by the ruins of a wall that had collapsed after a catapult shot had hit it. There was no chance he could free the entrance to the tunnel from all that rubble.

He turned back into the square, trying to reach the back of the cathedral. From there, he thought he could get to the rocky part of the hill and run down the steep cliff. He was just getting ready to run in that direction when he heard the heavy steps of many soldiers arriving from all sides to reach the top of the city's hill. He felt surrounded and stopped for a moment in fear.

Otto had to act again. With loud meowing, he got Colao's attention and ran toward the little door on one side of the Civic Tower. It was the only possible place to hide. They both entered, and while Colao was instinctively going toward the staircase to go upstairs, Otto instead went under the stairs where there was a trapdoor. Again, Otto stopped and meowed loudly. Colao ran back down to get his cat, saw the trapdoor, opened it, and they both descended those few steps into this little cave under the tower. It was used to keep spare ropes and other items needed for the tower bells.

Even through the thick walls of the tower, they could hear the soldiers' shouts of victory. In the distance, a roaring was audible, caused by the many roofs that had collapsed in the houses destroyed by fire. Frightened by all those noises, Colao and Otto remained close to each other. After a few hours, exhausted, they fell asleep on the coiled ropes.

The Amerians could not stop the invaders and had to surrender. Those who survived were taken prisoner and locked up. When things got quieter, Frederick II made his triumphal entrance into the city, surrounded by his jubilant soldiers. He reached the top of the hill and was captivated by the beauty of the view he could enjoy from there. He climbed to the top of the Civic Tower and was even more amazed by the view from that height.

Once Frederick descended, he ordered his secretary Pier Delle Vigne to warn his falconers. In the morning, he wanted to take his favorite falcon to the top of the tower to let him hunt the pigeons flying around. Frederick then entered the cathedral and ordered his men to dismantle it. He had the altars and everything else that was sacred or religious removed. To show his scorn for the pope and the Catholic Church, he decided to establish his residence in the cathedral. It was transformed into a military stronghold where his generals also found accommodation so they could be at the emperor's disposal at any moment.

The baptistery was turned into a kitchen, and a big oven was quickly built. Throughout the day and much of the night, the soldiers continued destroying buildings. Houses were robbed, and others burned down. The emperor gave orders to end this wave of violence, allowing his soldiers to continue to ransack the houses but not to destroy them. Wanting to fix his residence in Ameria for a while, he needed to have it preserved and not razed to the ground.

At dawn, silence reigned in the entire city. Exhausted from the battle and the victory celebrations, most soldiers were now deeply asleep, many still heavily drunk. Frederick himself retired to the sacristy, now turned into his bedroom. Although lying on a large canopy bed stolen from a nearby palace and quickly brought into the cathedral for his use, he could not sleep that night.

In the morning, Frederick decided not to wait for his falconers. He walked into the room where the cages with his falcons were kept. He took his favorite falcon on his arm with its *chaperon* still covering its eyes. Frederick left the cathedral, approached the tower, and climbed the spiral staircase to the top. He contemplated the incredible view made glorious by the first rays of the rising sun. Frederick was very glad he had decided to establish his headquarters there. From the top of the tower, he could admire the large dam built by the Romans, forming the lake below. Looking to the right, the isolated Mount Soranus caught his attention. He would soon march in that direction on his way to Rome.

Otto heard the emperor's footsteps and woke up before Colao. Frederick had already been at the top of the tower for a few minutes when the two fugitives lifted the trapdoor a few inches to look outside. Otto was swiveling his ears nervously in all directions, trying to perceive every possible noise. Nothing. He slipped out, and Colao raised the trapdoor to follow him.

They looked out of the tower door to be sure nobody was there. It seemed deserted and silent. They slowly exited into the large square. They looked around, but again, nobody was there. Side by side, they took a few steps toward the cathedral when, behind a corner, they noticed two soldiers whose legs were stretched out. The soldiers were talking to each other and did not realize they were being observed. The only way for Colao and Otto to escape was on the other side behind the cathedral. If they could make it across to the back of the cathedral and reach the rocky side of the hill, they could run away toward the valley. It was their previous night's plan and still the only possible way out.

At the top of the tower, Frederick took off the *chaperon* from his falcon's head and raised his arm. It was the signal for the predator to spread its wings and start hunting. Finally free to enjoy the height, the falcon began to fly loops around the top of the tower. Its hunting scream resonated in the silence of the morning. The emperor thoroughly enjoyed the beauty of his bird from this angle. It was very different from when he watched his falcons while standing on the ground looking up. From this height, he could admire the elegance of the falcon from the side and study its movements better.

At that exact moment, Colao and Otto started their run toward freedom, or at least what they hoped was freedom. The falcon caught that little shadow running on the ground below. The bird screeched loudly, scaring Otto, who started running faster and faster, moving away from Colao. Frederick heard the scream of his falcon and looked out from that side of the tower to see what had attracted its attention. He saw the falcon hurtling downwards toward a little animal. From that height, Frederick could not distinguish if it was a rabbit, a fox, or something else. He then noticed a boy running after the animal.

Colao felt the heavy rustle of the falcon's wings brushing his hair. He watched that large shadow flying quickly toward Otto, who was zigzagging across the square to escape.

Colao screamed loudly, "Noooooooo," as he jumped between Otto and the falcon.

The falcon almost grabbed its prey, but Colao shielded his cat with his body. The bird's claws, pushed away by Colao, could only grab Otto's skin, allowing Otto to wriggle free without being badly hurt. Not trained to attack humans, the bird was surprised by Colao's intervention.

Frederick had followed every movement and immediately brought his recall whistle to his lips. The thin hiss reached the falcon's sharp ears, and it returned to its master and rested on his arm.

Frederick quickly put the *chaperon* back on his falcon's head and yelled at the guards to stop that little boy. He then began to run down the spiral staircase to reach the ground. The guards reached

Colao, who, still on the ground, was cradling a trembling Otto as the cat pushed his little body into his human's chest. The wounds left by the claws hurt Otto, and two small blood trails stained his fur.

Colao felt two big hands lifting him from the ground. Unable to fight, he expended all his strength to hold his cat close to himself. He screamed, "Let me go! Leave me alone!" but the strong soldier kept Colao in his outstretched arms as he made his way to the cathedral entrance.

Once downstairs, Frederick ran to the cages to put his falcon back. He then approached Colao, kneeling in front of him to reassure him. "What is your name, little boy?"

Colao remained silent and held Otto even closer.

"You must love this cat very much to challenge my falcon's talons. Do not be afraid. I will not hurt you. Show me the cat's wounds; we have to take care of him." Frederick tried to take Otto from Colao's arms, but Colao would not let go. "Let's do it this way: Come with me, and I will show you how to help the cat."

Piero, the emperor's secretary, entered the cathedral to discuss some important matters with the emperor. Piero was surprised to see the emperor grappling with a child and a cat. Placing a large pile of papers on a table, Piero tried to get the emperor's attention. Without even looking at him, the emperor silenced him with a gesture and asked him to bring some clean cloths and a bowl of hot water.

Frederick kept talking in a low voice to that brave child and his frightened friend. "Come here, lay the cat down, and hold him." He dipped a cloth in the water and began cleaning the blood that had already clotted on the soft fur. "If you do not want to tell me your name, can you at least tell me the cat's name?"

"Otto," Colao whispered, without taking his eyes off his cat, who was lying on his side, his eyes half closed. Otto started to purr, a clear sign that he trusted this man who was cleaning his fur and his wounds.

"You were very brave in defending him from my falcon."

"Your falcon is really mean!"

"Oh, I see; you can talk if you want to! Now tell me your name!"

"My name is Colao Farratino."

"My falcon is not mean, Colao; he was just following his nature. He must hunt to survive. And you are lucky that he is well-trained. Do you see this whistle? When I use it, whatever my falcon is doing, he stops and flies back to me."

"Did you use it when he attacked us?"

"I did. I did not want him to hurt you." Frederick kept wiping the wet cloth against the cat's fur to clean off the blood and make sure the wound had stopped bleeding. "Here, Colao, your Otto is better now. Let him rest. He must recover from his fear and the wounds." Frederick looked at the two with great tenderness, stroking the boy's cheek.

The two friends were exhausted by the weight of the events of the previous day and the morning. They were shivering and hungry. The emperor ordered two of his soldiers to take them to one of the sacristy rooms, feed them, and then let them rest.

As Colao, carrying Otto, walked away with the two soldiers, Pier Delle Vigne was finally able to speak to the emperor. "What is it with this little boy?" the astonished secretary asked.

"I saw him from the top of the tower running to save his cat from my falcon. It reminded me of when I was in Palermo and tried to defend my rabbit from a fox. I failed to save it. I did not want this child to feel the same pain I felt back then. We probably killed his entire family. I did not want him to be left completely alone."

"Sire, you will never cease to surprise me."

"Make sure he is well fed, washed, and rested, as is his cat. Now tell me what you were here for."

In the next room, Colao ate his food voraciously. Otto did the same, devouring the food he was given, then starting his after-meal washing up. Otto tried to reach the wounds on his back; his saliva was the best disinfectant to heal them. When Otto finished cleaning himself, he approached his little human and crouched down on his legs. He meowed softly and started purring to reassure him.

They were almost asleep when the door to the small room opened wide. Following Frederick's orders, Pier Delle Vigne had gone to check on them. His abrupt entrance scared them a little. "Easy,

easy, do not worry. You are now under the protection of the emperor. Nobody will hurt you. Stay here, and you will be safe."

"Can I go and look for my parents?"

"You cannot, Colao. You better stay here. The city is full of soldiers. Not knowing you are under the emperor's protection, they might hurt you. We will look for your parents. Promise me you will not try to run away."

Seated on a large pallet, Colao nodded in silence, his hand tenderly resting on Otto's neck.

It Is War

In the following days, besides the vast bonfires set up to burn the corpses of the deceased from both sides, the emperor was mostly concerned with reorganizing his army to continue his march toward Rome and resolve his quarrel with the pope. He spent a lot of time with Colao and Otto, both now considered the mascots of the camp. They often ate together. As he tasted almost every dish, Colao repeated that his mother used to prepare it differently or better, and he described other dishes she used to make, stimulating Frederick's curiosity.

As a great lover of healthy food, the man listened attentively to the hazy notions of cooking the boy had about his mother's dishes. He asked his secretary to take notes and to write down the names of the dishes and ingredients that sounded new and interesting to him. Without creating suspicion, he asked Colao his mother's name. He was so intrigued by some of the culinary combinations the boy talked about that the following day, he asked the chief of the guards to go to the city jail and discreetly ask if, among the survivors, there might be a woman named Nofria of the Farratinos.

Frederick was well aware that many, if not all, imprisoned women had been raped by his men. It would not be easy to confront one face-to-face. However, he decided to do it for the love of this brave little boy. He himself had lost his mother when he was four years old. He only had a very vague memory of her.

In the afternoon, the guards arrived at the cathedral with a woman, her hands tied behind her back and her clothes torn and dirty. She was introduced to the emperor. "What is your name?" he asked.

"Nofria, and if you want to rape me as the others did, go ahead!" she yelled, spitting at him. One of the guards was on the point of hitting her, but Frederick stopped him.

"I apologize for what happened to you. But this is war. Be thankful you are still alive."

"And for how long? Was it not enough to kill my people? My family, all my friends, died because of your lust for power. You have destroyed everything!"

'Donna Nofria, I did not have you brought here to insult me. You speak the truth, but, as I already said, this is war. The ones on the wrong side must pay a high price."

"And who are you to decide which is the right and which is the wrong side?"

"Careful, Donna Nofria, you are disrespecting the emperor!" Pier Delle Vigne said.

"What do I care! I have nothing left to lose!"

Frederick interrupted her. "Believe me, you still have something to lose." He turned to his guards. "Bring the boy with the cat!"

As she listened to those words, Nofria's heart almost stopped beating. Her thoughts leaped about to a state of almost mystical hope. She exploded into uncontrolled tears of joy when she saw Colao entering the room, all cleaned up and unhurt.

"Mother!" he shouted, running toward her.

"Free her hands immediately!" Frederick ordered.

Mother and son joined in an embrace full of sobs and kisses under Frederick's melancholy gaze.

"Take them to the other room and give her the same treatment: feed her, wash her, and let her rest."

With her dirty cheeks washed by tears, she passed before the emperor, bowed, and murmured a subdued but sincere "Thank you." She had suffered physically and psychologically, her city destroyed, her husband and her other son killed in the battle. But now she felt reborn; now she had a reason to continue to live.

While she was cleaning herself up, Colao told her about their adventures, about how they had hidden in the tower, and how Otto had always remained close to him. He told her about the falcon's attack and about how Frederick had cured Otto.

"I am so glad to know you had your friend with you; at least you were not alone. I apologize for telling you at first to throw Otto outside. You were right to disobey me."

"Where are my father and my brother?"

"I believe they were killed in the battle. But we can be sure they died with honor to defend our city, or what is left of it."

"Do not worry, Mother, Frederick will not destroy Ameria. I heard him saying to Piero that he wants to keep it standing and camp here for a while."

"Frederick? Piero? How did you become so intimate with these killers in just three days?"

Colao recounted that they had eaten together every day and that Otto had become friendly with the emperor and Piero by jumping onto their laps. The emperor and Piero had started to joke about which of the two would be chosen after each meal for the cat's nap. In the meantime, Colao had listened to all their talk.

Nofria hugged Colao, happy to have him with her again and to see how much bravery he had shown in that dangerous situation. At the same time, she was frightened. How long would the emperor continue to show such mercy? For her, he remained a conqueror, a murderer.

The next morning, one of the guards came to summon her. "Donna Nofria, the emperor wishes to see you."

She stood up, reaching for Colao's hand.

The guard added, "Alone."

Nofria hesitated for a moment, not sure about what to do. Then she kissed her son on the forehead, telling him to wait for her and that she would come back soon.

"Sure, Mother. You will see that Frederick is kind!"

Worried about the guard's reaction, she said, "You should call him 'Emperor.' I do not think it is respectful to call him by his first name."

"Mother, he told me to call him by his name!"

"I can confirm it, Donna Nofria," the guard said. "Now hurry up. The emperor does not like to wait."

Nofria followed the guard down the central nave of the cathedral into the sacristy. When she entered, she saw him in an elegant dressing gown. She stopped for a moment. There were all the markings of a sexual encounter. She was ready to do anything to save her son's life. She bowed and murmured, "I am at your disposal, sire. Do whatever you feel like, but promise me you will spare my son."

Surprised by this statement, he reassured her. "What makes you think I want to take advantage of you?"

"Is that not what soldiers do when they conquer a city? Rape women?"

"I cannot control my men."

"You should!"

"I can assure you it is not easy to repress the instincts of men engaged in long battles, who for long months can only relax among themselves. They would turn against me if I tried to stop them from having fun when we conquer a town."

"You call it fun; we call it torture!"

"Donna Nofria, I understand your resentment, but this is war. We have already talked about it." He changed the subject before giving her time to reply. "Do not worry. I did not summon you to enjoy your body, even if I have to say you are a beautiful and desirable woman. Believe me, I feel sorry for the abuse you have suffered, but I wanted to talk to you about a different matter. Your son, who, by the way, let me tell you, is a very special boy, told me about some of your recipes that piqued my curiosity. I wanted to ask you if you could sit down with my secretary and tell him the most typical recipes of this city."

Her eyes widened, incredulous about what she had just heard. She was left speechless.

"Do not be surprised. I have visited so many cities, so many countries. I am fascinated by food and the different traditions about how the same ingredients can be prepared, depending on what each territory can offer. I am gathering all this information to prepare a treatise, a book, that can tempt people to try different tastes and, above all, healthy and wholesome food. Will you help me with this? Your son told me about your 'lassanie.' I think that is what he called the dishes. I would like to try them."

Still incredulous that a cruel emperor had just asked for her cooking recipes, without hesitation, she gathered the courage to say, "Sire, you can count on my help, but I have one condition."

"Please tell me what it is."

"I would like you to release the Amerians from prison. Let us save our city. If you allow me to talk to them and convince them not to rebel in exchange for freedom, we will serve you, and in the meantime, we can prevent our city from dying."

"What makes you think they will listen to you? Are you that influential?"

"I was the wife of Consul Giulianus. My husband was loved and respected. They will listen to me. In return, you will have all the secrets of Umbrian cuisine."

"You are asking for a lot in exchange for your culinary secrets!" He stopped for a moment, then added, "So be it, but I want the real cooking secrets! Now you can go give your son a kiss and his cat a caress from me."

Nofria asked if she could bring in two women whom she knew had survived the massacre, and with their help, the three women prepared many dishes the emperor had never tasted before. Nofria's "lassanie," prepared with different meats and vegetables, were the first recipes to be transcribed and ended up in his archives. Another one he loved was the breaded eel cooked in the oven with juicy anchovies, garlic, and onion sauce. So was the roasted woodcock with toasted bread covered with a paste of crushed innards cooked with garlic, parsley, bay leaf, vinegar, and lemon juice.

Frederick made sure all the recipes were transcribed and all the ingredients listed. Otto also enjoyed all those meals. The cat spent a lot of time in the baptistery that had been turned into a kitchen. During the preparation of each meal, Otto was handed several scraps of meat, such as some chicken hearts. Nor did he ever miss a meal at the table, where he got some delicacies from everyone.

The pleasure Frederick received at every bite of the food turned into curiosity about every detail of the preparation, about the herbs used, and about the processing of the ingredients. He constantly made sure every step was written down.

One night, during one of those meals, a messenger arrived from Rome and asked to talk to the emperor. The messenger reported the news that the pope had summoned a concilium of all the cardinals for the following Easter. The purpose of this meeting was to vote for the emperor's final excommunication.

After the messenger was dismissed, Frederick began to argue with his generals and strategists. He had to find a way to prevent this final excommunication from being confirmed by the concilium.

Stripping off the leg of a roasted pheasant and passing a piece of meat to Otto, Colao loudly whispered, "What is a concilium?"

Quietly, Pier Delle Vigne approached Colao's ear and explained, "It is a meeting with all the most important cardinals and bishops who gather in Rome from all over Europe, in this case, to vote against the emperor."

Without hesitation, passing another piece of meat to Otto, Colao asked, "What is the problem? Stop them before they get to Rome so they cannot vote."

Silence spread in the room. No one had thought about such a simple solution, and silence was the apparent admission that thinking too big can sometimes overlook a more immediate solution. Frederick broke the silence in the least embarrassing way for him and his generals. "We must find out all the routes the cardinals might use to reach Rome. By land or sea, we must intercept them and prevent their meeting with the pope. Piero, tomorrow, send out messengers and spies. We must know as soon as possible."

That night, while Nofria was clearing the table from the last leftovers and dirty plates, Frederick entered the room and talked to her alone. "Your son has a brilliant intelligence. You must be proud of him."

"I am, sire."

"Soon, I will be leaving Ameria. I do not know if or when I will ever be able to return. Be assured that I will arrange for you and your child to live comfortably. Do you have any idea if your house is still standing?"

"It is, sire, but it has been completely stripped of everything."

"I will give orders to supply your house with everything you might need to live and also give Colao an education. I cannot give him back his father, nor take his place, but I will make sure he will have everything he might need."

"You are very generous, sire." She bowed and added, "May I ask you a question?"

"Please."

"It is very difficult for me to understand your true self. On one side, I see the emperor: a violent, despotic, murdering conqueror. On the other side, I see a sensitive, benevolent man who loves good food, animals, and art. I would love to know how a man can be so merciful and cruel at the same time."

"You want to know the real Frederick?"

Otto appeared at the door. The emperor tapped twice on his leg, and with a quick jump, the cat was immediately on his lap. Otto crouched down and started purring. Immensely relaxed by those powerful vibrations, the tough leader started to recount his feelings like he had never done before in his life.

"I have never had the possibility to be what I really wanted to be, what I really am. At your son's age, I was already the King of Sicily. And believe me, I was not as bright as he is. My whole life was decided before I was even born. I was forced to follow paths I never wanted to. Yes, I love art, nature, culture, architecture. Every single day of my life, I try to dedicate at least a small amount of time to creating something that will be preserved in all those fields for future generations. Unfortunately, for the rest of the day, I am the emperor, and power and politics are never clean, never peaceful.

"I was heavily attacked when I tried to resolve things peacefully, like when I was asked to conquer Jerusalem. The pope sent me on a crusade, which I concluded with diplomacy. Do you think he was happy I did not spill a drop of blood? He was not. I was charged with conspiracy. I dream that people and religions can coexist. That is not the policy of the Vatican. They want to impose their *Dictatus Papae,* destroying other cultures and eliminating the differences that exist among cultures. I do not understand why they want to erase different traditions.

"I was fortunate to grow up surrounded by many different cultures, the Germanic, the Roman, the Arabian, the Greek, and each one has its own diversity, its marvels, its peculiarities. Each can contribute to the others. This attitude is not what the Roman Church wants. They think they are superior, that they are perfection, and this makes me angry and sad. That is why I am interested in the different preparation methods of the same food in the various countries I have the chance to visit. I want to preserve them and make them known to as many people as I can so they can try new ways of cooking and savor new tastes. But I am annoying you, Donna Nofria. And Otto here is not amused either."

Hearing his name, Otto raised his eyes to look at Frederick. He answered Frederick with a soft "Meow." Otto knew this man had always been forced to be cruel, but Otto had experienced Frederick's soft side when Frederick had treated his wounds. Otto trusted him.

"No, sire, you are not annoying me. On the contrary, I am glad to have known the man behind the emperor. I thank you for giving my son and our city a chance to survive. I do not know if I will ever be able to forgive all the pain and suffering you have inflicted on me and my people. I will try, however, to accept your motivation." She bowed and left the room to join her son.

Caressing Otto, Frederick continued to talk to him. "I will miss you, you little scoundrel. If this city has not experienced worse destruction, it is only thanks to you and that little boy. When I am done writing my treatise on falcons, I will study cats. You have fully understood the secrets of life. We should learn from you."

Otto's purring became even louder, and he looked at Frederick with his eyes half closed. He then lowered his head and slept as the emperor caressed him. For a moment, Frederick thought about how his life would be if he could drop everything, stay in Ameria, and marry Nofria. He would enjoy a quiet life, becoming a father to Colao. He was tempted for just a short time before his ambition and sense of responsibility, so deeply instilled in his soul, prevailed, and he shelved that pleasant thought.

He got up, still holding Otto in his arms, heading to his bed. Even though he desired to sleep with Nofria, that night, he only shared his bed with a fluffy cat. It was certainly one of the most serene nights of his entire life.

On the day of his departure from Ameria, the entire population, both the survivors and those who had fled to nearby villages but subsequently returned to Ameria, were summoned to the large square outside the walls. Pier Delle Vigne announced that Ameria would remain a stronghold of the emperor under the command of General Simone. A military unit would remain to rule over the city, thanks to its position as an important crossroad between the Via Amerina and Via Flaminia. The presence of the emperor's soldiers would ensure that the people of Ameria would have the chance to rebuild and resurrect their city without fearing possible retaliation from the papal army.

In his brief speech before leaving, Frederick asked the Amerians to collaborate with his general and added, "Your city and your valley are of rare beauty. The months I have spent here have allowed me to discover its tranquil and evergreen nature, which has allowed me to understand why northern populations love Italy and want to come here. I do not know when I will be able to return to Ameria, but I will ensure that your city will never suffer further destruction during my reign."

After he was gone, Ameria started a very slow rebirth. Some of the emperor's soldiers, injured during the long siege and unable to fight again, stayed and ended up marrying women who had lost their husbands in the battle, creating new families. Colao returned to his house with his mother and Otto, who never, ever left his side.

Every now and then, they climbed the hill to the former cathedral, now the military headquarters. At each visit, he asked if there was any news from Frederick, such as where he was and how he was doing. Colao was very proud to hear from General Simone that the fleet loyal to the emperor had stopped the ships headed to Rome. The cardinals traveling from Spain, France, and England never reached the port of Ostia to go to the Vatican. The concilium never took place.

It took five years for the new pope, Innocent IV, to summon a new concilium, during which not only was Frederick's excommunication finally confirmed, but also he was deposed as emperor. That same year, 1245, the imperial army left Ameria, which returned to being part of the Papal States. Nofria did not remarry, devoting herself to her son's education.

Saddened by Frederick and Piero's departure, Colao never fully realized how much his meeting with the emperor—a meeting well planned and directed by Otto—had been fundamental for the city's survival. They never met again. Frederick died ten years later. In those years, always with Otto by his side, Colao regularly contributed to the reconstruction of his city and, above all, to the maintenance of peace. The tensions between the Guelphs and Ghibellines quieted down for several years. A great desire for peace and reconstruction prevailed in the area.

Later on, Colao married Leandra, a younger woman born from the union of one of the emperor's soldiers with a widow of Ameria. Together, they had five children: Tommaso, Uliviero, Bartolomeo, Polissena, and Mirabile. The hereditary line of his first human was thus assured. Colao was only thirty-two years old when he was elected Consul of Ameria, one of the last to hold that title. From the first years of the XIV century, the leaders of municipalities changed their title to "mayors."

Otto had died several years before Colao became consul. Colao wrapped Otto's corpse in white linen. Alone and avoiding everybody, at night Colao walked up the hill to the Civic Tower. He chose to bury Otto in that spot where they had hidden so many years before. Colao dug a deep hole near the base of the tower and deposited his friend's small body at the bottom of the hole. He then filled the hole, trying to camouflage the spot on the surface so that no one would suspect Otto was buried there.

In his inaugural speech as consul, Colao dedicated his election to his father Giulianus, a two-time consul long before him, and to his beloved Otto, without whom he would not have survived the massacre. He would have liked to mention Frederick, but he realized it was better not to. His fellow citizens had a memory of Frederick utterly different from his own and would not have appreciated words of praise for a brutal conqueror.

Throughout his entire life, Colao carried in his heart all the greatness and all the lessons he had learned from Frederick. Even though their paths had only crossed for a few months, the emperor had left a deep imprint on his soul that he then carried all his life.

The End of the Middle Ages

Frederick II of Swabia's moral and political legacy was fundamental for the remarkable changes that would soon take place in Italy. The highly cultured emperor spoke German, French, Arabic, Greek, Latin, and the vernacular Sicilian. He concentrated mostly on the latter, understanding how easy it was to learn and to be spread to other areas. He started to use it in his literary efforts. During the following century, this way of speaking became increasingly popular, spreading from north to south on the peninsula, first conquering the northern royal courts until even the ordinary people started to use the new language.

It is not known exactly when or why it happened, but it was after that historical period that Ameria underwent its third and definitive name change. From the ancient name Amer, which later became Ameria, the Umbrian city began to be commonly called Amelia.

Frederick's legacy went far beyond spreading the Italian language. He had created a ferment in culture that found very fertile ground in peninsular Italy. The relationships he had created in many areas of life with his innate curiosity generated a growing evolution in taste and thought, leading within a couple of centuries to the birth of the Italian Renaissance, a period in which the arts, architecture, and culture found renewed splendor, a splendor not seen since the glory of ancient Rome. The backwardness and darkness of the Middle Ages gave way to the innovations of a major intellectual genius.

Tito's soul began to hover again, this time around the Civic Tower. His spirit was sort of imitating the flight of Frederick's falcon. He had no knowledge of when he would return for his sixth life, so he waited patiently for a signal to reincarnate. The Renaissance was coming.

Recipes
Taken from an Ancient Handwritten Booklet

Baked Breaded Eel with Anchovy Sauce

Take an eel, cut it into pieces, and put it in a casserole dish to boil with dry white wine, spices, fragrant herbs, and salt. When the eel is cooked, remove it from the casserole dish and let it cool down. Beat three egg yolks, adding grated bread, melted butter, salt and pepper, and nutmeg. Mix the sauce with the eel. Butter a pan, place the eel in it with the sauce, and put it in the oven to bake to a pleasing color. Take a quantity of anchovies you think might be enough, remove their heads, and beat them with a knife handle, then pass them through a sieve with some butter. Place the anchovies in a smaller pan with another pat of butter and a little finely ground flour and mix everything well; with a ladle, add some broth [...], then boil it for a quarter of an hour, adding a little pepper and nutmeg. Serve the eel with half a lemon squeezed onto it, keeping the anchovy sauce in a gravy bowl separate from the eel.

Fried Goat Sweetbreads

Take the quantity of goat sweetbreads, hearts, and throats that you need. Boil the meat in water for three minutes, then drain it and put it into fresh water. Clean the skin off the meat and marinate the meat in a terracotta pan with oil, salt, lemon juice, six shallots, and a little parsley, all finely chopped; leave the meat for two hours. Then, dry the meat with a cloth. Dip the meat in beaten eggs and flour. Fry the meat in lard, but not in too hot a pan, so that the meat is cooked and becomes a nice golden color. Place it on a plate with some fried parsley and serve.

Roasted Woodcocks

Take the quantity of woodcocks you want to roast. Remove their innards, which you cut finely and mix with onions, and then set aside. After beating the woodcocks enough, put them in a small pan with butter, four shallots, a clove of garlic, and some parsley, and let them fry for ten minutes. Season with pepper and nutmeg, over which you sprinkle a little flour with a small amount of broth and the juice of half a lemon. Cut some crusty bread into small pieces, fry the bread pieces in oil or lard, and then spread the paste with the innards on the bread pieces.

Frederick II of Swabia, "The Wonder of the World,"
from the Royal Palace in Naples

Chapter 6
The Renaissance in Amelia
Year 1513 AD
Meo and Giovanni Build a Palace

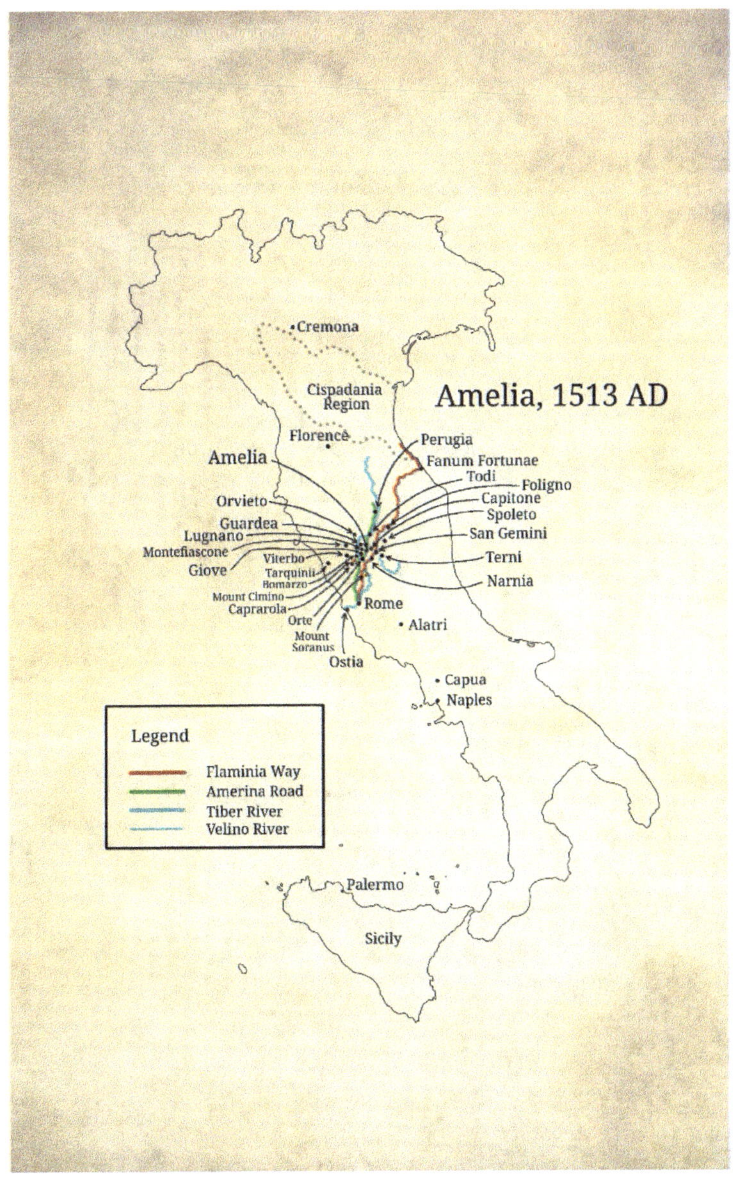

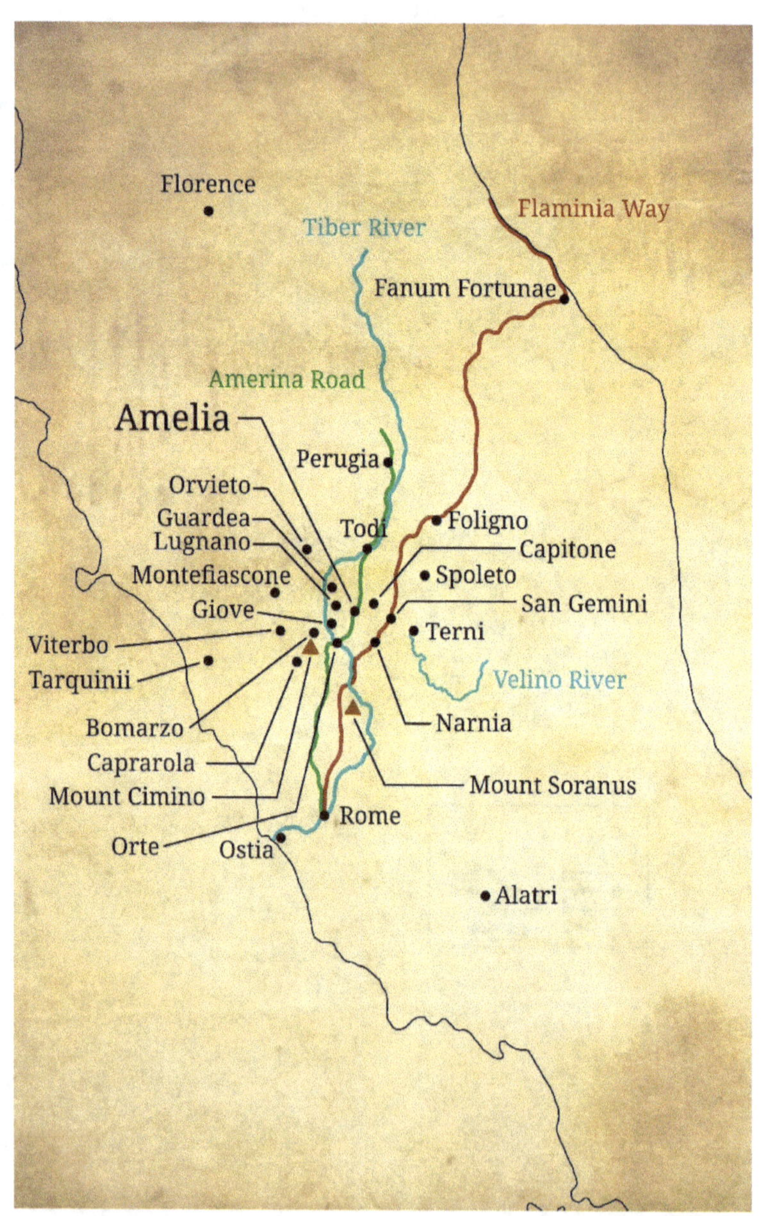

Florence
Tiber River
Flaminia Way
Fanum Fortunae
Amerina Road
Amelia
Perugia
Orvieto
Guardea
Lugnano
Todi
Foligno
Capitone
Montefiascone
Spoleto
Giove
San Gemini
Viterbo
Terni
Tarquinii
Velino River
Bomarzo
Narnia
Caprarola
Mount Cimino
Mount Soranus
Orte
Rome
Ostia
Alatri

Cast of Characters

Family at the Start of the Chapter

Giovanni: a large landowner and a member of Amelia's Council of
  Ten

Marianna: Giovanni's wife

Bartolomeo Farrattini: a bishop; Giovanni's younger brother; a high
  Vatican official

Pollemio: the youngest brother of Giovanni

Zaffinus: the father of Giovanni, Bartolomeo, and Pollemio

Perna: the mother of Giovanni, Bartolomeo, and Pollemio

Tito/Meo: a cat

Other Amelians

Aspria: the Farrattinis' housekeeper

Picts, Geraldinis, Virgilis, and Roscialtis: Amelian landowners

Historical Figures

Christopher Columbus

Queen Isabella of Spain

Alessandro Geraldini: a bishop; a native of Amelia

Cardinal Alessandro Farnese

Pope Julius II: from the Della Rovere family

Pope Leo X: of the Medici family

Agostino Chigi: a renowned banker

Marcantonio Flaminio

Pope Adrian VI (Adriaan Floriszoon Boeyens d'Edel): a Dutch Cardinal before becoming pope

Pope Clement VII (Giulio De' Medici): the illegitimate son of Giuliano De' Medici

Giuliano De' Medici: the father of Pope Clement VII

Lorenzo the Magnificent: the uncle of Pope Clement VII

Cristoforo Giacobazzi: the Bishop of Cassano

Bernardo De' Medici: the Bishop of Forlì

Giovanni Angelo De' Medici: the Apostolic Prothonotary

Charles V of Spain

Caterina De' Medici

Henry of Valois

Artists and Architects

Verrocchio

Donato Bramante

Sandro Botticelli

Giorgio Vasari

Ludovico Ariosto

Leonardo Da Vinci

Antonio Da Sangallo the Younger

Raffaello Sanzio (Raphael)

Populations

Landsknechts: mercenaries hired for the army of the Holy Roman
Empire

Family at the End of the Chapter

Fulvio, Baldo, Perna, Elisabetta, Simon Pietro, Cesonia, Zaffino, Tarsia,
Letissima, and Lepidus

Introduction

ONLY AT THE end of the XV century did Amelia begin to embellish itself again with new palaces, new churches, and a renewal of wealth accumulation. In those years, the Tuscan city Florence became a focal point of the latest trends in ideas and the arts that were initially stimulated by a man called *Stupor Mundi* (Wonder of the World). Under the influence of wealthy patrons and the concentration of some unprecedented talents, Florence became the center of an innovative concept of culture. Paintings, literature, and architecture were all enriched by the advances brought about by minds endowed with a preponderance of artistic brilliance. Masters like Verrocchio, Donato Bramante, Sandro Botticelli, Giorgio Vasari, Ludovico Ariosto, and Leonardo Da Vinci pioneered the richest era in Italian cultural history.

At the beginning of the XVI century, in addition to this cultural ferment, Amelia had a further small advantage over other Umbrian cities. When Christopher Columbus set out on his legendary trip in 1492, a great admirer and friend of his was Alessandro Geraldini, a bishop who was a native of Amelia. Spiritual advisor to Queen Isabella of Spain, this enterprising bishop was instrumental in convincing the queen to finance that epic trip. Columbus took two or three voyages before he realized he had discovered a new world and not landed in the Indies as he had initially thought. Bishop Geraldini announced the extraordinary news to the pope, and in response he got an order to travel there to bring the teachings of the Catholic Church to the new continent.

Once he arrived in a settlement initially called Hispaniola (now called Santo Domingo), Bishop Geraldini built the first church. He began writing to his family in Amelia, telling them about the new world. As soon as he could, he sent them products from that new land, so the Amelians discovered what potatoes, tomatoes, and pumpkins were before many others in Europe.

On another trip, Bishop Geraldini sent his cousin a couple of turkeys, a kind of giant chicken unknown on the old continent. The turkeys aroused the curiosity of the Amelians. The Geraldinis' farmers began to breed them, and at all banquets at *Palazzo* Geraldini the main course was always a big roasted turkey.

The Renaissance spread throughout Italy. However, the area between Florence and Rome experienced the greatest cultural ferment due to the continuous journeys between those two cities made by the many artists called upon to create countless important works of art and architecture. Amelia was not exempt from this cultural ferment.

Tito could not miss this culturally rich period. His soul felt a strong call to reincarnate and contribute to the fulfillment of an important project that would give fame and add luster to Amelia for the centuries to come.

Amelia's Renaissance

The bells of the nearby church rang punctually as they did every day at seven in the morning. Aspria, the Farrattinis' housekeeper, carrying a large breakfast tray, knocked on Giovanni's bedroom door. Lately, Giovanni's sleep had often been agitated, and she knew it. Aspria, a small but efficient woman, was always smiling, positive, and constantly trying to do the best for the family that had welcomed her since she was a very young girl.

Giovanni's wife, Marianna, had confided in Aspria about being very worried concerning the many duties her husband had in those months. In addition to the fatigue caused by his daily job managing the family lands and their products, including farro, olive oil, and wine from the extensive vineyards, he had the added responsibility of being a permanent member of the Council of Ten, an essential part of the city government. On top of all this, his younger brother, Bishop Bartolomeo Farrattini, dumped on his shoulders the supervision of the construction of the new palace the bishop was building in Amelia, which was a huge responsibility.

Aspria tried to make Giovanni enjoy every awakening. She had seen him coming into this world and watched him grow and transform into an elegant, extremely polite, cultured man. But for her, he was still that little rascal for whom she prepared a whipped egg for his snack every afternoon.

On the large breakfast tray, she had put a cup of delicious fresh milk sweetened with two spoonfuls of honey and two slices of still-warm baked bread with fig jam. A small plate held four almond cookies, Giovanni's favorite. To one side of the tray lay two envelopes that had just been delivered: one came from his brother Bartolomeo in Rome, the other from the nearby city of Terni, sent by the architect Antonio Da Sangallo.

Giovanni opened his eyes, yawned, and then, when Aspria opened the curtains with a quick flick, closed his eyes again, struck by the morning light invading the room. He sat up and moved to a table to enjoy his breakfast. He was initially happy to taste those soft almond cookies, but his mood changed when he saw the two letters. Giovanni was constantly receiving letters from both his brother and his brother's architect about the huge project that was overwhelming the entire family.

The letters were often peremptory and sometimes contradictory. While he was following directions from one, soon after, another letter from the other changed everything. Bishop Bartolomeo, at that time a prefect and treasurer in the Vatican, gave the commission for designing his new palace to Antonio Da Sangallo. However, the famous architect was involved in so many other projects that he could not follow the work in Amelia personally.

Sangallo was now head of the construction of Saint Peter's Basilica in Rome, a job which he had taken over from his master Donato Bramante, who had recently died. Sangallo came to Amelia every now and then, being also the principal architect of another huge project, the Farnese Castle in Caprarola. Another massive project he directed was the displacement of the Velino River to supply more water to the Marmore Falls in Terni. With all these jobs, Sangallo did not have much time for Bishop Bartolomeo's palace in Amelia. He delegated many parts of the project to Giovanni and his workers.

As a result, Giovanni had to discuss the project with the workers, meet with the city rulers to obtain the necessary permits, but above all, deal with his capricious brother who, enthusiastic about what was being created in Rome under his direction, wanted to repeat the same grandeur in Amelia. As Giovanni pointed out frequently to his brother, Bartolomeo did not realize that in Amelia they did not have the same means, materials, or expert workers Bartolomeo was used to in Rome. If Giovanni could have gone back in time, he never would have accepted responsibility for this venture.

While he was sipping his milk, those two letters remained in a corner of the table, staring him in the face. He looked away. His breakfast took precedence. He savored the creamy marzipan cookies melting in his mouth with their wonderful sweetness. His mind went back to the day his brother had first expressed a desire to build a new *palazzo* (palace). Giovanni bitterly regretted not having dissuaded his brother then.

Bartolomeo, three years younger than Giovanni, had moved permanently to Rome a long time previously when he was made Bishop of Sora and Chiusi. For several years, he was the ambassador of the Holy See in the Gallia Cispadania, the southern part of France. Upon his return to Rome, Pope Julius II (whose original surname was Della Rovere) entrusted Bartolomeo with important responsibilities. First, he appointed Bartolomeo to be a council member of the Tithes Commission as well as an Apostolic Collector, then he named him prefect for the construction of the new Basilica of Saint Peter in Rome, a project already started under the guidance of the architect Donato Bramante.

In February 1513, Pope Julius II died. The Catholic Conclave elected Leo X of the Medici family as Julius's replacement. The new pope confirmed Bartolomeo in the same duties, also giving him the regency of the Apostolic Chancery. Bartolomeo's commitment to successfully managing those grandiose projects brought him great notoriety and remarkable income. Always nostalgic about his hometown, Bartolomeo tried to return to Amelia as often as he could, but there was never enough time for the visits he craved.

Bartolomeo's older brother Giovanni managed the family lands and properties, a right Giovanni had inherited when their father, Zaffinus, died. Giovanni, Bartolomeo, and their brother Pollemio were the sixth Farrattini generation after their ancestor Colao, the one who had met Frederick II of Swabia.

In that fateful summer of 1513, after making sure that

everything was well organized and the new pope well established in his powers, Bartolomeo managed to take three weeks off. He left Rome for his beloved Amelia. In the warm evening hours of the day, he arrived. Although tired from the long journey, Bartolomeo decided to take a walk through the streets of Amelia, which had seen him as a child and then as a teenager. He wanted to settle his spirit by enjoying Amelia's atmosphere and the fresh evening breeze.

Bartolomeo walked toward the spring in the southern part of the city to sip some of that cool, fizzy water that so many centuries ago had attracted Khepri, the hunter and helped to give birth to the town of Amer. It was a very long time since he had walked in that direction. Their family home was located on the other side of the town, facing north. Bartolomeo refreshed himself with the spring water and then walked toward the valley, admiring the wonderful, pale, but still intense orange glow illuminating the lower part of the horizon behind the hill.

That particular evening, the sun seemed not to want to set. To his left, the sky was already colored an intense blue dotted with stars. He instinctively started to pray to the Lord, thanking him for giving him that highly spiritual view. He stood there reciting his prayers until the last ray of sunlight disappeared. Looking at the sky, now a dark blue cobalt color, he noticed a bright shooting star streaming down above him. It was an enchanting vision. At that exact moment, he realized how much he missed his hometown.

Walking back home, he started thinking about how he could spend more time there or leave a tangible trace of this love, something that future generations could appreciate. The following morning, at breakfast, he spent a long time with his brothers Giovanni and Pollemio.

Bartolomeo's two brothers overwhelmed him with many questions about what was happening in Rome and with his job and the new basilica—all topics he would have liked to forget so he could enjoy a deserved rest without having to think about the huge responsibilities he had left behind. Their curiosity was understandable, and he thought that maybe, if he told them everything all at once, he could then set aside all those concerns for the next few weeks. With this in mind, his responses to their questions were detailed and exhaustive.

"All of the projects are in full swing, my dear brothers. I have to take care of so many things that some days, I do not even have time to eat. The transition of power between Julius II and Leo X was not easy. We're lucky that Julius was, and now Leo is, a man of great culture and lover of the arts. They have summoned to Rome the best available artists, and this fills me with joy because it allows me to witness the creation of so many great undertakings.

"It is not always easy, though. I often find myself dealing with huge, touchy, and complicated artistic personalities. It takes all my diplomatic experience, and the help of our Lord, to handle specific situations. Imagine trying to arrange not having Leonardo Da Vinci and Michelangelo, who hate each other, in the same room at the same time! Michelangelo just finished painting the vault of the Sistine Chapel, which I do not like very much, but it is said to be a real masterpiece. Leonardo, now much older, is extremely jealous of Michelangelo's vigor and impressive works. I also have the feeling he is in love with him."

"What are you talking about, brother?" Pollemio asked with innocent candor.

"We have always known that Leonardo has a soft spot for handsome youngsters, and Michelangelo oozes sexuality from every pore in his body. It is not clear if Michelangelo also prefers the company of young men; he is very reserved. But one thing is certain: he is obsessed with male muscles—his paintings tell us this very clearly.

"Leonardo is now sixty-one years old, while Michelangelo is in his prime. I do not think Michelangelo has turned forty yet, and I am sure for Leonardo, it is not just artistic jealousy that he feels for Michelangelo. It is maybe for these reasons that the tension can be cut with a knife when they meet!

"Then there is Bramante, now seventy years old and not in very good shape anymore. I have not been able to see him for the last few weeks, even if seeing him was extremely necessary. Often, Bramante has sent in his place this assistant of his, a young man called Antonio Da Sangallo, who brings papers and drawings, but the poor guy usually cannot answer my questions, and so things have slowed down enormously. Sangallo always answers my questions, saying, 'I will have to ask my master this question. I will let you know.'

"And then there is this other very young painter, Raffaello Sanzio (Raphael), an unrepentant womanizer who should confess every single day given how much he sins! Actually, God bless them; all these artists should confess every day! The buzzing around, dear brothers… You have no idea! Nevertheless, Raffaello's paintings and frescos are of unparalleled beauty. He decorated all of Julius's rooms with magnificent frescoes. Now, Leo wants to entrust him with more commissions. If only Raffaello could concentrate as much on his art as he does on women!"

"It seems to me you have no time to get bored!" Giovanni commented.

"No, definitely not. And that is not all. Besides the organization of the projects and the careful tactics that I have to use with all these artistic personalities, I also must ensure that all the accounting and payments for their work go smoothly. They are all very demanding and smart. I must order my clerks not to talk about bills in front of them. If one of them found out he was being paid just one *baiocco* less than the others, you have no idea how much trouble I would be in! I have spent countless sleepless nights trying to fix this complex tangle of payments, meetings, and confrontations with all these difficult people!"

"But is it not very exciting for you to live surrounded by all that art? Promise me you will take me with you to Rome to see all those wonders," Pollemio said. He was still a student studying law.

"I will, my little brother, I will. But now I want to talk to both of you about something I realized last night when I was walking the streets of my beloved Amelia. I have a secure financial situation at the moment, and I would love to build a new home for our family— something great to remind all our descendants of my achievements. In Rome many bishops, cardinals, and popes are building wonderful palaces. I want to do it, too, but here in our hometown, not in Rome. I will need your help and support since I will not be able to be here to supervise such an important project. You will have to help me!"

Surprised by this unexpected news, Giovanni did not realize the possible negative consequences such a project would bring to his life.

"Do you want to tear our house down and rebuild it?" Pollemio asked.

"No, my brother. Giovanni, I want you to gather information about the large green area in front of the spring—all those gardens and sheepfolds, to whom do they belong, and can we possibly buy them? The view to the southwest is wonderful, and last night, the sunset was magnificent. While I was there, something magical happened. I was looking at the horizon, and at the exact moment, I was thanking the Lord for such an amazing view, a shooting star crossed the sky right above me. I know it was a sign from the Lord telling me I had to build our new home there."

Giovanni and Pollemio were speechless as they looked at the blissful expression on the face of their middle brother, who had enchanted them with the religiosity of that moment and his deep faith. Right then, the only thing they could do was to indulge his desire.

Bartolomeo's three weeks of vacation passed quickly. Before returning to Rome, he inquired again about the ownership of those parcels of land near the spring and left Giovanni with a substantial amount of money to try to purchase them.

After several months of negotiations, by March 1514, Giovanni had secured the entire area. He bought from the Picts, from the Geraldinis, the Virgilis, and the Roscialtis, who each owned a portion of that land. Right in front of the spring, Giovanni now had titled in his name an area of almost 25,000 square yards, which extended up until the edge of the city walls. He wrote a letter to his brother to inform him that the land was now their property and that he could proceed to the next steps: requesting city permits and choosing an architect.

In Rome, Bartolomeo had repeatedly considered asking Donato Bramante to design his new *palazzo*. However, securing the property had taken a long time, and the physical condition of the celebrated architect had worsened. He died on April 11th, 1514.

With Bramate's death, as prefect of the new basilica, Bartolomeo put aside his personal project since his main concern was to find a worthy architect to complete St. Peter's Basilica. Leonardo Da Vinci was still in Rome; he was an obvious choice. However, at that phase of his life, the Florentine genius was much more committed to studying physics, mechanics, and, above all, anatomy. In addition, besides not enjoying great popularity among the Roman clergy, Leonardo was an old man now, and Bartolomeo could not risk finding himself again without an architect should Leonardo die before the basilica could be completed. Shortly afterward, an anonymous letter was sent to the Roman Curia accusing Leonardo of witchcraft for his anatomical studies and research on dead bodies. This letter caused many problems for the great man, who decided to leave Rome and move to France.

Numerous long meetings followed between Bartolomeo and Pope Leo. The urgency to continue construction pushed Bartolomeo to suggest hiring Raffaello Sanzio for that position. Despite his rampages, Raffaelo was highly regarded for his art and talent. He was young and would ensure continuity in the long years still needed to build the basilica. Because of this crisis, Bartolomeo had to set aside his own project temporarily.

Bartolomeo had previously asked Raffaello if he would consider designing the Amelia project, but his quick answer was negative. Rafaello's huge commitment to the Vatican, plus a recently accepted project for Agostino Chigi (a renowned banker to whom no one could say "no"), made Raffaello refuse Bartolomeo's proposed commission.

It was Raffaello himself who suggested that Bartolomeo ask Antonio Da Sangallo to take on the commission. After Bramante's death, his former assistant had been making a name for himself as being among the major architects working in Rome, and he had been acquiring important commissions. Even Cardinal Alessandro Farnese contacted him about designing his own palace.

Since he was still on the Vatican's payroll managed by Bishop Bartolomeo, Sangallo, unlike Raffaelo, did not feel he could refuse to design a project requested by the person who was paying his salary for working on Vatican projects. In 1516, during one of his trips to Caprarola to supervise the Farnese project, Sangallo traveled to Amelia for the first time to see for himself the location of this important new project.

His first meeting with Giovanni without Bartolomeo being

present was not very pleasant. As soon as he arrived, this genius of Renaissance architecture immediately affirmed that building on such a steep lot would be impossible. It would be essential to level the section toward the valley with dirt. Then Sangallo abruptly asked Giovanni if he knew what could be hidden under that lot. The presence of Roman vestigial artifacts on a wall next to the spring proved the existence of nearby buildings from the Roman era.

"And how could I know what might be under there?" answered Giovanni, annoyed by the architect's arrogant behavior.

"Then excavate!" Sangallo said in an imperious tone. "When I come back a month from now, I want to have this whole area uncovered in order to figure out how to lay the foundation and orient the direction of the palace. You must excavate from here," and he began to take long strides for at least thirty-five steps, then pivoted and paced twenty-five more steps, "up to here!" He asked one of his assistants for a few stakes and planted them firmly in the ground.

Giovanni immediately became worried, wondering how many men he would have to engage in such a massive excavation. Also, the tone of this man, with his strong Florentine accent, was irritating to Giovanni, who was a kind and polite human being. Accepting orders from such a man would be repugnant. After the meeting, Giovanni immediately sent a letter to his brother in Rome.

Bartolomeo's answer was clear. He asked Giovanni to comply with the Tuscan's requests and said that he would soon come to Amelia to support him.

The Arrival of Tito

Several months passed, and finally, in the spring of 1517, Bartolomeo and Antonio Da Sangallo managed to arrange a meeting in Amelia. Those long months gave Giovanni the time to finish the entire excavation, as had been requested.

The scene Bishop Bartolomeo and the architect Sangallo faced once they arrived at the building site left them speechless. In between those four stakes that Sangallo had planted so many months before, a whole world had reemerged after having been buried for centuries.

Portions of stone walls with Roman stucco, cisterns, mosaic floors, remnants of statues, and marble ornaments were all revealed there, displayed for them to admire.

While Bartolomeo was more attracted by the decorative fragments and, in particular, by a beautiful elaborate frieze probably belonging to the columned portico of the ancient Roman baths, Sangallo immersed himself in an in-depth study of the walls and building methods used by the Romans. He had always admired their techniques and slowly began to scratch the mortar that had been holding together those stones for more than fifteen centuries. Sangallo wanted to know its composition. He saved a good handful of the mortar in a strip of cloth to study later on.

While the two continued to explore the Roman ruins, Giovanni walked toward the edge of the walls and left them to enjoy their finds. He already had had enough. The thought that his brother would soon return to Rome and leave him alone with that arrogant Tuscan did not make him very happy. He reached the long brick trough where animals went to drink water collected from the spring. He sat down on one corner of the trough, trying to enjoy the tepid heat of that early spring sun.

A quick movement on the opposite side of the trough caught his attention. A beautiful big cat was walking along the long row of bricks and quickly approached him, lying down next to him. "And who are you?" Giovanni said, stroking soft fur heated by the sun. The cat must have been laying in the sun for a long time to accumulate such heat, Giovanni thought.

The cat responded to Giovanni's stroking with a couple of meows, half-closing his big yellow-green eyes in which the thin vertical pupil was just visible. Giovanni could not understand the meaning of those meows, but Tito was telling him, *Hello, I am Tito, and I am here to help you.*

Tito had returned to life and, since his re-birth, had been hanging around that area for almost a year. He had left his sixth mother and had explored up and down his valley to figure out what to expect in his new life. He had seen and approached many people, but he had not yet felt that strange vibration he had experienced in his previous five lives. Ever since his experience with Hephaestus, his ability to sense the right human had enormously increased. Back then, he was wild and scared of humans. It had taken him a long time to get used to them.

It had been easier to recognize Tarzio and even easier with Marcus. Recognizing Lucius was so very easy. With Colao, it had been a dangerous game at the very beginning, but still, it was a game. When he saw Giovanni, sad and pensive sitting on that trough, he had no doubt once Giovanni's hand touched his fur—his whiskers started to vibrate. It was him, his new human! Now Tito only had to make the man understand he needed him.

Bartolomeo called over Giovanni, who stood up and joined his brother. Tito was a bit disappointed. His first attempt to approach his new human had not been as successful as he had hoped, but he had to be patient. He knew he would soon enchant him or, better said, capture him.

In the following days, the bishop and the architect spent many hours on the building site. Antonio Da Sangallo measured every single piece of those ruins and studied how to exploit the Roman foundations to his own advantage and harmonize them with the new building. Those Roman ruins, still solid after fifteen centuries, with the proper precautions would make a reliable base of support for the new palace for the centuries to come.

After Bartolomeo left, Giovanni remained as the person responsible for the worksite and for managing the agitated architect. Before leaving Amelia, to lighten his brother's load, Bartolomeo had written a letter to the city council, requesting permission for carts to enter the city walls, carts packed with the necessary quantity of dirt to decrease the unevenness of the land and with the materials needed for construction.

The disagreements between Giovanni and Antonio Da Sangallo began as soon as Bartolomeo departed. The architect's shouts filled the valley whenever an obstacle appeared during his busy schedule. Once, he was missing a specific tool, and another time, he was arguing with the workers, who were obviously not as trained as those he was used to working with in Rome. After offending them with typical Florentine expressions such as *grullo* or *bischero* or other words nobody knew the real meaning of, he turned to Giovanni and asked him to find other workers and supervisors.

At Giovanni's negative answer and response that these workers were the best in town, Sangallo raged without stopping. After every quarrel or discussion, Giovanni had to leave to calm down his nerves that had been shaken by the unbearable and often incomprehensible Tuscan's curses.

Whenever Giovanni approached the trough, Tito immediately approached him and laid down beside him, purring loudly. As soon as he caressed the cat, Giovanni felt calmer. It did not take long before he started to talk to him. "Why do you run here so quickly when I arrive so agitated? Are you a guardian angel sent by my brother?"

Tito answered with a soft "meow," which, of course, meant "Maybe!" Tito would have liked to tell Giovanni it was not Bartolomeo who had sent him, but someone long before.

The day came when Sangallo announced he had to return to Rome, where he was needed. This was a great relief for Giovanni, even though Sangallo's last day in Amelia was by far the worst day they had had until then. In only a few hours, Sangallo undertook to instruct Giovanni and the crew chief on what they had to achieve in the next six months until he could return to Amelia.

Annoyed by the heavy cursing and the countless *Maremma maiala, impesta'a e lurida* (a typical Tuscan derogatory expression), Giovanni could not help but think, "So now you want to teach me how to work?" Tito approached them and started rubbing on Giovanni's trousers. He stood on his back legs to reach Giovanni's hand with his little head. He wanted to make Giovanni aware of his presence. He stayed in that position with one paw resting on Giovanni's leg and the other reaching for his hand to make Giovanni notice him.

Trying with no success to have a normal conversation with Sangallo, Giovanni, without even realizing it, picked up Tito and held him in his arms against his chest. When Sangallo screamed another curse, Tito opened his mouth wide and hissed fiercely.

The architect was so frightened he stepped back, letting out yet another Tuscan saying: "Hey! Little one! I will take the ticks off your body!" which was a Tuscan way of threatening that "If I catch you, I will hurt you!" Sangallo was still disturbed by that powerful hiss when Tito, this time without opening his mouth, let out such a deep guttural sound that it seemed like it was coming from the afterworld. The sound was so powerful and frightening that Sangallo remained silent for a few seconds. He looked at Giovanni, who was as incredulous and surprised as Sangallo.

Giovanni had felt such a strong vibration in his ribcage after that guttural sound that he trembled. He felt defended by this cat he was holding in his arms, a cat that clearly had no intention of leaving. The conversation continued in much more controlled tones. Sangallo showed Giovanni and the crew chief many sheets with drawings and notes indicating the next phases of the project. Giovanni now listened without dropping his new furry weapon.

The meeting ended almost at sunset, and Giovanni walked home with Tito still in his arms. As he was walking, he spoke to the cat warmly: "I have to thank you, little fellow! You really helped me calm down that monster! He is certainly a good architect, but he is unbearable. For this, you deserve a nice dinner. I will take you home with me, and we will see what I can give you."

The cat continued to purr loudly the entire way. When they entered the house, Aspria and Marianna were not very happy to welcome a cat. The two women were already very busy with managing the many children running around the house. A cat was not in their plans, and Marianna was afraid the cat would scratch the children. Their six children—Fulvio, Baldo, Perna, Elisabetta, Simon Pietro, and Cesonia—with a seventh one on the way, were all between two and eight years of age.

To convince the two women, Giovanni told them how the cat had defended him from Sangallo. Amused by this story, they became more willing to accept the cat. Neither of them felt great sympathy for the Tuscan. Aspria, in particular, was not very happy to prepare impromptu meals for him since he often was not very appreciative. She was, however, indeed delighted to prepare some food for the first being who had managed to shut that arrogant man up. She was on the point of putting a saucer with some food on the floor when she stopped with the dish in midair, turned to Giovanni, and asked if the cat had a name.

"No, not yet."

Tito, who had been meowing loudly and looking at the saucer, stopped meowing and tried once more to make himself understood. With his big eyes, he looked straight into Giovanni's and intensely thought, *My name is Tito! Tito! Tito! Tito!*

"I am sure this cat is here by my brother's intercession," Giovanni said. "To remind myself of that, I will call him Meo. That was the nickname our mother, Perna, used to call my brother as a child, and that is how I will call you, my new friend!"

Aspria placed the bowl on the windowsill, and once again, Tito resigned himself to getting used to yet another name. Tito/Meo jumped up onto the windowsill and enjoyed the set-out delicacies. After a year of finding his own food, returning to a real kitchen like Setonia's or Artusia's was not a bad outcome at all, even with having been given such a ridiculous name he would have to carry for his entire sixth life!

Meo and His New Home

Although Marianna was still not very happy to have this new tenant in her home, Meo knew exactly how to win her over. He was now very experienced with humans. Tito was always very discreet, never imposing himself on them. He did not climb on beds, did not steal food from the kitchen even if the food was left unattended, and never dared to scratch anything or anybody. With his beautiful eyes and that sly, clever expression of his, Tito sat in a corner, watching every movement of his humans.

After a short time, having gotten used to Meo's presence, both Giovanni and Marianna ended up calling him to come to them. "Come here! Come here, and I will pamper you a bit!" they would say. Only then did he approach. He was very patient with the children and happy to play with them. When Marianna was sure she could trust him, she began to leave him alone with them. She educated them to respect him, as he was not a toy. Meo let himself be spoiled and amused by that small group of little devils without needing to escape to safety. He knew how to deal with children: he had done it with Fulvia and Marcus's children, with Lucius and Scilla's, and with Colao as a child. However, he always anxiously waited for Giovanni's call to escape them. As soon as Giovanni entered the children's room before going to the construction site, Meo stood up and followed him. Better to be an architect than a nanny!

A few months later, Marianna turned to him and told him, "Meo, you can now sleep here in the bedroom with us, but let me be clear on a few things. You cannot scratch or get anything dirty, and you will not get up until Aspria opens the curtains! Those are the rules, understand?" She paused for a moment, then pointed to the door and said, "Otherwise, you are out!"

Meo looked at her, torn between amusement and boredom. The expression on his face spoke for itself, clearly conveying a message: *So, you now think you will teach me how to behave?* Spending long days next to Sangallo perhaps had taught him a little arrogance!

Marianna never had to complain about the cat. Meo loved to sleep on the bed with its soft blankets. He did not need to get up early because, even if he sometimes felt hungry, he knew that on the tray Aspria brought in every morning, there was always a small bowl for him with some fresh milk or a few leftovers from the previous evening. He did not need to worry about finding food for himself.

Shortly after this development, Marianna gave birth to their seventh child, Zaffino, whom they named after his grandfather. Meo looked at the newborn from the edge of the heavy wrought-iron cradle. Later, they often found him asleep beside the baby, with the baby's little hand holding one of Meo's paws, both peacefully asleep.

Although getting a bit lazy and comfortably used to this new home, Meo never neglected his responsibility to assist Giovanni. He waited patiently for his human to get dressed, and, depending on his daily duties, if Giovanni said, "I am not going to the construction site today," Meo headed toward the kitchen or the children's room. If, instead, Giovanni simply said, "Let's go!" Meo, as a perfect assistant, followed Giovanni to help supervise the project. Whether it was cold, hot, rainy, or windy, he never failed to accompany his human. Meo followed Giovanni every single step and sat beside him when he stopped, with his white front legs perfectly aligned.

After their first encounter, as soon as Sangallo approached Meo and Giovanni, Meo would open his mouth and let out a menacing hiss, just to warn Sangallo that he was there and that Sangallo better behave. It seemed like a weird coincidence, but after Meo's arrival, the project proceeded with more tranquility, fewer quarrels, and more constructive discussions.

Sangallo and the Walls of Tarzio

Antonio Da Sangallo was traveling among his many construction sites. He always sent a letter to Giovanni to warn him of his arrival.

Sometimes he arrived from Montefiascone, where he was building the church of Santa Maria of Monte Moro (today called Santa Maria di Montero), or from Caprarola, where the construction of the Farnese fortress was in full swing. He stopped for a few days in Amelia when traveling again to Viterbo to follow up with the artisans involved in the wooden ceiling for the Sanctuary of the Madonna Della Quercia. Other times, he just traveled back and forth between Rome and Amelia.

Often tired and overwhelmed by all this moving around from one place to another, he was nervous and edgy. But by now, when he was in Amelia he had learned to be more accommodating with the workers and Giovanni.

Meo was always a step behind Giovanni, ready to hiss anytime Sangallo started to raise his voice. Meo was not at all happy to have to hiss so frequently. He had never had to do it in his previous lives, and it was not part of his normal behavior, but this particular architect needed to be constantly reprimanded. Any time Sangallo started to yell, he was scolded by an equally powerful hiss.

On one of his trips to Amelia, Sangallo had a few more days to spend there, so he asked Giovanni to take him on a walk to admire the city's walls. Ever since his first visit to Amelia, he had been fascinated by the beauty of the walls and wanted to take a closer look at the different methods used to build and restore them over the centuries.

Giovanni and Sangallo started their walk from the older part on the upper part of the hill, the section built with coarse stones of which only a small section was still standing. With his heavy Florentine accent, Sangallo commented on what he was admiring. "It shows here that the builders did not have a trained mind! Look at those stones! How could they think they would hold?"

Meo remembered how long Tarzio had studied the walls and how he had rebuilt that small replica stone by stone on his table to find its weaknesses. Meo followed the Tuscan's words attentively. Even if he was a cat and that choleric human spoke in a different way than all the humans he was used to being with, by now he understood enough Florentine words and expressions to follow any discussion. He thought, *You better not say anything bad about my Tarzio's work, or I will become dangerous!*

When they reached Porta Romana so they could walk along the lower part of the walls, Sangallo was entranced by such perfection. "I have seen many differently shaped city walls, but never one constructed so precisely! *Slutty Maremma* (a strong Tuscan swearing phrase)! Look at how those two stones almost kiss each other, so that not even the finest fern leaf could pass between them!"

Continuing the walk, Giovanni explained what little was known about the construction of those legendary walls. "This section seems to date back to the fourth century before Christ. Obviously, there is not any documentation about who built them or how, or at least not any documentation in any of the city archives. What we can be sure of is that their edges were added, and the walls restored by the Romans in the first century when Amelia was called Ameria and was an important Roman municipality."

Sangallo listened carefully to Giovanni's words as they were walking along the walls, with his hand tenderly caressing the stones, admiring the precision of the walls' construction. "Each and every one of these stones matches the one next to it perfectly! If after all these centuries they are still standing, it is because whoever built the walls knew very well what he was doing!"

Meo was happy. He could not stand this human, but now that Sangallo had praised Tarzio's work, Meo began to like him a little bit more. Maybe he would not have to hiss at him anymore. Sangallo continued to praise the walls to the point that Meo felt he had to rub himself back and forth against Sangallo's boots.

"What is this? A sign of a truce?" joked Sangallo, bending down to pet Meo.

Giovanni took the opportunity to say that probably, when Sangallo was not swearing and spoke quietly, Meo was not afraid of him. He could not know that Meo was only happy to see Tarzio's work appreciated, a project to whose completion he had contributed so many centuries before. And, yes, it also was a peace sign.

"He is more than a cat; he is your watchdog!"

Together, they headed home to enjoy Aspria's delicious meal before returning to the construction site.

At Bishop Bartolomeo's suggestion, the *podestà* (mayor) of Amelia and the city council, aware of Sangallo's presence in town, decided to ask him if he could propose how to reinforce the city walls. In the centuries following their construction, building techniques had made a lot of progress.

Sangallo had already explained to Giovanni that safer and more resistant walls could not be achieved solely by increasing their height. He could not know that Tarzio had given the walls a thickness of more than three human steps. Since the width of the walls was not visible from the outside, Sangallo could not be certain if the walls could resist attack by modern weapons. He spent a few hours designing a project to be presented to the *podestà* with his suggestions on how to reinforce the walls. Sangallo believed the many restorations that had previously been done and the creation of deeper moats were not enough.

He had had a recently restored section reopened to investigate its thickness. Once he realized the walls were indeed very thick, he concentrated more on the creation of a few vast, double-walled, reinforced embankments, a technique already in use at the Vatican and in other cities. The embankments would make the walls more imposing and robust, especially where there were curves and corners, the weak parts of any wall. Building an embankment would also create a much larger space to accommodate more soldiers and defense machinery.

Sangallo's proposal was very well received by the *podestà* and the council. Giovanni himself explained the details to them, but Amelia's financial resources were insufficient to cover the high cost necessary to complete this project. The council asked Giovanni if he could intercede with his brother in Rome to request financial support from the Vatican. Bishop Bartolomeo was the only one who could obtain results, but Bartolomeo was now extremely busy dealing with another huge problem.

When the lead architect for the basilica project, Bramante, died in 1514, Bartolomeo and the pope, despite having in Rome that immense genius Leonardo Da Vinci, preferred to assign the continuation of the project to the younger genius Raffaello Sanzio because of Da Vinci's old age. They could never have foreseen that Raffaello would suddenly die so young. On April 6th, 1520, under mysterious circumstances, Raffaello died at only thirty-seven years of age, leaving the pope incredulous and Bartolomeo again without an architect to continue the construction of the basilica.

Bartolomeo immediately dispatched a messenger to Amelia, knowing Sangallo was still there. He needed Sangallo back in Rome right away. The messenger delivered the news to Giovanni at his house. With Meo following him, Giovanni ran to the construction site to report the news. When he arrived, he saw Sangallo arguing with the workers. Giovanni shouted from afar to attract Sangallo's attention. "Antonio! Antonio!" Sangallo had never seen Giovanni acting like that.

"What the hell happened to you that you are so agitated?" Sangallo asked when Giovanni got closer.

"Antonio, a messenger has just arrived from Rome. Raffaello is dead. My brother wants you back in Rome as soon as you can get there!"

"What happened to that *bischero* (idiot, in Tuscan slang)?"

"They do not know. Rafaello reported being sick and was dead in a few days. They could not save him."

"*Maremma bu'aialal!*" Sangallo swore, using one of his strong Tuscan expressions. "Considering all the whores he took to bed, he must have caught something bad! Giovanni, make sure I can leave tomorrow morning. Your little brother must be in deep trouble!"

Now that Sangallo was usually speaking more calmly to Giovanni, Meo would sometimes move away from them, even if only to a distance from which he could still see them. He would wander among those uncovered ruins, and even though he knew something very significant was being built on top of them, he was concerned about what would happen to what had been found underneath all that dirt.

Jumping off a piece of masonry still showing the remains of red Pompeian plaster from the Roman era, he crouched on a mosaic floor with those little black-and-white tiles, which was the old floor of the ancient Roman baths. In those rooms he had lingered with Matron Lydia and Fulvia. He smelled that floor, closing his eyes and sniffing the unmistakable scent of the oils Fulvia had used to massage Marcus's body. That perfume had remained on her hands when she caressed him after finishing her time with the man she loved so much. The sensations and images of almost fifteen centuries before were still alive in Meo's memory. He loved being on that mosaic floor again. When the sun suddenly reached the spot where he was, he lay down. Soothed by the sun's warmth, Meo rolled on his back several times to pay homage to that life and to the memories of his "love mission." His eyelids closed.

Meo suddenly woke up, disturbed by Sangallo and Giovanni's voices approaching the spot where he was lying, along with the construction crew chief. "Here, you will cut down that wall to the floor," Sangallo said. "Then you will continue to raise the new walls like you have been doing up until now. When you reach a height of fifteen feet, you can begin to fill in the space in the walls with dirt. Then, start to build the wooden frames to set up the vaults. These steps will keep you busy for several months."

"And what are we doing with the mosaic floors?" the crew chief asked.

"Keep them! It makes no sense to destroy them and make new ones. If they have lasted all these centuries, we can still use them."

That news made Meo very happy. Along with Amelia's walls, he would now have more tangible artifacts of one of his previous lives.

When Sangallo left, Giovanni felt an even heavier responsibility on his shoulders. The project was underway and the construction crew chief well-instructed in what to do for the next few months, but the project was still a huge responsibility for him since he knew nothing about architecture. He was somewhat comforted by the fact that all the basement rooms could go through the same sequence of construction steps, which would keep the workers busy for months without them needing the presence of Sangallo.

The Family Gets Bigger

Seven years had gone by since Zaffino was born, and three more children had arrived to augment the already overcrowded rooms of their home. Two girls named Tarsia and Letissima and another boy named Lepidus brought up to ten the number of Giovanni and Marianna's children. Their very pleased Uncle Bartolomeo always managed to come back to Amelia to baptize his new nieces and nephews. When he visited Amelia he was always amazed by the progress on his new palace.

Giovanni often had to complain about the burgeoning expenses for materials and decoration. The workers were now raising the walls of the first floor, and Sangallo's design for the elaborate travertine window frames for the front and back windows was very expensive, according to Giovanni's standards. He tried to dissuade his brother from those excessive costs.

"Could we not make them smooth like the side window frames? Do we really need all those curlicues and spiral volutes?"

Knowing the much more exorbitant prices paid in Rome for the same kind of decoration, Bartolomeo was not swayed by the cost. He reassured his brother, telling him how much he had had to pay the stonemasons for the frames made out of precious marbles designed for the basilica in Rome. The costs for these window frames in Amelia were nothing compared to those in Rome.

"But are you sure we can afford them?" Giovanni retorted.

Bartolomeo was indeed concerned about how recent events in Rome would affect the *palazzo* construction. After Raffaello's sudden death, Pope Leo X had entrusted the basilica project to Antonio Da Sangallo. This development made Bartolomeo afraid that "his" architect would not have the same dedication to the project in Amelia now that he was again involved in the Vatican.

Sangallo himself reassured Bishop Bartolomeo. He would have to make several trips to Umbria, and he would stop in Amelia anytime he was close by. He was, in fact, still working in Terni on the project for the Marmore Falls.

But those were not the only concerns Bartolomeo had. Leo X was a very nice pope and a lover of arts and beauty, but he was also heavily criticized for his sexual behavior. Countless *pasquinate* (graffiti messages) appeared on the famous Roman statue about the pope's "private encounters." (The statue of Pasquino was used to hang anonymous signs denouncing papal and ruling class power.)

The pope's obsession with a young Venetian boy caused a considerable stir in the Roman Curia. Leo did everything he could to keep this beautiful boy, named Marcantonio Flaminio, in Rome. The boy had participated with his father in a private audience with the pope. His father had immediately understood the pope's intentions and took his son away from Rome. Not even the offer of a prestigious position in the Roman Curia could convince them to stay in the Vatican. The boy was a huge obsession for the pope and a constant worry for Bartolomeo.

Bartolomeo's concerns vanished on December 1st, 1521, when Pope Leo suddenly died. Initially, rumors that the pope had been poisoned circulated in the Curia. An autopsy confirmed that the rumors were just that—unsupported suspicions. The day after, another graffiti sign appeared on the Pasquino statue, making Bartolomeo saddened not only by Leo's death but also because of the repeated rumors about the pope's supposed sex life. The graffiti text Bartolomeo was handed read:

The poor man died, and don't tell yourself a lie,
*to have fuc**d one of his boyfriends too much in their a***

Bartolomeo knew the true facts very well. He had been aware of the pope's secret love for Raffaello Sanzio, a love that had never become public. The passionate artist's indisputable love for women probably caused his death and prevented the pope from making any moves toward him.

Leo had asked Bartolomeo to find an important position in the Vatican for the young Marcantonio, who certainly did not have the resumé required for such a job. He had also heard the pope's confession many times. Being aware of all this, he was not happy the allegations were now out in the public domain.

The Conclave was called into session, and Dutch Cardinal Adriaan Floriszoon Boeyens d'Edel was elected the new pope. He assumed the name of Adrian VI. Although he had studied and spent most of his life in Italy, this pope created a new set of problems for Bartolomeo.

During one of his visits to Amelia, Bartolomeo confided in his two brothers as he used to do. "I no longer know what to do. There has been an impromptu stop in the work on the basilica. This new pope has an incomprehensible cultural ignorance. He cut out most of the funds for any artistic project.

"I have to continuously argue with the artists and ask them to continue their work with reduced fees. Michelangelo has already threatened to leave Rome forever. Can you imagine that Adriano said he wants to have the original starry sky of the Sistine Chapel restored because he hates all those naked bodies painted by Michelangelo Buonarroti! I have not dealt with Sangallo yet. Certainly, he will not be happy to find out that his fee for his work on the basilica is now reduced by half. I am afraid he will ask me for more money!"

While telling these stories to his brothers, Bartolomeo was gently caressing Meo, who was crouched on the bishop's expensive robe. Bartolomeo was ready to walk to the cathedral for Sunday Mass. "Dear Meo! You are lucky! They gave you my mother's nickname for me when I was a child, and you do not know how much I wish I could exchange my troubled life for yours!"

Enjoying the caresses, Meo filled the moments of silence with his mighty purring. The strong vibration coming from his larynx had a pleasant effect on Bartolomeo. Meo's purring was sending the bishop a calming message: "Everything will be fine!"

Pope Adrian VI did not last long. Causing great (if secret) contentment on the part of Bartolomeo, Adrian died in September 1523, only twenty months after his election. In November of that same year, the Conclave elected a new pope, this one from the Medici family. At just forty-five years of age, Giulio De' Medici became pope and took the name of Clement VII. Giulio was the illegitimate son, later legitimized, of Giuliano De' Medici, who was killed before his son was even born. Giulio's uncle Lorenzo the Magnificent had entrusted Giulio to Antonio Da Sangallo to instruct. When Sangallo moved to Rome with the architect Bramante, Lorenzo again took his nephew under his own guidance.

Bartolomeo could not be happier with this choice of pope. This new pope would bring back art and culture to Rome. His long-term relationship with Sangallo would simplify the bishop's tasks.

Pope Clement and Bishop Bartolomeo developed a solid friendship in the following years. They spent a lot of time together even when not involved in the ecclesiastical-political obligations which at that time were decidedly intricate. The trust Clement had in him was such that Bartolomeo was invited along with Cristoforo Giacobazzi, Bishop of Cassano; Bernardo De' Medici, Bishop of Forlì; and Giovanni Angelo De' Medici, Apostolic Prothonotary, to the coronation of the Habsburg Emperor, Charles V of Spain.

Over the following years, the pope entrusted Bartolomeo with other delicate tasks. Bartolomeo traveled to France to accompany the pope's niece, Caterina De' Medici, to Marseilles to meet her betrothed Henry of Valois, future king of France. Bartolomeo was also in charge of supervising all the phases of the wedding preparations, from the signing of the necessary legal papers, to reaching the necessary complicated political agreements, to organizing the ceremony itself. To show his gratitude for the trust the pope had shown in him, Bartolomeo had the coat of arms of the Medici family painted within the frescos of his new palace, which was finally about to be completed.

Clement's papacy was not a peaceful one. In 1527, Rome suffered one of the most terrible, destructive invasions of the century when the Landsknechts, mercenaries hired for the army of the Holy Roman Empire, led by Emperor Charles V, laid waste to the city. During what has since then been remembered as the "sack of Rome," Clement VII and almost the entire Curia left Rome.

The pope retired first to Orvieto and then to Viterbo, while Bartolomeo took the opportunity to spend more time in Amelia. The roof of his palace had finally been completed more than ten years after the first stone was set in place. He could sleep for the first time in one of the rooms on the first floor next to the large ballroom. Many decorative finishing touches were still in the works, but the house was now inhabitable, and for a few months, he could finally enjoy it as his own.

He was very proud of the inscription Sangallo had engraved on the stringcourse (horizontal band) of the external façade of the first floor:

UT MEMINERINT POSTERI BARTHOLOMEUM
FARRATINUM ALIQUANDO FUISSE EX
LABORUM ET VIGILIARUM SUARUM
RELIQUIIS IPSE ET SUIS CASAM POSUI.

So that posterity will remember
Bartolomeo Farrattini,
who with a surplus of labor and vigilance
procured this house
for himself and his family.

Bartolomeo asked Giovanni to move in with him, but Marianna preferred to stay in their own home. She did not feel her numerous children would be safe in a palace still filled with workers engaged in painting or assembling wooden ceilings. Three of their children—Fulvio, Perna, and Simon Pietro—were already married and living with their spouses, but the other seven were still under her care.

During the long months of the sack of Rome, Sangallo also spent more time in Amelia. At that time, he was finishing the design of the elaborate wooden ballroom ceiling and the loggia. For the first of those, Sangallo was very demanding. Up until then, in all the palaces of Amelia, the main ballrooms had vaulted ceilings with frescoes. Sangallo had been the first to bring to Amelia the new, typically Florentine fashion of wooden coffered ceilings.

For Bartolomeo's palace he had designed a geometric scheme with fifteen panels, each including a large rose window. He insisted on finding a poplar with a sufficiently large trunk to be cut into thick slices. Each would be carved in the shape of a rose, each one unique, but by doing this, they would all have the same wood grain. It had not been easy to locate an appropriate tree, but one was finally found in the woods of Mount Cimino. Sangallo went to see it on one of his trips to Viterbo and gave his approval.

The carpenters carved fourteen large roses to decorate the fourteen ceiling panels. The fifteenth panel, right in the middle, would hold the family coat of arms.

The ceiling of the loggia, on the other hand, was divided into three large panels: two identical ones on the sides, while the middle one contained a very large family coat of arms surmounted by a bishop's miter. Sangallo was working on the design of this ceiling to pass it along to the crew chief and the carpenters when he received a letter announcing the peace agreement between Clement VII and Charles V, an agreement that allowed the pope to return to the Vatican.

Bartolomeo and then Sangallo had to follow the pope to Rome, the latter being called back urgently to resume his work on the basilica, which had been halted for almost an entire year. Both Giovanni and the crew chief again found themselves in charge of an imposing and delicate project that had to be performed without the presence of the architect. Nobody knew when Sangallo would return to Amelia.

On his last day in Amelia, Sangallo tried to explain to Giovanni and the crew chief the proportions of the delicate design of garlands, rhombuses, and other geometric figures to be placed on the ceiling, but he was not being understood. The three men were standing on the top step of the staircase holding several sheets of paper with drawings, along with measuring sticks and wood samples. They could not walk on the floor of the loggia because a casting of *cocciopesto* (a certain kind of plaster) had recently been spread and had not yet completely hardened. It would take at least another twenty-four hours before they could walk on the floor, and Sangallo had to leave that same day.

A walkway of long suspended wooden boards was created to allow them to cross the room. The crew chief was asking questions about how he could maintain the same proportions without a specific diagram. Sangallo tried to explain to him that he only had to quadruple each measurement given on each drawing. The design had to be carved in the poplar wood and applied to the boards already fixed on the ceiling.

Neither Giovanni nor the crew chief were convinced that they could convert those small drawings to a scale four times bigger and be sure all the pieces would fit together. Most of all, they feared that it would be very difficult to respect the design proportions once they had to nail the pieces to a twenty-one-foot-high ceiling in that room.

After another fifteen minutes of Tuscan curses and imprecations, the three men saw Meo silently passing next to them with a chicken bone tightly held between his teeth. He crouched on the floor, transferred the chicken bone to his paws, and started biting the last pieces of meat off the bone. The repeated small bites were leaving marks on the *cocciopesto* made by the lower part of the cracked bone.

Watching Meo, Sangallo had an unexpected insight. He ordered workers to immediately bring him two well-pointed iron rods, one at least three feet long, the other at least double that. He then asked the workers to prepare smooth and perfectly straight wooden slats and strong cords.

Giovanni looked at the crew chief. Neither of the two could understand what was happening. They had not grasped the subliminal message Meo was suggesting with his chewing and marking.

With quick and extremely precise movements, Sangallo walked back and forth along the wooden planks, resting the slats on the floor and moving the iron rod along them. The two still did not understand what he was doing.

Meo, tired of his completely stripped bone, walked away, leaving the bone in two pieces in a corner of the room. His task was finished, and, sated, he went downstairs to doze in the warmth of the sun.

Giovanni and the crew chief tried to ask Sangallo how they could help, but he shushed them and told them not to disturb him until he was finished. It took him nearly six hours before he called them back and showed them his genius. He had grown fond of Meo, and perhaps for the first time since they had met, he put aside his arrogance by acknowledging that Meo had inspired the creation of this technique.

With the tip of the iron rods and the help of the wooden slats, he had slightly engraved the not-yet-solidified *cocciopesto*. The design, in the exact same measurements as what had to be reproduced on the ceiling, was now visible on the floor. He had marked the outline of each single geometric part of that complex design. Rhombuses, squares, large circles, and everything else were marked on the floor in full size. Even a child could now assemble that impressive ceiling.

He turned to the crew chief and said, "Now, you just cut the pieces and lay them on the floor. When they are all ready, you will not have to do anything other than nail them to the ceiling. This way, there is no way you could go wrong!"

They headed downstairs, but before leaving, Giovanni stretched his hand out from the walkway to pick up the two pieces of bone Meo had left there.

Sangallo stopped him. "No, wait! Leave them there!" Leaning forward, he pushed the two small bones into the *cocciopesto* with the heel of his boot. Since the *cocciopesto* was almost solidified, it took some pressure, but he managed to mash them down in such a way that they remained embedded in the floor. "Here you are! So now we will forever remember that Meo suggested how to solve this problem. He put his signature on it! He is a great cat! He is not as stupid as you two!"

From the windows of the loggia, Meo, who had gone downstairs to the garden to enjoy the sun on the wall of the external staircase, heard Sangallo's words and rejoiced at having helped achieve another important goal. Once that ceiling was finished, only a few more details remained to be completed.

Giovanni had taken advantage of the presence of his brother in Amelia to have Bartolomeo instruct one of his sons, Baldo, who had great admiration for his uncle. Baldo's dream was to follow his uncle's footsteps into the Roman clergy. (Baldo, in fact, would become a bishop himself in 1559.) Another of Giovanni's sons, Zaffino, had the same wish. (He became a monsignor and Apostolic Prothonotary.) The two boys spent the entire time Bartolomeo was in Amelia during the sack of Rome living in the new palace, studying theology with their uncle, and listening to his teaching about diplomacy and political tactics. When Bartolomeo had to go to Viterbo to be with the pope and then return to Rome, Baldo and Zaffino stayed in the palace until they traveled to Rome to complete their ecclesiastical studies.

Giovanni's other two sons also moved to Rome. Fulvio and Lepido studied law and became respected lawyers.

Sangallo never returned to Amelia. He sent a letter to Giovanni while he was in Terni complaining about the monstrous number of mosquitoes there that prevented him from sleeping in that city, which also had an unbearable climate. He thanked Giovanni for helping him on many occasions and did not forget to send a caress to the cat, who, in a certain way, had domesticated him.

End of an Era

The years passed, and one after the other, almost all of Giovanni and Marianna's children embarked on their own lives. Only two daughters were still with them, but soon, Cesonia and Tarsia also got married and departed their parents' home. Giovanni and Marianna were left alone with Meo, now in his eighteenth year.

Meo, feeling weak and old, did not follow Giovanni around anymore. He preferred to stay in the few rooms into which they had settled in the new palace. Giovanni would carry him in his arms to the garden where Meo used to remain for hours in the sun, looking out at his beloved valley. His eyes were now cloudy, and the memories that crowded his mind sometimes began to overlap.

When a human came toward him against the sun, he had difficulty in recognizing the person. Once, he had the clear feeling it was Hephaestus; another time, he thought he had seen Marcus or Tarzio. Even if his eyes did not serve him well anymore, his sense of smell helped him, as did his whiskers. As soon as a hand approached to caress him, he immediately recognized whose it was.

Marianna loved furnishing and organizing this new large house. Her faithful housekeeper, Aspria, had died a few years before, and she had to hire three women to help her with all those rooms. New curtains, new beds, new furniture, and new amenities had to be brought in to keep the *palazzo* ready for visits that Bartolomeo might make in the future, and above all, the *palazzo* had to be ready to receive Clement VII, should he accept Bishop Bartolomeo's invitation to come to Amelia.

In 1533, Bartolomeo and Clement were returning from France after the marriage celebration of Caterina De' Medici and Henry of Valois. Bartolomeo sent a letter to Giovanni alerting him they would stop in Amelia on their way back to Rome. The preparations for this visit were frantic. Hosting a pope in one's home was not an everyday occurrence.

Marianna commissioned a majestic new four-poster bed and placed it in the room that opened onto the loggia. In the frescoes painted along all four walls, the coat of arms of the Farrattinis was alternated with that of the Medicis. Lions and angels symbolically held the coats of arms. Giovanni could not wait to show the frescoes to the pope and to receive his blessing as a recognition of his contribution to their creation.

When everything was almost ready, the visit was canceled at the last minute. During the trip back to Rome, the pope had suffered a recurrence of an illness he had already had a few years before. He traveled directly back to Rome. It was a big disappointment for Giovanni and Marianna, but nothing compared to what happened soon afterward.

The summer of 1534 became one of the most traumatic memories of their lives. When the news of his brother's death arrived from Rome, Giovanni was lying on his bed, gently caressing his beloved cat, whose breathing was becoming increasingly shallow. A few hours after he had received the messenger with the sad news about Bartolomeo, Meo, too, passed away. Meo was almost twenty years old, until then his longest life, while Bartolomeo was sixty-three.

Giovanni was even more convinced that his cat had been sent by divine intervention and that Meo and his brother had shared an invisible bond keeping them united in life and now in death. The fact that they died on the same day was more than a coincidence. To close the circle, a few days later Pope Clement VII also died.

Bartolomeo's corpse was taken to Amelia to be buried in a temporary tomb. The family had recently decided to build a chapel next to the cathedral to give him and the generations to follow a well-deserved burial place. Upon the coffin's arrival in Amelia, Giovanni had it reopened, and he placed the little lifeless body of his beloved Meo next to his brother. The two, linked by the same name that neither had loved, now would rest together for eternity.

Their souls started to roam around the rooms and the palace's garden. While Bartolomeo would always watch over the home he had built, Meo, now back to being Tito, was just waiting to be reincarnated for his seventh life, curious to find out what he would learn in his next life and who his next human would be.

Fresco of Farrattini coat of arms in the palazzo

Bones in the palazzo *floor*

Ceiling in Farrattini chapel in Amelia cathedral

Bishop Bartolomeo Farrattini, on his tomb in the cathedral in Amelia.

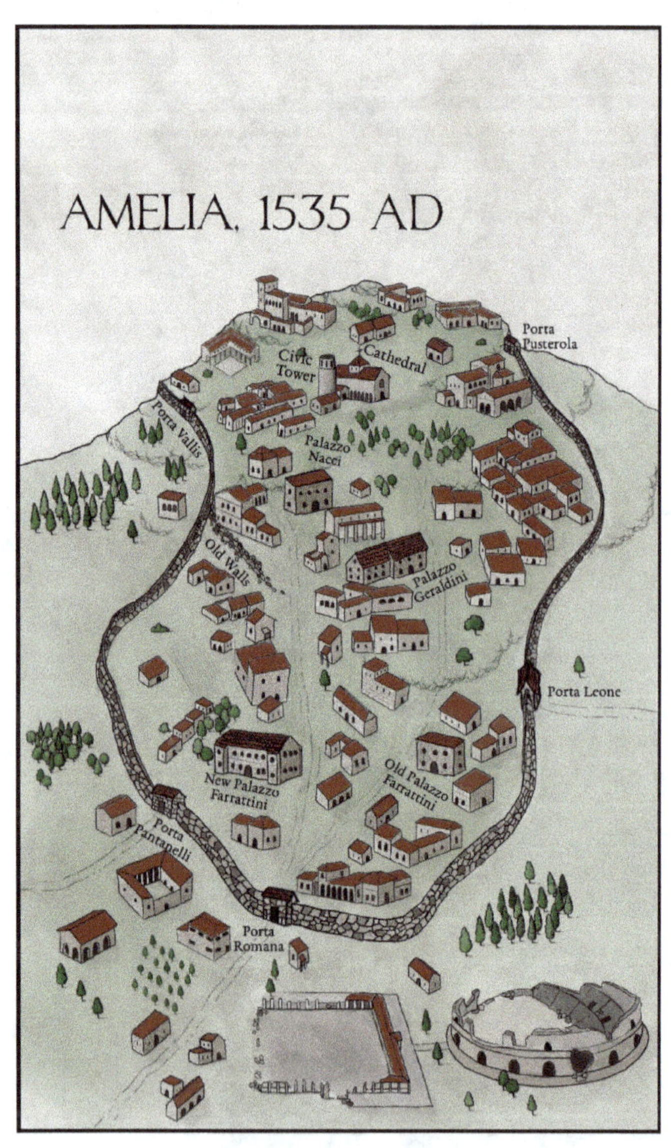
AMELIA, 1535 AD
Porta Pusterola
Cathedral
Civic Tower
Porta Vallis
Palazzo Nacei
Old Walls
Palazzo Geraldini
Porta Leone
New Palazzo Farrattini
Old Palazzo Farrattini
Porta Pantanelli
Porta Romana

Drawing of Amelia in 1564

Drawing of Amelia in the 18th century

Chapter 7
The Enlightenment in Amelia
Year 1722 AD
Ubi Helps Felice Idea Find Love

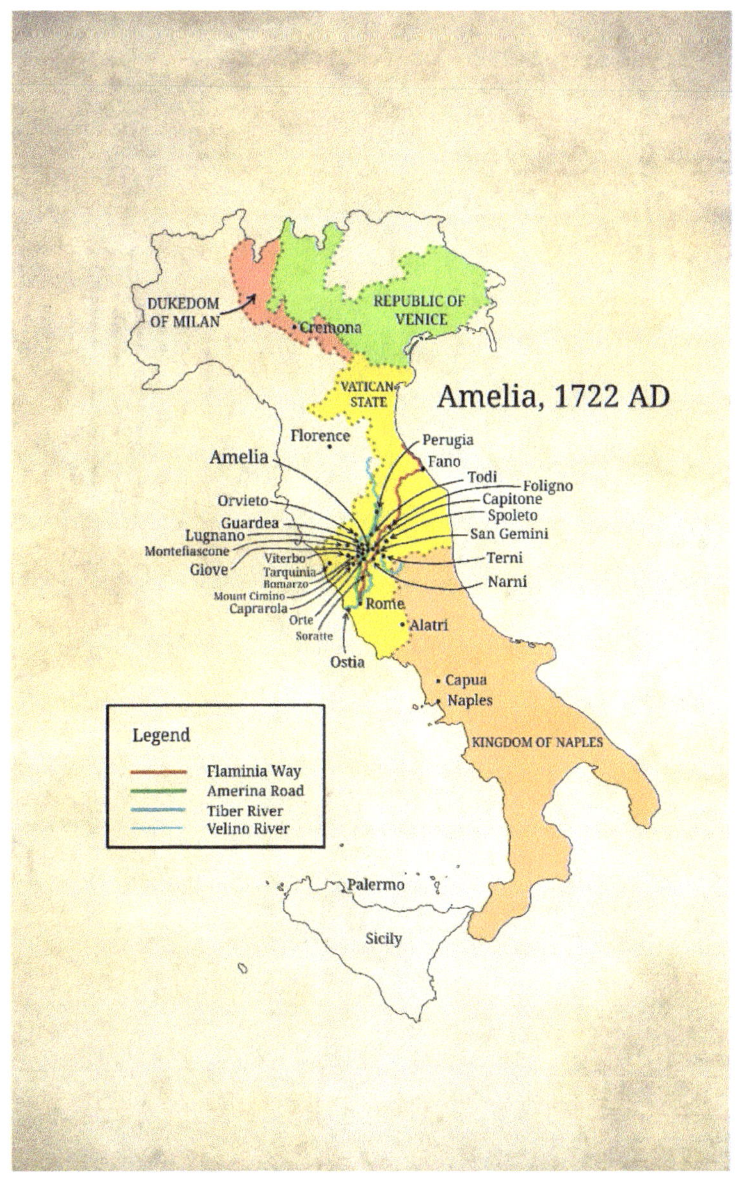

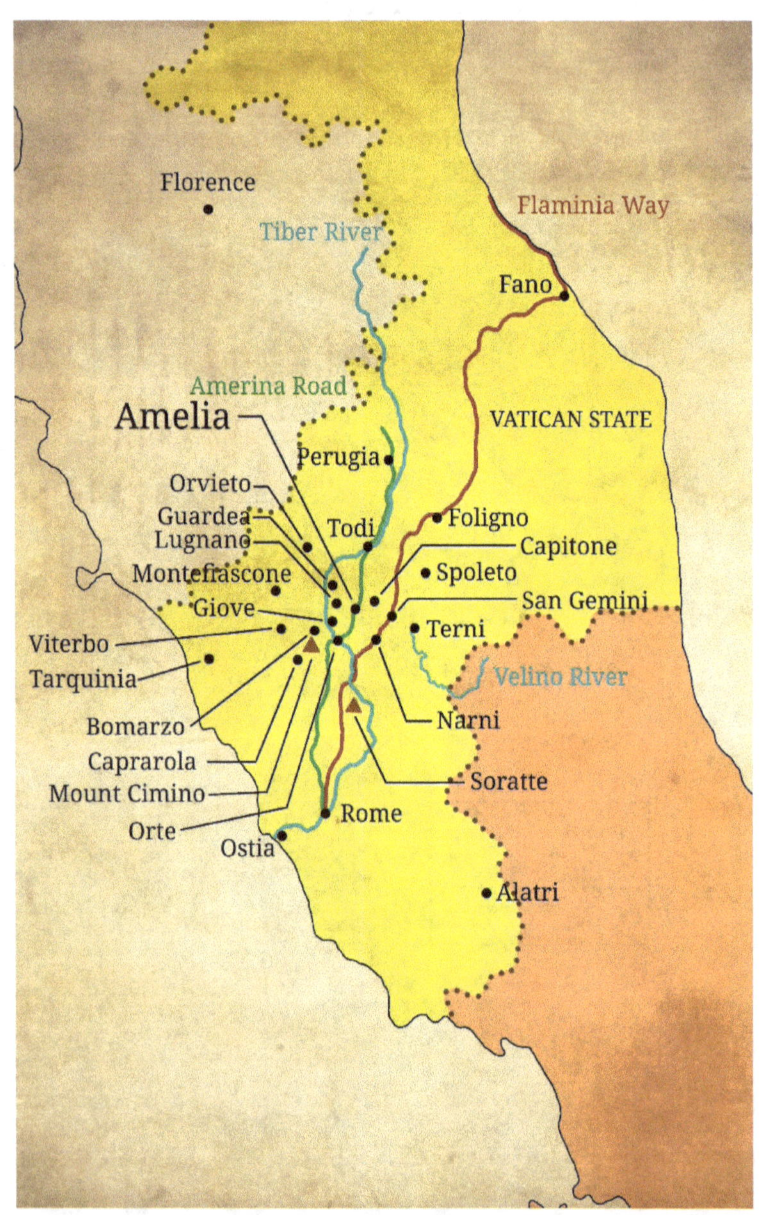

Florence
Flaminia Way
Tiber River
Fano
Amerina Road
VATICAN STATE
Amelia
Perugia
Orvieto
Guardea
Foligno
Lugnano
Todi
Capitone
Montefrascone
Spoleto
Giove
San Gemini
Viterbo
Terni
Tarquinia
Velino River
Bomarzo
Narni
Caprarola
Mount Cimino
Soratte
Orte
Rome
Ostia
Alatri

Cast of Characters

Family Between the Chapters

Fulvio: the son of Giovanni

Giovanni and Angela: Fulvio's children

Fabrizio: Fulvio's grandson

Giovanni

Family at the Start of the Chapter

Ubaldo: deceased father of Felice Idea, Maria Paola, and Francesco

Fabrizio: the brother of Ubaldo

Vittoria Cansacchi, the wife of Ubaldo

Felice Idea ("Happy Idea"): the elder daughter of Ubaldo and Vittoria; later called Fidea

Maria Paola: the younger daughter of Ubaldo and Vittoria

Francesco: the son of Ubaldo and Vittoria

Tito/Ubi: a cat

Other Important Characters

Gaetano Sandri: marries Maria Paola

Count Reginaldo Montemarte: the first husband of Felice Idea

Girolamo Benedettoni

Other Amelians

Geraldini family

Historical Figures

Grand Duke Leopold: the son of Maria Teresa of Austria; ruler of
    Florence

Bourbon dynasty: the rulers of the Kingdom of Naples

Pope Clement XI

Pope Innocent XIII

Jacopone Da Todi: a monk, poet, and philosopher; a distant relative of
    Girolamo Benedettoni

Pope Alexander VI (Rodrigo Borgia)

Giulia Farnese: the lover of Pope Alexander VI; wife of Prince Orsini

Prince Orsino Orsini: the husband of Giulia Farnese

Family at the End of the Chapter

Gian Lorenzo, Bartolomeo Carlo, Pietro Paolo, Anna Virginia, Anna
    Plantilla, and Giuseppe Angelo: Ubaldo and Vittoria's children,
    who all died before five years of age

Introduction

FOR THE FIRST time, after centuries of war and struggle of all kinds, peace seemed to have settled in Europe, both locally and internationally. The resulting tranquility gave way to significant growth in many fields.

Unlike the Renaissance, which was a very culturally rich period but still heavily influenced by Roman Catholicism, in the 18th century, science, art, and literature moved away from that influence. Although many areas on the Italian peninsula, including Amelia, were still under the strict domination of the Vatican, the ferment called the "Enlightenment" spread almost everywhere. New ideas on different ways to manage *res publica* (civic matters) started to gain power in various European states.

In Tuscany, the Medici family had, by then, already been extinct for three centuries. The Habsburg family ruled Florence in the person of Grand Duke Leopold, son of Maria Teresa of Austria. It was the first state where torture and the death penalty were abolished, decisive steps toward a more civilized society. Even the Kingdom of Naples, after the disastrous years of Spanish domination, saw notable changes under the Bourbons' guidance. The same situation prevailed in the Republic of Venice and the Dukedom of Milan, where social life and the economy continuously improved.

Not much of this ferment arrived in Amelia. In the Vatican State, time seemed to pass much more slowly than in the rest of the continent. After all, the popes at the beginning of the century, Clement XI and Innocent XIII, although engaged in complicated international diplomatic relations, did not leave much political or social room for the spread of the new movement, maintaining as they did a very conservative attitude.

The popes failed, though, in stopping those new ideas from circulating. Many newspapers and magazines were printed and distributed almost everywhere, reaching even the smallest towns. Publications entitled *Journal of Italian Literature*, *The Literary Whip*, and many others, mostly from northern Italy, moved throughout the peninsula. Such publications cautiously began to appear in Amelia, spreading new ways of thinking. The Amelians nevertheless remained politically and culturally under the heavy domination of the most traditional Catholicism.

~

Giovanni passed away in AD 1548, fourteen years after that sad day his brother Bishop Bartolomeo and his beloved cat Meo had died. He left all the family property to his eldest son, Fulvio. After Fulvio, other generations followed before Tito felt the call to come back to life for a new mission.

Fulvio, Giovanni's son, had only two children, a boy and a girl. Perhaps he had been traumatized by having been the eldest of ten children. He named his son after his father, calling him Giovanni, while his daughter was named Angela. The following generations had, as progenitors, Fabrizio (Fulvio's grandson), another Giovanni, and finally Ubaldo, who in 1699 married Vittoria, a much younger girl from another important Amelian family, the Cansacchis. They had a difficult marriage, not due to problems between themselves but because of the loss of most of their children at a young age. They had nine children, to eight of whom they gave a double name. Their eldest daughter was Felice Idea ("Happy Idea"), followed by Gian Lorenzo, Bartolomeo Carlo, Maria Paola, Pietro Paolo, Anna Virginia, Anna Plantilla, and Giuseppe Angelo. The last born, perhaps due to Ubaldo and Vittoria's tiredness, was just named Francesco.

Of the nine sons and daughters, only three lived beyond five years of age. The other six all died during their infancy. The three survivors were Felice Idea, Maria Paola, and Francesco, the youngest.

Ubaldo died when Francesco was only one year old. His wife, Vittoria, completely devoted her life to the education of her only surviving son. She was well aware of her responsibility toward her husband's family to secure the Farrattini dynasty. She was overprotective of Francesco and did not initially receive any help from other family members. (Although her husband's younger brother was still alive, he was not really helpful.)

Because of her focus on Francesco, Vittoria did not pay too

much attention to her two daughters. Her only goal was to find good husbands for them and to do it quickly. That was not an easy task, especially with the eldest, Felice Idea.

In 1722, a young girl could not oppose her parents' will. Despite her name, Giovanni's descendant Felice Idea was not facing a very happy future. That young woman, born with a rebellious soul, did everything she could to free herself from the restrictions then governing education, which were decidedly archaic. The new Enlightenment and liberal ideas that were spreading throughout Europe found in her a strong advocate. Her mother regretted the name chosen for her eldest child. It was, in fact, not a happy idea to try to impose her will on Felice Idea.

Tito's Return

Nearly two centuries had passed since Tito's last departure.

After her husband's death, Vittoria stayed in the family *palazzo* with her three surviving children. She knew she had to overcome any weakness and find the strength to manage the family's substantial finances until her son was old enough to take over control of family affairs. She dedicated herself completely to Francesco, seeking out the best tutors to give him an education and knowledge base that would be worthy of his ancestors.

For her younger daughter Maria Paola, she managed to arrange a marriage with Gaetano Sandri, the heir of another well-known Amelian family, the Sandris. Vittoria and Gaetano's father made the decision about their children's marriage without the two young people having the chance to say a word about it. They did not even know each other before they had to walk down the aisle to say, "I do."

It had been easier for Vittoria to marry off her younger daughter first since Maria Paola was quieter and more docile. Knowing the rebellious character of her eldest daughter, she knew she needed more time to find a suitable husband for her, one Felice Idea could not refuse. That would not be an easy business.

On her sister's wedding day, Felice Idea tried to convince her to rebel against this arranged marriage. She was helping Maria Paola do her hair for the ceremony, and she was not keeping her opinions to herself. "Sister, you still have time to say 'no'! How can you marry somebody you have just talked to a few times? I could never do such a thing!"

"My dear sister, how can I rebel against our mother's will? Since our father died, she has had too many responsibilities, and I do not want to give her any more new concerns."

"Yes, but then it is you who has to live with that man, not her! And what if he is boring and unkind? I will only marry a man I want to!"

"I would not count on that too much, sister! Now that Mother has arranged my marriage, her next thought will be to find a husband for you, too

"It would be better to go into a convent!"

"You? A convent? They would kick you out after just one day!"

Felice Idea made the sign of the cross in a funny and disrespectful way, and then she laughed and embraced her sister. They left the room to go to the cathedral, which was already decorated with plenty of flowers to celebrate the union of the two families.

Maria Paola knew very well that their mother was already in contact with a prominent family from Orvieto about a possible marriage arrangement for her sister, but she did not have the courage to confess this fact to Felice Idea, at least not on the day she was getting married.

In fact, about five months passed before Vittoria summoned Felice Idea into her bedroom to tell her that in two months, she would marry Count Reginaldo Montemarte from Orvieto.

"That is out of the question, Mother! I will never marry a man I do not love or even know!"

"You will obey me! He is the heir to a rich and powerful family. They have a beautiful *palazzo* in Orvieto, and he will be able to offer you a comfortable and quiet life!"

"Mother, I would rather become a nun!"

Felice Idea's mother knew her daughter would never be able to endure a convent life. She knew her daughter very well and did not plan to give her any choice. She dismissed her daughter with no sympathetic words, just repeating that everything was already arranged.

Felice Idea left the room in tears. Before slamming the door, she screamed, "If Father were still alive, he would never have done something like this to me!"

She ran to the garden and sat under the hackberry tree her grandfather had planted many years before. She used to go there to read on hot summer days to enjoy its shade. Felice Idea knew her father had been a very just man and very much in love with his wife. He had chosen Vittoria, and despite the great sorrow they went through together at the loss of six of their children, he had always stood beside his wife and never stopped loving her, just as he had loved his daughters. Felice Idea was twelve when he died, and she never got over his death. She was certain he would never have forced her into a marriage she did not want.

With her head lowered between her knees, her sobbing echoed in the silence of that late afternoon. She evoked her father's name, begging him to please make her mother change her mind. She felt a light pressure on her dress that made her raise her head. She saw the sweet and expressive little face of a cat staring at her. The cat let out a soft and comforting "meow" and hopped onto her lap, settling into the hollow space between her raised knees and her chest.

Tito had been back in his beloved valley for only a few months and had immediately started to examine the changes that had occurred since his last incarnation and also to seek out his new mission.

As Tito began rubbing his head against the chin of the sad young girl, his whiskers started to vibrate. He had no doubt about the young woman's heritage. By now, Tito had acquired considerable familiarity with humans, and he knew it was useless for him to waste time on preliminaries. He might as well just throw himself deeply into his new mission of saving this unhappy girl.

Tito began to purr loudly, kneading Felice Idea's lap with his claws as he had done until a short while before on his mother's teats. He knew no one could resist the soothing power of his purring. He did not give the girl time to react.

The cat's arrival was so brazen that Felice Idea hugged him

close to her chest, still sobbing, welcoming him, convinced her father had sent the cat to her. She did not believe it was just a coincidence that Tito had shown up just when she was calling to her father for help. She stopped crying, and a thin smile appeared on her face due to the energetic affection and sympathy Tito was offering her. Felice Idea got up while still holding Tito in her arms and walked back into the house, going directly into her bedroom.

Re-entering that *palazzo* after such a long time, a *palazzo* he had seen being built, gave Tito a strange feeling. He looked around at the many changes and the new furniture that had been added. Felice Idea's bedroom was the one Bishop Bartolomeo had used as his own the few times he had the opportunity to sleep in the house he had so strongly wanted.

Felice Idea sank onto her bed, and Tito immediately lay on his back to be cuddled and thus distract her from her sadness. He looked at her with his hypnotic eyes, purring to make her relax.

"My father sent you, did he not?" she asked him, caressing that silky, dense, and startlingly white fur on his belly.

He answered her with soft meows that seemed to say, "Do not worry; I am here now. You do not have to get upset."

Somebody knocked on the door, and Felice Idea asked who it was.

"Your brother! May I come in?" Francesco was eleven years younger than Felice Idea and, however spoiled, he was very close to his sisters. Now that Maria Paola had left the *palazzo* to live with her husband, he was sad at the thought that Felice Idea would also soon get married and leave. Francisco would remain in the *palazzo* alone with his mother. Even though he loved his mother very much, he sometimes felt oppressed by her constant attention. Approaching Felice Idea's bed, he immediately asked about the cat that was lying on it like it was his own.

"I found him in the garden. Well, it is actually correct to say that he found me."

"Sister, you have been crying. What happened?"

"Mother wants to force me to get married to someone I do not even know. At least Maria Paola's husband is from Amelia, and she had seen him a few times before their wedding. Why should I have to marry someone from Orvieto whom I have never even seen or met? I was just now praying, asking Father to help me change Mother's mind when this cat literally threw himself into my lap. I am sure Father sent him!"

"He is beautiful, and his fur is so soft…. Can I hold him?"

As soon as Francesco held Tito on his lap, Tito's whiskers again started to vibrate. He knew then that both these humans belonged to the same lineage he had known during all his past lives. He was in the right place. Tito just had to figure out which of the two was his next mission.

Francesco, still caressing Tito's fur, said, "You know Mother will not be happy about having a cat in the house."

"What difference does it make? In a couple of months, I will not be here anyway!" She ended that sentence with a lump in her throat. "I will take him with me, and in the meantime I will keep him here in my room."

"Have you named him yet?"

As soon as he heard that, Tito freed himself from Francesco's hands and stared straight into Felice Idea's eyes. He tried to convey his thoughts in a different way this time. Slowly he spelled out in his mind the four letters of his name, trying to send her a subliminal message telepathically. *T… I… T… O.*

Felice Idea remained silent for a few moments, then said, "I think I will call him 'Ubi' in memory of our father, Ubaldo."

Tito, resigned, crouched down again on the white linen sheets. As Francesco continued to caress him, he again thought, *What is the matter with this family to always choose these ridiculous names? First Meo, now Ubi!* At least now Tito/Ubi knew Felice Idea was the one he had to concentrate on.

Meeting Reginaldo

Two weeks after the wedding announcement, Vittoria told her daughter that her future husband was coming from Orvieto for a visit. He would stay in Amelia for two days to get acquainted and organize the wedding. She asked her daughter to be reasonable, to make both her mother and father proud, but mostly to behave like the young, educated lady her rank required. Above all, she asked Felice Idea to get rid of that cat that was no good for anything except spreading his fur on her dresses.

"Mother, you are imposing a husband on me. At least let me keep my cat! He has done nothing wrong, and he will help me bear the demands of your will. I will never get rid of him!"

"At least promise me you will leave him in your room when Count Reginaldo is here. I do not want that cat jumping around on everything, leaving cat hair everywhere, and making the Count think we are not clean and tidy people!"

On the day of Reginaldo's arrival, everyone was nervous. A table with rich food had been set up in the ballroom. Only a few guests had been invited to this first encounter. Maria Paola arrived with her husband Gaetano and his parents, along with Fabrizio, the brother of Vittoria's deceased husband.

Felice Idea lingered in her bedroom, looking at the new dress ordered especially for this occasion. Made of a lovely blue taffeta, it was lying on the bed, its skirt raised on the sides by two pads sewn into the accompanying underskirt. The beautiful bodice was adorned with elaborate laces, and puffed sleeves trailed down over the sides of the skirt. Next to it Felice Idea had laid out the dress she preferred: a simple, everyday, cream-colored dress with no laces or flounces.

She turned to Ubi and asked him, "Which one do you think I should wear? The blue one seems to me a bit too formal for a lunch, don't you think?"

Ubi jumped down from the armchair and up onto the bed. He took a few steps on the blue dress and then laid down on the cream-colored one, looking at her like he was saying, "This one! Wear this one!"

She also noticed the many cat hairs he had left on the blue one. She tried to brush them off, but they were stuck like glue to the fabric. Flounces, laces, and taffeta seemed to have a magnetic effect on his fur. The cat hair could clearly be seen everywhere on the skirt and bodice of the blue dress. The cream-colored dress had just as many cat hairs, but those were less visible.

Felice Idea put on the cream-colored dress and did not spend very much time on her makeup, nor did she wear her white wig. She just combed her hair into a very simple style. She wanted to look a little plain so as not to impress her betrothed, thus deluding herself that he would refuse to marry her.

When she finally entered the ballroom, Vittoria glared at her. Approaching Felice Idea, Vittoria whispered with not-very-hidden rage, "Could you not have put a little more effort into it? You look like a maid!" Then, turning to her noble guest, she forced herself into hiding her disappointment and pasted on a smile. "Count Reginaldo, may I introduce to you my daughter, Countess Felice Idea?" She moved sideways to allow the betrothed couple to get close to each other.

When he stretched out his arm to bow and kiss her hand, Felice Idea saw Reginaldo for the first time. The tight corset she wore was already limiting her breath, and now, seeing him, she almost stopped breathing entirely. He was not an ugly man, but he was at least ten years older than she was, a few inches shorter, definitely overweight, and she had the distinct impression that under his white wig he must be completely bald. He kissed her hand very elegantly while she leaned forward in a slight bow. She realized her plan would not work. Although she had not made any effort to improve her appearance, next to this little man she looked like a goddess.

At lunch they were seated next to each other but hardly ever exchanged a word. Despite Reginaldo's looks, which did not impress her, she had to admit he was a very kind and polite man. Most of the time he spoke with Maria Paola, who was seated opposite to him, to the point that Vittoria had to reprove her second daughter about monopolizing the conversation and preventing her sister from talking to her betrothed.

"Maria Paola! You are very talkative today! Allow Count Reginaldo to become acquainted with your sister."

Perhaps due to deep embarrassment or shyness, Reginaldo continued to talk to Maria Paola about books and poems they both had read.

For a moment Vittoria had the feeling she had made a mistake in assessing her daughters' affinities with the husbands she had chosen for them. Never having met Reginaldo before, she had not had a chance to ascertain whether he was intellectually closer to her second daughter's interests than to her eldest's. Vittoria realized Felice Idea might have been better suited to Gaetano, who had probably never taken a book in his hands, or at least not after finishing his education. Vittoria shelved that thought immediately, trying to think of any possible topic that might interest both Reginaldo and her daughter.

After an hour of delicious food and good Farrattini wine, the Count started sneezing and shedding tears. Worried, Vittoria asked if something in the food might have bothered him.

"No, Countess, not at all. Everything was delicious." He paused for a moment, then looked around the room and asked, "Is there a cat in the room? Cat fur does this to me, but I cannot see any cat here."

Felice Idea raised her napkin to her mouth to cover an impulsive laugh, then raised her eyes to the ceiling, whispering, "Thank you, Father!" Her dress was certainly covered in Ubi's fur. She had held him close to her heart before leaving her room, and, sitting next to her betrothed, the cat hair on her dress must have reached Reginaldo and caused his allergic reaction.

Vittoria stated categorically that there was no cat in the ballroom. She then glared at her daughter with an even more penetrating look of reproach.

Innocently, Francesco exclaimed, "Not here in the ballroom, but in her bedroom she has her cat!"

Reginaldo turned to her with his watering eyes and, between two sneezes, said, "My sweet bride-to-be, there will not be a place for a cat in my house. As you can see, I cannot bear it!"

Felice Idea immediately rose to the occasion and replied, "Then there will be no wedding. I am not getting rid of my cat. Father sent him to me, and I cannot live without him!"

Vittoria, who was by then incredibly annoyed with her daughter, tried to calm the situation by saying, "Do not worry, Count Reginaldo, that cat will stay here. He will not go to your house. Am I right, Felice Idea?"

"Mother, I told you! I will never part from Ubi!"

"*Ubi*! Oh, Lord! You did not name that cat after your father! Do you not have any respect?" Vittoria realized she had lost her temper and tried to calm down. She smiled at the Count and invited him into the adjacent sitting room for a cordial, hoping the drink would alleviate his allergic reaction.

After saying goodbye to her guests later that day, Vittoria was furious. She locked herself and her daughter in her daughter's bedroom, scolding her repeatedly. She yelled at Felice Idea that, despite being twenty-three years old, she was just an irresponsible, spoiled little girl who did not understand the importance of such a delicate situation.

"But Mother! Did you see him?" she tried to defend herself. "He looks like he could be my grandfather! He is short and fat! What ugly children I will have with such a husband!"

Resigned and exhausted after the long luncheon, Vittoria collapsed into an armchair. With a slight tremor in her voice, she let herself say, "Perhaps I will have to agree with you on that point." She remained silent for a moment, then chuckled and added, "Short, fat, and bald!"

"Exactly, Mother!" Felice Idea replied with a laugh. She began to walk around the room, bending her knees and imitating Reginaldo's belly with her arms.

Taking advantage of the humorous moment, Ubi jumped on Vittoria's lap. It was the perfect time to try to win her over with his charm. At first, she was surprised to have him on her lap, but still smiling from Felice Idea's imitation of Reginaldo, she started to caress him. To further win her over and help Vittoria maintain the fragile calm that had descended on the room, Ubi started purring.

"Daughter, we named you Felice Idea, but you did not really have a happy idea when you brought this young gentleman into your life!"

As had been true over the years with many other people, even her mother, every now and then, found a way to be sarcastic about her name, and this annoyed Felice Idea very much. But it was not the right moment to reproach her mother about her sarcasm or her atrocious choice of a name. Instead, Felice Idea said, "But Mother! Look how sweet he is! I am sure Father sent him to me to convince you not to make me marry Reginaldo.”

Vittoria just sighed and, still caressing the cat’s soft fur, told her daughter, “Felice Idea, my decision is made. Please do not make my life more difficult than it already is.” She stood up, letting Ubi jump on the floor. “Please get rid of this cat.” She left the room without giving her daughter time to reply.

The wedding plans did not change. Felice Idea’s marriage was confirmed for the end of September, and after long discussions the only concession Felice Idea could win was permission to bring Ubi with her to Orvieto, under a few strict conditions imposed by Reginaldo: Ubi could never go to the upper floor of Montemarte *palazzo*. He would live in a room on the ground floor, where she could visit him, or he could go out in the garden. She would have to change clothes before going upstairs so as not to bring along any fur into the family rooms.

With this concession, Reginaldo made himself appear very accommodating since he was agreeing to risk a few sneezes. *A cat is not eternal*, he thought. *Cats do run away, or they can be victims of accidents.* He did not tell Felice Idea that he kept two ferocious guard dogs in his garden that would put the cat on the run very quickly, if not kill him.

The Wedding Day

Felice Idea’s wedding day came sooner than she could ever have imagined. Maria Paola helped her sister put on her beautiful white wedding dress, telling her that she was growing attached to her own husband and that Felice Idea would, too. But Felice Idea was not happy. This day should be a day to remember all her life, a day of joy. As it was, she would prefer to run down to the stables, jump on a horse, and flee.

Before descending the staircase to go to the cathedral, she remained alone with Ubi for a few minutes. She held him close to her heart and spoke to him softly. He rubbed his head on her chin, keeping his paws on her chest. He was trying to show his affection and give her courage… and leave lots of cat hair on her dress. She kissed him and locked him in the room before going downstairs and walking with the others toward the church.

As soon as Felice Idea arrived, Vittoria, who had a wet cloth and a brush in her hands, quickly tried to clean away every single hair she knew would be on Felice Idea's dress. Vittoria double-checked very carefully to ensure that the dress was perfectly free of cat hair, and then she walked together with Felice Idea to the family chapel.

Uncle Fabrizio walked the bride down the short chapel aisle. Reginaldo kept his distance from her for the entire ceremony, approaching her only when they had to exchange rings and for their kiss. He did not want to start sneezing in front of all the guests. Despite his efforts to keep his distance, after an hour, his eyes had started to get red and tear up, although not too badly.

United in marriage, they turned around and walked together down the aisle to leave the church. As they passed, the numerous guests threw rose petals at them. About halfway down the aisle, Felice Idea saw on her right a handsome young man smiling at her. As she passed by close to him, the young man whispered, "For the most beautiful bride!" before extending his arms up high to drop a substantial handful of rose petals that fell on her veil from above. She answered with a soft smile and went on.

The wedding banquet was held in the large ballroom of the Farrattini *Palazzo,* where large tables covered with gorgeous pink table-cloths were decorated with sumptuous bouquets of white and pink roses. The lunch was most exquisite and included a large selection of the best traditional Umbrian dishes, including roasted marinated game with truffle sauce and various fried vegetables, plus a selection of dishes from the newly imported French style of cuisine and products that had arrived from America. Their neighbors, the Geraldinis, had offered one of their turkeys as a gift for the wedding feast. All the guests particularly praised the consommé.

For most of the banquet, Felice Idea almost forgot what they were celebrating. It was an enjoyable party with many very dear friends and relatives present. She hardly spoke to her new husband, and she tried not to think about the fact that soon everybody would leave, and she would enter a carriage and go toward her new home and her new life. Saddened by this thought, she chased it away whenever it entered her head.

The musicians started to play, and their music helped her not to think. A few couples gathered in the center of the large ballroom to dance minuets and gavottes. In the cheerful noise of the numerous guests, many with several glasses of wine in their bellies, Felice Idea's eyes met those of the young man she had seen in the cathedral. He was seated on the other side of the room, but she could see his gorgeous smile and how handsome he was.

She stood up and went to ask her sister, Maria Paola, if she knew who he was.

"His name is Girolamo Benedettoni. He comes from Todi. It seems he is a descendant of Jacopone Da Todi's family."

"And who is this Jacopone?"

"Sister! If you had paid more attention to your studies and the books I gave you, you would remember that Jacopone Da Todi was a monk but also a poet and a philosopher who lived more than four centuries ago. I gave you his books that include his prayers."

"Yes, of course, I remember now. And why is Girolamo here? Who invited him?"

"I think his family has business interests in common with Reginaldo. Well, your husband, he invited him."

Girolamo felt the attention of the two sisters. He raised his glass in their direction, smiling with a bit of irony. Feeling a hint of embarrassment, the two sisters parted.

Girolamo got up and walked straight to the young bride. He bowed and held out his hand, inviting her to dance. They joined the other couples in a minuet, and, during the graceful, choreographed, typical courtship steps of that dance, they alternately walked away from and then returned to each other and held hands.

Once, when they were close to each other, he spoke to her. "Your name arouses my curiosity, Countess!" The dance separated them. When they were close together again, he added, "And you, too, I must admit."

"I am afraid you will have to ask my mother about my name," she replied without having the courage to look him in the eyes.

At one point in the dance, when the man should look down while bowing, Girolamo lowered his shoulders but kept his head up so he could observe. He whispered, "And to find out about you, whom should I ask?"

Felice Idea froze as she was making her own bow, unable to find an answer that would prevent that moment from becoming even more embarrassing. What a terrible twist of fate to meet a handsome, gallant man from a noble family right on the day she got married to another man she did not love.

While the other couples continued to dance, she felt all the other guests' eyes on her, observing her to see her reaction to that man. She had to escape from that utterly uncomfortable situation. The only excuse she could think of was to tell him she had to check on her cat, who was probably scared by all the noise. She rose and offered Girolamo an apology, giving her cat as the excuse for leaving.

Before she could leave, he had the time to say, "I adore cats! I think they are the most sensitive animals!"

Amazed by that statement, Felice Idea turned to make her escape. She needed to leave the room immediately so as not to reveal her blushes.

She closed her bedroom door behind her, and Ubi ran to her. She grabbed him and held him tenderly. Her eyes shed bitter tears while she told her cat about that young man, asking herself why she had not met Girolamo before. She was a married woman now with no chance to escape a cruel future.

Meanwhile, Vittoria looked around the ballroom and, not seeing her daughter in the room, sent Francesco to look for her. Francesco found Felice Idea in her bedroom and told his sister their mother wanted her back in the ballroom since a few guests had started to leave the banquet.

Felice Idea wiped away her tears and went back to the ballroom. She looked around but could not see Girolamo anywhere. She asked her sister about him, and Maria Paola told her he had already left. Felice Idea was saddened but also glad he had gone. She would have liked to talk to him a bit more, but with him gone, she could avoid any more personal questions.

The inevitable moment for the newly married couple's departure arrived. Two carriages were waiting in the little square in front of the *palazzo*. Reginaldo walked toward the first one to open the door and hand Felice Idea in. Holding Ubi in her arms, she instead headed to the second one. Without giving Reginaldo time to say anything, she told him it would be better to travel in separate carriages. She would see him in Orvieto. Reginaldo got in the first carriage and closed the door.

Alone throughout that journey, she could not hold back her tears. For the first time in her life, she was leaving Amelia, her family, and the home in which she had been born. She watched the trees parading by along the road, wondering when she would see them again. Ubi sat on her lap, scared by the jolts of the noisy carriage. She hugged him and tried to reassure him. From now on, they would be alone and only able to count on each other.

Felice Idea and Ubi's New Life in Orvieto

They arrived late in Orvieto. The first thing she wanted to see was the room assigned to her cat.

Ubi was bewildered by the new home and by smells he had never breathed before. In all his previous lives, he had never left his valley. His senses were completely disoriented. Certainly, the constant barking of the two big dogs out in the garden did not help.

Felice Idea tried to calm Ubi down, and when Reginaldo came to accompany her upstairs, she asked him for some patience. She said that she could not leave Ubi alone; he was too scared.

"You want to leave your husband alone on our wedding night?" he inquired with disbelief.

"Dear husband, please try to understand. It is not just about him. I am very tired—from the wedding, the banquet, the journey, the new home. You are a kind and understanding man. Give me some time. We have to get to know each other better."

Before he could answer, he pulled out a handkerchief and started to sneeze repeatedly. He was unable to finish a single sentence without having a sneeze in the middle. "As you desire," he replied, and sneezed again. "I will see you tomorrow then." Another sneeze erupted. "Have a good night." He walked upstairs, still sneezing, with each sneeze sounding like a firework explosion in the vaulted staircase.

With the help of the Montemarte housekeeper, Felice Idea tried to create a better environment for her Ubi. Since the cat was supposed to be confined in that room, she had to prevent any possibility of him escaping to the courtyard where those two ferocious dogs would, at best, chase him. In the cellars, she found a large drawer from an almost destroyed old armoire. She had it brought to his room and filled it with soil. She planted a few seedlings and grass in it to allow Ubi to have at least some contact with nature and also to have a place where he could do his private business. She stayed with him as much as she could to help him get acquainted with his new environment.

After three days, even the understanding Reginaldo showed impatience. The night inevitably came when she was out of excuses and had to follow him upstairs. Before she left Ubi's room, she made sure Ubi was calm and locked in his room. She entered their bridal bedroom for the first time.

Their first night together was not one of the best nights she had ever had. She felt excruciating pain. Even though her sister had tried to prepare her by telling her what was going to happen, Maria Paola could not prevent the pain. As for the rest, it was like Maria Paola had described to her. The only difference was that when he was finished, instead of falling asleep, he started to sneeze, cursing poor Ubi and cursing her for being guilty of not understanding how unhealthy cat hair was for him. Reginaldo ended up collapsing into a heavy sleep. Felice Idea turned away from him to hide her tears. Her only wish was to hug her Ubi.

Eventually, the couple reached a compromise. She would sleep in Ubi's room for three nights in a row and then the three nights upstairs with him, but only after taking a thorough bath to remove every possible cat hair. The young bride had a wardrobe with clothes for downstairs and a separate armoire with a different set of clothes for upstairs. She had to try in every possible way to keep her husband from any possible contact with Ubi's fur.

One day Felice Idea found Reginaldo trying to get into the room downstairs where the poor little prisoner was held. She suspected

Reginaldo wanted to let Ubi out into the courtyard. Reginaldo gave a strong grunt of anger when he realized she had had the lock changed and nobody but her could open that door.

Their Second Meeting

A few months after she had settled into her new home in Orvieto, Girolamo reappeared in her life. Reginaldo had invited him to their home to discuss some business matters. Seeing Girolamo again was hard for Felice Idea. She had thought of him several times but just as a distant, pleasant memory. Having him right there in front of her made her realize how deep her attraction to him was.

And the feeling was entirely mutual. After greeting her, Girolamo asked her how her cat was. She told him Ubi had to be kept as a prisoner in his room. She explained the situation with the dogs and her fear that Ubi would suffer from not being able to enjoy his freedom. Girolamo asked if he could visit Ubi. He told her he was a cat expert and would know if Ubi was suffering so that she could be reassured about his condition. They took their leave from Reginaldo, who was busy with two of his staff preparing some accounting for Girolamo.

Felice Idea took a key from a small purse she kept hidden under her skirt. When she opened the door, Ubi immediately ran toward them, meowing loudly.

Girolamo took Ubi in his arms and rubbed his little head with his cheeks. "It is a way to calm cats down," he explained.

"So, it is true that you are a cat expert! And there was me thinking…"

"That it was just an excuse to be alone with you?" he interrupted. With Ubi still in his arms, he approached her and stole an unexpected kiss she could not refuse.

Ubi understood he had to jump down and leave them free to kiss and hug each other.

She was petrified but pleasantly surprised.

"Felice Idea, I have been waiting for this moment since I saw you walk down the aisle to the altar. I should have stopped your wedding right then, but I thought it would not be… a *happy idea*!” he said, emphasizing those two words with subtle irony that made her smile. “I am sorry to have to tell you that I cannot get used to this name of yours. Mostly because it does not suit you. I can see you are not happy at all. It is true that you are free to leave this room, but even so, you are more of a prisoner than your cat.”

“I know. But it is my name. I cannot do anything about it.”

Girolamo began to repeat the name “Felice Idea… Felice Idea… ” He paused for a moment, making a hissing sound with his lips, and suddenly it came to him, and he said, “Fidea! Of course! That is what I will call you. For me, from now on, you will be Fidea!”

She had the abrupt feeling she had been born for a second time into a totally new person, a person who wanted to run away with him. Reality quickly took over. “Thank you, Girolamo. I like it very much. But what can I do? I am a married woman. We must return to Reginaldo’s office before he asks about us.”

“But I want to talk to you, I want to see you, I want to kiss you. We have to find a way to communicate.”

“It is impossible, Girolamo. We cannot! Please do not insist.” She tried to keep a certain dignity. They left the room, and she locked the door to be sure Ubi would not sneak out.

Re-entering the room where Reginaldo was still busy working with his staff on his business papers, to avoid making him suspicious, Girolamo said aloud, “Countess Montemarte, you can be reassured, your cat is in excellent health. Yes, he should have more freedom, but he will be all right.”

“Thank you, Girolamo. Your words are such a comfort to me.”

They bowed to each other. Felice Idea instantly wanted to tell everyone in that room about her new name. Girolamo had correctly identified the problem. That horrible name did not suit her anymore. However, she decided to keep it a secret—at least for now.

Reginaldo escorted his friend to the door, confirming they needed to meet again the following week.

Walking across the courtyard to reach his horse, Girolamo paused for a moment, staring at the huge Cedar of Lebanon tree covering the entire courtyard with its long branches. The branches touched the boundary wall on one side of the courtyard, and on the other side, they reached the window of Ubi's room. He suddenly had a "happy idea" and started to count the days until he would see Fidea again and be able to tell her his plan.

When he returned to Orvieto, after discussing business with Reginaldo, Girolamo asked Fidea how Ubi was coping and if he could see him again. He knew Reginaldo would never follow them into that room. There, they could be sure they would be able to spend some time alone. As soon as Felice Idea closed the door behind them, they passionately embraced and kissed.

"Fidea, I keep thinking about you. I cannot accept that you are wasting your life with a man you do not love."

"Girolamo, I have never felt for anyone what I feel for you! But we have no future."

"But I need to talk to you. I need to know what you are thinking, and I need to tell you how much I love you!"

"Please do not insist. We must accept there is no chance for us!"

"Listen to me. I had an idea… " He stopped talking for a moment. "A very happy one!" He enjoyed teasing her, to amuse her. "It will work, believe me. Ubi will be our messenger!"

Hearing his name brought into the conversation, Ubi sharpened his ears and began to listen carefully to his humans.

"If we can teach him to climb the branches of the tree from this window, he can reach the boundary wall on the other side. We will tie letters we write to each other around his neck with a leather thong. Nobody will know we are exchanging letters. We will have the chance to be close, at least with our words."

"No, Girolamo, it is too risky. I do not trust sending Ubi outside with those horrible dogs. And how will I know you are there?"

"I will hoot like an owl. When you hear it, it will mean I am there."

It was a decidedly risky plan, but the only one that might work for them. They kissed once more. Girolamo then ran out to take his leave from Reginaldo and return to Todi.

It was very easy to teach Ubi to walk along those branches to reach the courtyard wall from the house. He immediately understood what to do, and with Fidea's letter tied to his neck he walked along the branch nearest the window toward the trunk of the immense tree to continue on the other side as far as the wall. Girolamo waited, standing on the saddle of his horse to reach the top of the courtyard wall. He caressed Ubi and exchanged her letter for one of his own.

At every exchange of letters, the dogs barked at Ubi, who really enjoyed taunting them. He often stopped to sharpen his claws on the big trunk. Every time he did so, a few pieces of tree bark fell on the dogs' heads, making them even more ferocious because of this insult.

The plan hatched by the two lovers worked for several months. The "furry messenger" began to recognize Girolamo's signal and ran to the window, waiting for Fidea to tie her letter to his neck so that he could go out on his mission. Not bothered by the two dogs, Ubi went back and forth carrying their letters.

Fidea kept Girolamo's letters hidden under the mattress in Ubi's room. She was sure Reginaldo would never go into that room. On the nights she was sleeping downstairs, she often took them out to read over and over again. They were full of love, making her sad and happy simultaneously since they expressed a love she would never be able to enjoy. In some letters he was sweet, tender, and exhibited his immense desire for her. In others he vented his frustration, wishing that Reginaldo would die so that they could be together.

When she received that kind of letter, Fidea tried to stop the correspondence, asking him not to write to her anymore. But the following letter would be so full of apologies and love that she could not help but continue.

Summer arrived, and windows were often left open to let in fresh air. For Ubi, it was time to add a little more cunning to their plan. He certainly did not want to spend his entire seventh life being a messenger! He had to act somehow. So, one night, after he had crossed over the courtyard to reach Girolamo, exchanged their letters, and returned to Fidea, he allowed himself a little more time on those branches. It was his only way to be outside in a safe environment.

Using the tree branches, he climbed to the upper floor and Reginaldo's room. He jumped on the windowsill, making sure nobody was around. He entered the room and went to rub against the armchair on Reginaldo's side of the bed, and on his side of the headboard, making sure he left just a few hairs so they would not be easily noticed. He repeated this surreptitious visit only on the nights when Fidea was sleeping downstairs so her husband could not blame her for his sneezing. The poor fellow could not understand why he sneezed more when he was alone than when she was there. He had the pillowcases changed every day, with no positive results. Even if he had wanted to, he could not have blamed Ubi for his allergy attacks.

Over the course of several weeks, an annoying cough began to accompany his sneezing. The doctor advised Reginaldo to spend a few days at the seaside since breathing the saltiness of the sea air would help clear his lungs.

Fidea took the opportunity to tell him she wanted to visit her family in Amelia. She had not seen them since her wedding. On the day of their departure, they exchanged goodbyes, each getting into their separate carriages, hers heading to Amelia and Reginaldo's to Tarquinia, the ancient Etruscan city which had become a holiday destination for many Umbrians.

But Fidea did not go directly to Amelia. She would not arrive there until the next day. She stopped in the small town of Bomarzo, where Girolamo had arranged a secret meeting. It had been difficult to convince her, but he overcame her initial resistance. Next to the Orsini family *palazzo*, he had discovered a discreet tavern with a few bedrooms for wayfarers. The owners loved to tell the legend that two centuries before then Pope Alexander VI (Rodrigo Borgia) used to go there to secretly meet his lover, Giulia Farnese. At the pope's suggestion she had married Prince Orsino Orsini.

It was the perfect place for Girolamo and Fidea to consummate their equally secret love. Girolamo joined her there, and they spent their first night together. Fidea, for the first time, discovered what it really meant to love somebody.

Before saying goodbye the next morning, they promised each other to meet there again as she made her way back to Orvieto, then Girolamo delivered a bag full of silver coins to the coachman to ensure his silence. She got into her carriage, still feeling his sweet embrace, but looking forward to returning to her family home.

As soon as they reached the walls of Amelia, Ubi began to meow so loudly that Fidea, amused by his excitement, struggled to keep him still. Once at the Farrattini *palazzo* he jumped out of the carriage and began to run in his garden and up and down the stairway of the *palazzo*. He was extremely happy to be back in his beloved valley. He now clearly understood his mission. The sooner he could achieve it, the sooner he could return home.

As soon as Vittoria saw her radiant daughter, she embraced her, believing that Felice Idea had come home to announce a pregnancy. She was too radiant *not* to be pregnant. Meanwhile, in her heart, Fidea thought it would be marvelous if she had conceived a child with Girolamo the night before. She was very careful not to reveal the secret reason for her happiness.

"No, Mother, I am not pregnant. Reginaldo left for the seaside for a few days, and I took the opportunity to come visit you."

"The seaside? And why did he go there alone? Why did you not go along, Felice Idea?"

"He went for those allergies he has. Recently he has also developed a bad cough. And, Mother, I have made an important decision. From now on, I do not want to be called "Felice Idea" anymore. Everybody, including you, must call me "Fidea." I am not a child anymore, and Felice Idea is no longer the right name for me."

"You are ridiculous!" her mother replied. She paused, then added, "Do not tell me he is sick because of that cat!"

"No, Mother, we have been very careful. And I am not joking. I want to be called Fidea."

How much she had missed her garden, her bedroom, her hometown! Orvieto was certainly a bigger city and could offer many more diversions to a beautiful young woman like herself, but returning to Amelia created a feeling of nostalgia she never would have expected.

Although she was very glad to be back home, during those few days in her childhood home, all her thoughts were concentrated on the night she would spend with Girolamo on her way back to Orvieto. She could not wait to leave.

They met again in that room where the overwhelming passion of Pope Borgia for the beautiful Giulia had been acted out so many times. Girolamo and Fidea, too, took full advantage of that second night together. They kissed, they hugged, and they had the most satisfying sex they could possibly have, all under the watchful eyes of Ubi, who slept on a chair. He did not want to disturb them by jumping on the bed. He was so glad to see his female human feeling such happiness, which, despite her name, she had never experienced before.

In the morning, Girolamo woke up before Fidea. He put on just his white linen shirt and sat down in the armchair at the side of the bed, resting his feet on the footboard. Ubi immediately jumped on his chest. Girolamo gently caressed him, looking sadly at Fidea, who was still asleep. Girolamo tried to fix her sleeping image in his mind, knowing that an occasion like this would not be repeated very soon.

When she woke up, Fidea saw that Girolamo had teary eyes and a sad expression. Ubi jumped down, and the two lovers embraced, declaring once again their love and their sadness at having to part. Girolamo took off his shirt, and they made love one more time.

After they got dressed, they went out to the little square where her carriage and his horse were waiting for them. It was a very sad goodbye. They had no idea when another chance like this would happen. After giving another bag of coins to the coachman, Girolamo stood in the middle of the road until the carriage disappeared behind the trees.

Although Reginaldo had always treated her with kindness and never with violence, with Girolamo she had discovered true pleasure. After that first night in Bomarzo, she would never again lie with her husband without regret and a touch of disgust.

The Unthinkable Happened

Upon his return to Orvieto, Reginaldo did not look well at all. His sneezing had subsided, but his cough got more congested. The doctor ordered him to rest and drink herbal and honey infusions. Ubi did not need to go to the upper floor to leave his hair to stimulate Reginaldo's allergies. The windows were now mostly closed, but Ubi's instinct told him that something more serious than a simple allergy was growing inside the man.

A month later, Reginaldo got a very high fever that seemed impossible to cure. He started to hallucinate, and at night, he could not sleep because of the unbearable burning feeling in his lungs. He had contracted tuberculosis. He died two months after he got back from Tarquinia, leaving Fidea a young widow at just twenty-five.

She was very sad about what had happened to her husband, who had tolerated the presence of her cat even with all the health problems the cat had caused him. Reginaldo had acknowledged before his death that he had had a much more serious health problem even before they met. After the funeral, Fidea decided to go back home to Amelia. She renounced her claim to any inheritance she was entitled to, leaving everything to Reginaldo's family. Fidea wanted to depart Orvieto as soon as she could and leave forever behind that sad part of her life.

Once home, her mother asked again if she was sure her husband had not died because of that cat.

"Mother, please! Stop with this nonsense! Poor Ubi had nothing to do with Reginaldo's death."

Vittoria could not resist remarking, with a mean smile, "Maybe Ubi gave him a little help?"

"Oh, Mother, I was not happy there, nor was Ubi. It was like both of us were in prison. Reginaldo's death was a miracle for both of us. I did not hate the poor man, but I was deeply unhappy."

Fidea and Girolamo exchanged only a few letters, respecting the traditional ten-month mourning period. After a year, they got engaged, and the wedding was celebrated in a very intimate and private ceremony as befitted a widow.

Vittoria asked them to stay with her in the *palazzo* in Amelia. Francesco was still underage, and she was starting to feel tired of all the responsibility that had been resting on her shoulders. She was also worried about leaving her son alone if anything should happen to her. Girolamo willingly accepted and also offered to join Vittoria in managing the Farrattini farms and products. Vittoria felt she was approaching the end of her days, and she was correct. Three years after the marriage between Fidea and Girolamo, Vittoria died in her bed after a short illness. She departed this world, glad to leave her son in the good hands of her daughter and son-in-law.

Fidea and Girolamo stayed with Francesco for two more years until he came of age, at which time Francesco became the legitimate heir to the title and family properties. After Francesco attained his majority, Girolamo continued to assist the younger man in managing the family farms, advising and supporting him.

Life in Amelia was decidedly happy for Fidea and Girolamo, even if they did not have children of their own. Ubi remained their greatest love, and the day his seventh life ended, he left them inconsolable. They never told anyone how he had helped them keep their love alive when they could not see each other. At least not until then. Once Ubi died, they began telling stories about how he defied the danger of crossing the courtyard with those two ferocious, barking dogs to exchange their letters for them.

When the time came to bury him, Fidea wished to place him in the crypt under the family chapel in the cathedral. It was not easy to convince the sacristan to lift a marble slab to allow the cat to be buried there. Girolamo convinced him by saying that for them Ubi had been more than a child. It also helped that Girolamo gave the sacristan a small bag of coins. At night and surreptitiously, they crept into the cathedral with a small wooden chest and, by candlelight, lowered it into the area under the marble slab at the bottom of the crypt, next to the coffins of other family members.

No one knew that Tito's sixth body was buried not far away. When he was called Meo, he had been buried next to Bishop Bartolomeo's corpse in that same chapel. And in the square just outside the church, his fifth body, when he was called Otto, had been buried at the foot of the civic tower.

At the end of this seventh life, back to being Tito, his soul resumed its ethereal form, waiting for the next call to reincarnate and continue to fulfill the prophecy of more than 2,700 years before. Amelia and the descendants of Hator and Khepri still needed him.

Chapter 8
The Restoration in Amelia
Year 1815 AD
Bat Rescues Sad Bartolomeo

Bartolomeo Farrattini (b. 1761), father of Francesco and Angelo Farrattini, and the grandfather of sad young Bartolomeo

Cast of Characters

Family Between the Chapters

Francesco Farrattini

Panunzia Poli: Francesco's wife

Bartolomeo: the oldest child of Francesco and Panunzia

Ubaldo: the second son of Francesco and Panunzia

Vittoria: the daughter of Francesco and Panunzia

Anna Geraldini: the wife of Bartolomeo and a descendant of Bishop
    Geraldini

Family at the Start of the Chapter

Francesco Farrattini: the elder surviving son of Bartolomeo and Anna;
    grandson of Francesco and Panunzia

Clementina Accarisi: the wife of Francesco

Ettore: the only child of Francesco and Clementina

Angelo: the second surviving son of Bartolomeo and Anna

Virginia Vettori: the first wife of Angelo

Bartolomeo: the son of Angelo and Virginia

Anna: the daughter of Angelo and Virginia

Caterina Fratini: the second wife of Angelo

Palmira Crocini: the third wife of Angelo

Tito/Bat: a cat

Other Amelians

Leondina: Angelo's housekeeper; the nanny for Bartolomeo

Ersilia: a maid for Francesco and Clementina

Architects

Stefano Cansacchi: designed the theater in Amelia

Gustavo Selva: Stefano's assistant

Historical Figures

Napoleon Bonaparte

Pope Pius VII: visited Narnia in 1805

Family at the End of the Chapter

Elena Nevi: the wife of Bartolomeo

Gilberto: the son of Bartolomeo and Elena

Gemma Claudia: the daughter of Bartolomeo and Elena

Zaffino: the son of Ettore

Tommaso: the grandson of Ettore

Ettore Bartolomeo: the son of Tommaso

Alessandro: the grandson of Tommaso

Fabrizio Pojani: the father of Plantilla

Plantilla Pojani: the daughter of Fabrizio; married Giovanni Farrattini
    in 1578

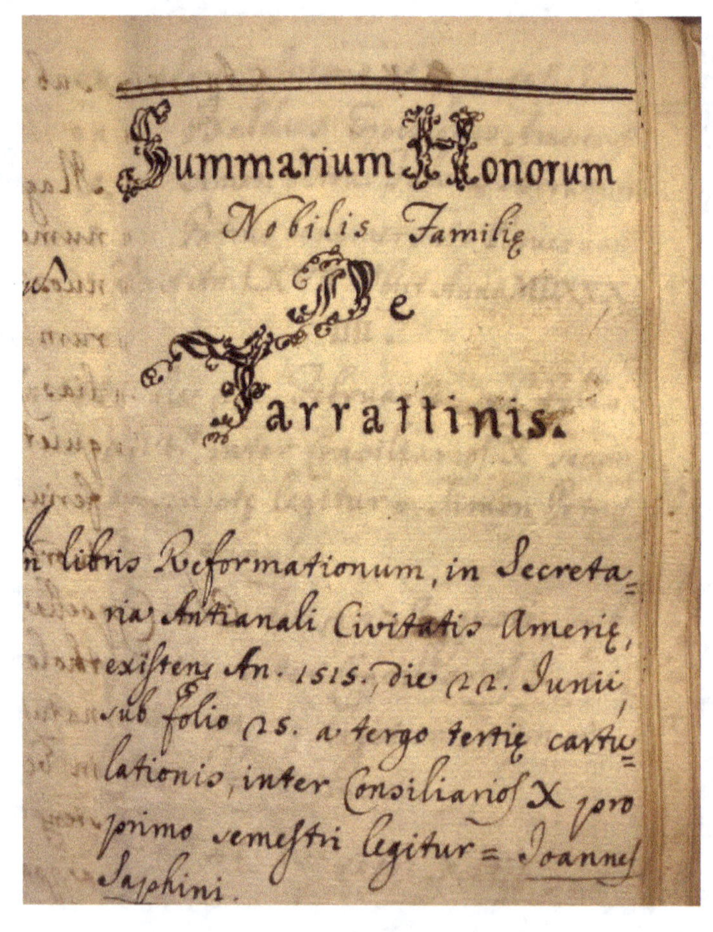

An ancient tome with information about the Farrattini family

Introduction

ABOUT A CENTURY passed before Tito's next reincarnation. Italy, previously mainly under Austro-Hungarian domination, was conquered by Napoleon Bonaparte. The French emperor quickly imposed his control over almost the entire peninsula, including the Vatican State.

In Amelia the new French laws replaced the pope's legislation. It was a rich but also uncertain period in history. Napoleon was most interested in imposing his reign over all of Europe. If he had stopped at some point at the territories he had already conquered, he might have reigned much longer. His constant desire to expand, in the end, cost him his throne.

After his fall, in 1815 the Congress of Vienna largely restored the former political order prevailing in the European continent, an order which Bonaparte had cast aside. Historically referred to as "The Restoration," this historical period saw the stark contrast between the supposed necessity to re-establish the pre-Napoleonic order and the new ideas that had been dramatically introduced to people by the French Revolution and Bonaparte himself.

At the end of the Congress, diplomats from all over Europe permitted very little of the new Napoleonic system to remain, restoring instead the pre-Napoleonic systems and institutions. While most of continental Europe was reunited under the German Confederation, Italy remained divided into many small states and duchies, nearly all under the control of the Habsburgs. Only the Vatican State and the Kingdom of the Two Sicilies kept their independence from the Germans and the Austro-Hungarians. And so Amelia was back under the pope's power, and the recent fresh air brought in by the brief French domination was completely swept away.

~

Under the guidance of his sister Fidea and her husband Girolamo, Francesco became the owner and excellent manager of the family properties. He married Panunzia Poli and had three children. He chose the recurrent family name Bartolomeo for his first child and then named the next two after his parents, Ubaldo and Vittoria.

The two brothers Bartolomeo and Ubaldo became very involved in Amelia's political and social life, and both were members of the Council of the Ten. Bartolomeo was also awarded the title of Knight of the Sacred Order of Santo Stefano. He loved arts and music. His passions led him to be one of the promoters of a notable initiative, undoubtedly the most important of the nineteenth century in Amelia. Together with other influential and wealthy families, the Farrattinis decided to build a theater. The project was entrusted to the architect Stefano Cansacchi and his young assistant Gustavo Selva. The latter treasured that experience to the point that he used this same project design to build the much bigger and more prestigious Theater La Fenice in Venice a few years later.

In 1805, Bartolomeo represented the citizens of Amelia in welcoming Pope Pius VII during his stop in Narnia while he was traveling back to Rome after Napoleon's coronation in Paris. That same year, Bartolomeo married Anna Geraldini, a descendant of the famous first bishop of the Americas. Together, they had seven children. Only two boys reached adulthood, and their chosen names were Francesco—Bartolomeo's father's name—and Angelo.

The two brothers had completely different characters and attitudes. Francesco was a rebel, and he loved nature and animals. He spent long days riding his horses in the countryside. His father was extremely disappointed in him. He did not see Francesco as the right heir to whom to pass along the vast family inheritance and responsibilities that, by tradition, were entrusted to the first-born son.

Tired of the persistent pressure from his father, Francesco removed himself from the line of inheritance. "Father, pass everything to Angelo. I just need a roof over my head, a good horse, and a small portion of our lands, just enough to survive. Leave everything else to my brother." Francesco moved out of the family *palazzo* and went to live in the old family home in the northern part of Amelia, leaving almost everything else to his brother Angelo.

Angelo was, in fact, an exceptionally good student. He

graduated first in law and then in theology. To Francesco, his brother was boring, a maniac about order, obsessive, and depressing. Francesco preferred to live in the open air and be in direct contact with nature. He spoke to his horses like they were humans and had an amicable relationship with his peasant workers. He treated them as his equals and had lunches with them on any and all possible occasions, such as during harvesting or threshing.

Angelo, on the other hand, was the classic authoritarian, an inflexible landlord who looked down on his workers. He was respected since he had never been unfair to them, but he was not as loved as his brother was.

Both brothers got married a few months apart. Francesco married Clementina Accarisi. They had one child, whom they named Ettore.

Angelo married Virginia Vettori. She gave birth to a son, and Angelo named him with the usual recurrent family name, Bartolomeo.

Francesco was very critical of his brother's choice of names. "With all the possible names available, you still chose Bartolomeo! Do you realize this will be the sixth or seventh Bartolomeo on the family tree? I wanted something new for my son's name, and there was not another Ettore in our family history!"

Angelo did not listen to him. He had inherited from his father a love of history and respect for the ancient customs and traditions. Although he was born four years after the conclusion of the Congress of Vienna, Angelo fully embodied the spirit of "Restoration" and remained a died-in-the-wool conservative. Francesco, on the other hand, was a son of the Revolution, open to the new and eager for freedom. He educated his son Ettore to love nature as much as he did.

After a second problematic pregnancy, Angelo's wife Virginia gave birth to a girl they named Anna, but neither Virginia nor Anna was in good health. In December 1860, the cold was intense, and there was no Christmas spirit in the house. On Christmas Eve, both mother and daughter got worse. Four days later, Virginia died, leaving Angelo in a deep depression and causing him to maintain a strict isolation away from everyone. After her death, he had a marble plaque engraved and placed on a wall in the family chapel. His last words for his wife were:

This prayer was not enough to save little Anna, who died a few months after her mother, increasing Angelo's pain and despair.

Meanwhile, Francesco and his son embarked on a special project in a grove located in one of Francesco's fields. They began to prune and shape the existing trees and plants to create a sort of labyrinth. They tied and cut the branches to turn them into arches and other shapes that resembled ancient Roman and Renaissance architecture. They planted many new trees in strategic positions to integrate with the existing ones.

The hedges became columns, branches were turned into arches, and using nature, they mimicked many more architectural forms. It was a project that bonded father and son deeply. It made Ettore a more serene and happy young man. He kept working on this project for many years, even after his father's death and up until his own death.

Ettore's cousin Bartolomeo did not have the same opportunities to work with his father. Tito heard the call to return to his valley to help this new Bartolomeo, another Farrattini with that name.

Sad Little Bartolomeo

Angelo's son Bartolomeo was not a lucky child. His mother, Virginia, died when she was just twenty-three years old, and he was only two. Bartolomeo certainly was too young to retain any fond memories of her.

Angelo, destroyed by his wife's loss, was not very affectionate with his son. His rigid, cold personality did not allow him to express his own suffering after his wife's death. To forget, he immersed himself in a large-scale project whose inspiration came to him following his own father's death. He decided to preserve his family's history, copying and collecting all the ancient documents present in the *palazzo* or in the city hall and ecclesiastical archives to which he could gain access.

In one of the rooms next to the ballroom, he had four long refectory tables placed against the walls and high shelving installed. In the center was his desk. In a very short time, those tables and shelves were filled with innumerable papers, letters, and documents of all kinds—contracts about buying and selling property, lists, maps, drawings, and lots of letters.

Angelo began cataloging the documents by date, subject, and ancestor to gather the most salient and significant ones in a volume that would retrace the most important events in his family's history. It became his obsession. He spent entire days locked in that room without realizing time was passing. For him, it was a remedy to overcome the loss of his young wife.

Every time he visited his brother, Francesco felt exasperated and remonstrated with him. "Angelo! Stop this nonsense! Enough of these old papers! Get out of this room, for heaven's sake! You are neglecting your son. When I visit, he is always with his nanny and never with you. Wake up!" he shouted, accompanying those last words with a quick gesture that sent a stack of papers flying all over the room.

Angelo kicked Francesco out of the *palazzo*, calling him superficial and irresponsible. "Go back to your little branches and your birds!" he yelled after him while Francesco was running down the staircase and then storming off on his horse. In his heart, Angelo knew his brother was right. He just could not find within himself the strength to express his feelings or offer the affection he wanted to give his son. Those emotions remained sealed inside of him.

Meanwhile, little Bartolomeo was growing up under the care of Leondina, the affectionate housekeeper and nanny who followed him as if he were her own son. She tried everything she could think of to make Angelo aware of his son's needs. She often took the lonely child into his father's room, but Angelo always had an excuse not to spend time with Bartolomeo. Leondina understood that the presence of his son only reminded Angelo of his dead wife.

Leondina and his uncle Francesco were the only sources of affection for sad little Bartolomeo. Francesco occasionally went to visit his nephew with his own son, Ettore, but the two cousins did not get along well. Like their fathers, they had completely opposite characters: one was always cheerful, vivacious, and overactive; the other was closed, unhappy, and melancholic. Ettore's exuberance intimidated his cousin, resulting in Bartolomeo withdrawing from any game they played together. He often ran away crying. Only Leondina's loving arms could calm him down.

On his sixth birthday, Bartolomeo was playing in the garden with his toy soldiers and some small bowling pins. He had learned how to play all by himself and retreated like a turtle when in contact with other children. In small garden alleyways covered in tiny gravel, Bartolomeo amused himself with his wooden bowling pins, and for hours, he would set them up and then knock them back down again and again, using a small wooden ball. He kept score of the points he made with little sticks he planted in the soft ground of the flowerbeds. While he was playing in the garden, Leondina was always nearby with her embroidery basket, darning a sock or sewing buttons back on.

A reincarnated Tito was also nearby, waiting for the right moment to make one of his memorable entrances. Back in his valley, Tito recognized his *palazzo* and its surroundings. After observing this lonely child for a few weeks, he wondered if Bartolomeo could be his new human. In fact, Tito was not very far from the big tree where he had first encountered the unhappy Fidea more than a century before. The only chance to know was to get close to the child's skin. He was certain that sooner or later, that little human would become his own.

He was not so sure about the nanny. He had to charm her before approaching the child whom he had to save from a miserable existence.

His experiences as a patient hunter and astute diplomat proved very useful in approaching the overprotective nanny. For days, he showed up only from a distance, just to get her used to his presence. He slowly began to creep closer, while keeping a safe distance. He stretched out in the sun, turning over on his back and repeatedly showing his soft belly with its thick white fur.

Finally, Leondina could no longer resist. She approached to caress him, and he immediately started his loud purring. The vibrations of his larynx passed through Leondina's skin and into her bones, instilling a hypnotic feeling of well-being. After a few encounters she began to bring him treats, and he started rubbing back and forth on her skirt. She was conquered and no longer a problem.

Tito sensed the young human was very timid and fearful, so he could not risk scaring him. If he did, he might lose him forever and waste a whole life. The only possible way to be accepted was to participate in the child's games and amuse him.

The right moment came. Tito hid behind the bricks which, standing vertically, bordered the flowerbeds in the garden where the boy played during those summer days. Watching Bartolomeo carefully line up the twelve wooden bowling pins painted black and white, Tito crouched as though he were stalking a prey—eyes wide open and fixed, restless paws ready to jump.

As soon as Bartolomeo threw the ball for the first time, Tito jumped out, hitting the ball with his nose and making it bounce between the two rows of bricks. Then he tossed it in the air and quickly caught it. Standing on his rear legs, he started a sort of acrobatic dance like he was a puppet. The young boy stood amazed by this performance and gasped when Tito threw the ball toward the pins, knocking them over.

After a moment of shocked silence, Bartolomeo burst out laughing. Leondina turned around, dropping her sewing. She had not heard him laughing so hard in a very long time. Bartolomeo put the bowling pins back in place and then again threw the ball into the middle of the alleyway. Tito again caught it and threw it toward the pins, scoring a strike. The game went on and on. Tito crouched in the middle of the alleyway, waiting for Bartolomeo to throw him the ball so that he could launch it at the pins, provoking loud cries of approval from Bartolomeo. Tito approached slowly, and Bartolomeo could not resist caressing the cat. The sudden, intense vibrating of Tito's whiskers proved him right. He was in the right place with the right person. Or at least that is what he thought.

The bells of the nearby San Francesco Church struck the hour, and Leondina told him it was time to go back inside for his afternoon snack. The boy timidly asked, "Can we get some snacks for the cat, too?"

Tito was happy. The connection had been established. They walked toward the steps to enter the house, with Tito running inside before them and straight into the kitchen.

"And how do you know the kitchen is that way, you naughty little one?" Leondina shouted.

He could not tell her that he had known the way for more than three hundred years!

Four years had passed since Virginia's death. Francesco was constantly trying to get his brother out of that gloomy and dusty room. He was impressed by the incredible work his brother was doing, but he was increasingly aware that it was a way to escape reality. Diving so deeply into the past was a way not to think about the present.

With immense accuracy, Angelo set down in his book an incredible series of important historical events, such as a protracted dispute that in the first half of the XVII century had involved Pope Clement VIII in solving a complicated lawsuit. The Roman Curia contested the ownership of Piediluco Manor by the Farrattini family. The manor arrived in the family's possession as an inheritance from Fabrizio Pojani. His only daughter Plantilla had married Giovanni Farrattini in 1578, and Fabrizio had arranged the marriage on the condition that the two distinct family surnames and coats of arms would be merged so that historical memory of his name, Pojani, would not be lost. So long as this condition was observed, he would leave his properties to his son-in-law.

Such a legacy went against the laws of the Roman Catholic

Church, which said that in the absence of male heirs, the church would inherit the properties of a deceased person.

Angelo carefully reconstructed the twenty-year-long lawsuit, paying great attention to every detail. Francesco was fascinated by the stories his brother Angelo told him but also wondered at the purpose of all this. While Angelo was going on and on with lengthy details, the two brothers heard loud laughter coming from the garden. Looking out the window from the first floor, they saw their two sons enjoying a game with Tito, who was using all his inventiveness to brighten the life of that sad child.

"I have never seen Bartolomeo so cheerful! What has happened?" Francesco asked.

"Honestly, I do not know."

"You do not know? Angelo, is there no way you can find the strength to take care of your child? This is not what Virginia would have wanted. He is not to blame for what happened. Come back to life, for God's sake! Listen, next week Clementina is organizing an evening at the theater. There will be a lot of friends here, and also people from Narni and Terni. You have to come. It will be an interesting evening, and it will help to distract you and get you out of this isolation. They will play Vivaldi's *Four Seasons*. I will save you a place. It will do you good."

Angelo went downstairs to say goodbye to his brother and nephew and then lingered for a moment with Leondina, asking her what had happened.

"*Signor* Angelo, it is a miracle! This stray cat arrived a few days ago and started to play with Bartolino." Leondina referred to the little boy affectionately by this nickname. "And since then, he has changed. He laughs all the time, and they play together all afternoon. He looks like he is another child!"

"I see, Leondina, but do not let that cat inside the house. Do not let him in! Have I made myself clear?"

He went back upstairs to finish his work on the chapter about the Piediluco lawsuit. After that, he planned to move on to another story. He had found the papers that proved the involvement of their ancestor, Bishop Bartolomeo II, in the marriage of Caterina De'

Medici with the King of France, Henry II. That story fascinated him, and he could not wait to start investigating.

Alone in the garden with his new friend, Bartolomeo asked his nanny: "When can we have our afternoon snack?"

"It is still early. In a little while," Leondina replied, looking for the right button to sew on Angelo's shirt.

"Please, let's go now! I am hungry, and so is he!"

Leondina did not make him repeat his request twice. Amazingly, he, the little wren, was hungry! It was usually torture to make him eat. Every meal lasted twice as long as it should have because of having to force him to finish each dish. There was nothing he considered appetizing. Hearing him say, "I am hungry," maybe for the first time ever, was an occasion she could not waste.

She put everything back in her basket, and the three of them walked to the kitchen. She made sure to close the door to the rest of the house tightly so as not to be seen with the cat inside the house. She did not want to disobey the orders she had received, but she also did not want to miss a good opportunity to feed the boy. She was tired of having to constantly repeat that he could not leave the table until he had finished his food.

While the boy and the cat enjoyed their snacks, Leondina asked him if he wanted to give the cat a name. Tito decided to keep eating. He knew by then that nothing he could do would give him back his real name, so he continued to lap up his bowl of milk on the windowsill.

"I do not know. What do you call a cat?"

Bartolomeo turned toward the window, where Tito was still working away at his milk. As he turned back, Bartolomeo bumped the arm with which he was holding his own cup of milk, almost spilling all of its contents on the floor.

Leondina called his name, planning to tell him to be more careful, and at the exact same moment, he said the word "cat." The overlay of the two words "Bartolino" and "cat" echoed strangely in the room, forming the word "Bat." The boy and the nanny looked at each other, amused, and from that coincidence Tito's name in his eighth life was born.

It was not easy for Bartolomeo to leave Tito/Bat outside in

the garden every evening when the big door leading to the garden was closed for the night. Leondina tried to convince him that the cat was an animal of the night and that he had to stay outside.

Bat decided he would not be able to use that excuse for much longer. He could not wait to win back a place on a comfortable bed or on one of the armchairs he had dozed off on with Giovanni and Marianna or with Fidea and Girolamo. However, he had to wait a little bit longer.

Every morning, on his way to school, Bartolomeo greeted Bat, and then Bat waited for him to return, lying on the low wall in the little square facing the *palazzo*. During those hours, he loved to sleep in the sun, listening to the perpetual sound of the refreshing water flowing from the spring—the same spring he had drunk from for the first time almost three thousand years before.

In his mind, he could see many images that lovely sound recalled to his memory. He remembered when the valley was all green with no humans living there. He remembered the long hunting days spent with Hephaestus and when, coming back with their prey, they stopped to refresh themselves at the spring. Bat could not forget Tarzio and Tarzio's friends, the twins that he had loved so much. But Bat also remembered the annoying curses of that irascible architect he nevertheless had managed to tame, as well as the tears of despair of the unhappy bride Felice Idea and those long trips between Amelia and Orvieto that had terrorized him so. All those memories and experiences made him who he was now: a sly, intelligent, shrewd cat who knew how to manipulate humans. True, right now, he was having a few difficulties with Angelo. He did not know that the situation was about to get much worse.

A New Mother

Angelo finally decided to go to the theater to enjoy the beautiful music that was planned for the performance. The joyous notes of Vivaldi's "Spring" filled the theater. He closed his eyes to better savor the music and let it bring him to a state of magical emotion. When he reopened his eyes, they locked with those of a beautiful woman seated in a box across from him. She was staring at him. He did not know his sister-in-law had organized that evening with the primary purpose of introducing him to that lady from Terni.

During the intermission, everybody gathered in the foyer to enjoy a glass of sweet wine before listening to the next two of Vivaldi's musical seasons.

"Dear brother-in-law, may I introduce Miss Caterina Fratini from Terni?" his sister-in-law Clementina asked.

Angelo's passion for history and his studies made him ask her, "Fratini... Farrattini. I wonder if we have some common ancestors? You know, I am doing research in old documents, and our family name has undergone several modifications over the centuries: Ferratino, Faratino, Frattino. I wonder if some branches of the family moved away in the past and gave birth to different generations with slight changes in the name. But I think I am boring you with these consider-ations. It is a great pleasure to make your acquaintance."

"*Au contraire, Signor* Angelo! I have always loved history and family traditions!" Clementina had given Caterina careful instructions on how to charm him.

The bell rang for the third time to remind everyone to return to their seats and boxes for the second part of the concert. Angelo and Caterina glanced at each other several times during Vivaldi's "Autumn" and "Winter."

Clementina, seated in a more central box from which she could see almost everyone, tapped Francesco's hand with her fan to show him how his brother was looking at Caterina. "I told you he would like her. You will see. In a few months, there will be a wedding."

And so it happened. Three months after that concert, Angelo and Caterina got married in a simple ceremony. Her arrival in the *palazzo* was not very well received by little Bartolomeo, mostly because he was still annoyed that he could not convince his father to let Bat into the house.

As a result, Caterina had a hard time being accepted by her husband's son. She was very nice to him and tried to play with him, but a bond was far from being created. The boy was much more interested in going out and playing with his cat than in playing with her.

When winter came with its intense cold, fearing Bartolomeo could get sick, Caterina did not let him go outside. She could not involve him in any games. He spent long hours looking out of the window at his cat crouched outside in the cold. One morning, he woke up to a heavy snowfall that, during the night, had covered the garden and the entire valley. He had never seen snow before, and he was worried about his cat. As soon as Leondina finished dressing him, he ran down the staircase to open the door and let the cat in, but Caterina stopped him at the door.

"You cannot go out! It is too cold. You will get sick!"

"Leave me alone! Leave me alone! I have to save Bat! He is going to die outside on his own!"

"You know your father does not want animals in the house, and you cannot go out in this weather!" To stop him, Caterina slapped him on the cheek.

"I hate you! I hate you both!" he yelled at her and ran into the kitchen to seek comfort in Leondina's arms. She tried to calm his crying.

Caterina regretted her reaction, but she did not know how to handle him. She went upstairs to talk to her husband. "Angelo, I do not know what to do. He does not listen to me; he does not respect me. You must talk to him. He lacks paternal authority. But I also must apologize. I slapped him, and I know I should not have done that."

Angelo was about to leave the room, ready to teach his son a lesson. But as soon as he opened the door, he found Leondina standing in front of it, ready to knock on the door. She was evidently furious and was trying to keep her anger inside without much success.

"*Signor* Angelo, *Signora* Caterina, please listen to me. Then you can also fire me, but for heaven's sake, stop making that poor child suffer like this!"

"Say what you came to say," Angelo said with his authoritarian voice. He could not tolerate being addressed like that by his workers.

"You know how much I love that boy. Ever since his mother died, I have always been by his side. I know him much better than you do." Her voice and whole body were shaking out of apprehension for the audacity she had found inside her heart to protect her boy. "I have worked very hard to feed him, to interest him in the world around us, to raise him the best I could, and I assure you it has not been an easy task. He has suffered so much because of the loss of his mother, but much more because of your indifference." She said those words looking straight into his eyes to make him feel guilty. "He is only six years old, for God's sake!"

"Exactly, he is only six years old, and it is from a young age that rules must be learned," he replied in a commanding tone of voice.

"You are right, *Signor* Angelo, but I can assure you that I have never seen Bartolino as happy as he has been since he met that cat!"

"You know I hate that nickname. Please call him by his real name."

"I will, *Signor* Angelo, but please, I beg of you! If you want serenity and do not want to lose his affection, please let him keep that kitty inside! They have formed such a bond that, when they are together, it looks like they are speaking to each other. That cat has something special, and he can only help Bartoli..." She stopped herself just in time. "... lomeo. Now, if you want to fire me, go on, but I had to tell you!"

Leondina stood still like a defendant waiting for a sentence. Before Angelo could speak, Caterina stepped forward. The last thing she wished for was for her husband to fire the nanny and leave her alone with the boy. She said gently, "You told the truth, Leondina. You do know him better than any of us. Thank you for your words. Now, please go downstairs and set the table for lunch."

Leondina closed the door behind her, crossed the ballroom, and walked downstairs, still trembling from her reckless initiative.

Caterina returned to her husband and spoke to him with sincerity. "Angelo, dear husband, perhaps we should listen to her. There is plenty of time to educate him about respect. But if we lose him now, we might lose him forever. His hatred and resentment will only grow. It is just about a cat! If that cat is so important to him, we should let him bring the cat inside."

"That will mean spoiling him and letting him get away with his bad behavior. If we start out like this, he will be spoiled forever."

"Angelo, do you want a son who respects you because he fears you, or a son who respects you because he loves you?"

Those words hit his heart like a gunshot. He plopped down on his favorite chair, tormented by that subtle dilemma. He remained silent for a few moments; his head lowered. He then extended one hand, reaching for hers. She took his hand, and he pulled her toward him, making her sit on his lap. With a sweet smile, he said, "Ah! You women! You always have more than one trick up your sleeve!" He hugged her, and they kissed. She then put her forehead on his and stayed like that for a while. Then they stood up, and walking to the door, he said to her, "Put on your coat. Let's go get that cat!"

Bartolomeo was lying on his bed, crying, with Leondina sitting beside him and trying to comfort him. They heard someone knocking on the door. When Leondina opened it, Angelo and Caterina swept in, with the shivering cat in Angelo's arms.

"Bat! Bat!" Bartolomelo screamed, running toward his father. He grabbed the cat and squeezed him in his arms. "You are so cold! Come to my bed. I will warm you up!" He took a blanket and wrapped it around the cat. Bat filled the room with his loud purring.

Leondina, her eyes full of tears she was not even trying to hold back, headed for the door. Passing near her master and mistress, she softly whispered, "Thank you!"

Caterina stopped her, putting a hand on her arm, not a usual gesture between a mistress and a nanny. "Many thanks to you, Leondina. Many thanks to you," she repeated.

The three adults exited the room, leaving the two friends to enjoy the moment. Bat had finally regained a comfortable and warm bed. He was happy to continue his mission, which was to make the no-longer-very-sad Bartolomeo happy.

A Cruel Fate

Several years went by. Bat was now a regular part of the family. Everyone accepted his presence, a position he had achieved thanks to his experience and discretion. While Bartolomeo was at school, he spent time with Angelo in his room full of dusty papers. During the summer, Bat better tolerated the heat by sleeping on the cool floor next to Angelo. In other seasons, he lounged on one of the chairs, if he could find one that was not piled high with books and documents. Angelo, even if he did not quite know where to put all those papers, had started always to leave one chair free for Bat. During the colder months, Bat slept on Angelo's legs, an exchange of heat that pleased both of them.

When they were together, Angelo started to talk to Bat, telling him the stories about his ancestors he was writing down. He found in Bat a much more careful listener than his own brother or son, who showed no interest in those stories.

The cat, half-asleep on his chair, listened to Angelo naming people and facts, trying to rearrange that complicated web of events. When Angelo was talking about Bishop Bartolomeo and Antonio Da Sangallo, Bat wanted to tell him that things had not exactly gone as he was saying. He wanted to tell him that if it had not been for his intervention, the construction of the *palazzo* would have taken much longer. He wanted to tell him all he had seen that was not written down anywhere except in his memories. Bat looked at Angelo like he was saying, "If only I could speak, you would never finish your writing!"

When Bartolomeo returned from school, Bat spent all his time with him. Bartolomeo had abandoned his toy soldiers but not his bowling pins. Every now and then, he took them out to the garden, and the two played a few games. With his stepmother, the relationship was more friendly and serene. It took time, but finally, they were at ease with each other.

Bat made his contribution by being very charming with the ladies. They were easy prey for him. With his innate discretion and the perfect manners of a very "gentlecat," he always managed to delight them. Intense looks, polite meows, and soft gestures impressed them all. His way of stretching his legs in front of him and making what looked like a real bow was always well received. His purring created a pleasant sense of peacefulness, and he had learned always to keep his claws sheathed, especially when he was next to all those laces and the voluminous dresses worn by Caterina. She became fond of him and was a little jealous when Bartolomeo called him and Bat ran away from her, even if he had just been deeply asleep beside her.

If the relationship between Caterina and her stepson was more relaxed, it was not the same between father and son. Bartolomeo was not interested in his father's work. He considered all those documents an obstacle keeping his father away from him. For his part, Angelo did not accept his son's lack of interest in family history.

His wife told him Bartolomeo was still too young and that maybe one day he would be more interested. Her two men did not make any great effort to get closer to each other. She worried about this and felt it was her duty to get them closer.

Caterina and Angelo had now been married for twelve years, but they had had no children. During those years, she had suffered two miscarriages that undermined her health. Very weakened, she spent most afternoons in her room, lying on a chaise longue at the foot of her bed. Bat never missed an opportunity to take long naps on her soft, voluminous skirts.

One day, she started to feel severe pains in her abdomen. The doctors could not find a cure. After a while, she rarely left her room, and Bartolomeo and Bat often stayed with her. They read poetry together, or she listened to Bartolomeo repeat his lessons for school while she caressed the cat's soft fur. A few days after Bartolomeo's eighteenth birthday, during the night, Caterina's pains became unbearable. She lost consciousness, and before dawn, she died in Angelo's arms in front of the very saddened Bartolomeo and Bat.

Angelo had to face a hard and lonely widowerhood once again. The poor woman, who with much love had tried to heal the relationship between father and son, left her life before achieving the aim she had imposed on herself. Angelo commissioned yet another engraved marble plaque to be placed in the family chapel.

DEDICATED TO THE BELOVED WIFE
CATERINA FARRATTINI
OF THE FRATINI FAMILY FROM TERNI
STOLEN FROM LIFE ON MARCH 22, 1875,
AT THE AGE OF 51

A few days before she died, while she was alone with Bat resting beside her, Caterina had spoken to him. "Bat, my dear Bat, I do not know how long I will live. I feel I will leave this world soon. I will leave you the duty of taking care of my two men. I know that, as long as you live, you will never abandon Bartolomeo, but please do not leave my Angelo alone. They both have already experienced this unfortunate situation. They need all the help you will be able to give them."

Bat listened very attentively, closing his eyes and meowing softly like he was commenting on her speech. He understood her words perfectly. He, too, felt she was close to her last days, and despite her initial hostility, she had helped him with his mission. He wished he could answer her, but there was no need since, through his purring and the gentle pushes he gave her with his little head on her hands and chin, she knew that he had understood her wishes. The night she died he sat formally on the chaise longue with his front paws always perfectly lined up. He comforted with a soft meow anyone who approached to say a last goodbye to poor Caterina.

The following days proved to be very hard for the family. Angelo isolated himself in his room. He spent days at his desk without writing a line. He lacked the energy to do so. Although his immense work on the family papers was close to a conclusion, he could not go on. The one volume he had initially planned had ballooned into three large volumes that traced the story of his ancestors. He was proud of his work, but now he felt annihilated. At the age of fifty-five, he was once again a widower.

Bat was not very young, either. He was almost thirteen, and he had to hurry to accomplish his mission before the end of this eighth life. He needed to find a new wife for Angelo and one for Bartolomeo. It was the only way to secure a chance for a happy life for his humans. He knew that, alone, they would never be able to find contentment.

The New Wives

A few days after Caterina's burial, Bat had already begun to think about what he should do. Father and son spent long days isolated in their respective rooms and rarely interacted. Leondina brought them trays with food, which she then took back to the kitchen almost untouched. Bat needed a partner in crime, and the only possible person was Francesco's wife, Clementina; he had to involve her. Having witnessed many afternoon teas between the two sisters-in-law, he knew they had exchanged confidences and had affection for each other.

Bat stayed very close to his Bartolomeo, but purring and showing his love in all possible ways was not enough to bring Bartolomeo out of his sadness. Bat ran out into the garden, approached the small wooden door next to the *palazzo*, and began to crawl on the ground until he could squeeze under it. Once on the other side, he navigated those narrow streets that centuries before he had taken countless times in the arms of Giovanni when the *palazzo* was still under construction.

He could not help but notice how much Amelia had changed! New houses and buildings confused him, but he managed to go in the right direction by observing the sun's position. He found himself in front of the house where he had lived during the Renaissance and sat down on a step next to the front door, waiting for somebody to open it.

Francesco was almost home. He had taken care of his horse in the nearby stable and arrived at his front door without noticing a cat sitting next to it. As soon as he opened the door, with a very quick leap Bat ran inside, up the stairs, and right into Francesco and Clementina's bedroom, the room he had stayed in for many years in his sixth life with Giovanni and Marianna. Sitting at her desk writing a letter, Clementina cried out in fear when Bat jumped on her lap. Behind him, panting, came Francesco, who had run after Bat up the stairs. "Sorry, Clementina, I could not stop this crazy cat, but let me catch him and…"

"No, wait, Francesco! Stop, that is Bat! He is Bartolomeo's cat. I wonder how he got here?"

"Are you sure?"

"Of course I am. Do you not see how he recognizes me? How did you get here, Bat?" Bat was rubbing his soft body against her chest and putting his head on her chin, meowing repeatedly. "What is it, Bat? Huh? What happened? What do you want to tell me?" she asked, caressing him. He continued to meow even louder.

"Maybe he just got himself lost and wants us to take him home," Francesco said without thinking.

"I do not think so! It seems clear to me that he knew the way here and came here for a specific reason. No, he is definitely not lost." She then asked the cat again, "Tell me, Bat, what happened? Tell me!"

"Come on, Clementina, now you are daydreaming! He is just a cat!"

"So? Do I have to remind you who talks to his horses and always says animals have a soul?"

"*Touché!*" he conceded.

"I am sure he is worried about Bartolomeo and came to ask for help."

"Now you are exaggerating, but in fact I wanted to talk to you about my brother. He is isolating himself again, and it is not good for him or for our nephew. We must do something, or I do not know if my brother and nephew will ever recover."

Clementina's eyes and attention were fixed on Bat's deep yellow-green eyes. Bat, in return, looked at her so intensely that he almost hypnotized her. For an instant, she had the distinct feeling that the words spoken by her husband had come out of Bat's mouth.

"Of course, Francesco! Bat came here to ask for our help. He knows how much they are in pain and that they cannot handle the situation alone. That is what he is telling me!"

"Well, actually, that is exactly what I just said."

"Really? I am sorry, Francesco, I did not hear you. I was focused on what he was telling me."

"Are you feeling all right, my dear? Since when do you understand cat language?"

"I am sorry, my dear husband, but I swear I heard him talking to me. Call Ersilia. Please tell her to get me that basket with the lid. We have to bring him back to Bartolomeo. He will be worried not seeing him around."

"I really do not think you will need the basket. In my opinion, if what you say is true, he will follow us back to the *palazzo*. Indeed, I am sure he can teach us a shortcut!"

"Stop teasing me! Come on, Bat, I will take you home."

He jumped down and was already standing next to the door. As soon as Clementina opened it, he ran down the stairs, turning occasionally to make sure they were following him. Once in the street, he started to run toward his home. Francesco and Clementina looked at each other incredulously. She was increasingly convinced he had come to seek their help.

When they arrived at the *palazzo* and knocked on the big front door, Bartolomeo came to open it, and Bat started to rub himself on his legs. Bartolomeo picked him up and hugged him tightly, asking him where he had been.

Clementina caressed Bartolomeo's cheek and asked, "How are you, dear Bartolomeo?"

He burst into tears, and Francesco hugged him. Through his sobs, the young man managed to say how lonely he was and how he wished his father would hug him like his uncle did. Francesco, stroking Bartolomeo's hair, told him that his father probably needed a strong hug, too.

Bat was still in his master's arms. At another time, he would have jumped down instead of staying and feeling uncomfortable in that narrow space between them, but he stayed there, purring as loudly as he could, creating a strong connection between the hearts of uncle and nephew.

That strumming vibration gave Francesco an impromptu idea, and he was surprised by what he said next. "Maybe Clementina, Ettore, and I should come and stay here with you for a while. You should not remain alone."

Clementina was caught by surprise since she knew how much her husband hated that *palazzo*. He had always considered it like a prison. Saying he would go there to live was definitely a big sacrifice for him, a sacrifice he would make only because of the love he had for his brother and nephew.

Bartolomeo hugged his uncle. Bat then jumped down and went to sit on one of the two long benches at the entrance to the *palazzo*. Clementina sat down next to him. "You must really love your young master. Thank you for alerting us. Do not worry. We will take care of him."

They moved to the *palazzo* that same day, and over the following months, their presence was of great help to Angelo and his son. A familial feeling was slowly growing, especially at lunch and dinner time. Being five instead of just two made it easier to get over the sadness of that period. The two cousins began to get to know each other more intimately. Several times, Ettore took his cousin to visit the wooded area he and his father had created so carefully over the years. Talking and studying together helped Bartolomeo open up a bit more to life.

After fourteen months had passed, much more time than the traditional period of mourning, Clementina decided she wanted to celebrate her birthday with a banquet in the *palazzo* garden. Angelo was not very happy with her request, but he could not say no to his sister-in-law. She spent weeks on the preparations, always thinking about the right people to invite. She searched among all her friends and acquaintances for anyone who had a daughter, a cousin, or a still-un-married relative or widow to introduce to her brother-in-law. If she had succeeded once, why not give it one more try?

Meanwhile, Angelo had completed his colossal work on their family history. His research was now consolidated into three large volumes, each with an excellent parchment cover. He placed the volumes in the center of the bookshelf in his library. Francesco helped him gather up all those papers and documents. They put them in some chests and stored them in one of the rooms on the mezzanine level.

Closing that door behind them, Francesco felt a profound sense of liberation. Going down the stairs, Francesco told his brother, "Angelo, you have finished an incredible achievement. Our descendants will be grateful to you for centuries to come. You have spent more than thirty years of your life doing this. You must be very proud, but now you must move on. Now you have to concentrate on yourself, your son, and the future of this family."

Angelo, looking down, replied, "I know that you cannot wait to get out of here, and I understand. You have never loved this house. But let me tell you sincerely, I will never be able to thank you enough for what you have done for me and my son. You are right. I must force myself to move forward."

On Clementina's birthday, in addition to their guests and friends from Amelia, others arrived from nearby towns. In her search, Clementina had not found any eligible "brides-to-be" in her own city. Only the Sandris had a possible candidate, but there were continuing rumors about her impossible behavior, which was probably the reason why she was still unmarried.

From outside Amelia, she had invited the Nevi family from Todi. They had a daughter named Elena, while from Perugia, the Crocinis arrived with their daughter Palmira, who had been a widow for three years. At the arrival of the Nevi family, Francesco and Clementina exchanged disappointed looks. Elena was much younger than they had been told. She could have been Angelo's daughter and was much too young to be his spouse. The Crocinis' daughter, Palmira, on the other hand, besides being the right age, was a beautiful woman.

Francesco was pleased to see how his brother greeted Palmira, exhibiting interest in her. He thought Angelo would not remain indifferent to such beauty. Palmira's elderly father was obviously impressed by the grandeur of the palazzo, and deep in his heart, he knew he could not wish for a better remarriage for his daughter. He spent time with Francesco, talking about his daughter's numerous outstanding qualities, including the substantial wedding dowry she would bring along.

Angelo had once again fallen into his sister-in-law's trap, inviting Palmira to dance a quadrille on the large lawn where the banquet was set up.

Clementina and Francesco were so busy promoting the union between Angelo and Palmira that they did not notice someone, a little further on, taking the same opportunity to implement his own plan. Bat walked toward a young girl seated on one side of the garden with a small saucer filled with sweets. He approached her and began his well-tested ritual to captivate women.

It was a beautiful sunny day, and Bat arrived stealthily at the feet of the girl. Without hesitation, he threw himself on his back, showing his soft belly and keeping his paws folded to look like a sweet little bunny. She could not resist and sank her hand into his soft, warm fur. She put aside her saucer to hold him in her arms and stroke him.

Bat was loudly purring and softly meowing when Bartolomeo, after seeing that scene from afar, approached the already conquered Elena. "I apologize. I hope he is not annoying you!"

"Oh, no! Absolutely not! He is so sweet! Is he yours?"

"Yes, he is my cat. His name is Bat. I am Bartolomeo. May I ask you your name?"

"Bat... What an unusual name for a cat!"

"It is a long story... Miss...?"

"Elena Nevi. I came with my parents. We live in Todi. Does Bat live with you?"

"Yes, this is my house."

"Of course, silly me! I should have understood. Who would go to a party with his cat!"

They smiled at each other. Bartolomeo offered to get Elena a drink, and over small glasses of sweet wine, they exchanged a few confidences, then promised to write to each other and meet again.

Clementina had invited both the Nevi and Crocini families, thinking of presenting two possible brides-to-be to her brother-in-law. She hoped one of the two would be chosen. She had immediately eliminated Elena due to her young age and concentrated on Palmira, not thinking about introducing Elena to Bartolomeo. In her mind, she still considered him almost a child, not ready to fall in love. Luckily, Bat had his own plan.

Six months after the party, Angelo and Palmira got married, and Clementina, Francesco, and Ettore could return to their own home. Leaving the *palazzo* was a great relief for Francesco, who felt like he had finally been released after a two-year prison sentence. He was extremely happy to have helped his brother and nephew, but he also had feared that the *palazzo* would swallow him up forever.

At his father's wedding, Bartolomeo met Elena again, and the two understood that the few letters they had exchanged since their first meeting were not enough. They decided to meet more often. Her parents invited him to spend a few days in their country home near Terni. It was the first of a few trips he made there. The two got officially engaged during one of those visits.

Bat was more relaxed now that he had accomplished his mission. His human was happy and "settled." Bat was feeling all the weight of the seventeen years of his eighth life. He had met Bartolomeo when the boy was six, and now his master was twenty-three years old. Even if the two were not married yet, Bat was certain the union with Elena would happen soon.

Bat died six months after Angelo's wedding, leaving Bartolomeo completely distraught. He decided to bury Bat in one of the flowerbeds where they had met for the first time, playing with the bowling pins he still kept safely stowed away in a drawer.

Bartolomeo married Elena a few years later. They had two children, Gilberto and Gemma Claudia. The lineage was assured until Gilberto suddenly died of pneumonia when he was twenty years old. His sister did not have any children.

When Tito/Bat had approached the young, sad Bartolomeo, he had thought Bartolomeo would be the one destined to continue the lineage. He had been misled by Francesco's previous renunciation of the heavy duties tied to the family inheritance. In fact, Ettore, Francesco's son, had the task of continuing the dynasty. Ettore's son Zaffino and grandchild Tommaso fulfilled Hator's prophecy, followed by two more generations in the 20th century, first Ettore Bartolomeo and then Alessandro, born in 1990.

Tito's soul resumed its hovering over his beloved valley, awaiting his next return. He certainly did not expect the tremendous change coming up in his next life, a change that would sum up all the experiences of his past lives.

Chapter 9
The Future in Amelia
Year 2026 AD
Tito Has a Very Different New Life

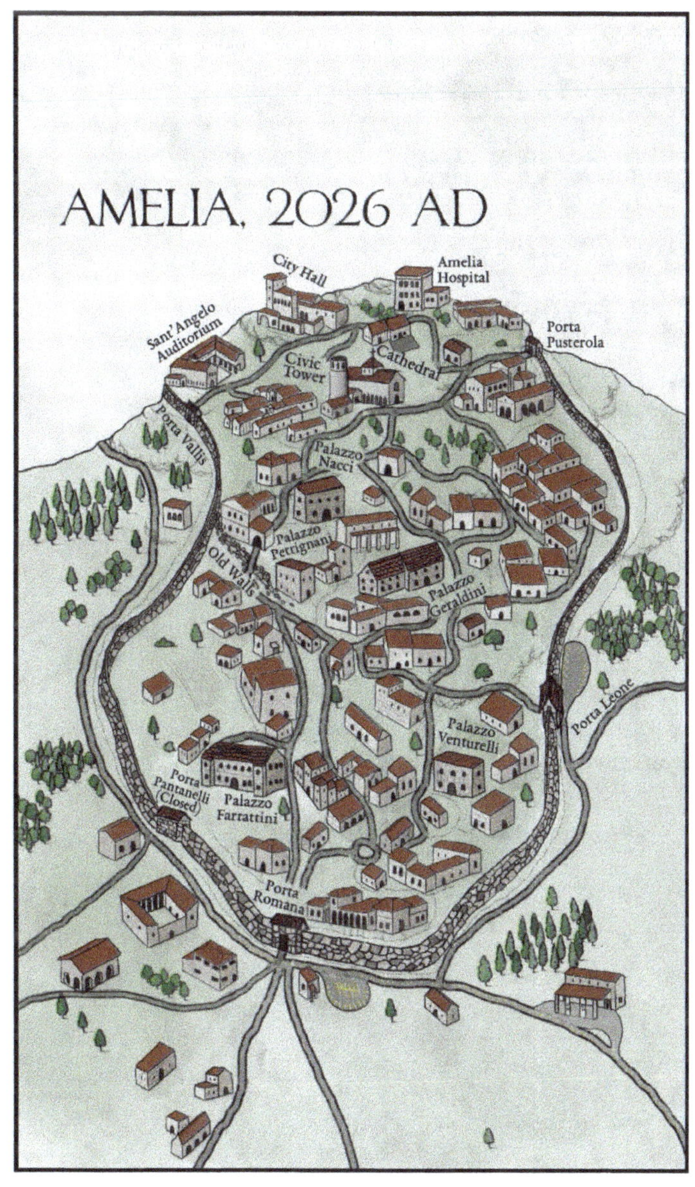

Cast of Characters

Family at the Start of the Chapter

Stefano Caspri

Giovanna Caspri: Stefano's wife

Luca Caspri: the son of Stefano and Giovanna

Other Amelians

Silvana: a neighbor of Giovanna and Stefano

Roberto: the organizer of the Amelia Film Festival

Alessandro Farrattini: film director based in London and son of the
author

Historical Figures

Zager and Evans. a singing duo in the late 1960s

Dalida: a singer in the 1970s

Piermatteo d'Amelia: a Renaissance painter born in 1445 in Amelia

Introduction

The delivery room in Amelia Hospital had not been used for years. Young mothers-to-be usually went to the bigger hospital in Terni or to other regional facilities. The hospital was now used primarily for rehabilitation and emergencies.

In a beautiful little house in the upper part of Amelia, not far from the hospital, lived a young couple expecting their first child. Their names were Stefano and Giovanna Caspri. On the evening of May 7th, 2023, Giovanna was quietly seated on her sofa watching television. Her husband was on his way home from work. According to her doctor at her last appointment, she was due in a couple of weeks.

She was watching a documentary about singers and songs from the seventies. The images and sounds from that era, mostly unknown to her, filled the room. Her attention was captured by a song called "In the Year 2525," sung by Zager and Evans, an American singing duo from that era. She did not know that version, but she remembered hearing the song when she was a child in a cover version sung in Italian by Dalida, who recorded her version under a different title, "Nel 2023" ("In the Year 2023"). Her father was a huge fan of that unfortunate artist who took her own life in 1987. It brought back many memories, and the thought that the song was composed more than fifty years before and that now it was the year 2026 made her smile.

Suddenly, she started to feel wet between her legs. She had the feeling she needed to go to the bathroom. It so happened that, with the weight of the baby in her womb, she sometimes leaked a few drops of urine. Going toward the bathroom, she felt warm liquid running down her legs. She murmured to herself, "Look how disgusting I am. I cannot even hold in my pee!"

She reached the toilet just in time to realize it was not urine, but her waters that had broken. She was close to delivering. She immediately called her neighbor to ask for help, and Silvana arrived to drive her to the hospital in Terni. As soon as she went out into the street, she knew she could not make it to Terni. She screamed, "Take me to the hospital here! Right away!"

"But your doctor will not be there!" Silvana screamed back in a state of panic.

"There must be a doctor or nurse who knows how to get this giant out of me! Take me there! I cannot make it to Terni!"

In a few minutes, they were at the emergency room entrance, where two nurses helped her lie down on a gurney and rolled her inside. Feeling an intense spasm of pain, Giovanna forgot all the preparatory exercises she had learned in the various sessions she had attended to prepare for the delivery. A nurse tried to calm her down and helped her begin the normal breathing rhythm to accompany her contractions.

She had not even made it into the delivery room when the little head of her child started to appear between her legs. To everyone's surprise, he was out in a few minutes.

Silvana had called Stefano to tell him to come directly to the Amelia Hospital. When he arrived, no more than thirty minutes later, their eight-pound baby was already cleaned up and resting in his mother's arms. He had immediately searched for her breast, which he was voraciously sucking, pushing with his little fists on both sides of her breast.

Stefano was ecstatic watching him. He walked over and kissed his wife, who had not at all been taxed by the fast delivery. He turned to the doctor and asked if there had been any problems.

The doctor, there for entirely different duties, was still pleasantly overwhelmed by this unexpected event. "I have never seen such a fast and calm delivery in all the many years of my career. Not even my cat churns out her kittens with such simplicity. He came out in a second! Impressive!"

"But is he okay? Are they both okay?" Stefano asked in a worried tone of voice.

"Yes, *Signor* Caspri, they are both fine, but maybe it will be better if your wife and baby spend this first night here in the hospital, just to be sure."

Sitting next to the bed, holding Giovanna's hand, Stefano apologized for not having been there at the critical moment.

"My love," she replied, "how could you know? I had no warning. Everything happened so fast!"

Knowing ahead of time that the baby was a boy, they had spent time choosing a few possible names for their child. They had decided to wait until they saw him before making a final decision. Only by looking at his face could they decide which name would be most suitable for him. The names they had in mind were Agostino, Sebastiano, Umberto, Renato, Luca, and Vincenzo, all names with an emotional meaning for them. The first four were their grandfathers' names, then the name of a recently deceased close friend, and finally, the name of one of Stefano's high school teachers he had been very fond of. Giovanna fell asleep while Stefano watched her and the baby with his heart full of joy. He finally fell asleep, too, on a chair next to the bed.

After a few hours, the newborn started to cry and woke them up. He was hungry and kept searching for his mother's breast. Once he was placed on her chest, the way he pushed his fists against her breast to get the milk out made them smile. "Look at him!" He looks like a kitten!" Giovanna said. "Remember we said we would wait to name him until we could see his face? I have an idea."

"Me, too! I was thinking about it while watching you two sleeping."

"Get two pieces of paper, and we can write down the name we thought of to see if we have the same idea."

So, they did, and after both of them had written down their chosen name, they exchanged the two slips of paper. They opened them, exclaiming in unison, "Luca!"

Luca had been Stefano's schoolmate. They were very close friends and practically grew up like brothers. Luca had been Stefano's witness at their wedding, and as soon as they learned Giovanna was pregnant, they had asked him to be their child's godfather. Three months afterward, he had died in a car accident. Since then, they had thought they might name their child after him, but only after seeing the baby. This little one, who really looked and moved like a kitten, had to have a short name. All the others were too long for him. Luca Caspri had arrived.

Little Luca Grows Up

Throughout his first six or seven months, little Luca woke up every night to breastfeed at least twice. He was always hungry. After being weaned off breast milk, his big appetite continued, but at least he slept through the night.

Other than always being hungry, he was a good baby: present and attentive. He learned to crawl very quickly. He often escaped from their arms even before they put him on the floor. He was particularly drawn to whatever rolled and rarely cried. He was usually silent, even if Giovanna tried to teach him a few words. While feeding him, she repeated, "Mum-my! Dad-dy! Lu-ca!" He remained quiet, watching her with those big eyes of his that were of an intense green, almost yellowish, color.

He was a big sleeper. As he got a bit older, he began to sleep at least ten hours every night and never missed long naps in the afternoon. Giovanna asked the pediatrician if it was normal for her son to sleep so much. Not that she was unhappy about it. The mothers of other toddlers often complained of the frequent fights they had to have to get their own children to go to bed. Luca never made a fuss; any time was a good time for a nap.

When he was almost two years old, besides the usual baby sounds that did not make much sense, he pronounced his first word. As if they came out of nowhere, he said two syllables: "Ti-to!"

Giovanna, surprised, turned around smiling and asked him, "And where is this coming from?"

Amused, banging his hands on the table, he kept repeating, "Ti-to! Ti-to! Ti-to! Tito! Tito!"

From that day on, he kept repeating those two syllables over and over again. His parents realized that if they called him Luca, he would not listen to them. If, instead, they called him "Tito," he immediately smiled, waving his hand up and down and slapping the tray of his baby highchair or the edge of his bed. Those two syllables excited him incredibly. It did not take long before they got used to calling him Tito. Seeing his excitement about the name, his grandparents and their family friends also started calling him "Tito."

Once he went to school, even though the teachers called him by his real name, Luca Caspri, his schoolmates ended up calling him Tito.

He was a very serious and attentive student. When he started middle school and began to study history in detail, he was fascinated by it. He read about all the significant events of history and was curious about events concerning his hometown.

A few years previously, his history teacher had made it a habit to take students to visit all the important monuments of Amelia in order to teach them the history of their city better. During their three years of middle school, each student had to delve into every aspect of a specific monument, reconstruct its history, and write a paper for the final exam. To prepare for these assignments, several school field trips were organized, and on one weekend, the students became tour guides for their families and for tourists to tell them the history of the monuments.

One of the first visits (and a main attraction) was to the impressive city walls of Amelia. All the boys, including Tito, had seen those walls countless times walking or driving by with their parents. Now, they took a closer look. While the teacher was talking about what little was known about the construction of the walls, Tito felt a strange sensation, like a shiver. He got closer than the others to the wall and placed his hand on one of those very big stones. At that contact, he felt something like a slight electric shock. It was like energy running all through his body.

During her lesson, the teacher mentioned a certain King Ameroe and told the story of the city's legendary founder. That name, which he had never heard before, sounded strangely familiar. Tito closed his eyes. In his mind, the image of the back of a seated, robust man suddenly appeared. His clothes were made of fur, and he was talking to a group of people. Tito could not figure out where that image was coming from, but he instantly knew that the man's name was indeed Ameroe. The teacher saw Tito with his eyes closed and called to him, "Caspri? Are you okay? Did you not get enough sleep last night?"

"Sorry, teacher!" He did not dare tell her about that strange image that had just popped into his mind, so he said, "I was just trying to imagine how life was back then."

They moved to the eastern part of the walls, where many years before, there had been an extensive collapse of a portion of the walls. None of the past city administrations had yet managed to complete the necessary massive restoration. One of the students asked, "But who built the walls?"

Tito's teacher recounted the legend of how King Ameroe had asked a Cyclops to build them since the Cyclops were the only beings strong enough to move such big stones. She also added that there were no documents, no evidence, that gave any verifiable information on how they had been built.

Tito once again placed his hand on one of those stones. That fur-clothed man appeared again. This time, Tito saw him turn around, look at him, and say, "I see we have a new king today!" That image was so real to Tito! It looked like it was happening exactly at that moment. How come Ameroe, until then a total stranger, had suddenly become so familiar, someone who talked directly to him?

The teacher called the students to line up. The walk back to school woke up Tito from those thoughts.

When he got home, Tito began questioning his father. He told his father what the teacher had taught them that morning and wondered why the walls had not yet been restored. Stefano told him that several mayors had worked on the restoration, but there had been countless problems, with bureaucratic hurdles and a lack of money being the first roadblocks on the list. Quarrels, misunderstandings, and a basic incapacity for collaboration between City Hall, the Archeological Superintendency, and the Ministry of Culture had so far blocked every initiative. For those reasons, the construction site had been abandoned for far too many years.

"It is a shame!" Tito exclaimed. "I cannot believe that after all the work done to build them, all the centuries they have been standing, now they have been abandoned like this. It is not right! Tarzio would be so fucking pissed off!" That name came out of his mouth without him having any knowledge of anyone named Tarzio.

Giovanna and Stefano initially did not pay attention to the

strange name, focusing instead on scolding Tito for his language. "Hey, young man! Who taught you to talk like that? Do not use that word ever again!"

"Sorry, Mamma, it just slipped out… but even so, it was well deserved!"

"Okay, okay, but do not get used to saying it since, once said, it becomes habitual, and I do not want you to talk like that. And by the way, who is this Tarzio?"

Tito was usually well-behaved and rarely cursed, unlike many of his classmates. That vulgar word came out of him from a very long time back, more than twenty-three centuries back!

That night, his sleep was very disturbed. He kept dreaming of that man. He also dreamed that he was draped on the shoulders of a younger man. He felt himself jumping down, walking beside that robust man who had been seated on the stone throne, exactly like he had seen the man in his mind's eye that morning. With another leap, he felt himself jumping onto a shelf and sitting down behind the man. Again, he saw that man turn to him and say, "I see we have a new king today!"

Tito suddenly woke up, feeling it was not so much a dream as reality. How was it possible to have the sensation that he had lived so long ago? Was it a movie he had watched that somehow had gotten stuck in his memory? He could not explain it.

The following week, in accordance with the scheduled program of visits, the students went to the Renaissance *palazzos* in the city, where they entered the ancient rooms of those impressive buildings. Their teacher told them stories about the construction of the *palazzos*. They first visited the Petrignani *palazzo*, then the Nacci and Venturelli *palazzos*, and the last visit for that day was the Farrattini *palazzo*.

The students walked up the staircase to reach the main floor. The teacher began describing the frescoes with the coats of arms painted on the upper part of the tall walls. She talked about the impor-tance of the architect who designed the *palazzo* when Alberto, Tito's classmate, said, "Look down in that corner. There are two bits of bones in the floor!"

Tito looked down and then knelt down to touch them. The

bones had been smoothed by the many centuries of people walking on them. As soon as he touched them, he was again pervaded by that energy, like a soft electric discharge, like the charge he had felt when he touched the city walls.

To his half-closed eyes, the room appeared slightly different, with no curtains or paintings on the walls. The three windows were instead three large arches that opened onto the garden. Three men were standing near the staircase with lots of papers in their hands. They were strangely dressed, and one of them was swearing in a heavy Tuscan dialect: "Eh! Are you a complete idiot? Cannot you understand that each piece must be four times bigger?"

"Caspri?" the teacher called him, but he did not react. She called to him again. "Luca! Are you with us, or are you taking a nap?"

That snapped him fully awake, and he stood up, apologizing.

A few weeks later, waiting for the bus to go home after school, he decided to return to the construction site where the walls had collapsed. At the walls, he looked around, and when he was sure that nobody was watching, he slipped into a narrow opening between a pole and a loosened board. He reached a spot where he could hide behind a couple of big stones. He sat down, closed his eyes, and touched one stone still in its original position. He felt that same soft electric shock he had felt the first time he had done it a few days before.

Suddenly, the image of a young man with a bundle of scrolls under his arms appeared before him. Someone was calling that young man. "Tarzio, come here! Hurry up! Another stone just arrived from the quarry." Tito recognized that name; he had blurted it out the other day without knowing who the young man was. Tito reopened his eyes and, a bit frightened by those images ran to catch the next bus to go home. During lunch, with an attitude of certainty, he declared to his parents, "I know who built Amelia's walls!"

His father, very knowledgeable about his city's history, said, "Oh, right. And who was it?"

"It was a man called Tarzio. He planned the entire project and supervised the construction of the walls.

"And how do you know this?" his parents asked almost in unison. "Did your teacher tell you?"

"No. She does not know… yet!"

Stefano smiled and ruffled his son's hair, saying, "Good! Continue with your research. There are many modern books you can consult in the library. When you are older, if you are interested, I will take you to the National Archives. There you can study the old documents. Right now, you are still too young." He reached out with his hand toward his son's upper lip, saying, "Even if I can see that your mustache is growing! I will teach you how to shave it off."

Tito answered that it was out of the question. He did not want to shave off his mustache and never would in his entire life.

Tito understood that no one, not even his parents, could understand the visions he was having. He decided to keep them to himself, at least until he understood what they represented. He was increasingly fascinated by the history of the walls. He felt a strong attraction to them. In all the research he did for his school project, never once could he find that name. There were no traces of Tarzio anywhere.

A couple of months later, he decided to go back to the construction site. He waited next to that pole again, and when he was sure no one was watching, he slipped through that narrow opening. He hid again behind those two rocks and, closing his eyes, touched a stone. The energy surged through him again, and the images came back. He recognized that young man called Tarzio, standing in the exact same position as the last time.

Tito managed to keep his hand on the stone a little longer. The worker was telling Tarzio they were ready to move the stones stacked on a sled that had just arrived from the quarry. The worker asked Tarzio to check if they had placed the stones in the correct order. Tarzio replied that he would do it immediately. He walked toward the worker, turning his back to Tito. He could see the leather bag Tarzio was carrying on his shoulder, from which the little head of a cat, comfortably seated in the bag, appeared.

The moment the cat's eyes met Tito's, there was an intense flash of light, and Tito found himself seeing that same scene but through the cat's eyes instead of his own. From time to time, Tarzio caressed his head while talking to him. "Look, Aker, look how nicely these stones have turned out. They join one another perfectly! I could not even pass a fern leaf in between them!" He sounded very proud, keeping his hand on the cat's head. Tito almost felt that hand on his own head, as if someone was actually caressing his hair.

He was suddenly awakened by the shout of a policeman who had noticed him from afar. "Hey! You there! What the hell are you doing in there? Can you not see it is dangerous? Come out right away!" The policeman recognized him. "You are Stefano and Giovanna's son, are you not? Go home now, and do not ever go back in there, or I will have to give you a fine!"

Tito now knew, so there was no need to go back there in the future. He was sure Tarzio was the one who had built the walls. He also knew that somehow he had been there with Tarzio back then. He could not understand or explain why he could see those images through the eyes of that cat. He told himself once again that it would be better to keep all that to himself. From that day on, he dedicated most of his time to his studies. He was not very interested in sports or in spending time with his friends. He dove into his studies with one specific goal: what could he do for his city and its walls?

Tito in Politics

The years went by quickly. After high school, he graduated from university with a degree in Cultural Heritage Conservation, and after that, he received a second degree in sociology. In 2047, around his twenty-fourth birthday, he began to show an increasing interest in public life. What made him sad was to see his city so neglected; it was being abandoned by his contemporaries, who were forced to leave to find jobs elsewhere. Foreigners had bought a few houses, but since they only lived there for short periods, they did not help much in keeping the city's economy going. Restaurants failed to survive because of a lack of customers. New ones would open but often closed after a few years with their owners deeply in debt.

Tito had to do something. He felt a deep attachment to his valley. On many occasions, the local situation became the overriding topic of discussion with his parents, his friends, and even the tourists he happened to meet. He could not accept that the various mayors who took office did little for the survival or growth of the city.

Over the years, he had had other visions, other dreams. They had all led him to have a particular point of view about those thirty and more centuries of Amelia's history that were buried in his mind. On one occasion, during National Heritage Week, Tito again entered Farrattini Palace, this time following a guided tour. The palace had been completely restored after the damage it had suffered during the earthquake in 2016. Descending into the cellars to visit the remaining Roman sections, after the rest of the group left the room, he kneeled down and touched the mosaics that had been created more than two thousand years before.

From those small black-and-white tiles, a jolt of energy ran through his body. His eyes closed. He saw in front of him two people dressed in white tunics exchanging a kiss. As soon as they appeared, he knew their names: Marcus and Fulvia. He could not explain how it happened, but he recognized them. At their feet, he saw that cat again. When his eyes met the cat's, a bright flash of light almost blinded him. The two humans suddenly became very tall. He had to lean his head back to look up at them. After they had kissed, the young woman bent over to pick him up. The strange sensation of being lifted up gave him a sense of vertigo that woke him up from that vision. He was extremely sure of one thing—they had exchanged that kiss thanks to him.

He still kept those visions to himself; no one would have understood them. The constant in all his visions was that cat. It was always the same. Whether they were visions from the time of the construction of the walls, from the Roman era, or from the Renaissance, that cat was always present. He heard him being called by different names: Aker, Bebio, Meo, Bat…

Any time his eyes crossed the cat's eyes, the flash of light happened, and he would begin seeing the same scene, but from the cat's point of view. He began to savor the idea that he had lived all those lives in a cat's body. Or, more believably, the memories of that cat had somehow been inserted into his own mind. He could not rationalize it, but they were there. At times, he was scared by the visions;

other times, he was amused by them, but he was always enriched by them. He learned to accept and assimilate them.

In that year, 2050, the election for a new mayor was coming up. He started to participate in various political meetings to decide whom to support, for the good of the city, for the following five years. Every assembly ended up in quarrels, fights, and nothing positive. Most of the proposed candidate lists were drawn up along strict, clear-cut political party lines.

None of the political parties' ideas were close to his way of thinking. He was very free-spirited and firmly believed in the good conscience of each human being. It was evident to him that his ideal of a peaceful and serene world where everyone could live together in peace and work to create a healthy and welcoming environment was just a grand illusion.

"Your ideas are pure utopia!" his father would repeat to him whenever they discussed these topics. Much more realistic than his son, Stefano kept repeating to him that things had gotten profoundly worse in the last few years. Respect for others, educational opportunities for all, and the possibility of constructive debate had become very rare concepts.

A noticeable rampant ignorance was growing at all levels, making Tito's desired model of union and collaboration fade away. After attending a second round of those political meetings, he chose to support a group that was a little bit closer to his ideals. Mostly, they talked about topics that were dear to him, like the necessary restoration the city needed to undergo. The problem in that group was that two leaders were vying for which of them would be the first on the list and thus become the new mayor, and neither would give up his battle to be listed first on the party list.

After another fight between the two, Tito found the courage to stand up and tell them their fights would only give the electoral victory to others. He tried to insist that it was essential to put aside personal selfishness and concentrate on what was best for the city. His intervention was so passionate that a lady seated in the back of the room took the floor and exclaimed, "We should all decide to take a step backward!" Turning to the two belligerents, she added, "Especially the two of you! Here is our winning candidate! He is young, he is politically clean, he is passionate, and we all know how much he loves our city!"

The lady's remarks brought a sudden silence to the room until another gentleman stood up and said, "Yes! He is the best candidate! We need fresh, young, and enterprising strength! I support his candidacy!"

Both contending party leaders stammered replies about how inexperienced Tito was and that he would not know how to maneuver to counter their political adversaries. They claimed he would be "gobbled up."

The lady who had so warmly proposed him intervened again, saying the two fighting leaders, as the second and third names on the party list, would also be elected and could assist and support him. She continued by explaining that they risked losing the election due to the mismanagement they had caused in the last few years by their fights. It was time they relinquished power and gave Amelia new possibilities.

Tito was flattered by those statements but refused to run for mayor. As much as he wanted to contribute, he felt the job of being mayor was too demanding for his capabilities. However, he agreed to be on the party list.

Three more meetings followed. The party met for the last, decisive time the evening before the deadline to present their candidate list. The group had not yet reached an agreement on the order of the candidates. Tito had no escape. In the end, the two contenders, to avoid having his rival's name listed first on the list as the mayoral candidate, begged Tito to apply. His name was then written in at the first spot on the party list for the filing documents, even though he was still saying he did not want to be mayor.

During the electoral campaign, the two intra-party rivals always followed him around, telling him what to say. They presented him with the party platform, which he read carefully, letting them know on what points he disagreed. He got in the game and started to go along so as not to lose their trust.

He turned out to be a good speaker at public meetings. His parents were surprised to see him talking with such knowledge about what must be done for the city. The walls were always one of the first topics he spoke about, but also the streets and the many churches now abandoned for lack of funds and priests to manage them. He would bring up the very few shops left in the historic center. He became eloquent on the importance of their city's history and the cultural heritage within the walls. He proposed that the important statue of Germanicus that was preserved in the city museum and the many archeological pieces found at different locations should be advertised and promoted more to revive Amelia.

The opposing parties based most of their campaigns on attacking Tito's political inexperience, saying he was just a naive young man easy to manipulate. Confident of their win, they did not present very engaging platforms. On election night, as the ballots were being counted, an exciting head-to-head race emerged throughout the evening. At some points it looked like it would be a tie, something that could not happen and had never occurred before. Victory was decided by a handful of votes. In the end, Tito was elected with 45.8% of the votes. The second-highest party ended up with 44.2%, while the third-highest party had to settle for 10%.

On inauguration day, Tito had to give a speech to the people of Amelia. His running mates instructed him to give a speech they had prepared for him. He listened to them carefully, did not say a word, just nodded, and when it was time to enter the room and stand on the podium, he was a bit scared but determined. He had the prepared speech in his hands, but as soon as he reached the microphone, after a moment of hesitation, he placed the speech face down on the table.

He looked straight into the camera, knowing his speech would be seen via streaming by at least 70% of the population. In a firm voice, he began to speak. "My fellow citizens, this is a significant day for all of us. A new chapter begins, and I am honored to be the one chosen to lead us forward despite my initial reluctance. I love this city that I have lived in all my lives…" He stopped, quickly correcting himself: "all my life, my short life. But I know it deeply, in each and every detail. I only want what is best for Amelia, which must return to being that wonderful paradise discovered by our founding fathers and enriched by all the others who have cared for it, defended it, and made it unique.

"I am talking about that first man who arrived on our hill and was mesmerized by it. I am talking about King Ameroe, who decided to settle here with his tribe. How can we forget all the men who dedicated their lives to building our beautiful and today battered walls? Then the Romans who made Amelia one of the most important municipalities of central Italy, or our rediscovered Germanicus statue, a silent witness to that wealth? Or all our ancestors who gave their lives during the Middle Ages battling the invaders?

"I want to remember Frederick II, nicknamed "Stupor Mundi," who was fascinated by Amelia. And Alessandro Geraldini, the first bishop of the Americas, one of the most illustrious Amerians! I want to remember Piermatteo d'Amelia and his fabulous paintings, and then the Renaissance that brought within our walls Antonio Da Sangallo, one of the greatest architects of all time. So many outstanding citizens born here have been distinguished in the arts, in politics, and in religious careers! Our culture and history are unique and rare.

"But these praiseworthy forbearers have been neglected and forgotten for far too many years. The youngest generation has had to leave the city to find a job elsewhere; many of them are friends I grew up with. During my term, I will try to concentrate on recovering our culture, which is an essential part of each of us and must be our primary interest. To do this, I would like to have each and every one of us contribute to bringing Amelia back to its ancient splendor.

"For that reason, I have decided to change the modus operandi of the city council. I ask all the council members to consider my proposal in the coming days and to meet again in a week to sign a pledge about a new way to rule the council. Will it be legal? I do not know, and I do not care. I just hope you will agree to follow me on this adventure for the good of the city and all its citizens."

A chilling silence filled the room, scaring the newly elected mayor. Maybe he had gone too far. He closed his eyes, took a deep breath, and continued his speech. "My proposal is very simple: in the city council over which I will preside, there will not be a majority nor a minority. We will be a group of people who will work together for the good of Amelia. No more infighting, no more stupid resentments between political alignments. Enough of the regrettable trend to block good proposals just because they come from another party. What is our main purpose? That Amelia should be a lively city, pleasant to live in, and functional. So why do we not all join together as a one-of-a-kind, united, strong team? We all have the same goal. Let's work together. We do not need quarrels, obstacles, or recriminations. That would just be a way to harm ourselves. And Amelia and its people will pay the price. That is why I will not entrust the various departments only to my political party list mates. If everyone subscribes to this agreement, the various activities will be assigned based on individual competence, regardless of the individual's party. Your political alignment, whatever color it is, let us leave it in a drawer for the next five years. Forget about it. For the next five years, there will be only one political color: the blue of the coat of arms of our city! Only one, for all of us!"

He ended his speech with such strong words that the room plummeted into an unreal silence. Nobody could say a word, completely undone by what they had heard. On that hot June afternoon, all the windows were open to let in a bit of air. Shortly afterward, the sound of ever-increasing applause started to fill the streets and the main square. Many citizens who had watched the speech on streaming services opened their windows and began to applaud. After the initial bewilderment, everyone in the city hall conference room stood up and joined the long and hearty applause.

People clapping and chanting his name quickly filled the main square. Those who knew him by his nickname shouted, "Tito! Tito! Tito!" while those who only knew him by the name printed on his campaign posters chanted, "Luca! Luca! Luca!" When he went outside to the square, he was carried in triumph in the most memorable electoral victory parade in Amelia's history.

Mayor Tito

For the first few months after his election to lead the city, a few changes already began to appear. The team he was leading, with all internal disagreements set aside, moved forward, united, in the same direction. They completely forgot the principle of opposition; they all moved into a very cooperative relationship. The general involvement of all groups lit a spark that resulted in everyone trying to find the best solution in every field. The single energy of individuals became synergies, all directed to a single purpose: the good of Amelia and its citizens. However, there were many difficulties and problems to overcome. The same refrain was repeated at every meeting: there is not enough money; there are no resources.

Tired of hearing it, at the end of a heated discussion, Tito slammed his fist on the table and shouted, "Enough of this stupid excuse! Problems are not solved with money, but with ideas!" Tito knew that neither Aker, nor Bebio, Otto, Pirro, Bat, Ubi, or Meo had needed money to fix the issues they had faced over the centuries. Each time, it had been a stroke of genius, an idea that had solved the problem. That lesson had remained within him and was, for him, the only way forward.

One of the initiatives Tito implemented was to listen to his citizens. He decided to give every citizen of Amelia a chance to meet with him, be heard, and offer their own opinion. This idea came to him from the first of his visions, from the image of that man seated on his stone throne, facing all his people. Each week, Tito dedicated one day to these meetings with citizens who wanted to talk about a specific topic regarding the city. They had to register on an online list stating their purpose and then had thirty minutes to express their ideas and suggestions. The booking list for the following six or seven months filled up in just a few days.

Tito wished he had more time to dedicate to his constituents, so after a few weeks, the sign-up list was reorganized to have citizens who were interested in the same topic appear at the same time as a way to shorten appointments. That page on the city hall website evolved frequently to give voice to everyone. The results of these meetings enriched a very valuable database of topics and suggestions that was; useful in establishing priorities for necessary projects.

Ever since the beginning of his term, Tito had focused on the reconstruction of the city walls, the revitalization of the historic center, and the promotion of the cultural potential of the more than thirty centuries of existence that Amelia could offer visitors. It was not an easy task, one all his predecessors had miserably failed to accomplish. He had long discussions and recurrent fights with his collaborators and advisers to try to resolve the project's many complexities while endeavoring to keep everything legal.

He was often told that, even if what he wanted to do was right, it went against this or that law. It drove him crazy. His goal was to revive those streets and those areas of the city he had seen in his visions. Although little by little he became more aware of the truthfulness of those visions, he still was not entirely sure he had lived those moments. They continued to reappear each time he touched a stone or a wall anywhere in the city. On each occasion, he acquired a new element, a new memory.

His fame began to spread beyond the city limits, and several reporters asked for interviews. He was never very happy about the media interest, not feeling comfortable about such attention. He slowly got used to it. On one occasion, a reporter wanted to film him in various city locations to show the city's beauty. While asking him questions about the monuments and their history, the journalist noticed that everywhere they went, Tito always had a hand resting somewhere. He asked why.

Without hesitation, Tito answered, "These stones speak to me. Touching them, I perceive their stories; they tell me what they saw. They help me understand what I have to do for my city."

A little perplexed, the reporter replied, "You really must love this city very much. From your words, it seems like you have been here since it was founded!"

"Maybe I do feel just like that!" He amazed himself with that answer.

Among the first proposals to better manage and revive the historic center, every citizen who had an enclosed space or cellar was allowed to turn it into a garage. Permits were given at no cost if the work just involved enlarging the existing entrances to allow cars to enter. To get this proposal approved, Tito embarked on a difficult battle with the architects of the city's Fine Arts Department who, close-minded, intransigent, and shielded by antiquated laws, refused to change their decades-old attitudes. Imposing his ideas, he finally succeeded in getting the permits. Within a few months, more than one hundred new garages were created in the old part of the city, resulting in a continual decrease in the number of cars parked in the narrow streets.

Many other new initiatives followed. The minibuses going around the city center were free of charge for riders staying within the walls, while a ticket had to be bought for outside-of-the-walls destinations. All city-related charges for opening a new business inside the walls were eliminated, and a reduced taxation rate for the first few years was introduced. An even greater benefit was accorded if the new business was opened by a citizen of Amelia under twenty-five years of age. That incentive fostered a considerable number of new enterprises, bringing back vitality and movement to the streets of Amelia.

On those same streets, little by little, the horrible asphalt was removed to restore the original cobblestones. Tito was also very strict about the restoration of the facades of all houses: a harmonious continuity of colors was established. Starting from the yellows and moving to the beiges, ivories, and pale pinks, Amelia was acquiring a set of facades in a well-balanced chromatic scale that was very pleasant to the eyes.

On Sundays, Tito loved to go for long walks in the surrounding countryside with his camera. He went to those locations where he used to go with Tarzio, Laertes, and Laertia many centuries before. He loved taking pictures of the city from afar and from every possible angle.

He then spent time on his computer enlarging the photos, rotating them, and cropping them to check on any detail that might interrupt the harmony of the view. He discussed his findings with the city technicians and architects and made visits to try to solve the problems he had discovered: a facade that had an excessively flamboyant color, a ruined or unsafe roof, a poorly lit lamppost that did not light the way. Tito had warm yellow bulbs restored to all the streetlamps. The existing cold, white lighting not only disturbed his sensitive eyes but also eliminated all of the magical ambiance of the old streets. Within a few years Amelia had completely changed its appearance, becoming beautiful, fascinating, almost sensual. Tourists and travelers were enchanted by its beauty. The reconstruction of the walls had resumed at full speed, with the archeologists studying the repositioning of each stone. A specific page on the city hall website was reserved for whoever had old photos of the walls and wanted to share them. The images were helpful to the archeologists in recognizing the stones and restoring them to their original placement. Constantly repeating to the construction site director how important it was to respect the original placement of the stones became his obsession. He was not totally aware, but deep inside of him he knew how much Tarzio had struggled to have the stones precisely fitted one to another. Although over the centuries the walls had suffered numerous restorations, the lower parts were still made up of stones from the 4th century BC, and for him it was essential to return them to their original location.

Whenever his duties gave him some free time, he walked to the construction site to follow the restoration project. He could not help it; those stones had a hypnotic effect on him. Once, during one of those visits, he overheard two workers discussing the use of a freight elevator. One of them, who had a very strong Tuscan accent, was trying to explain to the other how to direct the overhanging crane so as to place a big stone. The two did not understand each other. The first one exploded, swearing, "By that slutty Maremma, is it so difficult to understand?" That sentence made him smile; he did not know why, but it reminded him of someone.

Amelia: European Capital of Culture

The last move of Mayor Luca/Tito before the end of his term was to apply for Amelia to be the European Capital of Culture. He created the motto "CulturAMAmelia" (CultureLOVESAmelia). He managed to involve many artistic and cultural personalities in supporting this nomination. Important people in the arts, literature, and entertainment agreed to sponsor and participate in managing several events that would enrich a year of high intellectual, cultural, and other activities.

The many new events that had already started a few years previously got more financial support to make them better and more widely known, benefiting from more consistent investment and sponsorships. In addition, Amelia got its own literary prize and a festival for short films, along with many concerts and performances.

The auditorium of the historic Sant'Angelo Theater and other concert halls that had been created in the many abandoned and deconsecrated churches offered a wide range of concerts for every kind of music, attracting large audiences. Drama, chamber music, opera, jazz, pop music, and medieval and Gregorian chants each had its own space. The former soccer field was transformed into an arena to accommodate concerts for larger audiences.

When the new elections were held, it was almost useless to count the votes: Tito was reelected with 75% of the votes. Two years after his re-election, Amelia won the competition and was awarded the title of European Capital of Culture for 2054.

The musical, artistic, and intellectual events organized during that year brought tourists and VIPs from all over the world. Finding a house to buy in Amelia or its vicinity soon became impossible. More and more musicians, actors, writers, and other intellectuals wanted to have a home in Amelia. Tito could not be prouder.

In just over seven years, his city had rediscovered a splendor never reached since the Roman and Renaissance eras. The walls had been beautifully restored, and the streets and alleys returned to their original charm and authenticity. Commercial, catering, and hospitality businesses were thriving, and restaurants were always full.

During that important year in the history of Amelia, Alessandro, the last heir of the Farrattinis, returned. He had kept the house his father had left him, even though, due to his work as a film director, he had not come back in a long time. He could not miss that year since he had been asked to preside over the jury for the short film festival. From his adopted homeland, England, he returned to Amelia to spend his holidays there and to fulfill this prestigious task.

One of the events connected to the festival was a gala dinner in the Farrattini Palace, which had belonged to Alessandro's ancestors. Arriving at the dinner, the 67-year-old film director was introduced to the mayor and other authorities. The two met on the stairs that led from the atrium to the garden. The moment the film festival organizer introduced them, Alessandro and Tito shook hands, and an almost paranormal feeling overcame them both.

"Alessandro, let me introduce our mayor, Luca Caspri, though we all call him Tito." Turning to the mayor, the film festival organizer said, "Tito, this is Alessandro Farrattini, heir to the family who built this *palazzo*."

"It is a great honor to meet you," Tito said. He could not let go of Alessandro's hand. He received from it a powerful energy charge. It was different from the one he usually felt when he touched the inert stones of Amelia. He felt a strange sensation on his upper lip, as if his mustache was vibrating. It was like he had known Alessandro forever. He timidly asked, "Have we met before?"

"I do not think so," Alessandro answered, adding, "I have not been here for years; I do not think we ever did."

They could not let go of that handshake. Tito was receiving such a strong electrical charge that it almost took his breath away, and he lost his balance. To support himself, he placed his other hand on the bricks of the staircase.

Seeing Tito so pale, with a nod of encouragement Alessandro put his left hand on Tito's shoulder. He asked, "Is everything all right?"

This additional contact created a sort of spark, as if Tito had grabbed in his hands the opposite poles of two electric cables. On one side were the bricks his cat paws had walked on centuries ago, bricks that had recently given him so many visions. On the other side was the contact with Alessandro, whose cells containing that familial genetic code had made his whiskers vibrate in all his previous lives.

The concomitance of those contacts—the bricks, the handshake, the pat on his shoulder— provoked in him a subliminal manifestation of hitherto hidden truths. For the first time in his life, in this life, he was having physical contact with someone who descended directly from those who had known him when he was a cat.

Suddenly, everything became clear in his mind. It was like all those scattered images he had had since he was a child were making sense, and each one quickly took a clear position in his memory. They were like files on a computer being reorganized in a historical sequence. All the doubts and uncertainties he had accumulated now appeared obvious to him. It was the proof he had been waiting for. He had been a cat! He had been *that* cat!

Excusing himself, Tito took leave of Alessandro and the others to internalize this revelation. He walked down the few steps of the stairway and moved toward the garden in the direction of the sunset. At every step, he looked around to see the many guests present for the gala dinner.

Among them, he began to see all the humans he had lived with in his previous eight lives. Hephaestus and Khepri were there, as was Tarzio, in a corner chatting with Laertes and Laertia. Now, he recognized them. They were not just visions anymore. They were real people he had lived with. Still walking, he saw Marcus and Fulvia. Further on, he saw Lucius and Scilla.

They were all there in that place where he had shared joy, pain, adventures, and complicity with them. He continued, meeting Giovanni and Marianna next to the fountain, Felice Idea and Girolamo near the big hackberry tree, and sad little Bartolomeo near the flowerbed where they played with the black-and-white bowling pins.

All of his lives opened up to him clearly. He reached the highest point of the property to be alone and savor the realization that what he had always suspected but never completely accepted was indeed true.

From the top of the walls, he had below him the most beautiful view of his valley, where his story had begun nearly thirty-two centuries before. The sun had almost set, leaving a magical flow of colors in the clouds near the horizon. In the distance, the lights of the numerous houses built in the valley looked like the reflections of the many stars of that beautiful summer sky. He spread his arms and took a deep breath, tilting his head back with his eyes closed. He stayed like that for a few moments until he heard someone calling his name several times.

"Tito! Tito!" It was Roberto, the film festival organizer, running toward him. "Here you are at last! Please come; they cannot start serving dinner without you!"

When Tito turned his head and faced Roberto, his expression was ecstatically happy, and tears were running down his cheeks.

Roberto was petrified and asked, "Tito! For heaven's sake, are you okay? What happened?"

"Nothing, Roberto, nothing. I am so happy that I cannot hold back my tears. Look how beautiful this valley is! It has been a part of my life for three thousand years, and I will never get tired of looking at it!"

The real Lino/Titus/Tito

Epilogue—My Tito

Tito was truly a special cat for me. Previously, I was a dedicated dog lover.

Even though it had been about twenty years since I had had a pet in my house, I still had loving memories of my last dog, a long-haired dachshund named Robin Likealot. That little doggy initially could not stand me and barked at me constantly. He later became my shadow. He followed me everywhere and lived for me.

When my son Alessandro was born, Robin Likealot was already old and could no longer take long walks. When I went to choose a baby carriage for my son, I looked for one that had a basket underneath. I made Robin Likealot a soft foam pad so that whenever I went out with my son, Robin Likealot could enjoy our long walks comfortably seated in the basket.

The day I had to put him to sleep was very painful. I still have his collar in a little box on my dresser and still have his pedigree. I promised myself that if I wanted to have another dog in the future, I would go to England, seek out that same breed, and try to get one of his biological relatives. Has not genealogy been an important part of my family history?

Then, one day, Tito suddenly arrived in my life. We were sitting in the *palazzo* garden with friends and guests of my B&B, having drinks. He appeared and stretched out among us. I remember I immediately told everyone not to feed him. I did not want him to get used to getting food from us.

A few days later, I found out that he went for dinner every night at the pizzeria across the street. The owner, Valda, and the cook, *Signora* Lidia, fed him and placed a basket for him where he took long naps until closing time. They called him Lino, a nickname for "*Porcellino*" (little pig), a name given to him due to his never-ending hunger.

During the day, though, he was always with us in the garden, a garden that became more his than ours. He tried to be a little braver every day, stepping up to the door. I told him, "You will not enter here! You will stay outside!" I did not want him inside mainly because I wanted to avoid creating problems with guests who were allergic to or afraid of cats. Besides, it seemed cruel to me to get him used to the house when every year we would close it for the winter to go back to Rome. I did not want him to feel abandoned during the winters if he got used to finding food at the *palazzo*. During those summer months, our friend Elyssa often came to visit, and once she asked me, "How is Titus? Where is he?"

"Who is Titus?" I replied.

"What do you mean, who is Titus? Your cat!" she said, a bit surprised.

I turned to my partner Scott and said, "Did you give him a name?"

"Yes. I named him Titus from the name of our street in Rome, *Via delle Terme di Tito*. He does behave like a Roman Emperor!"

The cat was known as Lino on the other side of the street, Titus on this side, and then, of course, Tito. This special cat had gotten used to multiple names. Every spring, when we reopened the house, he was always there, punctual, greeting us like he was saying, "Welcome back! Everything is fine here. I guarded the place well."

Scott usually caressed him, pointing at me and telling him, "You do not have to convince me, but him!"

This routine went on for four years until, returning from yet another winter, we found him emaciated and in pain. Elyssa and another dear friend, Carol, two indisputable cat lovers, insisted I had to take him to the vet. So, I did, and we discovered Tito had contracted FIV, feline HIV, and he had developed an extreme gum inflammation, which caused him great pain. The vet told me that if we did not treat him immediately, he would soon be dead.

Lying on the vet's laboratory bed while purring at her, he looked at me with those incredible deep yellow-green eyes, and I clearly heard him say, "Take me with you. You will not regret it!"

I decided instantly and told the vet to do everything she could to save him. First, we had to have him sterilized, and then the second surgery was the removal of all his teeth to fight that irreversible inflammation. He was left with only his four canines, but that did not prevent him from continuing to eat everything without problems.

Back home after the surgeries, at the garden door, I explained to him, "Tito, now you can enter the house. Here is your litter box, and this is your sleeping basket." He was seated in the entrance hall, listening attentively. "Those are the stairs. You are not allowed upstairs. Upstairs there are the guests' rooms, so you cannot climb the stairs! Understood?" He never went upstairs. Even when there were no guests and I had to go to the upper floors, he would wait for me seated on the first step below.

On the second or third day that he was inside, I caught him scratching his claws on one of the sofas. I grabbed his paw and, giving him a little pat, I told him, "You cannot do this! You can scratch your claws outside on the trees, but not inside the house!" It never happened again.

To help his immune system, which had been undermined by the disease, I had to give him ten millimeters of an interferon solution with a syringe right in his mouth. When the vet told me how to do it, I told myself that it would not be an easy task. I distracted him while preparing his dinner, and before taking out the syringe in front of him, I explained, "Listen, Tito, we must give you this medicine. We must do it for seven days in a row, and then on alternate weeks. It is for your own good, understood? When I say open, you will open your mouth, and I will spray the medicine in, okay?" He answered with a soft meow. I bent down and said, "Open!" To my amazement, he opened his mouth wide, swallowed the medicine, and did the same every time. He knew it was for his own good.

In a very short time, Tito became the mascot of the residence. All the guests were won over by his charm, and his photos started to circulate on every guest's Facebook page. Thanks to his behavior, many guests began to tell me he must be the reincarnation of one of my ancestors.

At the end of the season, when it was time to close the *palazzo* for the winter, Scott was worried Tito would not adapt to being in a small apartment in Rome after being used to the outdoors. For Tito, it was not a trauma. He got used to it immediately. For him, it was essential to be next to me, and that is why he unhesitatingly endeavored to learn the rules. In all the years he spent with us, he never, ever harmed or broke anything. A simple "No" was enough for him to understand that he could never do whatever he was doing ever again. In return, he just asked for love, the possibility of sleeping with me on the sofa every afternoon for our nap, and, of course, his barely seared chicken breast for dinner.

After his passing on December 9th, 2019, he left me unbearably empty and devastated. Many people told me I needed to get another cat. It was not possible for me. I did not choose Tito. He chose me; it took him four years to win my heart forever. That is why I decided to celebrate him with this book. It was actually Tito who inspired me to write this book.

When, in January 2020, I delivered the final draft of my first book to a publisher, I began to think about the next one. The beginning of the pandemic and the lockdown presented the best opportunity to focus on a new book. My great passion for music and the magical influence it has had on my entire life pushed me to imagine a story related to music. After I had already written a few chapters, I was not very happy with the result.

One morning, seated in front of my computer, I searched for inspiration to continue without much success. On my computer screen, I keep as a screensaver one of Tito's most beautiful photos. Suddenly, I heard him again telling me, "Write about me! Write about us!" The inspiration for this story came to me instantly. I hope it will hold a special place in your heart and not just in those of cat lovers.

The first four chapters of this novel, albeit based on actual historical references to events and vicissitudes in the city of Amelia, are mostly fictional regarding my ancestors. Names, characters, and reconstructions of their stories do not have any documentation that could help me. The following four chapters are instead based on ancestors who really existed. I randomly picked a few that might have had a better connection to Tito's story and to Amelia's incredible history. Talking about all of my documented ancestors would have taken me many more than the three volumes my forebearer Angelo Farrattini transcribed in the XIX century that are now preserved in the National Archives in Terni. Those three volumes have been an essential source of information for this book. All the ancestors named in chapters five

302

through eight, from Colao onwards, really existed. Yes, even Felice Idea, that girl with an unusual name, existed.

Tito, I will never find the right words to adequately thank you for giving me all of yourself, but above all, for making me discover an aspect of love unknown to me until I met you. I will never forget that.

Now, I can go back to writing about music.

The author and Tito take their afternoon nap together

Acknowledgments

There are many people I want to thank, people who, in small or long-term ways, helped me to bring back to life, at least on paper, that magical cat, Tito.

First, my family, starting with all my astonishing ancestors, for leaving me such incredible history for inspiration. But also, the members of my modern-day family, including my partner Scott, my wonderful ex-wife Patrizia, my son Alessandro, and my sister Maria Claudia. Without their support, this book would never have been completed.

I am forever grateful to Anna Gentilini and the family Siciliano, artistic director and owners of the Armando Curcio Editore, publishers of the Italian version.

My indebtedness extends to all the students, art historians, university professors, and passionate history lovers who spent years looking deep into the archives, making my job sometimes easier but not less challenging.

A special thanks to all my English-speaking friends for their support and continuous clamoring for an English-language version after its publication and success in Italy. One in particular, Kathleen Boyd, for her personal commitment to helping me get this book to English-speaking readers.

Also, a special thanks to Julie Gianelloni Connor of Bayou City Press for believing in this story and its potential.

Last, but not least, to Tito, the real inspiration for these incredible but credible adventures. You have been one of the most important loves of my life.

Watercolor of Palazzo *Farrattini by* Thomas Lollar

Listing of Foreign Words and Special Terms

Baiocco: a coin used in the Papal States

Bischero: idiot, in Tuscan slang

Chaperon: the leather cap used to cover the eyes of birds of prey during training

Clepsydra: hourglass

Cocciopesto: plaster of a certain kind invented by the Romans, a mixture of ground lime, bones, and animal remains all mixed together that was used as glue

Dictatus Papae: papal dictate

Domus: a term of respect for a man

Donna: a term of respect for a woman

Farro: also called spelt, a species of hulled wheat whose scientific name is *Triticum spelta*

Focaccia: a type of flat Italian bread

Grullo: Tuscan insult

Lassanie: in today's Italian, lasagna

Maremma bu'aiola: a strong Tuscan swearing expression

Maremma maiala, impesta'a e lurida: a typical Tuscan derogatory expression

Necropolis: burial ground

Palazzo: palace

Pasquinate: graffiti messages on sheets specifically hanging from the Pasquino Statue in Rome, a statue that still exists. During this period, anonymous messages against the Pope were posted here and thus became common knowledge.

Patrician: upper-class Roman

Peristilio: peristyle

Plebeian: working-class Roman

Podestà: at first, commander; later, the title for mayors

Promissio Carisiaca: a deed that gave some formerly Byzantine holdings
    to the Vatican

Res publica: public matters

Saturnalicium Castrense: military Saturnalia celebration

Signor: polite title and term of respect for a man, "Mister"

Signora: polite title and term of respect for a woman, "Mrs"

Slutty Maremma: a strong Tuscan swear phrase

Subligaculum: an item of intimate clothing

Stupor Mundi: Wonder of the World

Titolo: job title

Triclinia: a couch for reclining diners

Notes on Sources

Although most of the books, articles, and documents I consulted to write this novel are in Italian, we decided to list them anyway to show the provenance of the historical facts recounted in The Nine Lives of Tito d'Amelia. *Some of the books were also published in English, especially those regarding Frederick II of Swabia. We have added informal translations of bibliographic information to help any readers who may want to delve further into topics in this novel.*

Farrattini, Angelo. *Notizie Casa Farrattini dal 1500 al 1777.* Volumi manoscritti da Angelo Farrattini 1830-1860 conservati nell'Archivio di Stato di Terni. (*Historical News about the Farrattini Family from 1500 to 1777. Manuscripts by Angelo Farrattini kept in the National Archives in Terni.*)

Di Tommaso, Angelo. *Guida di Amelia.* Terni: Editrice Annuari Guide Regionali Italiane, 1931. Second edition: Amelia: Riedita da Gruppo Ricerca fotografica, 1991. (*A Guide to Amelia, written by Monsignor Angelo di Tommaso and first published in 1931 and then re-edited and re-published in 1991.*)

Menchelli, Nazzareno. *Cenni Storici Intorno alla Nobile Famiglia dei Conti Farrattini di Amelia.* Amelia: 1896. (*Historical Notes about the Noble Family of the Counts Farrattini of Amelia, by the Canon Nazzareno Menchelli, published in Amelia in 1896.*)

Bolli, Luigi. *Amelia nelle sue origini e nelle sue mura pelasgiche.* Amelia: 1912. (*Amelia, its origins and its Pelasgian Walls, published by Professor Luigi Bolli in Amelia in 1912.*)

Bolli, Luigi. *Cenni Storici Intorno alla Nobile Famiglia Farrattini Pojani.* Amelia: 1927. (*Historical Notes about the Noble Family Farrattini Pojani published in Amelia in 1927.*)

Cansacchi, Carlo. *Antonio Da Sangallo il Giovane in Amelia: Il Palazzo Farrattini e le Mura.)* Istituto Storico e di Cultura dell'Arma del Genio, 1938. (*Antonio Da Sangallo The Younger in Amelia: The Palazzo Farrattini and the Walls.*)

Frederick II of Swabia. *The Art of Falconry, being the De Arte Venandi cum Avibus.* Stanford University Press, 1961.

—. *Storia Universale.* Milan: Rizzoli Editore Milano, 1965 (*Universal History, published in Milan in 1965.*)

Abulafia, David. *Frederick II: A Medieval Emperor.* Vintage (23 April 2002).

—. *La Storia.* De Agostini Editore, UTET Editore, 2004 (History, *written in 2004.*)

Monacchi, Daniela. *I Mosaici Romani di Amelia nel Contesto Urbanistico Antico.* Perugia: Annuali della Facoltà di Lettere e Filosofia dell'Università di Perugia, 1986. (*Roman Mosaics in Amelia in the Ancient Urban Context, published by the University of Perugia in 1986.*)

Contri, Tiziana. *La Fabbrica Edilizia come promessa dinastica: I Farrattini di Amelia committenti di architettura nel XVI secolo.* Università di Roma Tor Vergata, 2004. (*The Building of Architectural Projects as a Dynastic Promise: The Farrattinis of Amelia, Architectural Clients in the XVI Century, a Ph.D. dissertation by Tiziana Contri in 2004.*)

Bredekamp, Horst. La fabbrica di San Pietro: Il principio della distruzione produttiva. Einaudi, 2005 (The "Fabbrica" of Saint Peter: The Beginning of Productive Destruction.)

Martellotti, Anna. *I Ricettari di Federico II Dal Meridionale al Liber De Coquina.* Olkiski, 2005. (A Recipe by Frederick II for Cooking Chicken.)

Benedetti, Sandro. *Il grande modello per il San Pietro in Vaticano: Antonio da Sangallo il Giovane.* Gangemi Editore, 2010. (The Large Model of Saint Peter's in the Vatican.)

Yardley, Richard Bressler. *Frederick II: The Wonder of the World.* Pennsylvania: Westholme, 2010.

Cassidy, Richard. *The Emperor and the Saint: Frederick II of Hohenstaufen, Francis of Assisi, and Journeys to Medieval Places.* USA, 2011.

Farrattini Pojani, Ettore Bartolomeo. *500: Palazzo Farrattini 1514-2014.* Catalogo della Mostra documentaria e Iconografica in collaborazione con L'Archivio di Stato di Terni. Terni, 2014. (*Catalog of the exhibition organized to celebrate the 500 years of Palazzo Farrattini.*)

Arcangeli, Ilaria. *Il Palazzo di Bartolomeo III Farrattini a Roma e le altre committenze della famiglia.* Tesi di Laurea Magistrale di Ilaria Arcangeli. Università di Roma TRE, 2017. (*Bartolomeo Farrattini the III's Palazzo in Rome and other Commissions by the Family, a Ph.D. dissertation written by Ilaria Arcangeli in 2017.*)

Logo used for the celebration of the 500th anniversary of Palazzo Farrattini

Photograph, Map, Drawing, and Image Credits

The front cover photograph is by a friend of the author and was taken in the atrium of the *Palazzo* Farrattini in front of the main staircase.

The Farrattini coat of arms comes from *Palazzo* Farrattini. The photograph is by the author.

All maps of the Italian peninsula were prepared by Daniele De Vecchi.

All hand-drawn maps of Amelia were made by Carter Norman Phillips.

The drawing of the Amelia walls comes from a book in the Italian National Archives. The photograph is by the author.

The original photograph of the Germanicus statue was taken by Giovanni Carità.

The portrait of Totila is in the Como, Italy, Civic Museum and was painted by Francesco Salviati.

The image of Frederick II of Swabia ("The Wonder of the World") is a statue on the facade of the Royal Palace in Naples.

The photographs in Chapter 6 are by the author.

The drawings of Amelia in 1564 and the 18th century are from books in the Italian National Archives. The photographs of the drawings were taken by the author.

The portrait of Bartolomeo Farrattini was painted by an unknown painter and is in the author's collection. He photographed the painting.

The book is one of many that contains information about the Farrattini family that is in the Italian National Archives.

The two photos of Tito were taken by Scott Barnes.

The original watercolor of the *Palazzo* Farrattini is by Thomas Lollar.

The original logo was prepared by Francesco Persi for the celebration of the 500th anniversary of *Palazzo* Farrattini, based on a drawing by Thomas Lollar.

The back cover photograph of Ettore Farrattini Pojani and Tito is by Scott Barnes.

About Bayou City Press

FOUNDED IN 2019, Bayou City Press, located in Houston, Texas, has four areas of concentration: travel, history, international affairs, and Houston.

Bayou City Press launched its website in May 2019, showcasing columns penned by Houston authors about foreign travel and Houston. In October 2019, Bayou City Press threw open the doors of its new offices for the official launch of the company.

The first book published by Bayou City Press, *Savoring the Camino de Santiago: It's the Pilgrimage, Not the Hike*, appeared in late 2019. Written by Julie Gianelloni Connor, the book is a mixture of travel memoir and travel information about journeying down the French route of the Camino de Santiago in Spain.

While hit hard by the 2020 COVID pandemic, Bayou City Press continued operations, publishing a children's book on adoption: *The Baby with Three Families, Two Countries, and One Promise: An International Adoption Story*. While telling a fictional story about an adoption, the book explains the adoption process in a way that children can understand and gives parents a way to discuss adoption with their children as they read this story to them.

For a third publication, Bayou City Press launched another travel hybrid in late 2022. Written by Houston author Carrie Carter, the book takes a traveling author and her cat to Japan to visit a series of towns and sites. *Whiskers Abroad: Ashi and Audrey's Adventures in Japan* is a beautifully illustrated mixture of fact and fiction, with lots to laugh about along the way.

With this fourth book, *The Nine Lives of Tito d'Amelia*, Bayou City Press continues its tradition of publishing hybrid books, books that cannot neatly be categorized into a genre or even be listed as wholly fiction or non-fiction. Moreover, this is the first translated book Bayou City Press has published.

Bayou City Press maintains its focus on travel, history, international affairs, and anything Houston-related, but we invite book-length submissions on any topic for consideration. Submission guidelines are available on the website at BayouCityPress.com. Submit letters of inquiry to the following address:

Bayou City Press
10303 Scofield Lane
Houston, TX 77096